Two Corks in a Curse

A Huckleberry Hollow Witchy RomCom

By: Noelle Rider
Cover Art: Kaci Keyser

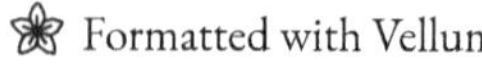 Formatted with Vellum

Two Corks in a Curse Playlist

My taste in music is eclectic and my brain is chaotic. This playlist represents songs that either have lyrics, moods, or inspiration for the chapters of this book. It will give you musical whiplash and make you wonder if I'm well... I'm not.

1. Like a Stone – Audioslave
2. abcdefu – GAYLE
3. Another Day in Paradise – Phil Collins
4. Fight Like a Girl – Evanescence ft. K. Flay
5. Another Bag of Bricks – Flogging Molly
6. Tired – Stone Sour
7. Look What You Made Me Do – Taylor Swift
8. Head Above Water – Avril Lavigne
9. It Ends Tonight – All American Rejects
10. Help – Papa Roach
11. I Put a Spell on You – Nina Simone
12. SOS – Rihanna
13. The Mountain – Three Days Grace
14. Have You Ever Seen the Rain – Creedence Clearwater Revival
15. Who'll Stand With Us? – Dropkick Murphys
16. Bad At Love – Halsey
17. Liar – Jelly Roll
18. Alone in a Room – Asking Alexandria
19. Unconditionally – Katy Perry
20. A Bar Song (Tipsy) – Shaboozey
21. Every Little Thing She Does is Magic – The Police
22. Take Me to Church – Hozier
23. Spiderwebs – No Doubt
24. Just Give Me a Reason   Pink
25. All the Small Things – Blink 182
26. Whatever It Takes – Imagine Dragons

27. I'll Make Love to You – Boyz to Men
28. Bitch Came Back – Theory of a Deadman
29. Mz. Hyde – Halestorm
30. Haunted – Evanescence
31. Words as Weapons – Seether
32. The Prophecy – Taylor Swift
33. Choker – SkyDxddy
34. Stabbing in the Dark – Ice Nine Kills
35. Heavy – Linkin Park (feat Kiiara)
36. Halo – Beyonce

Listen on Amazon Music by searching Two Corks in a Curse or eBook readers can click

Thank you to my dogs: Perry and Padfoot. Without you the darkness would win.

To my husband, for keeping me in coffee and snacks. Thanks to my mom for always being there to edit at the last second, you may not have done this one, but you're always willing.

Extra Special Thanks to Teresa and Martin at Free Dog Winery for hiring me for a year to pour wine, talk dogs, and pick your brains. I'm a member for life but I had to flex some serious customer service skills up in there.

PROLOGUE

DRAX

I stood watch outside my cave, rooted in place by the fractured beast I no longer controlled.

"Just five more minutes." He insisted from inside my head, where he had as much control over my body as I did.

"Come on, let's try again. Take that barrel and put it beside the cave. Just picture what you have, and where you want it, then... let yourself have it." Tempe gestured to an empty wine barrel. It was the dozenth time I'd heard the explanation in as many lessons. I rolled my eyes, trying again to force my wings out, only to be met with resistance. Still in good humor, she encourages the other woman. "You know what you want Lucy, now give me what I want!"

I turned around to hiss at my dragon. "We cannot do this! It isn't safe!"

"But..."

Lucy's blood-curdling scream cut through our argument and my boots carried me down the small slope to the field below. The magical barriers disappeared, a strange silence numbing my ears from the usual hum of magic and the woods surrounding the vineyard. Lucy's tears stung my nostrils, but the sun's light had dimmed, and the sky lost all light. While I watched the once vibrant life of Tempranillo solidify into a rose quartz pillar.

With the rat witch pinned against the ground by a scaled, clawed hand wrapped around her throat, it took a second for me to push my dragon back and find my words. She squirmed beneath me, but I struggled to rein him in.

"What the feck did you do, lass?"

Her whole body trembled beneath me. Weak fingers scratched at my claw as her breathing grew ragged, hazel eyes bulging. Fear tainted the air and brought me back, enough of a reminder that this wasn't who I am.

I was not a killer. Not anymore.

My hand contracted, obeying the dragon as I wrestled it for control. Another reminder why we hid, why we couldn't be with Tempe or her kind any more than a few fleeting moments.

"It-it was an ac-accident," she whispered, my hand finally leaving her neck. "She said to give her what she wanted..." Lucy tried again, but a hollow had opened in the shadows cast by Tempe's absence.

"Leave." My chest burned with bitter acid. Heart hammering, while the morning's breakfast slowly creeped back up my throat.

"Let me help! I didn't think what she wanted was..."

"I said leave!" I stalked over to the stone, my fingers brushing her frozen lips while my dragon flashed an idea. The same one he'd been begging for the past two full moons. Beneath my fingers, I sensed her life force thrumming and wild as ever, but her light didn't come through. Whatever Lucy had done, Tempe was no longer part of this world.

This is what she wanted most? Anger stomped around my head, fire licking the inside of my skull.

"Let me help!" Lucy was back in my space, shouting, angry, while the hanging rat in her hat quivered, retreating to the rear of the brim.

Flames licked out of my mouth, flickering toward her while caressing the air around what was once Tempe. My Tempe.

"I can make this right." She tried to push me out of the way.

"No, you can't." I sneered at her, bearing down on her slowly shrinking form. The only way to succeed was without witnesses. No one to tell Tempe about the sacrifice she would make to survive. Yet another in her life that she hadn't asked for.

In the rat witch's heart, I found her greatest insecurities right on the surface. A crap move, but for Tempe I would do anything, and I threw them in her face before she banjaxed the whole thing.

"Yeh can' do anything right, and yeh know it. Yeh've failed at every last thing yeh've ever tried. It's why even yer magic avoided yeh until it couldn't." Senseless violence coiled in my voice, a monster I'd thought buried in a coastal island off the north of Ireland pushing her back with the same force as a slap.

"What can you do? You don't have any magic!" She slapped me back, but she did not know the power of dragons. My eyes drifted closed, and I felt the nearly full moon lingering just beyond the setting sun. I'd been experiencing its growth for weeks, a reminder that I lived my life in twenty-eight-day cycles.

"There is far more ta magic than wiggling yer nose and castin' spells, rat witch." I scoured her with my eyes, but she didn't back down. "The strongest magics are those yeh cannot control. Like a fucking curse that splits yeh in two on a dying witch's lips, murdered by yer own claws to release the blood that seals it."

The witch swallowed hard.

"And what if you can't control it?" she shot back, somehow digging in her heels with the scent of tears lurking behind her eyes. "What if you're just as lost and powerless as I am?"

"I am lost, lass. And I cannot control this magic any more than yeh control yers." My eyes pinned her in place while the jumping pulse in her throat begged the feet beneath her to run. "I may fail, but only a magic as old as that of a dragon can reopen the path back to this dimension for her and ta share it, I must bind her to me. Tell no one, rat witch, yeh will not remember yerself. If I fail, this winery will burn to the ground, and yeh may find yerself in the ashes."

CHAPTER

ONE

TEMPE

ONCE UPON A TIME, I WAS A ROSE QUARTZ STATUE. It was a Tuesday, very much like this. The sun was shining, my back hurt because I'm in my thirties, and my hair was in a ponytail. Except today there was four inches of snow on the ground outside and a woman snapped her fingers in my face without so much as looking up from her phone.

Of the differences, no longer being a statue and the woman were the only two I considered a problem. Back pain was just part of decaying and inching toward death and snow usually meant fewer people like this woman. The reservation said Sarah, but her pixie cut, dark shaved sides, long bleached bangs teased and fluffed, said her name was probably Karen to anyone who encountered her in the wild. Why women of a certain age got the Karen cut and color baffled me, but her fake tan and over-use of bronzer said she wasn't doing it ironically. She had crafted herself to look that way intentionally... then followed through with a matching personality. As long as personality was defined loosely and I didn't have to go over there and find out if she had one.

The only similarities that I had with Sarah were our current location and being deeply irritated. The 'Love Potion on the Vine' tasting room, where I lived, worked, and... pretended to be a statue was not an optional locale for me–an irritated statue that needed our time together to end so I could be irritated alone. It was optional for her, and I would like her to opt the hell out of my establishment. Hopefully, sooner rather than later because the fake half-assed smile on my face was not as statue-like as the rest of me, and sooner or later it would fade and she'd see exactly how far I'd go not to look at her any more.

Petty, yes. Warranted, also yes.

However, Sarah-the-Karen's hand continued to stay in the air, snapping at me and I marveled at her dedication to arm day for the stamina to summon lowly peasants. Nothing else about her inspired me to do more than look up creative methods of homicide. Except homicide required both energy and effort, neither of which I had in ready supply. In fact, neither had been in my repertoire for at least two decades, if I'd ever had them at all.

Silent judgement, however, I had in spades. And when it came to Sarah-the-Karen, boy was I judging. She was both unoriginal and extremely obnoxious, but in a manner that failed to provide even a modicum of entertainment.

January in the tiptop of Idaho's stick meant she wore fur-lined boots, skin-tight jeans, and a waffle shirt that said *Country Girl* in some sort of glittery rhinestone script, equal parts tacky and boring. A calf-length puffer jacket was bunched on the booth seat behind her, despite the available coat rack, in a basic black, and a leather bag with far too many buckles clutched in her lap.

Her white-knuckle grip suggested she expected to get robbed at any moment. The speculated thief is a mystery for the ages, since everyone in the room today was as snowflake white as her, aside from my half-Latina ass, and most days I passed as white.

With how many "free samples" she'd asked for before selecting the glass in front of her, she'd already robbed me of both my sanity and two tastings' worth of wine. If anyone should be clutching their wares in fear, it should be me, clutching my bottles like she planned to grab them and dash out on those wedge-heeled boots... assuming she was sober enough not to trip or run into a wall.

It would be worth losing a bottle to entertainment costs if she committed some sort of bloody self-harm for the amusement of my other customers. Or my morbid, detached relationship to humanity was evolving and I alone found the idea of her bleeding on the floor entertaining.

To-may-to, to-mah-to.

Who cares as long as no one got arrested, and I cleaned up the blood to health code standards? Most effective would be to just poison her wine directly... but that was murder and back in the land of effort, energy, and pre-meditation, things I did not have the energy or patience for.

"Waitress!" She snapped her fingers again, and I closed my eyes, deciding she must have meant someone else. She might have been looking at me, but since I inherited this winery from my grandmother, I had absolutely zero plans to respond to someone snapping their fingers at me and calling me *waitress*. I qualified as owner, vintner, and boss bitch; though I'd accept bitch as a shortened title, I would not be answering to *waitress* in this timeline, universe, or quantum parallel.

Neither would my staff because witch, please. Not only was there only one person on my staff, but he was definitely male and not desperate enough for tips to cosplay as her waitress.

With my forearms balanced on the stone topped wine bar, I leaned over my coffee mug and inhaled the aroma. It had been a week since I'd slept more than a few hours. Longer still since I'd experienced anything resembling peace or joy, but petty vengeance brought me a type of joy that did not require giving up my spite. Peace would continue to elude me... as it had since that day.

The day I was really a statue and not just numb to the life around me.

I'd been teaching a witch from my coven how to control her powers. Lucy's magic bloomed later in life, and after a dozen lessons... let's just say it wasn't going well.

But when I was a statue... it was finally quiet. The anxiety, stream of chattering thoughts, missed social cues, and the sense of misplaced humanity, were all just... gone. There was no crumbling winery to worry about, no grandmother who jetted off into retirement without a backward glance, and no disapproving scowls from her fated mate when I continued to exist.

Then someone had to go and change me back, returning me to the land of Sarah-the-Karen snapping her fingers at me. Meanwhile, a bridal party on the other side of the room took wine tasting pours like they were shots, and unicorns only existed on the side of tie-dye hippie vans and the margins of my notebook where I doodled them on the regular.

My dream when I visited as a teenager, knowing I was expected to take over, had been a community space for magic and non-magic alike. I wanted to build a place for people to discuss their differences openly and tear down the myths and hatred surrounding them. But as I watched the Pixie-Cut and the bridal party, I had to accept that society hadn't gotten there yet.

Maybe we never would.

Despite being a weekday, people occupied almost every table in the winery. The plaster walls, yellow with grey marbled lines, expanded to windows high on the wall that let in the sun while hiding the fresh four inches of overnight snow. Black wrought-iron faux window detailing outlined an abstract painting of an Italian countryside. It was gran's weird obsession with their aesthetic that extended to the arbitrary shelf with a single bud vase holding a silk flower.

The effect would have been beautiful if I wasn't responsible for dusting it. Even with magic, keeping the place clean sucked. The only way to dust without breaking anything was to do it myself with a rag, Pledge, a stepladder, and a firm request to gravity that she not be a bitch about it.

Since moving here six months ago, my magic had been spotty at best. Simple spells, the ones that always worked for quick repairs, stopped working. Bigger magic, supercharged with crystals and herbs, never fixed or affected anything in this building despite working everywhere else.

Like the place was cursed.

Our tasting room was also drafty, cold, and I'd lost sensation in my toes an hour ago, when the space heater under the bar flickered out. Another thing to place on my endless list of shit that needed to be fixed, researched, or replaced.

A murmur of voices made me aware that my efforts at statuedom had not gone well, especially when a screech of celebration rattled the world to my left.

Just drink the coffee and think warm thoughts... like arson.

"Waitress! I'm talking to you!"

Like arson with a side of murder by setting Pixie-Cut on fire.

I flicked a glance over at Samuel, my one employee. The satyr wore a glamour to hide his hooved and furry lower half from my largely human clientele. Samuel, one of Huckleberry Hollow's diverse residents, enjoyed the perks of being an attractive male in a female-customer-dominated industry. He was friendly, efficient, and polite, all skills that made him invaluable as an employee and far better suited to the gig than I was.

Our eyes locked, his eyebrows contracting while he took a rigid step backward and held the wine bottle between us like a shield... or a weapon. Clearly, if I made him walk over there, he would quit. As he was handling the other eight occupied tables and trying not to get sexually molested by bridesmaids, it was the least I could do... or the most because the task may kill me.

I suppose if I couldn't be a statue, a corpse was close enough.

Elbows pushing me off the counter, I kept both hands wrapped around my coffee as I popped my spine up to the full five foot ten my driver's license promised. I walked around the counter, shuffling my black sneakers ever so slightly closer. My uniform of blue jeans and black work polo accentuated my ample hips, round belly and complete lack of shits given, appearing shabby beside her designer life but appropriate in my two steps up from death. The winery's logo stood out in red glitter, a single pop of color in my monochrome world. But the black on dark blue on black meant dribbled wine blended in, preventing red wine splatter from making me look like a murder victim.

Or perpetrator.

I kept my hands firmly wrapped around the coffee mug as I navigated the sawed-off wine barrels being used as tables between pairs of black leather chairs. Everything was made with either black leather or wood, a lived-in approach to the tasting experience that ensured no glass tabletops were harmed by clumsy witches. Sarah-the-Karen sat herself closest to the door with two other women, one with medium brown hair in a ponytail and the other sporting a pair of braids in her dark blonde hair. They both had on BSU hoodies and visibly shrunk as I got closer, but age and appearance suggested offspring and a familiarity with the woman I would not enjoy experiencing on a personal level.

My feet stopped at the edge of the table, and I drank my coffee, waiting.

Neighboring patrons lowered their voices, bodies trying to angle their seats toward us discreetly, for a better view of the inevitable carnage. A few of the supernatural guests tittered, always excited for a show I hoped would be disappointing. Since many of them had met me, my lack of social aptitude worn as a badge brighter red than the winery's logo, my hope was in vain.

The rubberneckers would get their casualties.

Three wine glasses sat on the tabletop. The two younger women were about halfway through the white wine they requested, while their mother was down to the last eighth of her red. Deep orchid lipstick stained her glass in three separate places, a choice that was going to force the poor cup to need at least two cycles through the wash.

And probably a jackhammer.

I took another drink of coffee.

Karen tapped her almond-shaped manicure on the table, pinkie to index. Her daughters shrank another inch in their hoodies. She did another round with her nails, and I drank again.

One more round, and it would be a hat trick. If this were alcohol instead of coffee, I'd be toasted.

"Well?" Her comment was directed to the space above my left ear, pursed lips and tapping fingers unlikely to get a break from their irritated tattoo any time soon.

I glanced behind me, but there was nobody there. My pulse kicked up, hands and feet aching to tap and twitch, but I forced myself still. Forced myself to be the statue.

"Aren't you going to ask what I need?"

Blinking, I looked down at my feet standing beside her table. Slowly, I brought my gaze level with hers and quirked an eyebrow. It was the only muscle I moved intentionally, but my face had subtitles and right now, they were cast in the villain role of a slasher flick.

"This wine is not what I wanted. Please replace it with another selection... I think I want the Malbec."

"That is the Malbec." I searched the room for something calming to focus my energy on. In my chest, the steady beat of my heart got just a little louder. Heat tickled my neck, and a dull ache settled into my clenched jaw as I fought the urge to let loose a banshee scream.

"No, it's not." She huffed and tapped a manicured claw on her menu. The eye roll and long-suffering slowed speech of a person communicating with the moronic. As though I had not poured it, entered it into the point of sale system, and secretly wished to curse the contents of her cup. "This is the Rhone blend."

I schooled myself to keep my hands wrapped around the cup, squeezing tight enough to test the tensile strength of coffee mugs as I envisioned them wrapped around "country girl's" neck. My brain started listing reasons not to live the dream: There were too many witnesses, murder is messy, and I promised myself when I was younger I'd never be on an episode of *Cops*.

"It is not because we do not have a Rhone blend." My over-sized orange cat appeared between my feet while I matched her tone, enunciating each word and decorating it with a sprinkle of

sitting back against her chair, arms crossed, and nose wrinkled. "I don't want this. Remove it from my bill."

"No."

"But I don't want it!"

"You *just* asked for it." I gestured at the menu she'd thrust my direction, her lipstick-stained fingerprint marking the spot beside the very wine in question. "Remember? You asked me to replace it with itself? You really do need to be cut off, I'm sorry."

"Because I thought it was something else! You tricked me!" She glared at the spot above my left ear, face scrunched and red. "But now that I know it isn't what I thought, I don't want it."

I doubted she had any thoughts, though I didn't say that aloud—if only just. Point for me, but only one because things were going to go downhill fast from here. "Nope. You drank it. It's yours."

Draigus Doherty, aka Drax, stepped out from behind the curtain. His six and a half feet filled the entryway before he slid to the side and held up the wall. Thick muscles corded his forearms, a broad chest offsetting the boyish freckles and slightly pointed ears beneath his close-cropped red hair. The short-sleeved black T-shirt he wore left little to the imagination, tapering into the dark green cargo pants he had belted around the tucked in shirt. Combat boots completed the look, and I'd have considered it a fashion statement if I hadn't searched the wine cave he used as a home.

The man only owned two pairs of pants, both cargos, and three shirts. All three were short sleeved, black, and decidedly as pretentious and obnoxious as the man who wore them. I'd tried giving him a polo shirt with the winery's logo, since he was co-owner and should actually support the place, and he'd scoffed.

Derisively.

Like I was the crazy person living in a cave and refusing to come out and help because it was "unsafe" for him to be in public. If he knew the number of murders I'd almost committed, he'd have figured out it wasn't any safer for me to be up here.

None of us wanted to deal with these people, but someone had to and the *least* he could have done was flip me for it.

Now I spent most of my time resisting the urge to flip... him off whenever he entered the room. Which recently had been whenever I was on the verge of breaking down or breaking some-one's neck. The addition to my ire rarely helped the situation, but I could appreciate the view.

"Are you listening to me?" Sarah-the-Karen snapped her fingers in my face again. My gaze flickered away from the dragon in the corner, but I felt him there. Waves of ancient crimson licked against my skin. Fiery hot with an edge of emerald mist at the core. His kaleidoscope of colors nipped at my skin, stealing my wrath and leaving the lighter weight of contempt, with the same efficiency as a hostile house pet.

A pet who could paint a masterpiece with magic and still not look alive, affectionate, or like anyone would adopt him if I shipped him off to the local shelter.

Pain in the fucking ass.

Sarah cleared her throat. "I said, are you listening to me?"

"Not really." I looked down at the cat. His green eyes narrowed, a reminder that my food stores weren't the only ones at stake if this place went under. "But it sounds like you drank wine, you want more wine, but you don't want to pay for more wine, and are too drunk to be allowed more. Is that accurate?"

The girl in braids tried to mask her snicker with a cough.

My lip twitched, and I nearly smiled.

"Excuse you! I'm a customer and you will not speak to me that way! For your information, I'm very wealthy and planned on bringing a lot of high-end clients here. I want to speak to your manager. Now!"

Corky and I exchanged a look, the cat giving me another warning glare that what I was about to do was as ill-advised as the fourth cup of coffee I had at midnight. But my brain ran the pros and cons like a computer excel sheet and I determined the universe owed me a bad decision.

Or perhaps I just wanted to be as much of an asshole as the other two assholes in the room, both of which were currently getting on my last nerve. One by running her mouth and the other by never opening his.

I learned secondhand that he'd seen some shit. He'd been used by the IRA over in Ireland as a weapon of mass casualty, and at some point, learned that no one's agenda was without hidden costs. It explained the outfit, the chip on his shoulder, his insistence that he was "too dangerous", and the accent. He just didn't talk about it.

He didn't talk about anything.

"We don't have a manager, but that's the owner," I gestured toward Drax. Every eye in the room pretended not to look, but I sensed the weight of their collective gaze leaving me to watch the Irishman. "Perhaps you can explain to him why you're 'very wealthy' and yet do not want to pay for your wine. Maybe while you're at it, explain to him what a 'high-end client' is, because that sounds fake and like something a person who's never known people with money might say, since a product is high-end, and a person is not. Ask me how I know."

I tapped a fingernail on my tasting menu.

Drax's eyes narrowed at me, his stiff posture yielding just enough that his shoulders hunched a millimeter and his folded arms took on a white tint as he gripped his biceps tighter. If looks could kill, he wasn't trying very hard.

I was, unfortunately, still alive and very minutely excited to witness his suffering.

"Sir!" Sarah-the-Karen snapped upright in her seat, staring intently in his direction. Chest out, shoulders back, and eyelashes fluttering strong enough to kick up a stiff wind, she was going for the boss babe flirt move.

A bold choice when your target looked like a professional murderer, but some people were into that.

Finishing my coffee, I picked up Corky and stuck him on my shoulder before turning away. I collected a couple of wine glasses on my way back to the bar and put everything on the plastic dish rack for washing. Back at my post behind the bar, I waited and watched while Drax glared at me.

Not a single muscle in his body twitched as the woman snapped her fingers. "Sir!"

The whole winery now openly gawked. No one had seen Drax in person for more than a few moments since we'd inherited this winery. Fewer still had heard him speak, and absolutely none of them had witnessed him interact with a customer.

I grabbed another bottle and poured the next tasting for a nearby table. Sarah was on her feet, marching toward the dragon with purpose, her hands still holding her purse in a death grip while her children shrank to approximately two feet tall.

I searched for some pity, but came up empty. Hopefully one of them had the car keys to drive her home, because she was probably not safe for motor vehicle operation.

"Excuse me, but your rude waitress is providing terrible customer service. She will not replace my wine, is insisting I pay for something I don't want, insulting me, calling me a liar, and has never heard of high-end clients." The woman reached out to grab his arm, and he finally tore his eyes away from me to look at the woman beside him.

The very short, very human woman beside him who suddenly couldn't pull her hand back fast enough. "What are you going to do about it?" She squeaked.

A soft growl came out of Drax's throat, and several non-human customers looked at me in concern. They all knew what he was and were uncomfortable about the prospect of being exposed as magical beings... or witnessing a homicide... in that order.

"Drax." His eyes slid to me, eyebrows popped in question. I tilted my head toward the woman, widening my eyes. Scoffing softly, he gave me a subtle eye roll. His look said, *This is what you get when I handle shit.*

Certainly something to remember at bad decision time, but I

probably wouldn't. It interfered with the *bad* part of a bad decision.

He let out another, even more feral growl and a small stream of smoke slipped from his nostrils.

Sarah backed up a couple of steps, stumbling slightly when she bumped into a chair. It clattered to the ground. The metallic clank of aluminum hitting concrete battered against me and I instantly regretted setting Drax on her.

The man was incapable of using his words, and he'd once again taken a simple problem and made it worse.

"Fine." Sarah stomped in embarrassment over to the table and threw down some cash. "Fine! I will post about this online! You will rue the day you spoke to me this way!"

Her daughters followed her out, slamming the door shut behind them.

A four-tiered wine shelf shuddered, and the glass bottles that were on it rattled nervously.

"Don't fall!" I infused magic into my command, and the shelf, tasting the burgundy vinaigrette of my request. The spell bounced off, and with barely a moment, I thought *gently* sending a flick of magic to the air around the bottles. It thickened into a dense cloud, holding them up while the shelf crumbled. Around the destruction, the bottles gently rolled to the floor in a slow cascade of dominos. Shelf pieces formed ramps, rolling the bottles safely to the ground, an orchestrated dance of disaster that avoided damage.

Attention diverted, I missed another telltale creak, and the floating shelf crashed to the floor, shattering a pottery vase. A stunned silence filled the room, and we all stared at the dust-covered fake flower lying above the bottles now sitting on the ground.

A flower for the corpse of my dead shelves and homeless wine.

Corky sauntered over to the bridal party, batting a plastic popper under the table. The popper collided with a woman's stiletto, and she impaled it.

A confetti cannon of glitter penises showered half my tasting room in anatomic cocks.

Laughter erupted around me while I gawked at the broken shelving. I hadn't been able to keep it from falling, nor the wine on the floor with no place to go, or the shattered pottery I couldn't afford to replace. My magic hadn't been able to prevent anything in this winery from collapsing, and despite the minor spells that spared product, life, and limb, I worried that whatever made me a witch was failing just as fast.

Searching the room for reassurance, I found nothing.

No one paid attention.

No one cared.

Normal business resumed while Drax slipped back out of the room, and I glared at the mess.

Fear of losing my magic grew as strong as my desire to say, "Fuck it," and dismantle this winery with a Midwest-style tornado. Except this place was really all I had.

Grabbing the broom from the corner, I started sweeping up the pottery and glitter as yet another blast of cocks coated my floor.

Once upon a time I was a statue...

CHAPTER

TWO

TEMPE

"Didn't we just do this?" I looked at Corky on the neighboring pillow, a ray of sun hitting him perfectly to look like an angel sent from heaven. On my right, my phone trilled a sound straight from the depths of hell and I slapped at it until the alarm went silent, and I waited for the usual dread. Every morning, the pressure would settle into my chest as my brain started listing for me all the things that needed to be done, that I needed to research to see if it needed to be done at all or I was just buying into hype, and a running total of how much all of it would cost.

Its consistency was almost reassuring... almost.

My phone trilled a second alarm, and I rolled up to standing, turning it off correctly this time without removing it from my bedside table. Several joints popped, and I wondered how I had cricks when I hadn't managed more than an hour or two of sleep. Just one of the mid-thirties perks no one talked about, like under boob rashes from sweat in the summer and feet that never warmed up in the winter.

If only I'd died before thirty, like I joked in elementary school.

The apartment and most of the furniture had been my gran's, left behind when she retired to somewhere warm. A floral chair full of not-quite-clean but not-yet-dirty clothes sat beside a white

19

dresser with metal handles on clawed feet. A matching white headboard stood behind the bed, two paperback-sized end tables bookending the mattress.

I hated this room and everything in it.

Without looking around more than was strictly necessary, I moved efficiently through the space to start my day. Standard morning order of operations happened on autopilot. I shucked my pajama shirt, swiped on deodorant, found a bra, shirt and pants in the least stain-showing colors, and donned them in the least imaginative fashion possible. In the attached bathroom, I pulled my hair into a ponytail without glancing in the mirror and left the room with my socks tucked under my arm.

Ambling to the kitchen, I poked the power button on the coffee pot I'd prepped last night, put cat food in Corky's dish and then grabbed a cup and coffee creamer from the fridge. Once again, not looking around the apartment to see gran's two armchairs, the kitchen table that seats six, or her atrocious taste in light fixtures that hung far too low for anyone not shrunken-old-lady sized. Reflexively, I moved the small blue bottle from one cabinet to the other, then back, then behind a box of white rice I didn't recall buying.

Then I waited for the machine to beep to the melodic crunching and swallows of tiny kitty teeth.

And waited.

And waited some more while existential dread creeped into my mind, telling me none of this was worth it and what was the point of coffee when it would just make me more energetic for the coming doom.

A loud clang came from outside my balcony, shattering the train of thought. My whole body leapt, but Corky didn't so much as blink from where he hovered over his dish. If the world ended, Corky was going out with a full belly, everyone else be damned.

"Don't worry, I'll check it out."

His head didn't rise so much as a centimeter.

I walked toward the French doors that led out to the small

balcony of my apartment, gathered my magic to myself, and prepared to fight or run. Similar to rolling a snowball up a hill, the raspberry sized ball grew into a burgundy cantaloupe that sat on my chest. Anticipation and anxiety thrummed against my ribs in time with my pounding heart as I held this potential energy at the edge of the downhill, waiting to be released as kinetic energy. I turned the handle and walked out in the grey-skied light of day.

Below me, Drax tossed glass bottles into the large metal recycle bin.

"What the hell are you doing?" I charged to the edge and glared down at him, but he refused to spare me a glance. Closing my eyes, I held the cantaloupe away from my chest and tasted the sweet sting of cayenne, imagining myself on the ground beside him. I let it go, feeling my body and the small amount of energy I'd recovered in two hours of sleep, plummet downward with my eyes closed. Wiped and exhausted, I opened my eyes to find I stood toe to toe with the dragon-sized pain in my ass.

"I asked what you were doing." My chest nearly bumped against his, and I saw a glimmer of gold in his green eyes. "Don't make me ask a third time, Drax."

"Recycling." He attempted to move past me, but I dogged his steps and remained between him and the bin, more or less where I wanted to be. While I was keeping him from his continued "recycling", I was also far too close and irritated with the man to be within hitting distance. One word was an inadequate response for an activity that could end up costing me money.

"Where did you get those bottles?" I pressed my hand into his chest, attempting to push him away from the metal bin. His skin crackled beneath my hand, heat sinking into the digits, and I became painfully aware of every ridge and plane of the man beneath the shirt.

He didn't move.

I put some magic behind it, drawing into the empty well for a crimson crumb to pressure him into compliance. The tart burst of a pomegranate seed pressed out of me, thickening the air and strengthening my arms for only a second.

Something ancient pushed back, wrapped around my magic, and sent tingles caressing the curve of my neck. Flashes of a red-winged creature danced in my maroon energy before slipping back out again and taking all the air from my lungs with it.

I jerked my hand back and glared at him. "Don't do that."

Boyish dimples smirked down at me. The man was over 100 years old, but dragon shifters slowed to practically not aging when they reached mating age and didn't continue until they found their fated mate. At most, he might be confused for a mature thirty, which was so unfair. Instead of addressing my comment, he let another trickle of magic tickle the edge of my nose. "Do what, love?"

"You know what!" I fisted my hands on my hips, grinding my teeth. "You're still doing it!"

"You started it." His magic wrapped around me a second time, turning the air near my ribs into invisible feathers that tickled my sides.

I squirmed in a mix of pain and pleasure that did unfortunate things to my insides. "And you clearly won, so why are you still doing it? Stop already."

"Why, *mo doineann*?"

" Don't call me that. I've already told you: Tempe is short for Tempranillo, not tempest. It's *Temp-ran-illo*, as in the Spanish wine grape. Seriously, for someone who is part owner of this winery, you ought to know your grapes." I'd turned around and stomped over to the recycling bin during my rant, deciding on the way that he was probably going to walk away before I finished, anyway.

Like most men.

Truthfully, if he'd thrown away the bottles I needed to fill and label, there was no point in explaining to him what he did wrong. I would just attempt to magic them back together, then succeed or fail, kick him in the nuts. Basically immortal, he and his junk would probably be fine. If no one had kicked his junk in a hundred years, it was time to remind him of the joys of being part human.

If it kept him from procreating, I'd send his mate an apology letter and condolences... for being stuck with him. Then throw a party to celebrate him being someone else's problem. I rolled onto my tiptoes, looking into the bin. Inside was a bunch of brown beer bottles glinting in the sunlight. I counted ten before I gave up and rocked back to the flats of my feet.

"Do you have a drinking problem?" I asked him, forgetting he probably walked away. When I turned around, he was still standing there. In place of his usual indifference, a slight frown aged him up to my thirty-five years and I felt like I was chastising my idiot brother. "And you chose cheap beer over the wine you sleep near? You know we have a higher ABV than any beer."

Drax looked torn between being a dick and seeking a conversation. I watched his indecision play out on his forehead as he weighed the merits of maintaining silence against asking questions. Whether his objection was to me or the topic was a mystery, and I should have left it alone, but I found myself asking anyway.

"Talk to me, Goose."

"I'm not a goose."

I kept forgetting the man hadn't had a civil conversation with me since moving here and even less familiarity with pop culture. "It's a movie quote. Just spit out your question."

"You want me to spit on you?" He tilted his head and amusement danced in his eyes. I was pretty sure he was fucking with me, and I didn't like it.

"Forget it. I don't have any idea why I bother talking to you. Wasted breath." I resisted the urge to look back into the bin and count the beer bottles. The number wasn't relevant. I had my answer and it was time to move on.

"I'm curious... Do you not share your family name?"

I startled and slammed my elbow into the dumpster. His hand

reached for my elbow, but I stepped back like he was threatening to cut me. "Ow! What?"

"The mailbox, says Verdejo, but your grandmother is not Verdejo."

"Holy crap, you can read?" I mimed pressing my hand to my forehead as though I would faint at any moment.

"Are you ok? That sounded painful."

"Not as painful as the heart attack you gave me by demonstrating you do more than stomp and brood and snarl. I should find you a gold star..."

"Aye, sarcasm aside, do you intend to answer me?" His eyebrow drifted up and briefly mesmerized me with the fact his face had muscles that moved.

"No, I don't. My mom was drugged out at the hospital and just wrote the two wines she missed the most while pregnant for my name, tempranillo and verdejo."

The dragon stood there, arms crossed, face blank. The dumpster lived on the edge of a dirt parking lot, serving the winery via a porch leading to the entry doors flanked by half wine barrels filled with seasonal flowers. Which in January, was snow.

The entire parking lot, usually dirt with wooden berms to mark where cars should park, was also covered in a fresh four inches of snow. Under the grey sky, it bounced and reflected the light into a brilliant morning that I found equally blinding and dreary. In less than an hour, I would need to find the strength to either magically relocate the snow, or shovel it so guests could park.

My bare feet were completely numb, and the hems of my pants were quickly taking on water. Putting on shoes and drinking coffee would have been a better idea than coming down here and engaging with Drax, but I hadn't been thinking. When it came to him, I was never thinking, and it ensured I made nothing but bad decisions and asinine comments. Wrapping my arms around myself, I shivered and started toward the offending mailbox.

The one I'd hand painted with our names when gran told me I'd be inheriting the winery with another person and the short-lived excitement hadn't yet met the reality.

Drax cleared his throat and reappeared beside me.

"Now what? Do you need me to explain pregnancy or alcoholism? Or drugs? What thing that I just said is escaping you?"

"Have yeh never considered changing it to match 'ers?"

"Why bother? It's not like I'm in danger of passing it on or seeing it on someone's wall of remembrance. I'm scheduled to die broke and alone with a cat, no one's buying a headstone or filling out a birth certificate for offspring that need my last name."

"A novel approach, if contradictory." He waggled his finger disapprovingly. "You are not alone if there is a cat. What about your gran?"

"She's not a cat." I started moving toward the porch again, hoping to get my feet out of the snow. Whether or not cold air was better than the snow was a surprise for ten seconds from now.

"Wouldn't you want your name to match hers?"

"No." Nine seconds to the porch.

"Are you two not close?" He trotted along beside me, not appearing the least bit deterred.

"Do you see her here?" Seven seconds... I started to worry about losing my pinkie toe.

"That's not what I meant."

"I know what you meant." Three seconds and a mental note to search the internet for symptoms of frostbite.

"And?" He prompted when I didn't go on.

"I stand by my answer. I'm not taking Damien's name, either."

He paused, seeming to remember his godfather had married my gran, making the family name I'd inherit his godfather's. "I suppose not. What about your grandfather's name?"

"Then it still wouldn't match anyone. What is your obsession with names?" We'd made it to the porch, and I shivered. Shaking the snow off my feet, I wondered how many hours it would take for them to feel warm.

Based on past experience, I would die first.

"Just trying to understand you, love." Drax stood beside me, so still, I could mistake him for a statue. "You haven't been very enlightening."

"Sorry, you feel that way. I always strive for transparency with absent business partners who claim to be a threat to my safety, don't help out, provide one-word answers when asked reasonable questions, and then keep me outside, barefoot, in the snow. How tremendously rude of me."

"You cannot apologize for someone else's feelings." Now his smooth, freckled face contorted into a scowl that brought out his wrinkles. There was something comforting about seeing his otherwise flawless body show signs of imperfection.

"A - Surprised you learned that. And B - you can if you don't care about said feelings because of ALL THE OTHER THINGS I SAID!"

"Who said I have feelings?" All the frown lines had smoothed out and a single cocky eyebrow sat elevated in its place. "Or cared about you being transparent with me? Though I am sorry about your toes, they look cold."

"You... I..." Everything I said replayed, and I rubbed my forehead, trying to piece together the nonsense that led to him accusing me of accusing him of having feelings. The sun peeked through the clouds, reminding me I'd already verbally vomited twice, and the stupid loud birds needed to head south. A wide yawn slipped out and Corky appeared on the balcony beside the porch awning. With a single meow, he reminded me why this day had already gotten away from me.

"Forget it. I hate you and I need coffee." I turned around and moved to the door, adding this to the list of memories I shared with Drax that would taunt me in the back of my mind.

"You left your residence un-caffeinated?"

Startled, I turned to see him following me to the main winery doors. I used a smaller amount of magic to unlock it, far less than it would take to transport my matter back up to my apartment.

Magic was like spoon theory for mental health, if you got adequate sleep and ate well, any witch performing a reasonable amount of magic wouldn't experience a crash. As I wasn't sleeping, hadn't had coffee, and was probably going to eat pumpkin spice oatmeal, I was in for a day of doing things the human way.

Not that my magic had been much help these days, anyway.

"Yes. If you don't care, why are you following me?"

"Aren't you... very attached to coffee and caffeine as a life substance?" He elected to ignore my question.

"Also, yes. Why are you following me?"

"Is it safe to be near you if you haven't ingested any?"

"Probably not. Stop following me." I rolled my eyes and frowned, annoyed at the line of questions. The man barely came around but had somehow gained an accurate knowledge base of facts about me. He'd been watching, getting to know me, creating a discomforting sense of intimacy between us. All while I'd been standing around... hating him. And doing everything in my power to keep him from leaving me. Goddess, what a fucking pair of issue packed weirdos we made.

"Should I start preparing bail money for the inevitable homicides?" He continued to follow me through the tasting room to the faux wall that led to my apartment. "Or were you planning to just bury the victims in our vineyard?"

"I told you to go away and I hate you."

The man's sudden chattiness made me uneasy. Chattiness of any kind made me uneasy, but now, venturing into discussions of casual murder, my queasiness returned.

He shrugged, like he knew I didn't actually care if he listened. "I heard yeh, but I decided you were lyin'."

Somehow, we'd gotten too familiar, too close. I turned around and realized we were *really* too fucking close. "You're the only one here, Fireball."

"So, you were hoping I would help you bury them?"

"I was implying you would be my murder victim, genius." I tossed my hands in the air. The cocky dragon made innuendo an art form but missed subtle allusions to his downfall. I tried to fight exhaustion and depression, rubbing my eyes and knowing it would do little to clear either.

Drax took another step closer, his hand extended toward my face, reaching for me. I pulled back, and he paused. Like he was catching himself before trying again with his hand floating in the air between us. Instead, he curled his fingers in toward his palm, eyes tracing the lines of my face.

"Would you really kill me, *mo doineann*?"

"No... Just... because you're the only one here, the law of probability.... and you're annoying, so you won't be around to post my bail... It was a joke. Also... can I kill you?"

"No, but it would amuse me to watch you try. Was it really a joke, Tempe?" He tilted onto one shoulder against the wall, crossing his arms. "Or was it the pre-coffee version of '*in vino veritas*'?"

Sweat pricked along my shoulders and under my arms, everything got very warm, and my slippery palms might drip sweat at any second. The dragon leaned slightly closer, nostrils flaring to remind me that my sweaty palms were not a secret problem. It made me wonder what flop sweat smelled like and if it differed from exercise sweat.

I blinked at him. "We're in a winery, technically everything in here is 'truth in wine'."

"You're evading."

"No, I'm thinking about sweat." I flapped my arms, trying to get some airflow to the space.

"Because it's running down your spine and through your hairline?"

I swiped my brow, and it came away damp. "Very astute." The *asshole* at the end was implied.

"Have you thought much about my death, love?"

"Not yours, per se. Just death, in general. I guess the good news is if I kill you and bury you, your body would probably be excellent nutrients for the grape soil, assuming the dragon fire means your tissue is rich in sulfur and not normal human toxins. Humans are really super toxic because their food is full of chemicals, but they're so tasty... the chemicals, not humans. I've never eaten a human..."

I sucked in air and tried to stop the words spilling out of my mouth.

"No?" Drax stepped in my path, not quite touching but once again sharing more of my air space than enjoyable with the sweat dripping down my index finger.

Normally, I would back away. But there was nowhere to go, and I... didn't want to? It defied reason, and I wasn't sure if I should blame magic, sleep deprivation, or his thick accent calling me his storm in the most gorgeous Irish... Despite the death threats I... liked him? Kind of? This was weird and too much for my pre-coffee brain. A thousand fire ants singed the underside of my dermal layer, threatening to tear me apart and I needed to run away before I lost control and melted down.

Except a literal dragon stood in my path, looking immovable and smug.

"Still waiting on an answer, love."

I struggled to remember the question. "Chinchilla teapot?"

"Have you ever eaten a person?" His repetition of the question indicated my answer was unsatisfactory.

"Nope." I popped the p and waited. "Cannibalism is frowned upon in these parts. No *Modest Proposal* ambitions for me. Did you know that author?"

He smirked but didn't answer.

"Would you move?" I crossed my arms, leaning away from him slightly. My foot-cicles might have stuck to the floor, but I still had a fully functioning upper body.

"I've got quite the appetite for... certain parts of people, historical satire notwithstanding. Though it's been a while since I've had anything with that salty goodness on my tongue. How about you?"

I swallowed, throat bobbing and flexing while my brain processed his words. "Have I had any..."

"Human parts..."

"In my mouth?" I finished the sentence.

"Recently." He was just a hair's breadth away, following my retreat and I couldn't move away.

I rubbed the dry sandpaper that used to be my tongue against the roof of my mouth, gaze drifting between each of his stormy green eyes, searching for some clue what part of people he used to chow down on. If it was feet, he needed to go wash his mouth, like now. Otherwise, what other parts...

An audible *Oh* fell from my lips, and it stayed there a moment longer than appropriate, considering what else happened in this position. I caught myself glancing at his mouth, wondering if he...

"Are you flirting with me?"

"If yeh have to ask, love..." He chuckled lightly, the sound sliding down my spine and circling the very parts a man might put in his mouth. Eyes flicking to my lips, I got the impression he would settle for either set.

"Shut up and move, so I can go upstairs. I don't want you to flirt with me."

"Off to drink your mandated coffee before any mortal beings arrive?" He studied my face again, fingers flexing at his side like they'd just traced the very places his voice left tingling. But he didn't make a move, just stared at me with a look of amused concern that suggested everything was in my head. I blinked so long it might have been a micro nap.

"Tempe? The mortals?" he prompted.

I groaned. "Are you really immortal?"

"No, but I'm extremely difficult to kill. Are you going to drink your coffee?"

"Are you going to pour it down my throat if I say no?"

"Would you like me to pour things down your throat, *mo doineann*?" His eyes trailed from my eyes to my lips, lingering before they drifted to my neck, and he swallowed. "And yes, I meant that to be flirting, lass."

"I... don't..."

His eyes dropped to my lips, watching my mouth fail to form words. I swallowed a knot in my throat, his hand reaching for me again, only to pull back. "I suppose you'll need more time to think about my offer then. Yeh know where to find me."

Without another word, he turned and walked away, through the kitchen until I sensed him moving through the magical barrier and back to his cave.

I shivered at the heat running through me with his passing and tried not to hyper-fixate on his words. The offer hovered in the still air while my brain worked overtime.

What the fuck was that?

CHAPTER
THREE

TEMPE

DEATH WOULD BE BETTER THAN FINISHING THIS work day.

It was 4:40PM, and the winery closed at 5. Despite 6 cups of coffee, I was on my last leg and every second ticked by with the ominous echoes of doom. Each of my heartbeats throbbed through my still cold feet, the bruised and bandaged fingers of my left hand, and the exhausted weight of my snow-shoveling arms.

Should I have asked the dragon in my cellar to melt the snow with his fire? Probably. But I didn't, because he was dumb. After a scalding shower, I reached the conclusion he was fucking with me. I was the ugly girl at the bar that some dude was dared to ask out by his douche-y friends, and I wasn't asking him for help with anything.

Probably.

Three sets of customers continued to hang around who had not only already finished their tasting and settled their tabs but were now just staring at videos and social media on their phones. With the heater on the fritz and our lack of free Wi-Fi, they would be better off, and warmer, burning their data literally anywhere else, but no. Here they sat, and here they chose to remain. I was this close to asking if they had squatters rights.

In front of me was one of my notebooks, this one filled with tasting room improvement ideas. Lucille Goodwin, a friend and coven mate, had suggested guest WiFi as a way to increase traffic. As I watched the zombies seated before me, I crossed the suggestion off the list.

We would offer free WiFi over my frozen dead-footed body.

I stared at the rest of the list, shelving mocked me as a line item on at least two different pages. The bottles I'd saved from crashing yesterday now sat lined up like sentries along the bar. I'd spent an hour scouting potential alternate locations for them and came up with nothing. Their old location had the only available space and the shelf needed to be rebuilt. Sadly, my attempts at manual shelving repair turned out less successful than my attempts at magical shelf repair.

Who knew hammers were dangerous? I flexed my bandaged hands, wondering if it was my fault or the tool as old as time.

A merchandise shop was also listed as a suggestion, and I looked at the available floor space. Technically there was room beside the fireplace for a few barrel displays and a table, but who would want to display their goods here? Did I know anyone who made stuff that wasn't food, odorous, or directly competitive with a neighboring artisan's offerings?

Did I have neighbors? A question for the ages because I would not look for them and I played dead if someone knocked on my door.

My head fell onto the bar top and I banged it once. Somewhere in the room, a man cleared his throat, and a phone started to autoplay a news story before the viewer silenced it. Leave... I tried to will them out of my establishment with an internal, ghoul voice. Corky was snoozing on the bar, and I wondered briefly if he'd be useful at coercing the squatters to depart. Like an attack tiger, or a former Army canine with a gas problem.

I should not work in the service industry, my inner critic decreed. I named her Captain Obvious. Because *obviously*. There was a reason I'd gone thirty-five years without a single job that forced me to cater to others. Even, ironically, when I worked in catering. I just made the edible arrangements and threatened to skewer anyone who questioned my bamboo rod technique.

"Tempe?" A guest approached the counter beside me. "Would you please take a picture of us?"

I counted to five before turning around, my face contorted into a semblance of friendly that would send moms with small children crossing the street. It was the female half of one of my parties of two, practical jeans and sweater as endearing as her willingness to drink water and exercise patience. My forced smile melted, and my shoulders relaxed away from my ears as I followed her over to the table they'd sat at.

She held up her phone and gestured to the man across from her. The reservation had been Carrie, Christy... Possibly Barbara? The pair had been cute, her explaining the reds to him while he offered her a goofy smile and nodded. He'd taken careful note of which wines were her favorite and when she went to the bathroom, bought the top three.

It was adorable... and disgusting.

"Of course! Do you want it at the table or something else in the background?"

She considered the wall of random shelving and then the bar, before settling on the wooden X-racks on the wall beside the door. "Could we go over there?"

I nodded, and we waited for her partner to stand.

She encouraged him to bring his empty glass for the photo, and he rested the other on the small of her back while being led into position and through a series of poses. First, raising it up to cheers, then linking arms, and finally just holding it in front of them. With his thick dark hair, braided beard, and abstract geometric tattoo circling his calf, I'd guess him as Samoan. I'd also guess this weather was not his cup of tea, but the loving way he smiled at Carrie, patiently performing pose after pose, made me stand a little straighter, try a little harder, and hope for a little more.

If not for myself, then for the people like them that didn't belong where they found themselves but made it work... For love. Or great sex, no judgement.

After snapping ten different pictures from a few angles in portrait and landscape (for the 'gram), the couple thanked me and collected their things. Dropping extra cash on the table, the man pressed his hand to Carrie's lower back and walked her out while holding the bag of their purchases. Tucking her to his side as they stepped into the cold air to keep her warm.

I studied the too-cute couple until the door closed, torn between wishing someone would keep me warm and hoping he'd left enough money on the table so that I might afford to fix the heater. Or the washer and dryer upstairs. Perhaps for the dishwasher making the sounds like it was *this* close to giving out. Or a ticket to somewhere far away, then I'd abandon this place and leave it to be someone else's problem.

The eternal war in my brain between romanticism and practical dreams.

I stared at the place they'd been standing and considered adding "photo booth" to my list. They sold ring lights that held people's phones, and then they could be in charge of their own pictures... but it required a power source.

Gravel crunched in the parking lot, and I physically recoiled. No way was it the couple leaving yet, it had to be a vehicle arriving. Not just any vehicle, based on the sound, a large one.

There had been a closure on the "usual circuit" of the wine region, cutting off one of the standard stops for transit vans and buses. Though there weren't many wineries out here, there was enough for at least two tour companies, and we'd hosted three tour buses so far today despite my adamant refusal to be included in their route, brochure, and lifestyle.

If a fourth one just pulled up, I was turning off the lights and playing dead on the floor until it left, loitering patrons be damned. There was not enough money in Jeff Bezos's pockets to convince me to serve another bus full of tourists who couldn't tell a grape from a raisin.

Sneaking to the wooden door, I spotted the back side of a lifted black pickup truck. A large flagpole jutted out of the rear bumper with some sort of branded message on it. Looking phallic as fuck jutting up from the ball hitch, I wondered if the branded content was for butt plugs or assholes. The driver also had actual testicles hanging from it for a reason I assumed was both immature and idiotic. Also, not very aerodynamic.

On the rear window of the cab, a decal of an oversized truck that said, 'Lifted trucks, because fat chicks can't jump' stood out against the tinted windows in a bright cherry red. Nope. Not today, Satan.

I started to lock the door when another of the couples approached me from behind.

"Thank you so much, we had a lovely time!" The woman, Paula, gushed. She looked genuinely happy while clutching her reusable bag filled with six new bottles of wine. Paula had chosen some of my favorites and appreciated each one with a gusto I neither faulted nor fully comprehended. Normal people *liked* things, but loving things should be reserved for fluffy creatures and people you've known for most of your life. Who goes around with boundless enthusiasm for... everything? "You really have some excellent varietals out here. Will you be expanding your offerings?"

"We... I have a plan?" I tried to engage while keeping one eye on the lot. A heavyset man with an oversized belt buckle, a red ball cap and graphic hoodie had just slithered out of the driver's side. "I've got some space set aside to experiment with other grapes but was planning on playing with some potential blends tonight if there's time after I run the numbers and get the wine put away. And there's a lot of barrels downstairs waiting for me to get bottled."

I gestured to the now homeless bottles.

"Ooh, have you considered a GSM?" She was bouncing on the balls of her feet, radiating the energy of a much younger woman. A GSM was the common name for a blend of Grenache, Syrah, and Mourvèdre. I'd experimented with them some, but I really like Mourvèdre on its own and the crop had been meager at best.

"It's on my list," I said, going for a partial truth. "We'll see what I can get to really sparkle this growing season."

"Well, we can't wait to come back." Her husband joined in the enthusiasm, head bopping to a beat only he could hear.

"We look forward to having you." I plastered a fake smile on my face. The lie was necessary because I looked forward to very little in terms of human interaction. Even pleasant humans drained my social battery and that sucker hadn't been holding a charge since the Power Ranger birthday party I went to second grade. "Drive safe!"

Paula pulled open the door and walked out, her husband following behind. He paused, giving a curt nod and holding the door open for three people: truck man, a woman in jeans and flannel, and a second man who may have been related to one or both of them.

"Did you see that rainbow fag flag on that Subaru in the lot? There's a lezzo in here somewhere." The man in the red hat scratched at his belly, rattling my windows with a boisterous laugh. The other two chuckled, eyeing my bridal party in the corner with equal parts concern and apology.

Samuel, bless his heart, decided to pull out a bottle from nowhere that they 'just had to taste', dancing a Charleston and improvising a grape stomp to keep all eyes on him. Laughing, the brides to be and their friends clapped along, enjoying the love and affection they had for each other, but Samuel remained tense. A muscle in his jaw ticked and the hand not holding wine stayed balled in a fist at his side while he sent furtive glances telling me to handle this shit before they ruined his lady's good time.

Despite the current group not being interested in men,

Samuel always knew how to make sure women had a good time. I was pretty sure the dude polluting my doorway had never found a clitoris and thought missionary was good enough, but I wasn't sure what to do about it.

I chewed my lip, gripping my bicep with the opposite arm while my heart pounded in my chest. My eyes darted between Samuel, the table of customers, and the group in my doorway.

Everyone here was a normie, and without magic, I wasn't sure I had the strength to force them out.

I wasn't sure I had the strength to kick them out *with* magic.

"Oh look, they think we're gonna let them get married and desecrate the sacred..."

My patience, a fragile little eggshell, shattered into a million pieces. Anxiety faded and my vision filled with the bright red of the man's hat. I zeroed in on it like a bull, nostrils flared to take in more air. Fire flickered in the corners of my eyes, blazing hot in an inferno that, if fed a single tinder, would engulf them whole and leave nothing more than bone and ash. It raged through my bloodstream and sent heat to every nerve ending until I was burning alive.

Ready to incinerate everything.

"Shut up and get the hell out." I squared off against all five foot seven of his well-insulated frame. I tried not to shiver as Drax's essence slid against me, crossing the barrier. Moving swiftly and silently, he appeared almost instantly to hold up his favorite wall. The same fiery rage I felt was mirrored in his eyes, an oil pastel of vengeance. "Now. I won't tell you a second time."

"I don't have to leave, fucking half-blood. It's a free country as long as you aren't some savage border hopper, stealing jobs. No fat bitch or dyke is gonna keep me from taking a seat and grabbing a drink."

He tried to move around me to get a table, but I cut him off. Heat rolled off me in waves, a new and weirdly comforting natural force field that pushed him backward. The skin nearest me turned red, sweat pebbling along the surface.

"Look here, fucker. You're right, this is a free country. I'm not ashamed of being half-Latin, but I do have a sign that says I reserve the right to refuse service to anyone. Refusing service to you is the choice I'm making, and it makes me super happy. The same way you choose to wake up and be an ass nugget, a choice it looks like you make every day of your pathetic, insignificant life based on your face, your truck, and your pencil dick. Religion, politics." I pointed at his hat. "All choices. Your identity, not a choice. Who you love, not a choice. No one just wakes up one day and says, 'I'm tired of not being hated and treated like a second-class citizen, I think I'll be gay'. I can assure you, if it was that easy, there would be a hell of a lot more lesbians. Dick is dumb as fuck."

I gave him a scathing once over.

The bridal party let out a whoop, saluted me with their tasting glasses and downed their pour. Samuel looked ready to back me up, and I refused to acknowledge Drax. It felt like a dragon was raging through me, it stampeded through my body with the force of a wildfire. I couldn't control it, couldn't bring myself back from the heat and fire pouring out of me when exhaustion held my magic too far to access.

"Big words for such a wittle-"

"Careful what you say next, asshole. Since I'm feeling generous, you get exactly two choices. Get the fuck out of my winery or get thrown out of my winery. You pick and keep in mind—I don't believe in being gentle."

"You can't throw me out, fat bitch. I'll crush you!"

I pulled at my magic, fighting fatigue and hoping it would arrive.

But Drax was on him in a second. Beside the raging beast, all three were the size of Lilliputians and Drax fisted the front of the truck driver's shirt. Muscles bulged under his t-shirt while he moved the man backward until he was flat against the wall.

No one exhaled.

"You were saying?" The growl sent shivers down my spine even as anger licked at my feet.

I fucking had this. Mostly...

"We're cool, man. We're cool. I was just joking!" His lip trembled, hands gripping Drax's wrist with pale ineffectual claws.

A cruel laugh echoed around the room. Drax's smirk called the fire out of me and left a soothing balm in its place. The exchange calmed some of my exhaustion, letting me have back a smidgeon of strength from the bottomless fire. We were a balanced equation, one where we would never leave the other wanting.

I trembled with the loss, but no part of me was cold.

"You were not. Do not lie. Admit you were wrong, apologize, and then leave." His grip on the man's shirt didn't waver, not a single vein in his arm popped from the stress. Under his grip, the seams snapped, giving up under the weight.

"S-sorry, man. Lady."

Drax dropped the front of his shirt, immediately stepping back so the sad sack ended up in a heap on Spanish tile. His friends stood to the side, immobile, while the red-hatted creature tried to get back up. Drax turned to them, and they physically flinched, grabbing their fallen comrade and dragging him out the front door.

Quietly, I whispered a memory charm and sent the relaxing message outward to cloud the specifics for both the customers remaining and those in the lot. We could not afford a lawsuit, and I could hardly stand when it was done.

"You didn't need to do that." I snapped while the remaining guests began to pack up in a cheery stupor and my whole body grew far too heavy to continue fighting gravity. As they marched out, Drax gave them all a polite smile that would scare children. "I had it under control."

My legs gave out and I slowly sank onto the stool behind the counter. My head drooped forward onto the bar, and I stretched out along the smooth stone surface.

"The polite response is thank-you." He smirked, locking the door behind the last visitor and flipping the sign to closed. Samuel had joined their departure, mouthing that he'd see me tomorrow while fleeing with the rest. I was pretty sure he high-fived Drax, but I was also pretty sure I saw a yellow canary floating in the corner, so my sight was unreliable.

"Thank you? Why would I thank you for interfering where you don't belong? You waltz in here like some kind of macho neanderthal after months of being little more than a damn shadow and I'm supposed to thank you for swinging your cock around like it was for anyone but yourself? You want appreciation, do something useful! Fix something, make something, hell, tell me a damn story. But taking away what little stress relief I get standing up to assholes..." Trailing off, my voice had lost most of its fire. It wasn't all that much relief, if I was honest and I was too exhausted to lie.

After a too long blink, Drax was crouched beside me. His breath warm against my cheek, caressing me without actually making contact. It steadied me to the befuddlement of logic and reason, but I needed him. The sensation of being wrapped in fire returned, but instead of a blazing anger, he wrapped me in a comforting blanket that sought to soothe and heal.

"I was not swinging my cock around, but if you would like a private showing later..."

"You are missing the fucking point!"

"No, love. I was attempting to make you laugh. I cannot help you if you cannot admit that you need me, *mo doineann*. Tell me you need me. Tell me *what* you need." His voice was barely a whisper and carried visions of stark cliffs and green fields beside stone cities and ancient castles. I wanted to crawl into the world his words promised, the Ireland of the past.

"I don't need anything or anyone." I jerked myself away when I realized I had leaned closer. An attempt to invade the world he created.

He is not your friend! He is just another damn burden of this winery!

"No one believes that, including you. This place can't survive on caffeine and spite alone. You need to let me help you. If not for your own sanity, then for those who depend on you. I wasn't sent here to be a pretty face."

"My sanity? You want to talk about my help and my sanity?" I pulled my head up and he took a step back. "You said you were dangerous, and look what you did! That's battery in this country. You can't just pick people up and drop them on their ass! What if he pressed charges? What if I wasn't here to make him forget? You think having you here is good for me? You think on top of everything else I want to be babysitting you too? Making sure you don't accidentally kill someone?"

"I would never accidentally kill someone!" He took another step back.

"Just on purpose? Isn't that what you used to do? What your job was? Is it still your job, Drax?" He pulled back, face red and angry. Gold and green flickered through his eyes, hands clenched at his sides.

"You nearly used magic in front of non-magic beings, how is that different?" He scowled down at me.

Maroon sparks danced above the surface of my shaking hands, but I had no control over this magic, and I stuffed them under my thighs. "The difference, Drax, is that yours is a crime. If I get caught using magic, I'll have to defend my actions to a council but as long as no one gets hurt, it'll be fine. If that man reports that an out of control, rage monster lives at this winery, cops will come down on this place. Is that what you want? Is that what you're here for? To ruin my gran's winery?"

He fisted his hands at his sides, clenching and unclenching them while his jaw ticked under the scruff that grew throughout the day.

"No. I'm here to help and repay a debt to an arsehole, love."

"Fat lot of good you've been doing at that, huh? Just... go

away." I waved him off, leaning back onto the counter. He lingered beside me for a few moments.

"I don't kill people anymore." His words lingered in the air while his footsteps carried him through the kitchen, back to the cave he chose to live in.

Behind me, the dishwasher made a pained screech and stopped, water pooling on the floor beneath it. A tear ran down my cheek. "And I don't know what I'm supposed to do anymore."

CHAPTER

FOUR

DRAX

MY CLAWS FLASHED IN AND OUT OF MY HANDS. THE sharp points sparkled in the lights ran through my converted wine cave, a space I'd occupied with the same indifference I occupied life. I wanted to crush something, destroy it and unleash the fury still pacing my chest.

"I'm not a killer anymore." The bed beside me remained indifferent. As did the dresser, the bookcase, the rug, the fridge, and the chairs all delivered into the space by Tempe. Everything I had that made this place more than a temporary stop-over on my way to death—was from her.

When I'd moved here and lived outdoors, I'd brought with me a single burner camp stove and a cooler for rashers. The wooded area bordering the winery held many plants similar to the native Irish vegetation I'd foraged for years, and I was hardly starving. But one of my first trips back to the island had seen a larger multi burner propane stove installed with a small refrigeration unit that dispensed water toward the rear of the cave near the cellar's ventilation unit. Tempe kept it stocked with rashers, cuts of chicken and beef, and a sack of spuds always at the ready.

At first, I thought they were the product of a promise to my

44

godfather and her gran, a repayment of sorts for the protection I was sent to provide the lone lass of the household. It would have been a major shift in character, but not one I'd turn down. That idea was quickly dismissed when I saw neither hide nor hair of the couple for months and she struggled to find answers in the mess left behind. She didn't need my protection, and she hadn't been asked to provide for me. Tempe took care of people because she did not know how to take care of herself beyond immediate threats.

"It was easier when meh job was murder."

"We could make an exception for that man." Crimson scales flashed through my mind, the voice of my dragon half echoing through me like a fleet lost at sea, come home to anchor in the bay. *"He'd never darken her nor anyone's doorstep again."*

"No." It was a plea delivered as a command. One I'd made before in the old country to another dragon. "Whatever Damian's intent for requiring us to be here, it was not to kill anyone. It was just a slip. Too close to the full moon and you are irrational about her."

Smoke blew through my mind, the snort grating against my senses. *"So are you."*

I sat heavily on the bed, my head in my hands as I tried to find a sense of calm. Tempe had never shouted at me, but whatever I'd shown her, whatever she felt was enough to break her stoic indifference. Seeing her come to life, seeing her lose control and feel... I liked it.

I liked it a lot and I wanted to piss her off to bask in the fury again.

"You gave her the dragon's fire." A flash of scales, he preened inside of me, and I missed when he was just part of who I was but when I started to ask how, he disappeared into the back of my mind.

My dragon had nearly granted her the power to burn the assholes to a crisp. How the fucker had given her the dragon fire was not something I'd been taught. There were no lessons back in the old country about sharing power across species but faced with a wanker who embodied toxic masculinity to the core, my dragon had arrived for her. He'd given over strength without either of our consent and calmed the ache of her own exhaustion when he left.

"I need to try harder to win her over." My dragon snorted in my head, and I flipped him off. As he was part of me, I just stuck my middle finger in the air for no reason and looked like a bloody fool. I needed to do something for her, something to prove to her that I wasn't a burden, or a monster. I needed to do something to end this tense stalemate we'd been existing in.

"Are we done pretending to be a threat?" The scaly bastard was back.

"We are a threat. We are a threat to her! But we can't live like this..." It was my fault we were here, but fuck if I knew how to fix it without time travel. After nearly seventy-five years alone on an island, I expected having an actual human nearby at all times would be grating. Instead, I found that I liked her and was socially challenged enough to feck up every interaction. When I brought her back to life but still could not join her completely without risking everything, it only got worse. I was so beyond fucked in all of this, but we were bound and ignoring the bond was not working.

I closed my eyes and counted backward, soothing the beast for the moment. There were a few more days until the full moon, but every hour leading up to it was increasingly more trying. He was taking over second by second, and without my mind at the reins, his activities were unrestrained and unknown. I'd seen nothing more terrifying than a destroyed land mass after a full moon, not knowing if my dragon had been the cause.

I blew out my breath. It had taken a solid two months to get permission to move around the American pack's land. Once I had permission, I was bound by the same magic that sucked the energy from Huckleberry Hollow. Trips into the township left me weakened and drained of my power. Once the Council was annihilated and I could feel Tempe's safety was restored, I was willing to carry the debt and the curse if it kept her clear of both.

Until Tempe had turned to stone and my heart had been ripped from my chest.

I'd known who she was the moment I laid eyes on her despite my denial, but I couldn't and wouldn't bind her to me. Not with my history of slaughter and the dying witch's decree. With every separating of man from beast during the lunar cycle, I would be a danger to her until I died. But when it became the only way to save her, I'd kissed her under the fullest moon and poured some of my magic into her to save her life.

Except she didn't know.

"Bloody fekkin hell." I shoved up, hastened back into the barrel room and looked around. This area was technically a cellar, where cases of wine sat on pallets beside an industrial washer and dryer for the tasting room linens and a full bath that my godfather had installed for when it was too warm to sleep indoors. Wooden cradles of wine barrels stacked in columns filled one corner, waiting for their time to be served, a forklift parked beside them. I'd never seen it operated and wasn't sure it or the system of conveyers and labels were still operational. There wasn't anything in here I knew how to work and even less I knew how to help her with.

Hurrying up the wooden steps, I followed my nose to the office space just off the small kitchen area. No food was cooked onsite, and the kitchen was nothing more than a stainless-steel surface for slicing meats and cheeses that would be plated with crackers, fruit, and nuts. A prep table with color-coded cutting boards sat beside a large sink with a retractable hose and then a counter filled with used wine glasses pressed against the fridge. The opposite wall had the large dishwasher, drying rack, and a supply shelf. Considering how often Tempe dropped glassware, I had a feeling this setup was troublesome for her, and she'd benefit from all dishwashing operations being on the same side—unfortunately I did not think I could accomplish that with her in the next room, but I earmarked the idea for later.

Tempranillo was seated at a flat screen computer with a picture of a slightly ingested apple on the back. Her hand dragged the mouse, eyes unfocused as they stared at something just beyond this world. Three notebooks sat open on the desk beside her mousepad and I glanced at the pages, moving further into the room.

The first had a numbered list and was labeled "Stuff to Fix". Top of the list was the space heater behind the bar to 'not lose her toes'. There was also the upstairs laundry, which explained why she was cleaning her clothes downstairs, farming equipment, the dishwasher 'making an awful sound', wobbly plumbing fixtures, and the fence to the rear where delinquents were entering to steal grapes.

I'd already checked that one off for her, making me question whether or not this list was regularly audited or she copied items over from one day to the next assuming if she hadn't done it, it wasn't done. Had I any knowledge of modern appliances, I would attempt some of these, but it was likely I'd make them worse.

Plumbing for the winery, however, I could look into and made a mental note of which areas were experiencing issues. That technology had developed little since its advancement by the Romans thousands of years ago. Tools may have gotten better, but gravity, water, and flow rate were still basic physics and if I got pissed off and nearly burned something, water was readily available.

Next to the first list was a second notebook that said "Ideas for Grapes". Tempe had listed blends she wanted to try, drawn a diagram of the vineyard and labeled the empty space with varietals she wanted to grow. She had notes about soil composite for each type to flourish and paired them in rows.

Her final notebook was a dated planner. Lunar cycles, coven meetings, shopping lists, payroll... everything was on there in her neat script, planned down to the exact hour of its execution.

February 4th, however, was blacked out.

On the screen, Tempe had the days' sales reports open side by side with an Excel sheet. I'd seen the bastard boxes dozens of times, but instead of filling in data or reconciling reports, the witch was highlighting D3 through E6 over and over. Clicking off and repeating, a weird repetition that seemed to bring her comfort.

Stimming, my brain supplied. A word I'd learned at the behest of my godfather, who had informed me Tempe was *different*, and I'd do well to learn all about her *abnormality* to best survive our time together. He was a bloody arse, but at four hundred, he hardly had the vocabulary to grow past murderous, manipulative git. The lesson was all part of his great plan for me to ingratiate myself to her, but I was simply grateful that my debt was paid without him underfoot.

"What's happening February fourth?" I asked into the still room, and she leapt a foot into the air. I steadied the chair and the woman within it, taking a quick sniff of her hair. Her musk of a day spent sweating mixed with sandalwood and plum shampoo, an intoxicating hit that sped up my heart.

"What the hell is wrong with you?"

"Asks the woman clicking the same boxes on a spreadsheet. Pot, meet kettle." I came back, noting the dark circles under her eyes and yet another cup of coffee on the desktop in front of her.

"I was... thinking." She crossed her arms, sitting back and pouting. I offered her my least believing smile, arms crossed over my chest. "Shut up."

"I said nothing, lass." But the smile crept up my face anyway.

Her nose scrunched, the freckles crinkled beneath her narrowed eyes. "Your face did, and it was being rude." She shut the planner that was laying open on the desk. "And don't call me lass."

"I can't help that you don't like my face. Plenty of other people do, *lass*." I threw in the name just to see if she'd take a swing at me, show me the signs of life and fire that I'd seen when she yelled at me earlier.

"I'd do anything to feel her touch." One of the few times my dragon and I agreed but it wasn't for us to decide.

"Then go bother those people." She went back to playing with her computer mouse. Aside from that one hand, she was reminding me of when she was a statue again. Glowing under the moonlight in rose quartz with her life force just out of reach.

"But you're right here and you're so easy to bother." I smiled at her, watching the muscles in her jaw work. I found myself silently begging her to let it out. Shout at me, throw a punch, break down.

She remained silent, clicking her squares more rapidly. I waited her out, sending my dragon into and out of her space until she cracked.

"Proximity doesn't equal permission, Fireball." She shuddered as the dragon danced over her skin, giving a flush to her cheeks and a pink tint to her chest.

"True. But when we met, you immediately gave me a pet name. On some level, yeh consider me worth companionship, if not company. I'm nay an expert on social interaction, but if you wanted to get rid of me, you could have. Admit it, you like it when I bother you, at least a little. You can even consider me your pet like that arse of a cat you keep."

"I admit nothing. You're being weird. I told you to go away, and here you are. Acting like we didn't have an argument about your anger issues." She stopped clicking to look at me. "And if you were at the pound, I would not adopt you."

"You wound me, love. Aye, short term memory loss. I am over a hundred years old. Did I remember ta put on pants and a shirt? Where are meh readers?" I patted myself down, inching closer to her as I did so. "Did I leave the kettle on?"

A smile tugged at the corner of her mouth, her head shaking in humorous dismissal. "I think I liked you better as a brooding, silent, asshole. What do you want?"

"What's February fourth?" I asked again, still holding the back of her chair. Warmth from her back seeped into my digits and my finger extended of its own volition to stroke her hair.

"None of your business." She jerked away from my touch, but her skin pebbled above the neck of her shirt.

"Mine." The scales flashed in my periphery.

"We share this business, so I believe it is." I decided to press my luck, sliding my hand along her shoulder, down her arm and separated her hand from the computer mouse. Soft warmth greeted me, her skin a welcome relief from my own inner hell. Every inch of our flesh meeting felt like heaven, and I wished for a second kiss. One where she kissed me back and it wouldn't ruin her life.

"You can tell me," I whispered against her hair. "Yeh can tell me anything."

My fingers stroked her wrist, pushing into the soft flesh to watch it turn white and then red when I released it. Small reminders she was alive, that no matter what Damien did with my oath, what the witch did with the splintered pieces of my soul, I had done this.

I had saved *mo doineann*.

Slowly, I lowered my head and inhaled her scent. I pretended to read the screen, knowing none of it would register beyond the rising heat. When she didn't pull away, I tried again to get her to talk to me, to trust me.

"In a hundred years, I've never blabbed a single secret. Trust me. I was sent here to help, but I can't if you don't let me into that pretty little head of yours."

"Do you tell me everything?" Her eyes were closed, jaw set, prepared for a lie or a dismissal. Everything was a give and take, but I was not familiar with how to proceed. I wouldn't endanger her with too much information, but I'd give her everything I could.

"What do yeh want to know?" Her pulse jumped under my hand, surprised by my willingness to offer myself. I held still, waiting for whatever questions would come out of her mind.

"Where did the glass come from?" She didn't look at me, but she seemed to relax into touch. To let me in.

"That's what yeh want to know, love? Where the recycling came from?" I tried to hold in my laugh when she nodded. "Cleaning up around the vineyard. Heard some youths out there on the lash and found the bottles this morn buried in the snow and more in the earth beneath. Fixed that fence as well." I inclined my head toward her book. "Shun' be able to nick the grapes anymore, though it could do with some magical touch-ups when you've the energy."

"Thanks." She exhaled, sitting back into me with shoulders a hair lower. Just a bit closer, a mite more comfortable, but I'd take anything. Any sign that we were moving past the wall I'd built. "Do I owe you for lumber?"

"Nay." I let my other hand work into her shoulder blade, pressing on the knots. A moan slipped through her lips and went straight into my cock. If not for her chair, she'd feel every thick inch attempting to steal all her woes.

And give her new ones yeh eejit, I reminded the beast within. He seemed to forget that outside of one moonlit kiss where he granted me control against the century-old curse, we still could not promise her safety.

"Do you ever wish yeh could just hit people like those who came in today?"

She laughed. "Yes. But I want to hit a lot of people, so it's not much different other than that if I had brass knuckles, I'd have used them." She relaxed into me a little more. "I know killing people is wrong, but I don't believe all life has value. Some people just harm and hate and do nothing but tear down the world. It might be bad Karma, but I would go on a vigilante killing spree if getting out of bed wasn't so damn hard."

"Yer nay thinking about that man from today, are you?" I stilled my hand against her. Every muscle tensed as I waited for her to again remind me of my past violence. To ask more of me.

"We will do them." My dragon vowed and I struggled to swallow the bile in my throat.

"No. I was thinking about Neo-Hitler and his Reich of morons... someone should end them. Wouldn't even be hard to find them."

I forced a laugh. "Shall I just fly over and burn the house to the ground?" We were getting steadily closer, my hands drifting around her arms and shoulder unimpeded, but my stomach had slimy green acid burbling through it. "Wouldn't be my first foray into contracted death."

Her hand squeezed mine, a flash of her eyes over one shoulder.

"No. I can't be another asshole asking you to kill for my cause, whether or not you've done it before. You deserve to be free, Drai-gus, to just live your life without people asking you for murder. If I can't do it myself, I'll just have to keep lighting candles and waiting for the universe to provide." My chest fluttered awkwardly at her statement. Words I hadn't known I needed, healing a decades old ache that still rutted inside me. "Though with the way my magic is failing, I can't count on that either."

"Your magic is not failing. I can sense it right..." I let my dragon slide through her, glide along the maroon ridges of her gift and sent sparks floating out around us. Almost immediately, the magic was pulled away, sucked into the ether as though it had never been. "Here. It's always been here. You're just too tired to sustain it."

Her body shuddered against mine, confirming she felt it, but still the woman was stiff and resistant to the idea. "Maybe fading isn't right. It just... doesn't work? I couldn't fix that shelf so it wouldn't fall. Couldn't fix it after it fell. The only reason dozens of bottles didn't smash on the floor was because I slowed their descent." Her eyes drifted down in shame. "Life was already hard, just existing and trying to get people to like me. If I don't have magic... who am I? And is she even worth it?"

"You are worth it, with or without magic. And I like you

either way, love." I leaned in to hug her but was blocked by her chair. Before I could turn her around, confess that I more than liked her, she drifted further away from us.

"You have to say that. You're not allowed to leave." Face dropping into her palms, she scrubbed at it. "If the winery fails, though, you can run far and fast. Or fly... I guess. So, silver lining for you. You can go home. This is all I have left."

She kept her face in her hands, resting on her elbows.

"I don't have a home, love." My hands wrapped around her torso, holding her to me even with a chair between us. Mouth right beside her ear, I encouraged her to let me in. "Tell me about the business, tell me anything to lighten your mind."

Her head shot back and slammed into my nose, arousal wafting off of her mingled with embarrassment and fear.

"Oh my gosh, I'm so sorry. Are you OK?" She gripped both of my cheeks, angling my face for inspection despite the lack of blood. It had been a century since I'd seen my mortality. "Oh crap, here."

Pulling several tissues from the box on her desk, she passed them to me, and I blinked. A warm metallic taste dripped into my mouth, my tongue flicking out against my lip to capture the tickle that ran down.

"I'm bleeding?" I stared at the red stain. Tempe pressed it back against my face, checking me over while I stood rooted.

"I'm so sorry. I'll get you ice." She dashed out of the room returning a moment later with a threadbare white cloth holding ice cubes. Rising to her tiptoes, she pressed the scratchy cloth against the bridge of my nose while her soft belly melded into my own hardened abs.

The hand not holding tissues beneath my nose lifted to rest on her hip, unconsciously trying to bring her closer. My fingers sank into her, pressing harder until I felt muscles and tendons, kneading them and hoping to distract her back into our moment.

"What do you need?" She lowered the ice when I pulled the

tissues away to have a look. Folding them over, I swiped again, and it came back clean.

"I think it's done."

Immediately she pulled away, foot catching on the wheels of her office chair. Before her arms could windmill into me, I grabbed her waist more firmly, sliding my arm all the way around to pull her up, back flush against my front where her round ass could tempt the raging beast that lingered beneath the surface. Back in my arms, where I could inhale her intoxicating mix of wine, plums, and sandalwood.

"Damn proprioception." Her voice was breathy as she tried once again to get away from me. Once again, I had to let her go and the loss of her warmth dimmed the room around me.

"Why were you surprised to see your blood?"

I raised an eyebrow at her.

"Why is February Fourth blacked out?" I countered. Whatever spell cast by our admissions had broken, and the bristling, irritated Tempe was back. In one move, I'd undone everything we'd worked on in the past twenty minutes.

"Can't you just answer my questions?" She dumped the ice in the trash and tossed the washcloth by the door, presumably to take to the wash later.

"I did, this is a give and take, love. You can't just take and expect to never have to share anything about yourself." I reminded her, though recycling and a blacked-out date were likely not on par with one another. She'd also shared more than I expected this evening and given me too much to think about.

I opened my mouth to tell her when she did the same. Anger colored her cheeks, the fiery storm that battered me harder than any I'd seen on the shores of Ireland, and I prepared for another brutal tongue lashing.

"It's my mom's birthday, OK?" She slammed the two remaining notebooks closed and stacked all three in a perfect pile. Beneath her waves of indignation, embarrassment, and sadness, was desire. She was mad that she wanted me, wanted to spend time near me, but as soon as she mentioned her mom, it all went quiet. Every scent, every salty flick of her taste in the air, evaporated under her wilted frame. Though she remained upright, every light inside her went out.

"So, is it blacked out to remind you to call her? Are you leaving to go visit?" I looked around for some sign that I was missing. Something to explain the complete shift from inferno to... statue. It reminded me that the spell her friend cast had more to do with it's target than the spell itself.

"Ehhh!" She made the sound of a loud buzzer. "You're out of questions, but thanks for playing. I'd ask if you knew you were very annoying, but I refuse to answer any more of your prying questions."

"I've heard that a time or two in the past century, an answer you can have for free." I crossed my arms over my chest to keep from brushing her hair from her cheek. Despite standing before us, she was already gone, and I had no intention of making it worse. "Not recently, as my social life has been as active as yours. Well, as inactive as yours, since I've lived on a deserted island for the past seventy-five years."

"What? Why?" She paused halfway into reaching for her coffee cup. "Because of the murder thing? Was that your prison? The place they send bad dragons?"

"Of a sort. I sent myself there for public safety. But if you'd like a bad dragon..." My mouth twisted into a smirk when she snatched up her coffee cup, only to find it empty.

"Damn it... that was the last of my coffee."

"Should I alert the Guarda of your impending rampage?" I joked. "Perhaps get the villagers to safety?"

"Don't bother. The nearest villager is miles away, so not only won't they hear you scream, but no one really knows you're here, so they won't notice when I murder you." She left the room as lifeless as she'd been when I entered it.

Once the sound of her footsteps faded, I picked up the phone and dialed the pack alpha's son. While the line rang, I studied the tissues in the trashcan-my blood shining back at me.

I was no longer frozen in time.

Despite the lack of a mark, we had bonded enough for all the magical benefits and dangers to kick in. It was how my dragon had shared his fire and knew she was distressed. Gifted her the ability to understand Irish and many other languages.

At the sight of my blood, I knew I would age alongside her. Then, beside her, I would die.

Tempe was my mate, but unless something between us changed, I would never be hers.

CHAPTER

FIVE

TEMPE

"C'MON, PLEASE?" I BEGGED THE DISHWASHER. FLIPPING the switch once, twice and a third time with a tiny pinch of magic before it sputtered to life. "Goddesses bless you."

A jeering chorus of cat calls accompanied Samuel arriving at the large table in the corner, and I physically recoiled. I was not equipped for this today. Most days it was hell, but today, I was heading toward a future where I burn this place to the ground.

Beyond the bridal table, a couple made goo-goo eyes at each other over a shared bottle of rose that I had in an ice bucket. They didn't seem to want an interruption, but their cell phones buzzed incessantly from either a pocket or a purse. Above my head, the fan ticked softly from a slight imbalance related to the angle of the ceiling, and the electric heater in the corner would not stop buzzing.

Can you call in sick from life?

I pondered this as a squadron of geese honked overhead, somehow permeating the ceiling to add to the cacophony of noise. Stemware scraped across a nearby tabletop, and I fought the urge to curl into the fetal position and cry out.

Once again, I didn't sleep.

And once again, I was being forced to behave like a func-

58

tioning member of society. Calling on my inner therapist, I gave myself a pep talk. I won't have a meltdown, I'm a grown ass woman now and I know what the problem is. Having a meltdown is for children who can't verbalize what's wrong. The problem is sensory over-stimulation.

Lucille, the witch who'd turned me to stone, looked at me from the corner seat in the winery as the bridal party let out another chorus of *whoooo*! Her gaze swung between the guests and me with interspersed looks of guilt and frustration. She had long, light brown hair and constantly wore a crocheted, conical witch's hat with a floppy point. Her familiar, an opossum, hung out in the brim and she fed him little bits of cracker from the remnants of a charcuterie board on her table.

While most people couldn't wear a witch's hat year-round without attracting attention, Lucy made it work. I wasn't sure if it was her "who cares" attitude, or her quirky sense of style, but she never looked like she was about to get the witching community discovered. Instead, she looked like an eccentric with kick ass stories, candles and a bunch of cool rocks. Despite that, or maybe because of it, she struggled with dating—always choosing men who treated her like she should be grateful they talked to her.

They should be grateful I didn't walk around with sharp objects to cut them.

I took a long drink of my quad shot hazelnut mocha and waited out another jovial squeal from their corner, wondering if Lucy remembered how to turn me into stone... and if she'd do it again.

Probably not, since the first thing she did whenever we saw each other was apologize.

Two people scraped their chairs against the floor tiles and I nearly screamed. None of my techniques for managing overstimulation were working and neither my internal longing nor my external frustration would go away for another... I glanced at the clock. Two hours and fifteen minutes.

"I'm getting married!" The blonde in the center of the table squealed, the five blondes around her doing some sort of shimmy and foot stomp that would have been cute if it wasn't fucking loud... and I wasn't afraid they'd fracture something. The six of them together had a total weight of under seven hundred pounds. And when offered charcuterie, cheese, hummus and veggies or anything with substance, they informed me they didn't eat solids.

Didn't. Eat. Solids.

Like that was an honest to goodness weight maintenance strategy leading up to a wedding. Not that the alcohol's empty calories seemed to bother them. I winced as they tapped the round bottoms of their stemmed wine glasses against the table and then raised it to their lips as one, chugging the last tasting Samuel poured like it was a shot and squealing again. They beat their feet on the floor, squeeing again as three of them reached into their pockets and tossed penis confetti onto my floor.

Those bitches.

"Should we put some food on their table or something?" Samuel asked, holding the next tasting bottle. A 2015 Malbec, the grapes I'd personally encouraged my grandmother to plant when I started learning about wine in the early 2000s. It was a staple in the area, given the freezing point and soil content, but gran had planted none before then, barely tending to the plants that were already here. This vintage had a smooth, jammy front with a peppery finish that warmed from the bottom up.

There were nine cases of that year left, and until I could sample and confirm the barrels downstairs, that was all there would ever be of that varietal. We really didn't have enough wine to be wasting it on women who couldn't or wouldn't notice the flavor.

"They don't eat solids." I mocked the pinched and bitchy mean girl from the early 2000s movie. Furrowed eyebrows aching, I rubbed the space between them, shaking my head. "I'm being an asshole. Truthfully, I have no idea if they're healthy, but I don't know how you can fortify your bones to not fracture without calcium-rich foods and they keep stomping their limbs."

He cocked his head to the side, and I realized I hadn't actually spoken aloud my fears that they'd break their bones stomping their feet. Now that I saw his reaction to the surmised speculation, it seemed more ridiculous than I thought.

"Never mind. I'm just... tired."

"Also, they're loud and you're overstimulated," he added, and I nodded. "Think you should call it?"

The sandy haired man stood at about five-five in his human glamour. His satyr form was just a little shorter, and while I appreciated his way with the ladies and customer service skills, the real benefit in employing him was his willingness to just cut through the bullshit and say what needed to be said.

"Everything in this room is so fucking loud." I curled in on myself, trying to be smaller. "But I've got this. I won't abandon you."

"You're not abandoning me. You're basically useless, Tempe. Let me handle this." He gave me a pointed look that stabbed at my sense of duty. The winery was my problem, and I couldn't leave it to him. Not with all these bride enthusiasts.

I removed the wine from his hand, grabbed an empty wine bottle and filled it with grape juice from a jug I kept under the counter for children. Reaching for my coffee, I let out a sigh when I found it empty. Death would be preferable at this point. "I can do this. I thought we banned bridal parties?"

"You tried." Samuel snickered at his own memory, and I eyed him sideways. "It ended with your winery being Jordan-almond and taffeta-ed. It was on the heels of a dark moment when you ran out of coffee... like this one."

I shuddered when it came back to me.

So much glitter.

"Thankfully, you seem to have planned ahead this time." He filled my ceramic mug that declared me a "Grape Bitch" from the drip pot behind me and I blinked in confusion. Though I knew I owned a drip maker, when and how I had made the pot was hazy, since I was pretty sure I'd bought the to-go coffee this morning because I'd consumed every bean I owned last night. So either I'd failed to look thoroughly, or I'd manifested coffee like a total boss witch, but neither explained how the mysteriously appearing beans had been brewed.

Am I losing time? Can you lose time when you don't really sleep? Or go anywhere? Or have any memory gaps and know for a fact you did not make that damn coffee or have any? Instead of examining my life any further, I drank the coffee and pulled out a jug of cucumber water.

Because nothing said *bougie winery,* like flavorless vegetables in your water. If I hadn't mastered growing cucumbers in high school when my mom blew through our grocery budget on tequila, I probably wouldn't have bothered. As it was, I had a magical greenhouse filled to the brim with cucumbers, corn, tomatoes, and zucchini.

"You sure you should swap the customer's wine for juice? I'm not saying they need more wine, but..."

"They are wasted and not even tasting it. Offer water first, and if they start acting like people who don't plan on puking in my parking lot, we'll go back to wine." I waved my hand at the bottle and altered the color to mirror the rich burgundy of the actual varietal he was meant to pour. It was an illusion any witch could see through, but we were outside the Huckleberry Hollow boundaries and these women weren't part of the community. In a peace offering, I pulled a pre-plated cutting board of cheese, veggie sticks, and hummus out of the mini fridge as well. "I won't insult them by putting crackers on it but see if you can get them to eat something and I'll give them bonus pours. Kids these days have no damn sense."

"You realize those women are only seven years younger than you, right?" He chuckled, and I scowled at his back. Thirty-five hadn't felt ancient until I was tired and lonely as fuck. Now I was staring at a table full of Stepford Sisters looking into their future of the wedded bliss that comes from the married tax bracket and dual-income households.

"Do you wish it was you?" Lucy asked, and I glanced over my shoulder to see her seated at the bar. I raised an eyebrow in question as I watched her languish over a glass of white. Her aura still held secrets, but not nearly as much as it did loneliness. "The wedding, getting married, having a bachelorette party? Do you wish it were you?"

"Not sure it's in my future." I shrugged, watching her grey eyes mist over. Lucy was one of the few people I knew who wasn't jaded by life. Her parents had been happily married forty years, her grandparents seventy years, and when she looked at bridal parties, she didn't see income taxes and lust fulfillment—she saw hope for the future.

I saw glitter dicks and torture.

"Why not?" Lucy took a sip from her wine glass, and I tried not to wince at the sound, but she caught me anyway and plucked a plastic straw from behind the counter. I watched her insert the juice box bendy straw into her glass and drink silently.

"Bless you, you're a goddess among men."

She laughed, the sound a soft thrum against my frayed nerves that didn't cause harm. "I feel like you'd be a wonderful partner, even if you keep everyone at arm's length with sarcasm and humor."

"Ouch. Hitting hard today. Honestly, between keeping this place together and keeping my brain together, I just don't see how anyone could want to take this on. And if they did, what could I offer them to stay? I'm not really someone people stay for, but I have a cat... Cats are good. Though he's kind of an asshole and I think I need a dog." I glared at the cat in question as he started swatting a cork closer and closer to the brides in an effort to get the confetti cocks. Between glitter and plastic bags, his intestines were basically artificial and festive.

"What about your dragon in the dungeon?" Lucy waggled her eyebrows at me, and I laughed.

"You're ridiculous, you know that right?" I wiped down the counter and then held up a finger to pause our conversation. I quickly poured the next tasting for a couple of tables, putting on my best socially competent face. "I sicced a Karen on him the day before yesterday and he's still here."

"You did not! What happened?"

"He growled at her and blew smoke from his nose. She stormed out of here swearing to annihilate me on the internet. The ushe. How did your date last night go? You didn't text me."

She turned pink and then puffed out her cheeks in an exhale.

"Tourist Tom turned out to be a dud?" I asked, refilling her wineglass with the taster. With magic, I materialized the cheese-board from where it sat discarded behind the wedding party to between my friend and me. Though the winery was filled with non-magic mortals, no one noticed. As usual, people were too self-involved to care about anything as strange as moving cheese plates.

Unfortunately, between that and camouflaging the juice, I was spent. I dragged over my own stool and sat down heavily.

"Worse than a dud. He had an unhealthy relationship with his mother, which didn't end with just living in the same room where his crib used to rock as an infant... she burped him. On our date... where he invited her!" I snickered at my friend's horror and tried to mask it with a cough, but she glared heavily at me through grey eyes turned stormy. "It's not funny!"

"I mean, it kind of is. His last name is Janowitz. If he was any more of a Jewish male stereotype, he'd have a Beatles haircut, ride a red Vespa, and been created by J. K. Rowling." I shook with laughter while her cheeks shifted from pink to flaming red and heat warmed my arm in proximity. "Oh shit, please tell me he didn't?"

"You know, I always had a thing for Howard..." she answered, squirming awkwardly on the stool.

"The haircut or the Vespa?"

"Both." She tucked her chin, and I cackled. "Shut up! I froze my tits off on that ride."

Opie ambled from the brim of her hat, wrapped his tail twice around the rod by her left ear, and lowered himself down to hang beside her. A normal possum was the size of a raccoon, but Opie remained the same size as a small field mouse and while I suspected unintentional magic had played a part, the creature was neither distressed nor unhappy, so I minded my own business.

"You're adorable, but seriously. If you need a date, there's a single dragon in my basement."

She jerked backward. "Hard pass. If anyone in town is going to hit that it's you."

"How dare you! And after I gave you wine and cheese." I pressed a hand to my chest, clutching at my imaginary pearls, mouth agape. The front door opened, and a slight breeze blew in with a solo guest joining her friends. It slipped by us toward one of the barrel tables and it quivered. The bolts rattling in their housing. "No!"

Lucy whispered beside me, and I felt both our power glide over to the bolts. Her citrine and my maroon caressed and coaxed the wood, the bolts, the metal bands, but it bounced off. As gentle as the breeze, our magic ghosted away into the ether and the table crashed to the ground into a splintered pile of planks and hardware. The sound reverberated through the winery, my brain, and the shaking bones in my arms.

"I'm sorry!" Lucy gasped, pressing her hand to her mouth.

"It's not you." I sagged against the bar, taking my seat back and shaking my head. "It's this winery. Something's wrong. My magic isn't working on anything here..."

Lucy wavered, mouth opening, to offer a suggestion when her eyes slid behind me. Her face jerked out of my reach as the air around us rose several degrees. Wild eyes darted everywhere and then toward the door as my friend prepared to flee from what must have blown in off the farm. Corky, the ginger harbinger of dragons, jumped on my shoulder just as all the air left my tasting room and I knew exactly what the cat dragged in.

"I should probably head out," Lucy whispered, gripping her

purse. "See you at the coven meeting later? Maybe they know how to help."

"Lucy, you don't have to-"

The woman was already at the door and halfway out it before I could even form the words to call her back. I spun around on my heel and glared, noting the man was wearing the same cargo pants and a black tee.

"Stop chasing away my friends with your face, Fireball."

CHAPTER
SIX

TEMPE

Two women across the bar knocked over their wine goblets, a man walked into a door frame and the walking rage monster arranged himself against the far wall for all to see. Gaze zeroing in on me, I tried to stare back in defiance but quickly lost my nerve when everything felt like a sizzling skillet in the wake of his presence.

I grabbed a rag and hurried over to the spilled wine. I mopped it up, watching the dragon through the mirror behind the counter. His smirk twisted into a scowl as his gaze swept my face and body. When I collected the glasses with a yawn, the scowl took on a level that could only be described as loathing.

Instead of dwelling on how I'd managed to piss him off in ten seconds, I collected the glasses and stacked them near the dishwasher. Then I poured tastings for other guests, all while avoiding eye contact with the Prickly Dragon.

"What happened to the table?" Drax's voice carried over the din to where I stood a few feet away. I jumped slightly, unaware I'd gotten that close to him. I snuck another look and saw him standing with his arms crossed, eyes boring into mine. His biceps were practically bulging out of his shirt while he flexed.

"It fell down. We couldn't save it." My mouth dried out,

stinging in the corner of my eyes threatening tears. "Someone opened the door and there was a breeze."

Drax frowned, looking at the splintered pieces. Something red and scaled flashed through my periphery, his dragon getting the lay of the land. There were three parties of non-normies in the room, two of witches and one harpy in a glamor. None of them had looked up when the barrel went down or when Lucy and I tried to stop it, but the dragon drew everyone's eye.

"Where do I get me one of those?" I glanced at the bridal party and saw all of them practically ovulating onto their chairs. With the confetti penises underneath them, it looked like a creepy clown porno where the dildos shrank and turned into a real man.

"Hell-lo! Is that my stripper-gram?" The bride's eyes were wider than the base of my wine glasses and I arched a brow in Dax's direction, curious to see if he'd take off any clothes for them. While I wasn't flush with cash, I could spare a few dollars for the show.

"Actually, Mr. Doherty owns the winery with Ms. Verdejo." Samuel smirked, filling in the details of Drax's identity. "But he rarely works with the wine, so maybe that's his real job."

The satyr might have had a bit of a mean streak...

"Your name is Tempranillo Verdejo? It's like fate that you work in a winery!" The bridesmaid beside the bride smiled widely, excited by name. She was cute in the same way they all were, and I decided this wine outing was probably her idea if she knew those were both wine grapes. I also decided I hated her because she was the reason I was in this hell and would need a vacuum exorcism to clean my floor.

"Own... well, inherited this winery. Took over? My gran isn't dead..." I pondered this, head tilted to the side as I moved around the table collecting glasses of unconsumed water.

"So, you got your name because your family is in the wine biz and they're all named after grapes? That's so cool!" A second woman, who was drinking grape juice like it was ten-year-old Cabernet. The sniff at the end with an eye roll said she did not, in fact, think it was cool. "Must be nice to be born into a future instead of having to work for it."

I glanced at her grape juice and reconsidered my stance on poisoning people and murder. "Actually, my mom has a different last name, and so does my grandmother. My mom named me after those two varietals because they were the wines she missed the most while being forced sober for 9 months and I had too many X chromosomes to be Jose Cuervo." I shrugged like it was no big deal, but I caught Drax watching me closely, maybe hoping to learn more. Under his scrutiny, I continued despite all the reasonable sirens screaming at me to SHUT UP! "She was too high on morphine while filling out my birth certificate to think my last name should match hers."

Wandering back to the bar, I grabbed a glass and poured myself some wine to keep from saying more. Taking a sip, I realized it was the grape juice and considered spitting it out but decided against it. My punishment for poor life choices was juice... Also, the grape juice was kind of good. Maybe toddlers were onto something.

"Ouch. But at least you got a cool name out of it! Is she proud you run this winery now?" the bride asked, though she was still staring at my business partner.

"No clue what she thinks. She died of alcohol poisoning ten years ago next week. If you like alcohol enough to name your kid after it, don't have kids. Pro tip." I shrugged again, kicking myself and trying to find something positive to end on. "But... my grandma established this winery, hooked up with his godfather at some point, and they retired together into the sunset and now we run it, and I have a cat. So, dreams come true for some people."

My gesture to Drax drew the attention back to him. He was still staring at me, and I resisted the urge to scratch my itchy skin. I didn't like the attention, but I liked even less that I'd just over-shared... again. Over shared and was now on the receiving end of pity... pity that said I was not emoting correctly for what I had just shared.

I needed a mirror and an expression manual for this shit.

"Wait! So, you guys are married and own a winery together!" One woman exclaimed, though I couldn't tell which one because I was now only looking at a small crack in my wall. It hadn't been there yesterday and if there were any justice in the world, a voice would call out that 'Prisoner zero has escaped' and a blue police box would appear and crush me. "That's so cute! Why didn't you take his name if yours isn't in your family?"

No sounds came from the crack and the only thing crushing me was anxiety.

"Not married. Drax is actually single, ladies." I ignored the burning rising up my chest at the thought, probably acid reflux. "Not sure what brought him up here, but if one of you wants to keep him company, he..."

The words were barely out of my mouth before they were on their feet. Five chairs scraped along the floor as every blonde, but the bride, rushed over to my co-owner.

"Whitney-"

"Back off, Whitney, you're dating my brother. I'm Elsie."

"Elsie has two baby daddies and zits on her butt. I'm Brayann."

The third elbowed her way in and Corky let out a loud yowl of displeasure when a fourth came over to drag her back by the hair.

"You can help him if you want, but blondes aren't really my department," I told the cat. Leaving Drax to his own demise, I met an older couple at the door and seated them at the far end of the room for their tasting. After a brief intro, they chose the red flight, and I caught Drax's eye on the way back to the bar.

I'll kill you, he mouthed as two of the women tried to get one hand under his shirt while the other was clawing at her supposed friend. It was like watching two grown-ups in the 90s fighting over a Furby at Toys "R" Us. It would have been comical if I wasn't partially in charge of cleaning up the bloodshed, in addition to the confetti penises gracing my floor.

I wondered if bloodstains could be cleaned the same way I cleaned wine stains... I pondered, eyeing the black towel. When one screeched and dumped a clump of blonde extensions on the floor, I gagged and grabbed a broom.

"Keep it civil, ladies. If there's any bloodshed, I'll have to throw you out."

Drax rolled his eyes, flashing his fangs in my direction and hissed as fingernails left red marks on his cut abs. He gripped the woman's wrist, his green eyes flashing predatory gold—a warning from his dragon that startled the drunk bridesmaid and sent her stumbling backwards into her friends.

"Wh-what was..."

"How about an extra tasting?" I called out, glaring daggers at Drax as I held up a port fortified with extra brandy. Angry red lines criss crossed his abs, and a gust blew my hair around me as he pushed down his shirt. The unnatural wind sent the women stumbling backward and maroon smoke billowed around the space, threatening to fill the winery and consume all the blondes.

Outside, the sun blinked out. Darkness overtook us, swallowing nearly everyone inside while the maroon smoke rose higher. It slunk around the table of blondes, nipping at their heels, pulling against their hair even as it was sucked into the floor and walls.

Soft fur caressed my skin, and I startled. Glancing down, I saw the orange cat rubbing his cheek and sides against my arm. My free hand automatically reached out to pet him, settling the raging storm and I blinked into the still air.

Light slowly filtered in, maroon dissipating back into the ground with the rising sounds.

Did I...

Magical traces clung to the air, and I tasted my own energy. Shit. Shit, shit, shit. I'd used magic unintentionally. Despite my control and regimented practice, I'd nearly used magic unintentionally against... *who*?

I searched the space and inspected each patron closely, praying to the goddess that all would be unharmed. Breathing out a sigh, I took a long inhale when I determined everyone was fine. It must have been a discharge of excess frustration, or a magical manifestation of my overwhelm. No harm, no foul.

Around me, the winery carried on, oblivious to what I'd almost done, with two exceptions. The golden eyes of Drax and the curious gaze of Samuel, both demanding answers in their own way.

Taking a few steps forward, Drax spoke first. Inches from my ear, his thick accent caressing my spine as it carried heat down to my core and settled deep into my soul, his words carried on a breath of smoke and pepper. More light streamed in, and my nerves settled.

"Defending my honor, *mo doineann?*"

"Your... honor?" I choked out. My eyes darted to the bridesmaids. Had I attacked them? They looked fine... If I'd attacked a mortal out of jealousy, they would take away my magic.

"Do you deny I have honor or are you unwilling to claim me?"

"Honor? C-claim you?" I looked around, wanting something to break this tension.

Green eyes flashed gold, then back to green and he relaxed his shoulders.

Trying to pull in air, I fixated on the spot above his right ear and tried to count bottles of wine on the wall. My knees knocked against each other while my feet were planted with concrete bricks of weight beginning at the ankles.

"Do you like the shelves I built for you?" Drax redirected me to look at the west wall. The bottles that had lined my counter were now on freshly built X-shelves decoratively stacked on the floor. Somehow, the stress of the day had rendered me blind...

"You made those?" I took his hands in mine, flipping them over and inspecting both sides like a seasoned detective. "With your hands? And didn't sustain injury?"

"Aye, love. I can do a lot of things with my hands. Would yeh like me ta make yeh a list?" His eyes shifted to gold again, and I dropped his hands faster than a hot cauldron. A single finger trailed down my arm before he clamped his hands back on his biceps so tight the fingertips turned white. "Or I can arrange a demonstration?"

"N-no?" I guessed, not sure if that was the right answer. "Yes? Where do we put the shelves?"

"If yeh wanted the shelves, you'd find somewhere to put them, Tempe." Irish lips caressed my name, and I wanted him to say it again. Wanted him to caress me.

His nails dug deeper into his arms, and I could swear I saw a vein pulse in his neck. Like his words were as effective at arousing him as they had been on me. Despite my frustration with him, my bitter resentment at being forced into this collapsing death trap with a not-so-useless man who builds shelves, I couldn't mask my desire. And I couldn't give into it either.

"I have to go." I turned on my heel and fled, Corky racing after me while the cocky dragon laughed, and the dishwasher died.

CHAPTER

SEVEN

TEMPE

I glared at the numbers in my notebook, my foot bouncing on the edge of the chair, while the silence stretched. There must have been a mistake, despite asking twice if there was really meant to be four zeros in his answers, I must have misheard him.

"It can't possibly cost that much to inspect a dishwasher." Though I wasn't a Jedi, and I wasn't trying to mind trick anyone, I hoped the reiteration would make him realize he'd quoted me for the repair of a fleet of flying vacuums and not a half decade old appliance. "The thing isn't even broken! It's just... a little sad! You know... like having the sniffles?"

"Commercial washers are tricky. That's the price, and if there's something wrong, it'll probably double. You can call us back if you want to set something up." With an ominous click, the line went dead beside my hope, and I considered purchasing them a shared tombstone while I slumped in my chair. I picked up the paper cup I'd been nursing for an hour, intending to take a drink of my peppermint mocha and put it down.

Not even coffee could fix this.

There was no way the winery had enough money to fix every-thing that was broken. I didn't know how much we had, but if this was the cost for one measly dishwasher, I was terrified to find out what everything else would be. Technically, we had two, the small one behind the counter was for glassware throughout the day and the much larger one in the kitchen for cutting boards and water service, but I needed both.

"It feels like I'm meant to fail." I confided in the cat, his tail swishing back and forth from the chair beside me. "Like gran broke everything before she left and was just waiting for me to take over, run it into the ground and collect the insurance money from the smoking crater left behind."

"Aye, lass, don' be gi'in the cat ideas." Beside the table, an older man in a kilt stood barely two feet taller than the edge. If I were standing, he'd maybe come to my shoulder and while my first thought was that he was adorable, I had zero interest in making a friend. "Yeh can' trust him nay to make good on the speculation."

I forced a smile at him, the red hair on his head reminding me of my coven mate, Penny. His thick Scottish accent overlapped some with Drax's northern Irish, and I found myself wishing I hadn't run away. Until I remembered the obnoxious smirk and the weaponized flirtation used to distract and disarm me from... what?

"Bee in your bonnet, lass?" The man's wedding band sparkled in the café lights, his open smile and gentle attention not something I'd experienced before. Strange men approaching me would be grounds for immediate departure on a normal day, but for some reason, this man didn't inspire my usual urge to flee. Whether it was his similarity to Penny, the odd echo of his voice reminding me of stark seaside cliffs, or just the way he spoke without expecting anything—I wanted him here.

"Not a bee, but the cat's Corky. He's pretty fond of cat food and pillows, I can't see him setting himself up to lose either. But I will keep a lock and key on my world domination plans and unicorn doodles." I doodled a unicorn beside the obscene number I'd been quoted. Then I drew the horn extra-long impaling the name of the shop who'd quoted it. "If only I'd thought to do that with my coffee, I might not have to go to the store on top of everything else... I hate the store. So many lights., so many people."

The man shook his head and chuckled, eyeing my drawing. Despite the violent nature of my depictions, he maintained a light, jolly demeanor.

"Aye, but some things only have value when you can access them. Can I share ye table?" He asked, gesturing to the chair across from me. Glancing around the room, I noticed a number of vacant tables, I cocked an eyebrow. "My wife is out of town, and I could use a chat."

Swallowing a bout of nerves, I nodded and shifted in my seat, the non-verbal agreement at odds with my brain screaming no. I needed to make more calls, I needed the quiet, I needed... he slid into the chair, and I stopped listing the things I needed.

"Arran." He offered me a hand, and wavered, carefully reaching over to touch just the tips of my fingers to his and then jerking it back.

"Tempe... Well, Tempranillo Verdejo. But people call me Tempe." I took a drink of coffee to stop myself from rambling.

"Aye, yer Maple's granddaughter? Liv's kid?" He blew on his drink, an ineffectual task through the small hole in the lid. I opened my mouth to suggest removing it when steam billowed toward me with the weight of fog, scented with the perfume of mossy rocks and whiskey. It pulled me through time, loosening something in my chest wound tight around secrets and memories. Back to the past when cops and bartenders would leave my mom on the doorstep, confirming the address with a single name.

Liv's kid.

It had been so long since anyone had called me Liv's kid... so long since anyone but me remembered she'd once lived. "Y-yeah." I swallowed a lump in my throat. "What did you do?"

"Hmmm? Sad ta hear 'bout her passing. Can' have been easy. Wha' with yer gran bein' who she became after your granda' passed. Those two were always much closer and his death was sudden." He studied me over the top of his cup, and I felt the first tear fall down my face. She'd had an addiction, her brain and body betraying her under the weight of life, but people acted like her life needed to be erased.

"What do you mean they were closer? They were married, of course they were close." I asked, head cocked to the side. "And why does it smell like a loch?"

His face broke into a wider smile, the bright red of his cheeks showcasing wrinkles and sunspots. "Old siren's trick. Not your gran, though she liked 'im better than most. I'd heard yer ma had qui' a bit more in common wit' her da than with her gran. Wasn' a problem til he pass'd but I don' reckon that affection transferred to Damien." He squeezed my hand across the table, and I didn't pull away. "Is that what brings you down today? Too many memories up there?"

My brows drew together, and I tried to dig up a memory of my mom talking about her dad. She'd always come across as distant, not wanting to share too much, afraid of being affectionate where people could see. I knew she loved me, in a way, but she was scared of people knowing about it. "No... I don't think she spent much time there... if any. I think they bought it after her? Thoughts of her usually keep me up at night. When it's quiet. The cruel irony that I crave quiet and that's where the hauntings happen is not lost on me."

"Nay, lassie, she grew up there. Not surprised she ne'er mentioned it, but someone shoulda. Half this town has never left, none of them said an'thing?" He rested his elbows on the table, eyebrows twitching.

"I don't talk to a lot of people... people suck. But no, no one said anything about her. Does she have any old friends still in town?" Hope bubbled up in my chest, the promise of a connection to her bringing me a small spot of light.

"Wish I could say yes, but I don' think she hung around much in town withou' magic. The old Council di'n approve. I'm sorry." He leaned in, patting my arm. "Hadn't meant ta taunt ya like that."

The hope bubble deflated, replaced by the oppressive weight of life and loss. "It's fine. Wouldn't have brought her back anyway."

"Nay, but I know what it's like to want a connection to home. Is that all that's got yeh down?"

"I'm... they're..." I sucked in a breath and the loch grew stronger. For a moment I was on a tiny dingy, being battered on all sides by the deep tumultuous waters. It pulled against the pressure in my chest, unwinding my words.

"Have you been to the winery?" I wasn't sure where to start, but maybe if he knew something about the place, I wouldn't have to try so hard. "Before when Gran Maple was in charge?"

Arran nodded. "Aye, we went up a time 'er two. Hardly e'er seemed to be open, but when it was nay a vacant seat to be found."

"How did it look then? Did... was... Things keep breaking. A small breeze destroyed a table today. Two days ago, a shelf collapsed when the door closed. Dishwasher, laundry machines, fences, and plumbing, it's all just falling apart. Was it always? And she wasn't even open that often?" My voice had gotten progressively louder, hands shaking and face getting warmer, but I couldn't keep it in. "I'm working my ass off, did she?"

Looking up at him, there was knowledge behind his eyes. Another wave of mossy stone washed over me, a gentle mist that splattered on my cheeks with the tears sitting in the corners of my eyes.

"I don' recall her havin' near tha' many difficulties. When di' it all start?"

I shrugged, trying and failing to pull the first memory forward. Had it started when I'd arrived? Before that? The end of summer when I couldn't harvest the grapes in time, and they rotted beneath the vine? When the forklift broke and I couldn't move the wine barrels? "It wasn't right after gran left... I don't...

she was still up there for a few weeks after I got here. Here but not, like a zombie, she just fluttered around and wouldn't or couldn't tell me anything. Damien had left first... I thought it was weird he didn't want to greet his godson. Like he didn't want to be in the same room. But that wouldn't make sense, would it? I think it was before I was turned to stone..."

"Yeh turned to stone, lass?"

"Yes... well, a statue. I remember seeing it happen from the bottom up and I remember watching myself slowly return to being human. It was nice." The sigh slipped out while my gaze lost focus into the past. "Being a statue, it was nice. Quiet."

"I hadn' heard abou' this. When did it happen? How'd you come back?" He drank from his cup, a paper tag hanging from the rim.

"Late summer, early fall? About a month after Drax got there. I don't know how I came back, just the quiet. The peaceful sense of... nothing." An image flashed in my head, and I squinted to try to bring the memory into focus. "There was a full moon. Something... flew across the moon and cast a large shadow. But then the noise crashed into me... everything was so loud. Lucy doesn't remember anything, she said she was in a trance for a day."

The Scotsman stared at me, his face unreadable beneath a drawn expression and an immobile body. Only his eyes moved, sliding back and forth across my face, plucking knowledge and truth from my head with or without my ability to verbalize. "Is tha' the one time yeh've had magical mishaps up there?"

I shook my head. "A bridesmaid attacked Drax today... well, attacked is strong. They were trying to undress him, and one clawed at his chest. She left a mark, and I saw red... literally. Corky brought me back from that one."

Arran looked away and then into his cup, tapping the edge against the table while his teeth worked on the lower lip of his mouth. "Have ye talked to anyone about that overwhelm?"

"What? No!" I pulled back, chair legs scraping the tiles. My elbow caught a passerby, and I quickly apologized. "Who... what are you?"

"That's a repeat question. I did tell you I was siren, love." He winked at me. "Fer now, yeh should prob'ly head over to Sue's fer ya meeting. I'd suggest askin' them to help yeh with yer winery and yer overwhelm. They can be quite the help."

Glancing at my phone, I confirmed the meeting was inching closer and stood with my empty cup, plotting where to get a refill before I had to head over. Corky jumped onto my shoulder, and we'd nearly stepped away when awareness kicked in.

"How did you know about Sue's meeting?"

He smiled, arms crossed over his chest. "Meh daughters in yer coven. She'll be pleased someone else was victim to my siren's truth song. And a bit miffed that I used it on 'er friend."

"Your daughter?" I kicked myself for not shielding against the siren's call for truth. I was too distracted, too tired.

"Yeh, Pen-eh," he answered, standing up to leave himself. A barista called my name, and he gestured toward the counter. "That's yers. Consider it an apology."

Patting my shoulder, he disappeared while I tried to pick apart his thick accent and figure out who the hell Pen-ay... Pen... Penny?

Penelope.

Shit.

"THIS IS PROBABLY TOO MUCH," I said to the sky. Staring at the slowly appearing stars, I waited in vain for the sky to either open up and swallow me or assure me it was a good idea to turn around and go back home. "I can't do any more people-ing today. So either end it or give me a sign I can leave."

Corky mewed from beside me, and I stared between the orange cat and the townhouse outside my passenger window. The grey and brick affair sat in a perfect row with dozens of other carbon-copies. Four steps leading to a small stoop, a burgundy door and a two-story house currently blanketed in a layer of snow. Remnants of the Yule festival remained on the porch, ribbons and boughs of pine garland distinguishing Sue's house from her neighbor's.

On the driver's side was a forest, the homes worked into the trees seamlessly to exist with space. Treehouses and mushroom capped dens housing sprites and woodland nymphs peeked out of the darkened forest to wink in mockery at the regimented structures across the way. It was like looking at someone's game shelf and seeing a domino set across from a unicorn terrarium, both technically toys, but only one inspired joy.

The other made you think of rows of Nazi dominos marching side by side, waiting to be knocked over to reveal some intricate design. I'd kick the townhouses down myself to reveal the underlying beauty if it wouldn't make several people homeless. There was also a high probability that the whole thing would make a tremendous amount of noise and reveal absolutely nothing interesting.

The former would be enough to keep me from ruining everything, but the latter would send me on a one-way trip to a mental institution.

All the noise, noise, noise, I wanted to scowl like the Grinch and hightail it back out of the hollow. To my hill and my dog... after I got a dog and plotted the demise of... something.

I need something to hate... Drax and his dumb, handsome, shelf-fixing face, maybe? Did I need my heart to grow three sizes? I glanced at Corky and wondered if you could hate things with your cat or if it was a redundant exercise since cats weren't overly fond of anything to begin with.

Behind the Subaru, my winery winked on the hill in subdued lighting. It didn't look like a cursed business venture with a surly dragon shifter and insufficient money to hire farm hands to till and tend the crops. When I'd first taken over, I thought maybe Drax was the answer to farming more grapes without incurring debt. A dragon could easily do it, but my grandfather didn't shift and Draigus was apparently not into helping me keep the family legacy alive.

"Shit." I banged my head against the steering wheel. "Shit, shit, shit. It's *my* family legacy. It doesn't matter if they're here or they care. I have to care. Which means..." I stared through the side window at Sue's townhouse. "I have to ask for help."

Corky flicked his tail against the back of my hand. The cat equivalent of *a duh, bitch*, I assumed. Picking up the coffee from Penny's dad, I took a fortifying drink and made direct eye contact with the cat.

"Are you in this with me? We ask for help to understand why the winery defies my magic and we listen, and we don't judge ourselves?" Corky purred softly, butting the top of his head against my forearm. I reached over, scratched the top of his orange head and lifted him to my shoulder. A Doberman appeared in the front window, watching us exit the car and walk carefully up the icy walkway. Max kept his eye on us until we made it to the front steps and then withdrew into the house.

I reached for the knocker at the top of the two steps, only for the door to be pulled open.

"I heard you could use some help." Penny smirked, her familiar Grim beside her with Max and Sue waiting behind them.

There's no turning back now.

CHAPTER

EIGHT

DRAX

THE BLASTED SATYR TEMPE HIRED HAD JUST FLIPPED the sign to "closed" and I still hadn't figured out why the table had fallen over. We'd cleared the pieces away after the last guest departed, only for a chair to collapse when the saved wood bumped it on the way past. There were no more clean towels after draining and drying the floor beneath the dishwasher, and the claw marks from the bridesmaids still stung from where they'd broken the skin.

"Do you need something for the scratches?" Samuel's nose worked in my direction, his glamour dropping and the furred chestnut legs and hooves coming into view. He still wore the winery polo shirt, but without the illusion, it hung below his waist like a tunic. Curved horns protruding from the light brown hair on his head were sharp enough to impale, though he did not appear to suffer from bloodlust. "Antibacterial goo or a plaster?"

"A plaster?" I lifted the plastic tray full of dishes and started toward the kitchen. Without the smaller dishwasher, we'd been running loads to the neighboring room, a task for two workers, an impossibility for one. "Are yeh fekkin takin the piss?"

He shook his head and pulled a rectangle from his shirt pocket. Using the internet, he pulled up a picture of a sticky strip

83

with gauze in the center used to absorb blood and prevent infection.

"I can't get an infection, and I don't bleed." Or I didn't, but that wasn't for this man to know. Though we'd worked quietly in tandem, his presence made me uncomfortable. A being from the old country, he had the same energy signature of Ireland and guilt clawed at my insides, sticky and sharp.

"Are you sure?" His nose worked, eyes narrowed my direction. "Smells like you might. Like maybe you've rejoined the timeline and are in denial about it."

"I did not kill that boy's family." But I couldn't believe the scaled beast. There was no way he remembered all that he'd done, not like I did. Their faces haunted me both asleep and awake.

"Nay still... frozen in time." My throat worked around a lump, the man in front of me not buying the lie. Half lie, as it were, since I was frozen in inaction—uncertain what to do about the woman I needed to accept me for us to move forward. The dishwasher signaled completion, and I dragged the wet glasses back to the counter while the horned child watched. "Shouldn't yeh be headin' out?"

"Evasive much?" Samuel's pocket rectangle emitted a barrage of sound, and he pressed it to his face. "Yeah, I'm here with him. Do you want to talk to him?"

Silence stretched into the room. It weighed on my chest, in Samuel's eyes, and in the small step back he took before grunting affirmation. He placed the device back in his pocket and put up his broom, eyes not meeting mine.

"Who was that?" A tight band wrapped around my chest, an uncomfortable sensation of my skin crawling over itself tickled my scalp.

Samuel spared me a look and pulled a small satchel from under the wine bar, collecting his tips from the past two days and slipping them into the front pocket. "It was Arran Odenberry. He's on his way here to speak with you."

"The father of Tempe's coven mate?" I blinked in surprise,

fumbling with the dish rag as Samuel continued to increase the distance between us. "What does—"

"I have to go. Tell Tempe I'll see her tomorrow." He waved me off and walked out, leaving the door unlocked behind him.

Resigned to lock it once I was done with these glasses, I continued to dry them and curse flighty youths. The door creaked behind me, and I called out. "Did yeh forget something or did yeh realize you were bein' ridiculous?"

"Nay, I'm here to speak with you, sonny."

My eyes shot to the mirror above the bar, connecting with the short red-haired man in a kilt standing in the center of the room. He'd locked the door behind him, a move that had my blood pounding in my ears. My weight shifted to the balls of my feet, and I had a strange urge to flee. I had a foot and a hundred pounds on the lad, but I had a feeling he'd hand my arse to me just as easily as any warrior.

"Mr. Odenberry, I'm guessing?" I set the glass down and turned, leaning against the bar with my arms crossed. I tracked his movement across the room, each step a calculated advance that swam with the misty magics of the isles. My dragon stood, scenting the damp stones and responding with a sulfuric warning. "Yer a siren, then?"

"Aye, lad. I see your dragon will keep me from using that talent. Let's see if ye'll be honest without it." He pulled out the barstool and perched on the edge. A finned fog swam through the room, touching each item, tasting the surface and the power underneath. It was the same thing I'd done earlier, searching for hidden talents or traces that would explain the damage. The same as before, the mist was sucked away into the walls and floor, a passing show that faded.

"It's all her gran's." I confirmed what his own power would tell him. My arms relaxed, and I placed one of the wine glasses in front of him and lifted a bottle of red. He consented, and I poured. "There's nothing here, but there's also nay an explanation for the slow structural demise and the steady loss of magic in the air."

I set the wine bottle beside the glass and stared at the label. Tempranillo.

"Seems yeh know why I'm here after all. Want to tell meh about the day she turned into a statue or who your godfather really is first?" He took a sip without looking away.

I pulled another glass out and poured wine for myself. After a long drink, I stared at the shelves I'd built for the woman in charge. "He's nay my godfather. I owe him a debt. One that is repaid by remaining here a year, to what end was not made clear."

The Scotsman raised a furry eyebrow at me, the red caterpillar equally entertaining and threatening. "But yeh never intend to leave this place, do yeh?"

I shook my head, drinking the wine and swallowing the growing sense of truth to his words. "Nay. I can't leave her, not anymore."

He nodded, my secret in his eyes. Our eyes stayed locked for another moment, and I broke away first to drink my wine. He pulled a tote bag out from under the counter, one I hadn't seen at first, but he'd brought in with him. "Yer lass expressed distress over being out of coffee and I kept her from having time to visit the shop. I acquired some for her as an apology, unaware that my son-in-law had already helped you. But I can't imagine this goin' ta waste."

I looked into the bag and saw an additional dozen bags of coffee. A laugh slipped out, one that bounced off the walls and melted the stern expression from the man in front of me. His genuine smile split his face, filling his round cheeks and highlighting the deep lines of joy carved from years of laughter.

"Yeh used siren magic on her?" I tucked the bags away, adding the remaining supply I needed to deliver from my own arranged purchases to her apartment later. "Imagine that went over as well as Nessie in a union jack."

"She won' be comin' near me without a shield spell in place

anymore." He leaned forward to look at the dishwasher, then sideways into the kitchen. "What debt do you owe Damien, son?"

My fingers tapped on the bar, considering while blood rushed to my head and I felt slightly sick. What I cost him was worse than death, but what he'd done... "His dragon. He claimed I cost him his dragon."

Arran pulled back, head cocked to the side. "That don' sound righ'."

I shrugged and poured more wine into my glass. Despite all the flavors and effort *mo doineann* had put into this bottle, I couldn't taste a thing. Sandpaper and sawdust had replaced my tongue. When half the glass was empty, I tried again. "The debt was incurred before I knew the truth. But a blood oath cannot be taken back over something as trivial as the truth."

Bitterness coated the words, the acrid burn souring the air between us.

"Bit of unsolicited advice?" He'd taken a long pause considering how to proceed, and I decided whatever suggestion he made, it had to be better than my plan... as presently there wasn't one.

I nodded, toasting him with the last of the wine in my glass and swallowing it.

"If yer debt and your bond depend on her surviving this winery, yeh'll want to stack the deck in your favor." He handed me a paper, and I unfolded it to see a list of names and phone numbers. "Everyone there wants to help, but she' hasn' asked. Yeh should see about changin' that for her."

Arran finished his wine and offered a hand. We shook, and my dragon shuddered under the sudden mist that traveled through the line. His gaze hardened, pulling back and staring into my eyes while heat patched my skin through his renewed grip.

"You have more than a debt, sonny." It wasn't a question.

"Aye. But if I fulfill the debt, I can do something about..." My dragon floated to the surface, taking control, taking over. With a groan, fists clenched on the counter, I fought him back to see Arran on his back. "Shite. Are you—"

Mr. Odenberry rose, dusting off his kilt. I couldn't smell blood, nothing was broken, and yet... *What did you do?*

"What I had to do!" He snarled, pacing the caverns of my head, fangs and claws flashing.

"Aye. How often do you lose control?" He studied me the way a child might analyze an insect under a magnifying glass. The neutral expression was worse than disgust, because underneath, I suspected he may pity me.

I kept my hands anchored on the counter, my stomach knotted. "Every full moon. For seventy-five years."

A soft whistle escaped the Scotsman. "If yeh need assistance..."

I nodded. He took that as his cue and walked out the front door. I followed him out and locked the door, carrying the coffee we'd arranged for Tempe. While the old man watched, I shifted just the flesh of my back. Six-foot-long wings expanded from both sides, and he let out a low whistle while I examined the winery Tempe had been making our home.

"What are yeh doin' son?" He leaned back against the car while I lined myself up with Tempe's balcony.

"Putting this away." I held the bag aloft. Bent at the knees, I crouched low and shot up, taking two short strokes through the air before landing on the balcony outside her living room. The space was dark, but I could see through the windows that she kept it as tidy as the rest of the winery. As expected, the handle was unlocked, and I let myself in to the amused departure of Penny's dad.

Her scent punched me in the gut, warming and lurking in every fiber of the room. I leaned over a chair and inhaled, wishing I could bottle the soft musk that came with everything she touched. Light glinted off her coffee maker, the one appliance that didn't match, and I studied every piece in her space.

From the scarred wood table to the generic white stove, none of it looked like her. Even the armchair bearing her scent was laced through with Damien and Maple. I ran my hand along the counter, seeing the cat's dishes were repurposed ramekins in vibrant colors brought a small smile to my face. It was a tiny thing, but it was one of the few signs she lived here.

I set the bag on the counter, unloading the bags of coffee Arran brought and the ones I'd added from my earlier purchase via Artemis. Together, we'd purchased about twenty bags for her apartment, and I turned around to find the correct home in her cabinet above the stove. The first I opened had a small blue bottle behind a box of rice.

"Why is that there?" I scanned the shelves, removing the bottle and finding no place that looked like it belonged. In the neighboring cabinet was a large empty shelf, the residual scent one of coffee and flavor, with sufficient space for all twenty bags. "I could have bought her more."

"There is still time to bring mate tokens." I chuckled softly at the notion of a dragon bringing his mate coffee a hundred years ago. Flowers, gemstones, and any manner of jewelry were the standard then, but our mate... *"We'll bring her coffee."*

It was as good a place to start as any. My hand started to close the cabinet, and I blinked at the blue bottle. I'd placed it beside the bags of coffee. Frowning, I took it down again and opened another cabinet, finding dishes and containers for food storage. It looked like a more reasonable home, and I reached for the bottle to place it inside, only for it to be gone. Back inside the cabinet beneath the coffee beside the box of rice.

"Where..." I caught sight of one of Tempe's notebooks and abandoned the cabinets. Flipping through the pages, I saw sketches and a list of ideas for the outdoor patio to be used as additional seating. Another notebook stuck out under her armchair, and I pulled it free, reviewing her suggestions for a new experimental growing region.

An idea formed. A way to use Arran's suggestion and my need to do for her. The dragon and I went room by room through first her apartment and then the entire winery and collected all the notebooks Tempe had tucked into every corner. After the first two, it no longer mattered what was inside, only that she had all of them available to her.

Tomorrow, we would pick one, any one, and make a change. Make this place hers... ours.

Ready or not, she was done trying to hold this place together on her own.

CHAPTER
NINE

TEMPE

The Coven of Misfits technically didn't have a name. Two women, Sue and Andrea, had been having coffee in the early nineties with their dogs when the town's old Council had bound all the magic within Huckleberry Hollow to their life force with the dark magic of the demon realm. With her home just beyond the border, Sue's house was a neutral location for magical creatures and beings to gather where the Council couldn't siphon their magic or manipulate it into hate. The coven grew as witches who'd grown up in the area came of age and started asking questions, finding themselves on the outside with no support. One by one, Sue and Andrea had collected the outcasts, the beings with innate magic, and their pets until we were a coven with the joint goal of... eating cheese and fucking over the patriarchal group of skeletons.

At least, that was the lore I'd been told. Unlike the others, I'd ended up in the coven because my gran doubted my ability to make friends and guilted her own into including me. It was the only explanation for why a woman in her sixties would shlep up the hillside to invite a stranger to her coven meeting—pity and obligation to an old friend.

Sue's townhouse had three stories, with the front steps

entering to the main living area. The hallway was wider than the narrow structure would lend itself to, breaking off to a living area on the right and a kitchen straight through, angled towards the left. To the left before the kitchen was a carpeted staircase leading up to the bedrooms and another leading down to the garage and laundry area. Cinnamon and anise permeated the air, undercurrents of citrus tickling my nose, and I wanted desperately to sink into the comfort and protection the herbs and fruits usually offered.

But I couldn't relax tonight, knowing I'd come in to admit everything was not okay and I needed... other people. My track record with other people wasn't great, so the chances this would end the same place it started were pretty high.

The good news was I had a frequent flyer pass to nowhere, and they knew me there.

"Ladies, into the circle please!" Andrea called out into the hallway. She was wearing her large, wire-rimmed glasses and a bandana holding back her curly grey hair. As usual, she was wearing a rainbow of colors, drinking a rosé, eating cheese, and sharing cheddar with the black Kelpie who was never more than six inches from her person. "We haven't got all night."

"We literally do," I muttered and felt a small hand clap against the back of my head. "Ow!"

Sue gave me a look from a foot below me, where she was somehow also seven feet tall. The short woman was Andrea's opposite, forgoing whimsy and color for the function of jeans and flannel on her tiny frame. Max, her Doberman, panted beside her. His wide, smiling mouth appeared to laugh at me.

"Don't get smart with us, Tempranillo. Just because you had a poor upbringing does not mean you will behave poorly." She continued into the room, the weight of her declaration settled on my chest while my scalp smarted from the hit.

Shuffling into the room, I took my place across from Lucy and Penny on a favored, weighted meditation pillow filled with beans. A half dozen chairs sat around the perimeter, but nearly all of us sat on the floor. Either because we needed to feel grounded or because it was a shorter fall when we got drunk and inevitably lost balance. No one had ever sat in a proper chair besides Andrea and Sue.

Butterflies danced around my guts and I started to reconsider my request. What seemed like a good idea talking to a siren in a coffee shop was feeling more like humiliating myself in front of the only people who tolerated me. Yes, they were all nice, but did that mean they wanted to help?

The coven had about fifteen members, a number that fluctuated based on who was in town, who remembered to show up, and whether or not there was booze. Penny, Penelope Odenberry, was our newest member of a few months, a witch and a psychiatrist, with red hair, a large black dog and curves for days. She was born in the Hollow, bullied into running away, and then forced to return where she kicked some serious magical ass.

Naomi, a wood nymph, was her one quasi friend besides her fated mate and she was in attendance this evening. The woman made a 6/4-time signature look slow and held grudges, like they alone powered her universe. Jen, our resident Harpy, perched in her usual seat beside the window. Though she rarely shared, or spoke, her magic brought the taste of creosote and juniper to every coven meeting that re-established us into the natural order. Curtis was a dick, and no one wanted him here, but he was a coven-less witch, which meant we had to take him... or kill him.

I'd personally voted for kill but narrowly lost the vote. I had high hopes one day the tides would turn, and we could string him up by his toes to use as a pinata.

Hayami snickered beside me, the Satori tattoo on her arm dancing in the light. The tail appeared to weave back and forth, a soothing metronome of metered hypnosis measuring my breath into a stable pattern. I watched it for several minutes, letting its antics lull my mind into quiet for the first time today, settling the weight on my chest and granting me my first deep breath.

My gaze shifted between the ink and its owner, but she

appeared to be paying attention to Naomi, the woodland nymph and sandwich shop owner, telling a story about a cursed olive that tried to eat her hand. Still, I watched. The Japanese folklore surrounding the monkey-like monster was shrouded in fear-mongering heresy. Hayami had thick straight glossy hair and a timelessness that meant she could be twenty or two-hundred and no one would know the difference. I had never learned much about the quiet woman or her relationship with the legendary mountain creature, and she'd never brought it up.

But I now wondered if she descended from the Satori, or if she was the original and they were immortal.

Hayami's gaze flicked to me, and I went back to looking at my shoes. Scolding myself with a stern reminder to mind my own damn business.

Being hyper observant was a drawback of autism. One of many. No one likes it when you notice and remember small things, and they like it even less when you call them out on their hypocrisy when they try to refute the thing you remember. Pattern recognition and reasonable extrapolation of predictive models make you look like a witch, even when you haven't developed magic yet... or known that magic exists. When you actually are a witch... let's just say I was a few centuries shy of being used as tinder. From what little I'd learned of the rest of the coven members, they'd have been burned alongside me.

"Let's get started." Andrea opened the meeting, and we all turned our faces toward the ceiling, looking out into the universe. The flavors gathered together, a prismatic rainbow of color and scents, dancing in and out of each other until we were our own nighttime spectacular. "Blessings to our sisters, blessings to the Earth, and may fortune follow us safely down our path this winter's eve. So, mote it be."

"So, mote it be." We returned the magic to her, and I watched it all expand and recede into the circle. I concentrated on the intention behind the words, hoping to get something deeper. To really connect with the coven and the sentiment. I'd felt our magic, felt our community, but mostly it felt like fortune was a stalker and the only blessing the Earth really needed was humanity to get the hell off of her and die already.

"Now, there are several orders of business. I believe we should begin with Tempe, as I understand there has been some trouble she's dealing with." Andrea looked over at me and Corky jumped into my lap. His warm weight countered my urge to run, forcing me to remain seated, as everyone knows you cannot move once a cat settles into your lap. Sue entered the room and passed me a glass of wine before taking a seat in the floral armchair opposite Andrea.

I took a long drink and set the glass away from me. Staring into the shades of orange in Corky's fur, I stroked down his back twice before finding my voice.

"I was overstimulated." I cleared my throat when the words came out muffled. "Am still overstimulated. There was a bridal party in the corner that was... really drunk. They wouldn't eat, or drink water, and the cozy couple was whispering, the penis confetti on the floor, the fluorescents humming, birds honking overhead, and the space heater wouldn't stop clicking..."

Corky began purring in my lap and I focused all my energy on the steady vibration.

"A table collapsed. In the middle of the room, on a breeze, Lucy and I tried to stop it, but we couldn't. Yesterday, a shelf fell over, and the dishwasher started to die. The day before, an entire shelf of wine collapsed, and I couldn't save the shelf. I slowed the wine, so it didn't break, but my magic has no effect on the items attached to the walls or of long-term living in the winery. I think there's something wrong with it, or me, and I don't know what to do. I need... help."

Silence filled the space, and I took another drink of the wine. It was one of mine, a Cab Franc, and I wasn't sure if I'd brought wine or it just lived here at this point. After another minute of staring at my wine in silence, I glanced up to see everyone looking at me.

"That's the most you've ever talked to us. I actually thought you might be a retard—" Andrea smacked Curtis on the back of the head and Grim stood up, growling at the thirty-year-old male witch who reinforced the belief that B.O.B.s were better than live ones. "What? She looks half dead most of the time!"

Andrea smacked him again, but several other coven members snickered, and I felt my stomach bottom out. Despite doing my best to help others, I was a joke here, and no one cared enough to help. This was why it was never better to show vulnerability, you learned how little people cared when you asked them to support you and all they did was laugh at your expense.

"Forget it. The winery is all I have of my family, but if you don't want to—" I started to pick Corky up, but Hayami placed her hand over mine, the Satori tattoo stilled to listen.

"You said you saved the bottles, so your magic saved the bottles?"

I shook my head. "It worked on the air. I thickened it to slow their descent and keep the shelves slightly aloft to roll the bottles to the ground. Anything attached to, mounted, or associated with the winery, however, just... it absorbs the magic."

"Absorbs it?" Sue leaned in, her flannel shirt hanging off of her small shoulders. "It doesn't bounce off or break something else?"

"No... I don't..." I looked to Lucy for confirmation. "It got sucked in, right?"

She nodded with her agreement.

"What is the biggest magic you've done there recently?" Naomi leaned forward to make eye contact, and I spared her a quick glance, immediately shifting to watch my finger trace the rim of my wine glass. Sensing my reluctance to make eye contact, Naomi tucked herself back into the circle.

"I haven't been able to do any big magic recently. Not enough sleep, so mostly everything's been done the normie way." An image of the sky blacking out and maroon magic snaking around the tables crept into my periphery. "Except..."

I fell forward, closing in on myself and Corky with a gentle rocking gesture.

"Tell us what happened, love." Sue's calming voice and use of Drax's preferred term of endearment broke the dam in my chest.

"I jokingly told some bridesmaids they could hit on Drax when he came upstairs after the table collapsed and they thought he was a stripper. They started fighting over him, one had her hand in the band of his pants, the other had his shirt halfway off. It was somewhat funny until I turned around and there were scratches... on his chest. Deep red marks and the sunlight went out; maroon snakes of magic slithered around the room trying to murder them... Corky pulled me back. I was horrified and confused, but all the magic was gone just as quick."

"They marked him?" Penny drew up sharply, angling her head to give me the full force of her emerald gaze. My heart hammered in my chest and the very tip of her mating mark peeked out of the collar of her shirt. I'd seen it before, but in this context...

"They were normies. I don't think they were trying to claim him as their mate... the way those bitch witches were with Artie." Andrea frowned in the armchair and at least two other coven members sat back on their hands. "What?"

"Is your magic always *weird* when he's around?" Sue was careful to phrase her question neutrally, but the extra emphasis on weird gave me pause.

It always felt like his dragon was pressing against my magic, pressing against me. Whenever I'd feel anger and he'd appear, it would be amplified. Excitement, and it would double. He brought fire and energy to all of my feelings, was he the reason I felt burned out?

"I'm not sure. We never spent much time together in the beginning. But after I was a statue, he came around more. And when he's around, it's all just... more. Do you think it's him? Do you think he's the problem?"

No one spoke, either because they were contemplating my statement or they were bored with the topic. I was bored with the topic, but I'd been living with it, so it seemed unfair for them to be over it so quickly.

"How do you feel about him, Tempe?" Andrea looked at me meaningfully.

I blinked at her. "Like... the whole wanting to rip his pants off cuz he's hot or rip his head off because he's a pain in the ass? Cuz other than those two feelings, I feel... like I'm glad someone else is out there because being alone sucked?"

Andrea and Sue exchanged a weighted look. A conversation passed between them, and I felt like a child being talked about by grown-ups while sitting in the room, but no one wanted you to hear.

"I think we should do a cleansing." Penny gestured between her and Lucy. "We'll come up and banish the demons!"

Everyone laughed out loud at the ridiculousness, but I welcomed them anyway. "Sure. Maybe while you're at it, you can figure out how to deaden the noise in there too. Maybe all of this is in my over-wrought brain."

"I don't think it is, but do you need us to place protections around your space to help with the noise?"

I looked at Racina, one of the coven members who rarely spoke but often had more insight than we did. She was one of our coven's less finite magical beings, a multi-generational crossing of mythical and magical whose talents, and age, weren't easy to pinpoint.

Brow scrunched together; I thought about the possibilities. Racina's suggestion focused on something tangible that could be adjusted to help my brain cope, and didn't require it to suddenly understand or behave differently.

"Is there a way..." I started, letting my gaze drift four inches from the cat to the carpeted floor of the room. Asking for help with a trigger had never occurred to me... why had I never thought to do something about the noise?

"Could we put noise canceling speakers or something in the

place? Something to... cancel the noise so it doesn't carry?" I stopped when I realized I'd just said the same thing twice.

"Yeah, but technology is less reliable than magic. I can send my cousin out that way the day after tomorrow, she specializes in technology and mechanical witchery. Her son has issues with sound and her whole house has this cool noise canceling deal. It's a trip." Racina had leaned forward, warmth lighting her face as she talked about her family.

"Thank you. Do you know if she has experience with farm equipment?"

"You can ask when she gets there." Racina smiled brightly in my direction. "Kaci will be thrilled to see you and the farm again."

"Thanks." I smiled and went back to looking at the floor, wondering when I'd met a Kaci and if perhaps she was confusing me with another desperate and lonely winery owner. "Just give her my number?"

With that settled, Sue and Andrea moved on and I felt the first tenuous sparkles of hope.

CHAPTER

TEN

TEMPE

"Shhh... he'll hear you!" I locked the tasting room door behind us and gestured behind the bar. "You get the wine; I'll get the candles!"

Penny and Lucy giggled in response, stumbling into chairs and tables despite the mostly full moon.

"Shhh!!!" Spit dribbled out of their mouths, their attempts at shushing each other drowned out by a chair crashing to the floor.

Laughter bubbled out, and I flicked on the overhead lights. If Drax had slept through everything we'd done so far, the lights would not wake him up. I righted the fallen chair and looked at Lucy and Penny, both as tall as I was, struggling to sit on bar stools. "Maybe we should have a floor picnic before you guys break something."

"Seconded." Artie appeared in the doorway, and I cocked my head at him. He'd driven all of us here after we shared three bottles of wine, but I was pretty sure I locked him outside when Penny shouted, 'no boys aloud' and made a break for it. He was her fated mate, and her best friend, but also not permitted in girl talk and seances. "You locked the door, you didn't close it."

I leaned sideways to check and stumbled, the world tilting on a new axis while spinning, spinning, spinning. The wooden floor

100

planks grew, getting bigger and bigger until they filled my entire line of sight, and my mouth, and... "I fell over."

"You did." Artie's boots advised. "I'm not sure if I should help you or leave you there where you can't hurt yourself falling over a second time."

Penny's leather booties appeared along with Lucy's fur-lined boots. Before I could ask for help, boots turned into thick calves in leggings, thicker thighs, sweaters, and finally the two faces of friendship I wasn't sure how I made.

"Sup?" I slurred, sitting up to swipe the drool off my chin. "Come here often?"

They both laughed, Penny passed me a bottle of wine and I took a slug directly from the bottle. Artemis let out a sigh and draped himself on one of the booth seats between the bar and the door. I passed the bottle to Lucy and took a deep breath, picturing the picnic blanket in the hall closet upstairs. It featured a yellow and white checked pattern, wrapped with a brown faux leather Velcro strap, a crepe texture, and a somewhat squishy depth... the blanket was in my hands.

"Wait, is that your blanket or the winery's blanket?" Lucy leaned over, her face pressed against the surface. Her round glasses pushed into her eyes, suctioning slightly to the orbital, while she made investigative sounds. "Watson! A clue! There are long dark fibers poking out of this! Evil spirit haunting this house, we banish you!"

Penny pulled her back and gestured Artemis over. "Those are your eyelashes, weirdo. Can you please set this up for us?" She batted her eyelashes at the half-demon, half-bear shifter. His face softened, the gooey look of love dripping out of every pore enough to make me vomit wine.

"Aww...." Lucy clapped her hands in delight. The large black husky mix took that as an invitation to come over and Grim stuffed his head into her arms. She squeezed the dog, murmuring ridiculous baby sounds into his head. Corky, seated on top of a wine barrel table, stared at us in disapproval.

We scooted onto the blanket and Artemis returned to his seat, taking the large dog with him. Two more partial wine bottles appeared on our picnic blanket, and we passed them around while Penny summoned candles from her house and Lucy checked her purse for matches. Everything accounted for, we assembled a pentagram with a wine bottle at three of the five points, the two black pillar candles at the remaining points, and a tarot deck in front of Lucy that no one asked for.

"What's the deck for?" I eyed it suspiciously, not appreciating the possibility of having my inner thoughts read by the cards. In general, I was fairly transparent and had a tendency to over-share, but I really didn't want to risk having some bomb dropped or emotional trauma flashback on the floor of my workplace.

Lucy stroked the deck, a perfect pet to do her will. "In case the spirits have something to say."

"Do you feel spirits?" I eyed the corners of the room, my voice dropping to a low whisper. "Is there someone here?"

Lavender smoke drifted around the room, circling the perimeter and fluttering the lit candles. Merlot shimmer joined the swirl pattern and citrine waves danced between the two, our three magics scanning the room for abnormalities, but after a moment, it faded into the wood and leather, leaving a pulsing remnant of never being there at all.

"That's... not normal, right?" Artemis picked up Corky and held Grim closer. "Maybe I should take these guys outside while you gals... do this." He darted out the door before we could even comment, Penny's eyes rolled to the back of her head.

"He just wants to continue listening to his spicy audiobook but needs constant company. Since we moved in together, he's taken to stealing Grim whenever he can—bribing if necessary. Looks like Corky is on his list now." She let out a sigh and smiled. "I need... quiet time, but he hates it. So it's our weird compromise. Now... Maybe we should try to hold a séance? Who would haunt this winery?"

Penny and Lucy looked at me and I popped the stiff joints in my neck, leaning back onto my hands to stare at the ceiling. "My mom, maybe? I just learned she grew up here from your dad, which fuck you very much for." I glared at her, but without any real heat. "I could have used a warning that he was a truth siren going around interrogating people for fun because your mom's out of town."

Penny put her palms in the air, leaning back slightly. "Sorry! I didn't think he'd start hunting down my friends for entertainment. What did he say?"

"That my mom and grandpa were close before he died, closer than she was with gran. Maybe he could be haunting this place? Maybe they're haunting it together?" I violated the pentagram and took a drink of the open tempranillo. "He was asking about the day I turned into a statue—if you apologize one more time, I will throw corks at you!"

Lucy closed her mouth again; cheeks pink in the candlelight. "I don't remember what happened after and it bugs me. It was like I was in a trance for a couple of days. I only remember... fury."

Penny and I jerked back. "You never mentioned that before. Whose fury?"

Lucy's brows drew together. "Drax. He was so angry and... yelling."

"That... that can't be right. He leaves at the full moon, and it was at the full moon." I chewed on my lip, glancing toward the kitchen. "But if he was mean to you, maybe we should—"

"No! Maybe I'm mixing up something else. He just makes me nervous, ya know? What about your dad?" Lucy's posture shifted from slumped over to almost forced upright. Penny gave her a long look and then took a swig from another bottle. "Or a famous rockstar?"

"What about them? They make you nervous?" I tilted my head at her.

"No! The haunting! Maybe the ghost of like... Elton John is

haunting you! Wouldn't that be cool?" Lucy's excitement vibrated, the awkwardness from before gone.

"Why would a famous person haunt this place unless gran's been killing people and burying them in the wine cave... then I think they'd go for the dragon sleeping out there before the furniture. Why does he sleep outside? There's a second apartment upstairs I made for him... I mean, all that stuff's out there now, but geez. Rude."

"Were you serious about wanting to rip Drax's pants off?" Penny let out a hiccup, and we all giggled. "I mean, I missed the shirt removal earlier, but you went straight to pants? That's next level."

I glanced toward the kitchen again, lowering my voice. "I've washed his underpants." We all squealed, rolling onto our backs, laughing.

"Would you... hook up with him?" Lucy took a drink from the third bottle, and I had to assume the séance was doomed. I wasn't sure if I was relieved or disappointed.

"Umm... yeah? It's been... a long while and dude is ripped. Even if he just laid there. We have chemistry, its volatile, but it would make him a damn good fuck." I fanned myself, the room getting warmer as I felt his hands on my waist. "But then I'd have to look at him the next day."

"So date him." Penny shrugged, like this was the most obvious solution. "Maybe the reason it's weird is that you're trying too hard not to like him. Just... try liking him?"

My lip curled, and I leaned away from her, plucking the wine from her hand as I went. "You're cut off. Clearly you are too drunk to have any more. Maybe we should try talking to the dead before you kill me with dumb suggestions."

We all laughed, and I placed the bottles back on the star points. We joined hands and called out to anyone who might be haunting the winery. When no one answered, Lucy pulled out the tarot deck and tried to make a simple read on Penny that ended when the cards almost caught fire and we all ended up sprawled on the blanket with our heads on each other, mostly asleep.

"So what are you going to do next?" Lucy yawned, cuddling in closer when Artemis opened the door and let in a blast of cool air.

"Sleep hopefully." I yawned and rolled over.

Penny moved first, Artie lifting her and carrying her out to the car while Corky took her place on my tummy. I shifted to get off Lucy, letting her pull her boots on as grown-up sleep-overs never lasted the whole night on work days.

Lucy stood, stretching tall and then squatting to squeeze my hand. "Even if you don't see it yet, we're not all going to leave you, Tempe. And I think that includes your dragon." Artie reappeared and helped half carry Lucy out with a hand squeeze of his own and an ear scratch for Corky.

"Book have a happily ever after?" I yawned, snuggling into the blanket.

"It ended in with a four way and a lot of orgasms." He escorted Lucy out and I smiled.

"Sounds like a good night." When they finally left, I pressed my magic into the air around the lock and forced it to turn closed. Nothing happened, because it was part of this winery and my magic was useless.

"Fuck it, don't let me get murdered, Corky." I burrowed into the cold floor and let my eyes drift closed again.

Soft footsteps tapped the ground around me. They went to the door, clicked the lock into place, and then moved closer. Candlelight flickered out, the clink of glass being placed on the bar top, and then I was airborne.

"Murderer." I tried to shout, but the murderer smelled like ash trees and lava rock. He was warm, hard, and his hands light and protective where they connected with me.

"Aye lass. But not in this century."

"You're warm and you smell good." I rubbed my face against his chest, the muscles stiffening beneath me. His arms rigid, I felt his grip tighten and he pulled me closer. One of his hands shifted, the air and light changing with additional moonlight. The soft tick of the ceiling fan in my bedroom greeted my ears, bringing visions of pillows, blankets, and... "Water?"

"I'll bring you some." His voice rumbled through me, the vibrations tickling my neck muscles and the very tip of my nose.

"Are you taking me to bed, Drax?" I was carefully lowered onto the top of my blanket, his blazing heat kneeling beside me.

"You're playing a dangerous game, love." My boots disappeared, and he tucked my feet under the covers. "I'll be right back."

When he left the room, I got up and removed my pants, shirt, and bra. Grabbing my sleep shirt, I went into the bathroom, changed, and brushed my teeth. When I exited, Drax was standing there with a glass of water. I chugged half and then went to my bedside table for medications, his stormy gaze staying fixed on me the entire time, making sure I swallowed the last drop of water and every evening pill.

He took the cup, and I slid under the covers, shivering at the chill of the empty bed.

"Cold, love?" I heard him return the water cup to my beside table, refilled in the time it took me to situate myself under the blankets.

"Yeah... Could... would..." The bed dipped and his heat permeated the blanket through the covers. I moved closer to the center, and he filled the space I emptied, sitting with his back on the pillows and providing heat for the length of my body through the blanket barrier. "Thanks."

"Anything you need, love, I'm at your service." He brushed the hair from my face, and I drifted to sleep easily for the first time in weeks.

CHAPTER

ELEVEN

TEMPE

I woke up with a splitting headache and two pairs of eyes on me. One in a furry orange head that I expected, and the mirth-filled eyes of an obnoxious dragon shifter who looked far too well-rested and perky for... something o'clock in the morning.

"What are you doing?" I reached for the water beside me and found medicine bottles beside it. Allergy, pain, upset stomach, and acid reflux, all lined up. After a drink, I cracked open the pain pills and swallowed two. "And can you do it somewhere else?"

"Watching yeh sleep, love. So, nay, I can only do that here. Is that the one for pain?"

"Yes... and that's oddly honest. Also creepy, what the fuck?" I drank more water to avoid looking at Drax. The bottles made sense if he placed them there. Over-the-counter pills were probably not something he spent a lot of time with. "Who just watches people sleep?"

"I don' watch people sleep, love. Just you. Since yeh wan' ta rip off my pants, I felt it granted me some leeway." His smirk lit up the words and I started to glare at him. The move strained at my hangover, and I decided instead to hate him in facial indifference. "For the record, I can wash my own knickers."

"Eavesdropper." I was too hungover to be embarrassed about what he could have heard. The man was a shifter with shifter scenting. If he hadn't already known I harbored a physical attraction to him, it was his own fault. "How did I get up here?"

His eyes sparkled, and I returned an eye roll, my nose detecting fresh brewed coffee that may or may not have come from the insufferable Irishman in front of me.

"Yer a bit prickly this morn'. I thought getting sleep and havin' someone bring yeh coffee in bed would improve yer disposition." Drax continued to lean in the doorframe, his arms crossed over his broad chest showcasing all the muscles in his arms. "Did yeh nay get summin' else yeh wanted?"

I pointed at the water glass. "If you mean that, it's not coffee. It's called water. Though water is a key ingredient in the beverage of coffee, if you don't run it through the magic machine, it's missing crucial components. Namely caffeine and the will to live."

His head bobbed toward the other nightstand, and I turned. A coffee mug sat on the other end table with fresh brew, creamer, and a small amount of cat fur, though I doubted it was placed there by Drax.

"Aye, but that is. I am familiar with water and coffee makers but thank you for the sarcastic rendition. Fair warnin' yer cat stuck his face in it while yeh were still in the land of the dead. I can dump it and get yeh a replacement, but I heard tales that yeh murder for that."

A soft growl left my throat, and I grabbed the cup, taking two lukewarm gulps and consuming half of it. After a quick breath, I downed the rest and set the cup back down.

"Thanks. What flavor is that?" I checked I was wearing clothes and slid out of bed. After a series of stretches and pops, I turned back to the dragon. His jaw muscles ticked, body rigid, I watched his eyes work their way back up from my exposed legs.

"Irish cream." He bounced his eyebrows twice, and I rolled my eyes again. His tense shoulders remained unmoving despite the joke. His gaze swept the room, from my cat on the pillow to the floral drapes by the second balcony window. A crease formed above his eyebrows, his lips disappearing when he pressed them together.

"Something wrong?" I searched the room as well, curious if I'd left tampons and vibrators in plain sight. I wouldn't apologize for them, but I would explain to him what they're for if he needed a lesson.

"Just... doesn't seem like you in here. No unicorns or severed body parts." He shrugged and inched into the room, carefully avoiding contact to grab the coffee mug and take it back to the door frame.

"What can I say, they were on back order the day I set aside for decorating and I couldn't be bothered to reschedule. I need a shower." I ducked into the bathroom and shut the door. Feeling awkward about being naked with Drax in my apartment, I locked the door and showered as fast as I could. Usually, if I forgot to shower the night before, the morning shower was all about foot warming and muscle relaxation, but I'd woken up warm and relaxed today. A phenomenon I was not ready to explore the source of.

Towel wrapped around my torso; I paused with my hand on the bathroom door. I hadn't brought in clothes, and now I was trapped between walking out in a towel or dying naked in my bathroom to avoid potentially being seen by a hot man while wearing a towel. "I did not think this through."

After another moment of hesitation, I decided to woman up and opened the door. Immediately I was confronted with Drax in the doorway, holding a fresh cup of coffee. His brow went up, a single up and down appraisal that made the towel feel invisible.

"Thought you might need this to remember yer knickers don' go on yer head." He extended the coffee ever so slightly and I reached for it with one hand while my other had a death grip on my towel. When I was barely an inch from him, I realized he'd slowly moved the cup inward until we were nose to nose. "But since I heard yer confession, I thought it only fair to say I wouldn't mind seein' them on the floor. And if yeh've got an itch to scratch, I'm here to assist." He pressed the mug against my palm and wrapped my fingers around it, brushing a soft kiss to my cheek before leaving the room and shutting the door behind him.

"Oh, and yeh might want to hurry. We've got a bit o' work to do before we open. I've fed the cat."

Corky yowled in protest, declaring he had not been fed, but that meant absolutely nothing in cat land. He could be fed to the point of bursting and still screaming about starvation. The other kitty in this house, unfortunately, was suddenly starving... for Drax.

WE STOOD in the closed tasting room, and I knew Drax regretted his offer. Around us, on nearly every inch of the bar, were notebooks.

He'd collected all of my notebooks last night, but this was the complete collection of my insanity. Aside from not counting them, I also don't think he knew how much was in each one. Each book held a list of something that needed to be done, organized by type, with diagrams, and potential tools. Barrel room notebook, office notebook, kitchen, tasting room, bottling, farm equipment... I had a notebook for everything. In my head, I believed that if I organized everything that needed to get done, I could chip away at it until it was done. Step one was writing everything down to clear it out of my head so that I could make space for the action steps, and my brain wasn't just bursting with lists of things to do.

Once I made the list, the sheer number of items on it was so daunting that I shut down and did nothing. Then a new batch of ideas would surface, I'd get a new notebook, and the cycle would repeat until I had a million ideas both on paper and pinging around the inside of my skull like a pinball game that never ended.

Only I wasn't the one playing pinball, I was the thing the ball bounced off of, slowly going mad.

"What the fuck, Tempe?" Drax exclaimed, staring at all the notebooks. "Now that I've flipped through all of them, I think your system is banjaxed."

"I'm aware." I grumbled, crossing my arms under my boobs and glaring at both the dragon and the notebooks. "But I haven't got any other systems."

Drax remained silent beside me, and I glanced at him. His eyes were firmly fixed on my tits, that were being pushed up and almost out of the shelf bra camisole I'd worn for a day of trying to get my life in order. Were my boobs too big for a shelf bra? Yes. Did I wear them anyway to keep my boob skin from touching my rib skin without having to endure an actual bra? Also, yes.

Instead of the foggy, Irish green, his eyes flickered gold. Drawing a line from the swell of my cleavage to the exposed skin of my neck where his dragon wet his lips with a flash of fangs.

Desire flooded my body, and I sucked in some air. I regretted my clothing choice as much as I regretted ever letting him see the first two notebooks. If I hadn't promised myself I was going to get the winery in order, I would just go back to bed... with a vibrator and a mental picture of the look Drax was wearing right now.

"Tempe?" Drax pulled me away from my fantasy. His green eyes shimmered with amusement, either from reading my thoughts or smelling them. Probably the second one, since I was pretty sure he couldn't read minds.

We were closer, an inch apart, and his hands were fisted at his sides, fighting the urge to reach out and touch me. Every muscle in his body screamed at him to get closer, move closer, and it was all written in the human green of his eyes. If he could read half of what I was thinking on my face...

Instead of answering, I let my hand trace the curve of his jaw. Small patches of stubble scratched against my hand, Drax leaning into the touch like it held the air he needed to breathe. My thumb rubbed at the dark circles under his eyes, while his lips pressed a kiss against the pulse point in my wrist and the rest of him remained eerily still.

"Why does it feel like something between us is different today?" I swallowed the urge to take it back as soon as I said it. From waking up with him in my apartment to the casual contact between us, it was like we'd been visited by three ghosts and decided we *did* want to be better.

"Because, *mo doineann*, I was visited by a man in a kilt last night who brought you a sack of coffee and yeh held a drunken séance for ghosts. Because furniture is breaking without cause and I don't have any idea what's happenin'. I promise to work with yeh, work through all of this, with you." He kissed my palm, my wrist, while rubbing his cheek against my hand. "It's just... really hard not to touch yeh since yeh bashed my nose in and said yeh want to fuck me."

"Sure. That's how I get all the guys, violence and crude declarations of lust." I laughed and he let loose an agitated growl.

He took my wrist in his hand, lacing our fingers together. "Maybe don't mention any men who came before to me, love."

"Why? Are you ashamed that I have a past?" I tried to take my hand back, ready to read him the riot act for thinking women should be celibate little virgins waiting for some seed spreading farmer who'd never given an orgasm.

"Neigh, lass, more like I'll hunt them down and rip off their hands for touching yeh. But we need to handle the business, see if we can sort through repairs and improvements. Maybe if there's time after, we can work on my jealousy of men you knew before I met you. Or yeh can give me a list of names of who yeh wouldn't mind seein' murdered." He took hold of my shoulders and turned me to face the notebooks. "Choose one, the sooner you start, the sooner it's over."

"Heard that before." I sucked in some air and felt him quietly laugh behind me.

"Clock's ticking, love. If you want to be done with one thing before we open, you need to get started." Leaning back against the counter, he crossed his arms and waited for me to begin. I stared at all the notebooks but didn't touch them. None of them had what I really needed for us to get started.

"The problem with basically... everything is that it starts with money." I gestured to the financial notebook and the tablet that tracked sales. "And we *probably* don't have any."

"People are in here all the time, love. How do we not have money?" Drax cocked his head to the side, and I released the breath I was holding.

This was happening, we were going to fucking master business-ing business. Now he would know that I was Unikitty in the *Lego Movie* with a fake tie drawn on and no clue what I was talking about.

"Well..." I opened the electronic tablet. Opening last month's sales reports, I showed him the numbers. "This is what we brought in, in revenue, across tastings and sales, less the cost of tasting bottles opened, salaries, estimated damages, and insurance costs." It was not an insignificant number, and I'd be pleased if I had any frame of reference. "If I've accounted for everything, we have a decent profit margin, but not enough for capital improvement."

Drax nodded, and I patted myself on the back for using 'capital improvement' correctly.

"Show me the sales reports from before Maple left." He leaned in behind me, not quite touching but warming my entire back. "Are we better, worse, or the same?"

"No idea. She didn't use a point-of-sale system or provide me with any of the receipts. Now, on days Samuel works, all tips go to him. Technically, people aren't supposed to tip me, but when they do, it goes into my personal banking account for... coffee and cat food, mostly. Probably student loans if I've been paying them... Don't remember." I pressed a few more buttons. "This is an estimate of what we have in inventory, but we need to count because I know this is wrong. I did inventory when I built this system and there are several recent releases missing because I had no time and also there are some losses that didn't get put in."

"What kind of losses?" His hand was on my shoulder now, massaging the muscles. I hadn't quite believed him when he said it was a struggle not to touch me, but the bare skin of his hand against the smooth exposed flesh of my shoulder sent zips of electricity dancing through my nerve endings and I wasn't sure how I survived without his touch for the past twenty seconds.

"Gravitational. We need to restock the tasting room before the week starts, but that's a monday job. Clean the displays which haven't been revamped in months, and some displays need to be replaced because the wine listed is out of stock. Then we need to check the barrels and see if they're ready to be bottled. If they are, then we need to bottle and plan a release. If we can get regular allotments, then I might offer subscriptions, but there's nothing to offer people right now."

Fingers worked their way into a knot at the seam of my shoulder blades, and I tried to relax them. While he rubbed my back, Drax hummed and stared at the tablet in my hands. It wasn't so much a song as a melody, but it carried away my words on a rain-soaked breeze across a scraggy shore.

"I don't know shite about numbers, accounting, memberships, or appearance expectations, love. I can build you some shelves if you tell me what you want them to look like, and I've fixed a bit of your plumbing issues. You studied business, how much money do we need to accomplish your goals?"

"A lot." I turned off the tablet and set it down.

"How much do we have?"

"No idea... some?" I leaned back into him.

"How much money is in the business account?"

He dug into a knot, and I let out a squeal.

"I don't know." I folded into myself, trying to be smaller. "I lost the password."

"Can you reset it?" His hands were now massaging the area around my neck, effectively distracting me from the usual panic that came when the subject of money came up. We never had money growing up, my mom drank it all or blew it on extravagant fun that turned into creditors calling at 2AM and repossessing her car. If his hands left me for even a second, I was going to crumble faster than a gingerbread house in the rain.

"I tried. The email on file is my gran's, and she doesn't respond to my texts. Or forward my password reset request emails, assuming she gets email in... fuck, wherever they are." My voice caught and Drax moved his hands down my arms, massaging the muscles in my biceps and forearms, tracing the tattoo inside my wrist.

"What system is there for if you get locked out and cannot access your email?"

"You have to call." I huffed out a breath and dropped my head to my chest. "And I called. But I was on hold for an hour and when someone finally picked up, my phone died and dropped the call. The next time, they were closed. Then another I had to give up while on hold to help a customer–that was pre-Samuel. It led to the whole 'need to hire help' chain of events, and the months long process that led to our satyr."

"Alright, and after Samuel started?"

"Then I forgot."

"Tempe..." The soft whisper of my name was so full of emotion, and it broke something down inside of me.

"I know, ok!" I threw my hands up and paced away from him. "I'm a mess. My brain is a mess, my life is a mess. My family... I don't fucking have one. But I'm trying! That's why I have two dozen notebooks! I'm trying! I never wanted to own and run a business, but I took the classes because gran insisted one day I would. I don't like people! Customer service is not in my skill set, but she didn't leave me any employees, so now I do that too. Hiring people and interviews? No fucking clue, but I managed. The only part of this I know about and want to do is the planting, smashing and aging grapes. But most of the grapes rotted because I was too overwhelmed and backlogged to get them picked or hire anyone to pick them because I didn't have a list for who she hired for that either! I'm failing at the only part of this I was supposed to be good at and no matter how hard I try, I can't dig myself out of this hole."

Angry tears streamed down my face, and I stalked back and forth in front of the bar. Corky leapt onto the counter, testing notebooks with his nose and tapping different ones with his paws. Behind the counter, Drax watched, face impassive as he worked through everything and tried to parse out what, if anything, could be done.

"Do you have a bank card for the business?"

"Yes," I said, pointing toward the cash drawer behind the register. Corky gently nudged a unicorn notebook filled with ideas for parking lot beautification and floral, closer and closer to the edge of the bar. When it was precariously perched on the verge of falling off, he paused and began grooming himself. Orange statue picture of indifference.

"Is there a number on the back of it?" He dug into the drawer and pulled out the blue bank card.

"Yeah."

"If you call it, do they give you the account balance?" His hopeful expression was endearing as he walked back over, setting the cart on the counter.

"They do... if you know the four-digit pass code."

"Do you know the four-digit pass code?" His expression pinched at the corners of his mouth. Corky turned suddenly, batted the notebook, and dropped it on Drax's foot. The dragon shot the cat a stern warning, but my feline licked his paw, the picture of innocence in the face of accusation.

"I did... but I lost it."

"Can you reset it?" His whole body was rigid, finally comprehending how truly fucked this whole thing was.

"You can... online. With the password."

"Fucking technology." He scrubbed his hands over his face and stared at all the stuff in front of him. "Can you reset it with magic? Or use your gift to access your account? I mean, is it breaking in if it's yours?"

On cue, my phone dinged with an email from the magical IRS, a section of magical auditors aimed at keeping magic and paranormal safely out of sight of the normies. One of the ways they managed was by preventing the use of magic in normie finances and monetary transactions—i.e. you couldn't magic away your debt, and you couldn't use it to reset your pin. I read the message to him.

"You cannot use magic to interfere in human finances. Please use the established non-magic process or you will be fined with a forty-eight-hour power loss and a review of all magical activity." The signature at the bottom looked like a horse eating an ass, and not the donkey, but I decided not to mention that part.

"Bloody hell, those fuckers are fast. Are they listening to your every word? Do they know yeh think fucking me would be amaz-ing?" My cheeks turned pink, and my email dinged again. He turned his head to read the message.

"We do not invade people's privacy, but calling us fuckers is rude." He glanced at me and then the room as a whole. "Like fucking hell, they don't."

I nodded my agreement and set the phone back down, slightly farther away. Corky took a few steps toward the device and laid down on top of it, purring softly.

We stared at him in silence for a round of heartbeats before bursting into laughter.

"Better than a faraday bag, I guess." My cheeks ached with the effort.

"A what?" Drax asked, head tilting again, and I wondered if it was a dragon thing or if he'd spent too much time with dogs as a child. Did he have pictures of him as a child? "Never mind. Look, Tempe, I don't even own a phone. I can sit on hold for yeh, but I think you need to hire someone to handle the business parts. Money people, who will keep track of the finances and give you complete reports that the little box can't. A legal advisor to guide you through the mess of business practices here. If there are no receipts, I'm afraid..."

My stomach hollowed, and I shook my head.

"Look, love, I know yeh don't think we can afford it, but what we can't afford is for you to fall apart and turn into that little girl on the tricycle talking about red rum. Delegating is your best bet. How many of your friends have their own businesses? Penny has 'er practice, Naomi owns that insufferable gnome place. They can refer you to someone trustworthy... why are you shaking your head?"

"I can't ask them for that. What if they think I'm using them? Or that I'm a failure who can't handle things?" I whispered, but he already had my phone in his hand, the displaced cat giving him the worst side eye I'd ever seen.

"The point of friends is that they care about and want to help you. Yeh aren't asking them to do your taxes, you're asking them for a name. It's the same as searching the internet, but you know whoever answers will be familiar with magic and business. They want to help you, love."

Panic filled my chest, a variation of this morning's hangover, but instead of my head pounding, it was my heart. I had a feeling whoever I hired would find what I did, and it wasn't going to be a positive experience. During a preliminary check to see how the business was doing, I'd tried to pull past tax filings.

There weren't any.

Not only had the US standard IRS never heard of us, but he also started quacking like a duck and hung up on me. I knew inside the boundary of Huckleberry Hollow they had to get creative, since the place technically didn't exist, but the residents did. And the residents could be put in jail if they didn't file taxes and report income.

"Umm..." I shifted from foot to foot, not looking at my phone. I moved closer to him, wishing I had telepathic magic instead of garden magic. "I don't know if gran filed taxes."

My lips brushed against his ear, and he shivered, from the

prospect of being a felon like the president or my flesh brushing against his was anyone's guess. I watched goosebumps pebble along his neck, skin getting warmer against my chest pressing against his arm. Turning his face toward mine, our noses brushed, and I had a fleeting moment of panic that he was going to kiss me before he pulled away.

Did I want to kiss him? Yes, which was hard to admit to myself. But our first kiss being the moment I found out I might become a felon? That was not ok.

Even if this was just lust and physical attraction, I had some standards. They were dirt low, but a first kiss while I was about to have a stroke was beneath that.

"I think that means we definitely need that accountant, then love." He handed me my phone and forced my hand closed around it this time. "And if you're a good girl and make the calls, I'll start another pot of coffee."

I swooned. Maybe my standards needed some adjusting, because I could definitely kiss him for that.

CHAPTER

TWELVE

TEMPE

"I need a nap." I flopped across the bar top, defeated and deflated.

"You haven't done anything yet, love." Drax took my hands and hauled me up, forcing me upright with my arms around his neck like a dancing corpse. He swayed with me gently, eyes traveling the room while I fought to stay upright. "Do you have the magical shields up all the time?"

"Yeah, why?" We spun around and he placed me on the bar top.

"Lower them."

"What? Why?" Worms danced in my belly at the thought of losing my protections. "They're what keeps intruders out of your cave."

He cleared his throat and shifted his hand into a clawed talon. "I can keep intruders out of my cave, love."

"You're not always here. You leave every full moon. Case in point, you're leaving in the morning, most likely. If I take down the shield, you could come back to raccoons, hunters or—" I shuddered. "Teenagers having sex in your bed."

"You... know that I leave?" He brushed a strand of hair off my face, leaning into my space.

120

"Yeah... I mean. I didn't put it on my calendar or anything." I cleared my throat, hoping he didn't look at said calendar because it was in there. "But I notice when you aren't here for several days."

He lifted his chin, cocky smirk in place. With a hand on either side of my hips, he bracketed me into place. "Good to know. But I'm here now, love. Just... try dropping them. I'm worried constant magic is sapping yer energy. You shouldn't be this tired, ghosts of the past haunting your sleep or not."

"But... once they're in place, there's no magic required to maintain them. So—"

He pressed his finger to my lips, stemming the flow of words. "Humor me, lass."

Heaving a sigh, I took a deep breath and felt for the edges of the protection shields. The one blocking the apartment staircase from view was the closest, but instead of a strong burgundy edge, the edges melted into the attached walls. My magic was being sucked into the walls of the winery.

"That's weird." I tugged at the wispy spool, encountering resistance. The walls fought to hold on to the edges as I struggled to take back the spell. On a final metaphysical yank, the doorway collapsed, and I fell forward on Drax's chest, panting. "What the hell?"

Tackling the one between the kitchen and the barrel room, I was given yet another fight. There was an even greater struggle, all energy devoted to holding onto the first shield, now dedicated to the second until I was forced to surrender.

"I can't take down the second one." Sweat dripped down my face, my limbs tense and achy as though we'd been in a fight. "The winery... it's pulling back on the magic, drawing it in. Drawing it out of me. I don't understand."

Drax's face went red, gold flashed in his eyes before he carefully reorganized his expression into gentle concern. "Perhaps we should try again, working together?"

"I don't think dragon magic works that way, does it?" The

throbbing in my head returned, and I reached around him to get the water bottle I kept beside the register. I probably hadn't cleaned it recently enough, but I still needed a drink. "I mean, most shifter magic works to shift and to mate. Can you really lend me power?"

He took the water bottle from my hand and laced our fingers together. "Yes, *mo doineann*. He's been doing it for days. Are you ready?"

"No! What? How did he, I mean you—"

Drax pressed the fingers of his other hand to my lips. His eyes closed and with an irritated huff, I did the same. Taking another deep breath, I reached back into the shield. Feeling for the edges in the wispy fog of my magic. When I had a grip, I squeezed Drax's hand and heat slid into my body, up my arm and through my veins to the very edges of my mind. Clawed talons cut along the edge of the door, breaking the tight seal of magic and slurping it back into me with the grace of saucy spaghetti.

"One more, love." Drax's voice pushed me out into the sunlight of the winery, and I felt the edges of that barrier. Solid and unmoving, this protection was all mine without interference.

"It doesn't need to come down." I opened my eyes, and he did the same, heat leaving my body through our joined hands. "That one is mine. It hasn't been hijacked."

Drax gripped my chin, angling my face this way and that. "You look better. How do you feel?"

A knock sounded on the winery door, and I glanced over to see Lucy, sporting dark sunglasses and a hangover. "Like you're about to see why asking for help is a bad idea."

Lucy, Penny, Artie, Arran, Sue, Naomi, her wife Leila, and Samuel were all in the winery before I even had a chance to organize my thoughts. It was unclear why they had *all* shown up, but after my texts for accounting recommendations and a string of apology messages for asking, they'd taken it upon themselves to come over. Drax was still on hold with the bank to update my email address and reset my password, but I had suspicions. Suspicions that looked like a six-foot tall dragon who knew more than he let on.

"Whoa, that's a lot of notebooks," Lucy said, picking up the one labeled *Office* and flipping through it. Her eyes read and scanned so quickly, I wasn't sure whether she was reading or just looking at the doodles I occasionally put in the margins when I couldn't come up with the words. "Andrea wanted to come, but the cold weather is doing shit to her joints. So once we get an idea of what you need, she'll send some stuff along."

"Come for what?" I asked, while everyone shed their outer layers and draped them over the chairs. Lucy was thumbing through her notebook, giving Drax a wide berth and looking a little uncomfortable to be sharing his air. But she was still here, either a comment on our friendship or a sign of progress in their relationship.

"Huh, this is actually really well organized and super straightforward. I've got office." Lucy started toward the kitchen that connected the tasting room with the behind-the-scenes areas.

"What do you mean, 'you've got office'? And why wouldn't it be organized and straightforward? I'm not a chaos gremlin!" I let my eyes rove between all the people in front of me like they were the less furry and cute versions of Cerberus. "What is this?"

"We didn't know you needed help with this. You bring so much wine to the coven, and you're constantly helping us. Like Lucy with magic lessons, me with not cursing Yasmin, Naomi with remodeling and helping all the people pushed out by the old Council rebuild. You show up for people in this town and take care of business. You never let anyone help you, even when we outright ask and tell you how we can help you. So, we're just going to help." Penny picked up the notebook for farm equipment. "Is this a small car or a big golf cart?"

"Maybe save that one for Kaci. She's still coming tomorrow, right?" Sue asked, and I looked at her bewildered.

"Who?"

"Racina's cousin, who's familiar with sensory issues?" Sue checked my head for signs of trauma and came up blank.

"Maybe? I thought Racina was just being nice."

Penny set the farm notebook down.

"I think you could be useful here." Sue handed Penny the kitchen one and the brain witch flipped through it. I couldn't remember what I wanted to do in the kitchen, but it primarily had to do with organizing. Nothing was in an accessible place, and it was impossible to find things when I needed them. There was also no airflow and the distance between dishwasher and drying counter made the probability of broken glass pretty high. "Arran, would you like to take a crack at building some shelves?"

"Yeah, organizing a kitchen should work. When are Numbers and Double Talk showing up?" Penny switched from talking to Sue to talking to Artie. He was watching Grim sniff around the tasting room, despite being here a few hours ago, the dog seemed convinced something new had occurred. Corky took a flying leap from the counter, landing on Grim's back. In the back of my mind, I could hear him shouting 'Onward to fuckery'.

In the front of my mind was just a whole lot of screaming, sweating, and decapitated chickens.

"Aye, I can build shelves. I assume you were intending to help, lad?" He looked over at Drax, who nodded while holding the phone to his ear.

"What's a numbers and double talk?" I asked, watching the familiars disappear to do... whatever familiars did and wondering if I could follow them.

"In about an hour. I told them we needed some time to get access to the accounts before they could start going over everything." Artie answered Penny.

No one answered my question, instead Artie grabbed the notebook labeled barrel room.

The bear slash demon skimmed the contents and handed it to me. "I know nothing about wine flavors and varietal signatures. I think this one is all for you." Then he chose the one labeled tasting room and skimmed the contents. "Hauling wine upstairs and making it look good, I can do. These little sketches... are they what you were thinking of for shelf labels and layout?"

"Yeah but, I don't have a printer or a designer." I stared at the doodles with Leila, Naomi's adorable wife. At three feet even, however, I had to crouch to make eye contact with her, and my knees were too old for this shit.

"I can sketch these out. And then, if I recall, you are a witch? In fact, several of you are. You can replicate the designs sized correctly on the paper you choose. Like magical Kinkos." She giggled, the sound alone brightened the room, and I was entranced by her in a way that made me concerned the wood nymph would murder me with her punk rocker rage. "It's amazing how little you all rely on your magic for the mundane. You know that instead of saving it for the big stuff, you can just... use it to make your life easier? Then, when the big stuff happens like this, ask for help?"

She practically danced away on the points of her feet like an extra in The Nutcracker.

"Water sprite magic," Nay said from beside my elbow, and I jumped. "I'm a muralist, but she's the sketcher. The whole brightening the world, everybody loves her, that's equal parts water sprite magic and just genuine kindness that radiates out of her like stupid radiates out of MAGA. If I didn't love her, I'd waste all my time trying to destroy her joy and probably become exhausted. Nothing can steal that woman's light. Part of why I love her."

I could feel sweat pooling in my palms. Naomi was insanely cool, and I was insane...ly awkward. No words were coming out, I just stood there next to her, staring at her wife and trying not to make fish-face almost speak.

"Sorry. I know this is a lot for you. But we're all super cool, and chill. I promise. Except Artie, who's a dirty rotten STD..."

"NAOMI!" Her wife scowled at her and she smiled, shit-eating and busted. "For the love of nature, let that shit go. He is your friend's mate and a good man. Why are you holding on to high school grudges?"

Before I could have a complete breakdown, Drax appeared behind me and pressed my cell phone into my hand. It was warm, his smell engulfing me and calming some of my socially anxious panic.

"Your customer service agent's name is Delilah, and she is not at all happy to help you, but you should pretend to believe the lie," he whispered, before disappearing into the barrel room.

CHAPTER

THIRTEEN

TEMPE

FACING ARTIE AND HIS TWO PROFESSIONALS IN DRAX'S bedroom, I felt like a trespasser. The dragon had insisted he didn't need to be here for the money chat, and his bedroom was the only place free of electronics and any sort of magical or electronic monitoring.

That we had to meet out here was a bad sign for whatever Numbers and Double Talk had found after I'd finally reset the password and gave it over without bothering to look at the accounts. I needed coffee and a drink, so I'd switched to sampling barrels and was slightly buzzed as I watched the three beings in front of me, sweaty and jittery.

Double Talk was Artie's attorney, Chance, a non-binary witch who radiated fuck around and find out energy while looking impeccable in a dove grey suit, peacock feather earrings and a braided plate that went halfway down their back.

It was so punk rock corporate I wanted to cower in inferiority.

Numbers the Accountant was actually called Numbers. Their species' native language comprised sounds the human mouth couldn't replicate, and while in this dimension, the half-shadowed spirit declined being referenced as more than the function it performed on this plane.

127

Artie's ability to communicate with Numbers came from his demon half, but even he couldn't explain what exactly Numbers was, only that the shadow being had a CPA, filed taxes on time, and was happy to be paid in magical castoffs.

Which apparently was achieved just by standing in dwellings where witches did magic, so I was paid in full... for like a year because I did a fuck ton of magic in here, as had gran, and this place hadn't had a magical cast-off cleansing in well over a century. According to Artie, my walls were leaking so much power, the place could rocket to the moon in a moment.

"Alright, Tempe, I stole this $5 from your petty cash drawer." Chance held up the bill. "So, you've officially hired me and I'm now your attorney. Everything said here is subject to attorney client privilege and cannot be repeated."

Chance gave Artie a pointed look, and the half-bear shifter bounced on the balls of his feet, hands raised in surrender. The familiarity said the friendship was probably more motivating for them to be standing in a drafty dragon's cave than any real dedication to my business and law.

"It was an accident!"

"Every time?" The lawyer was giving him dark looks. When they switched to looking at me, I had to fight my urge to cower and apologize. Court room killer flashed in metaphorical neon above their head, and I decided to never go against them. "Artie is a shit secret keeper. We'd never let him in the room with us if we didn't need him to help communicate with Numbers." The spirit wavered in acknowledgement, and I felt more than heard it.

"I don't enjoy this any more than you do."

"Harsh," I muttered, and Artie turned to me. "You're not that bad. A little too sunshine and joy for my liking, but someone has to be. We can't all be dark and twisted, someone has to bring us coffee and sing *Annie* songs."

"You heard that?" Artie peered at me a little closer, like a dog who'd just counted backward from one hundred.

"Felt more than heard..." I glanced around the room. "Can't everyone?"

Lawyer Chance shook their head, as did Artie, and the spirit laughed slightly. *"Someone else to talk to."*

A shiver ran up my spine, and I shuddered again. My own voice in my head was normal, if a little obnoxious, but the cool caress of a nocturnal other was like using a cotton swab when your ear itched—pleasure and discomfort at once.

Drax walked into the room and eyed Numbers warily. Taking a seat in the armchair beside his bookcase, he leaned back without any fanfare. "I was unaware you were meeting with bananach."

"Another one... are you the reason she hears me?"

Drax nodded, and my eyes flashed between the pair of them.

"Excuse you, I hear things because I'm a witch." I fisted my hands on my hips. Drax waggled his hand in a *kind of* gesture, and I glared at him. "Don't act like you know everything, Fireball."

"Well, now I feel left out." Chance propped a hip on Drax's bookshelf. "Can we get on with it since I'm the only one who can't talk to the dorcha?"

The specter laughed, and I shook my head at the absurdity my life had become. It was the opening to one of those weird jokes that could be offensive but was probably going to require explaining that made the whole thing lose any comedic value. A dragon, a specter and a half-bear shifter walk into a bar...

"Any-way." Chance redirected our attention to them. "You don't have a business license, you haven't filed taxes ever, this property might not be legally deeded, and your liquor license is possibly fake."

My heart stopped, and blood drained to my feet. "A- we- huh?" I was not prepared for the band-aid they'd just ripped off. Or in this case, the post-op staples holding two chunks of my person together.

"What part did you miss?" They were being smug, basking in the radioactive waste following the bomb they detonated in the middle of my room. "That none of this is legal, or that none of it is yours?"

"Just..." I took a breath to avoid throwing something at their head. Chance knew what I meant and was being an asshole on purpose. "How the hell have we been operating? Who does it belong to?"

"Best guess?" The lawyer checked out their manicure. "Magic. From what I know, your gran is old enough that she may have been able to skirt some rules and get by on grandfathering and fuckery—some puns intended. This region was originally part of the Hollow, so maybe she was being up and up at first, but—"

"I inherited a criminal enterprise!" I whisper-shouted and everyone laughed. "It's not funny, I'm not equipped for prison! It's loud in there! And I can't be a crime boss! Do you know how many people they have to intimidate? I rely on him to handle my Karens!" I hooked a thumb at the smug dragon shifter.

"The good news is that Canada isn't far if you want to evade."

"Shut up, Numbers, you know I don't have run-away-to-Canada money! And I definitely don't have criminal enterprise enforcer muscle money if someone slays my dragon." I rubbed my hands up and down my face. "Who owns this mess?"

"Unclear, without further research, but it's someone in your family at least. But I'm pretty sure you'll be dead if your dragon is, since he's—"

Drax let out a warning growl, and I glanced between them.

"What the hell?"

"Never mind them for the moment. Ask Chance for the print-out." The specter gestured toward the lawyer, and I shivered again. Communicating with shadow demons was probably going to take a while to get used to.

"There's a printout?" I accepted a small stack of papers from the lawyer and scanned the account transaction history. Utilities, paychecks, small transfers to my personal account and one coded as grans... current balance...

"Holy shit." I gaped at the number and then at the group in the room before me. "This can't be right. Did I steal it?"

Artie glanced over my shoulder and shrugged while the lawyer inspected their manicure again. When I shook the papers in their face, I received an exasperated sigh. "You rake in sales, Tempe. You have low overhead, and honestly, most of this has come in since you took over ten months ago. Your gran operated in the black, but she wasted a lot of money in the past forty-ish years on dining out, luxury goods and... I don't want to say sex toys, but now that I have..."

"There's a million dollars in here!" I hissed, looking at Drax. "Did you rob a bank and forget to tell me?"

Once again, everyone chuckled, but sweat was beading on my skin in all the places that would chafe or stain.

"I suspect there'd be more if you got all your ideas implemented."

"Or the IRS would have found me faster." I sat down on the edge of Drax's bed and put my head between my knees. When I counted to ten, the world had stopped spinning, and I looked up to find it wasn't a dream.

"Joking aside, witch, you are very competent at what you do."

I flushed at the double compliment, not used to people continuing after I brushed off the first attempt at flattery. Drax let out a soft growl, and the specter seemed to turn toward him.

"Down, boy, I don't want your mate. That was actual accounting feedback."

"I'm not his—"

"If we have access to the money and the operating costs, can we hire you to file the nonsense that will keep the government off our property?" Drax interrupted me. I stared at him, Artie glancing between us while the specter seemed to laugh through all of us. Artie's eyes shifted from amber to a golden brown and back again, his bear and demon halves investigating something in the air.

"Smooth, eejit. You're playing with fire. I've been paid what I

need to handle taxes and finances. As well as your obituary, when she finds out and kills you."

"Kills him for what?" I looked between them.

"Yes, and I'll get started on the legal protections and asset management. Rather than worry about back taxes, I'm going to throw your gran metaphorically under the bus and begin everything from when you took over, a brand-new business that sprang up now, well, six months ago. We can even rename the winery if you want and have a whole fresh start. *Love Potion on the Vine* is fine, but it's hardly your brand." The lawyer glanced between Drax and me. I didn't love the name, but I wasn't sure I should change it without talking it over with gran. Of course, she also wasn't talking to me and hadn't given me a single fucking instruction or heads up, so maybe I could do whatever I wanted.

The endless possibilities were both exciting and crippling. Just thinking of them made me want to hide under the blanket on this bed until everyone left and I could lie in the dark and quiet.

Fuck, I was spiraling and missed the last five seconds of conversation.

"You don't have to, Tempe. Just something to consider. Especially if you want the brides to stop throwing glitter dicks on your floor. Perhaps move away from the love and romanticism to something more... I don't know, magic, wine, darkness, and brooding. Something more like the two of you. It's yours now, or it will be when I figure out what the hell is up with the deed, what do you want it to be?"

I rubbed my temples, at a loss. All this time, I thought this was my legacy, my responsibility, but we didn't even own it on paper. "I didn't fucking want it. Taking this place over has basically been a curse. I'm a garden witch, I thought I would just be growing plants, smashing grapes and drinking wine. Not dealing with money, government crap, and asshole customers." I laid back on the quilt I'd placed out here for Drax. The seams made me itchy, but I got the impression he'd slept on a hay pallet in his former life and wouldn't mind.

It felt good to say it all out loud. Maybe if I said it enough times, gran would pop back in and take her business back with a judgmental lecture. "Between my cursed brain, family and existence, his cursed and sketchy past, we're more like two peas in a cursed pod, stuck here without a clue. I'm still not even sure why the hell we were forced into taking it and now you're saying legally it might not belong to either of us?"

"I'm not saying that, but you should be prepared for the possibility that somewhere out there is a person who may come and claim this land. If you want it, want to fight for it, then you need to ready yourself. Perhaps calling it *Something Cursed* would be more appropriate." Chance stroked their chin, and I let out a laugh. "Or perhaps *Two Cursed Souls for Eternity.*"

"Yeah, people will definitely want to come drink wine from a place boasting curses and eternity. You wouldn't catch me booking a room at the Hotel California, and you wouldn't catch me rubbernecking cursed souls for a sip of wine."

"You'd be surprised what people are willing to do in the name of adventure and alcohol." The specter and Drax exchanged nods. *"Also, you'd rubberneck if it wasn't your life. The boring are always entertained by the extraordinary."*

"That makes them extraordinarily stupid. I guess we can consider it. For now, can we just become legally compliant?" I spread my hands on the bed like I was making a snow angel and then turned to the side to face them. The lawyer nodded, and the accountant agreed. "Great. What do we need for that?"

"Business account, which you have, but I'm going to switch up some things to get you better ROI, business license, tax ID, and permits for alcohol. You'll need a business name eventually for the licenses and in the event your gran's choices come back to bite you, I'd suggest renaming your *ass*-ets." The twisted turn of phrase caused Drax to smirk, and I was moderately annoyed. In a room full of beings with decades on me, they were all immature as hell. "For now, you'll need an LLC to protect yourselves, and it needs a name. Any ideas?"

"Aside from 'I should have taken creative writing instead of business and plant biology in college so I could name all the crap you keep asking me for'?" I snarked, and the lawyer gave me a saucy smile full of perfect pearly whites. "Absolutely none. My cat's name is Corky because he was playing with a cork. I'm named after booze. His name translates to dragon, though that one's not on me. You got anything, Fireball?"

"Perhaps you can name it after yourselves?"

"Numbers suggested naming it after us, is that an option?" I asked, and the lawyer waggled a hand.

"Tempranillo Verdejo for a winery is questionably asinine, Draigus Dougherty would work but leaves you out. Dougherty and Verdejo, LLC could work but is honestly boring as fuck and filing the paperwork would kill me, so I refuse and if I won't do it, the answer is no."

"You suck and make life unnecessarily difficult."

"My job as a lawyer, sweet cheeks." They finger gunned me and I rolled my eyes, glancing at Drax, who was looking at me.

"Shall we just name it after you, love?" The lawyer opened his mouth and Drax shot him a look to shut it again. "If you do not wish to be *mo doineann*, perhaps this place can be our storm."

"The thing that attempts to drown us?" I scoffed, and he shook his head, eyes steady on mine. "I guess it will probably eventually batter me until I'm shattered on a rock somewhere. So why not?"

"No, love. The thing about storms is in weathering them, you learn things about yourself and those who remain beside you through it. When they end, and they always do, you're stronger for the journey."

"So, this is the thing that, if it doesn't kill us, makes us stronger?" I asked, thinking it sounded dumb but better than anything I had. "I'm glad to know this whole time you thought I'd kill you."

"No, *mo doineann*, you challenge me and remind me I'm alive. This winery will be the thing that makes us stronger, together."

FOURTEEN

DRAX

"I'M FUCKING KNACKERED." I PRESSED MY FACE INTO Tempe's hair as the last car disappeared and we stood under the moonlight. We were on the last sliver before the first night of the full moon and Tempe was right, I would have to leave her tomorrow.

"Stay! Stay with mate!" My dragon begged inside my head. He'd been quiet today, less of a nuisance since I took a chance this morning and touched her. She'd willingly granted him access, and he was permitted to help her destroy something to save her life. All of his hedonistic urges satisfied, the beast had rested peacefully in my mind. What had not been peaceful were the massive amounts of people who'd come in for wine, snacks, and screaming.

"Yeah... that was a day. Chance said they filed our LLC paperwork today, we are officially Mo Doineann, LLC. May I never have to pen it on a doc because I can't spell that to save either of our lives." She nudged me with her shoulder, and I followed her inside. Though we'd been unable to make as much progress as we wanted, Arran and I had built shelves separate from the building and the more artistically inclined set up the display. The chairs and tables were taken out and replacements were brought in from the Huckleberry Hollow Community Center surplus, a creepy facility that Sue alone knew the location of. Working outdoors, the witches had transformed the serviceable furniture into gothic modern pieces that revived the space and gave them a protective coating of anti-magic that kept the winery from weakening the structures.

Samuel had just collected his bag when we walked in, cash tips tucked into the front pocket of his jeans. "Weird to have you up here all day, dude. I think you gave two ladies spontaneous orgasms and one old gay man a heart attack."

Tempe scowled, a low rumble in her throat as she crossed her arms and glared daggers at the now empty table the women he mentioned had once occupied. "I don't know if I should file sexual harassment charges against them or not. So freaking inappropriate."

Samuel laughed, starting for the door when Tempe placed a hand on his arm. "Do you have a moment?"

The satyr looked between us, face scrunched and hands tapping his thighs. "Yeah, what's up?"

"Do you wear your glamour anywhere else but here?" She studied his legs, and then the walls surrounding us. I leaned in a little closer, needing the same answer she did.

"Yeah, a few places. College and the movies, but I mostly party with shifters and magic people in case they rub against me. No way I can convince a normie I'm always in fuzzy pants, y'know?" He gestured toward his lower body with jazz hands.

I chuckled slightly, and he gave me a small smile. Our time together when Tempe left yesterday had been trauma bonding, if nothing more solid.

"Aye, I can see that being a problem in summer. Do you feel more exhausted after holding it here than yeh do elsewhere?" I picked up Tempe's questioning when her focus drifted away. I knew she was exhausted, the day far too long, but answers were needed. "Like it requires more energy?"

Samuel's horns dipped to the side, his face pinched. "It's hard to say. I'm energized by lust, and there's no shortage of that around here. But on slow days, or days with just happy couples, yeah... it can get... sloggy. Why?"

Tempe considered him, then the walls again, and finally me. "I think something is sucking the magic out of people who come here. Any magic done is being pulled from the source and into the walls. If it's ever too much, please go to the office and let the glamour fall. You are not expected to suffer."

"Is that why I can see the entrance to your apartment?" We all turned to see the staircase, visible and freshly painted to match the walls this morning. Leila, Naomi's wife, had a way with colors and texture that defied logic.

"Yes. There's also no longer a protection to the barrel room, so if you ever did... over PG-13 activities in there before, please refrain." Tempe's exhaustion made her sound so serious and professional that Samuel backed away from her.

"Is she OK?"

I laughed. "Aye, but I should get her to bed."

He waved us off and left through the front door. I locked it behind him and then approached my mate with caution. She had said this morning something shifted between us, and it was true, but I wasn't sure if I was invited into her chambers for the evening meal.

When she continued to stand there blankly, I wrapped my arm around her shoulders and tugged her toward her doorway. "Are yeh hungry lass?"

She nodded as we walked up the stairs. I kept her slightly in front of me, providing balance and satisfying my need for contact. At the door she stared at her lock in confusion, thrown off by the sight. "There's a keyhole?"

"Aye, love." I pulled the key from her pocket, careful not to stray further than necessary. I unlocked the door and ushered us inside, hanging the key beside the door. "We put it in to reduce magical use in the building."

She walked into the apartment, staring at the furniture and

decorations with a weary sadness. When the cat appeared beside her, she bent down and scooped him up, holding him close. "Why did she do it?"

I swallowed my words, unsure what to reveal about my guess.

"Why did she enchant the winery to steal magic and siphon power? Gran had immense magical potential all on her own... I found her book. Her grimoire? She'd put down all these spells and ideas, hypotheses and speculation. From what I read, she could do everything she needed to and more. There's no reason to take, to harm others, for power—is there?" Tempe's eyes begged me to explain it to her, but I couldn't. I'd never met Maple, not officially, and while it was her signature charming the walls, I doubted it was her spell casting that placed it there.

Not when she lived with a leech.

I wrapped my arms around Tempe, holding her close and stroking a hand up and down her back. "I don't think we'll know until we talk to her, love. Grab a shower and I'll make us some supper. Do you have any preferences?"

"No." Her nose was buried in my shirt, and I could feel her inhale against me. My dragon sat up, pleased she found comfort in our scent and wanting to offer her more.

It is not the time I reined him in until the beast pouted in the corner.

She pulled away and I let her go, pretending not to notice the tears glimmering in the corners of her eyes when she made to wipe them away. When she was nearly out of my arms, I pressed a kiss to the top of her head, the only reassurance I could offer.

"We'll figure it out, love."

With a half smile, she trudged into her bedroom, then the bathroom, and started the water for her shower. Her cat looked between me and the open bedroom door, trying to decide which of us could be manipulated into giving him something he wanted.

I turned to her fridge to see what was inside, settling on chicken and broccoli pasta. In the cabinet above the stove, I reached for the pasta. A small blue bottle sat on the shelf above it, but when I went to inspect it, the cat let out a high pitched "mew". Pasta in hand, I turned and saw him seated beside his partially empty cat dish. The bottom of the ramekin visible in the very center.

"Yes, I suppose I should refill your dish as well. I'd hate for you to starve with only a half bowl." I reached behind me and closed the pantry, fed the cat, and then got to work on dinner.

ONCE TEMPE WAS SHOWERED and fed, I tucked her into bed. "Do yeh need my heat again, love?"

She yawned wide and nodded, lifting the edge of the blanket for me to join her underneath. Kicking off my boots, I crawled under the covers and wrapped my arms around her, pulling her head onto my chest and stroking her hair.

"Why do you sleep in the wine cave?" Her question startled me, and I took a moment to recover.

"It's too warm for me to sleep indoors. Dragon's fire." I felt her relax against me slightly and I released a breath, sinking into the pillow beneath me and the feel of her heartbeat and steady breaths on my chest.

"Sounds like a dumb thing dudes say to get out of cuddling." She yawned and burrowed in a little deeper.

"Says the woman cuddling with me. I might add that of the two of us, I still have all meh clothes on." I stroked her hair, patting the little wisps back into place among the mass of hair at her crown. "Yeh didn't even try to rip off meh trousers, I'm insulted."

"You should be."

I tickled her sides, forcing her to squirm over me to the detriment of my sanity. After a moment, everything quieted again.

"Will you ever stay the night with me?"

"Of course I will, love. But not tonight." I kissed the top of her head, enjoying the weight of her pressed into my chest.

Holding her just a little tighter, I counted her breaths and waited for the sandman to cart her off to dreamland.

A half hour later, I was startled awake when the cat jumped on the neighboring pillow. His green eyes shone, daring me to challenge his claim on the comfort square. After turning once, he curled into a cat ball and laid down, glaring at me.

"I fed yeh, why are yeh looking at me like that?"

Tempe had rolled off my chest and was now curled against my side. I ran my finger down her cheek, savoring the uninterrupted opportunity to explore her face. Memories of her mom had kept her awake, plagued her attempts at sleep, but without the barriers draining her magic and pulling at her while she slept, the woman appeared restful.

Brushing her hair back, I kissed her temple and stood. In the moonlight from the window, I watched her hands reach for me. A temptation I struggled to resist, but there was something that I needed to do before I left for the duration of the full moon.

Walking into her living room, I studied the walls and wondered if the enchantment continued up here. If, beyond absorbing the magic, it was also listening and feeding information to the man in question.

It was too important to risk. After looking in on Tempe one last time, I bolted the front door with her new lock. Sliding the metal chain into place, I tugged on the handle and confirmed my mate was secured in her home. Walking over to the balcony doors, I opened them to the night, stepping out onto the terrace to take in the frosted landscape. Below us sprawled Huckleberry Hollow, all the lights long since extinguished beneath the last of the waxing moon. Funky rooftops side by side with row houses, surrounding the fairy lights of downtown that reflected in the snow coating the ground.

It was desolate, but peaceful, its own kind of magic that the residents could comprehend but not name. A resonant glow from spending the evening with my witch sliding over me and making even the mundane just a little less dreary. Time with Tempe, however irritated she may get, was time to treasure.

Just my wings emerged, and I shut the doors, flying down three stories to coast into the mouth of the cave. They rejoined my human form as I took in my space, wondering not for the first time how much better it would be if Tempe were here with us.

A shadow stopped outside the cave, and I studied the small creature. It was too hairy to be a coyote, and too tall to be anything but a dog. It whimpered softly, and I shook my head, going into the barrel room to grab some ground meat and veggies Tempe kept in a large fridge.

I dumped it in a bowl and placed it at the cave entrance, walking back to the sitting area. On the shelf beside the dragon-themed paperbacks was a small box of thick paper, and I took one out. Setting it on my kitchen table, I went to the corner of the room where my old duffle was folded and stuffed in a foot locker . Cautious of spiders, I opened the case and gently unfolded the green canvas, checking each pocket until I located the phoenix quill.

"Bloody impractical lot." I carried the feather to the table and stared at the paper. There wasn't a way to begin this that didn't make me sound like a hatter, so I just went for broke. In the phoenix feather fire, I penned a short message to the war tribunal for supernatural crimes.

I believe something has gone amiss, and a new leech has been activated that answers to the old. I'm uncertain how, but I believe he intends to suck all the magic out of Huckleberry Hollow.

UNCERTAIN IF THEY'D even read a message from me, I called forth a single flame from my dragon and singed the edge of the message. The dragon fire called to the phoenix flame, and the message burst into a small green cascade of sand that disappeared before hitting the table.

"We did what we could." I saw the dog eating at the mouth of my cave and turned away to not frighten him. "It's up to them now. But if there is another, it must be related to the first."

CHAPTER

FIFTEEN

TEMPE

THERE WAS FAR TOO MUCH HEXING SUNSHINE IN MY bedroom.

"It would be super great if the sun could just... die already," I muttered to the cat, sunning himself on the pillow beside me. He batted a paw toward my face, and I assumed I was expected to shut it because the sun was his favorite and I was unnecessary. A wide yawn stretched my mouth, and I buried my face in the pillow. Beneath my own smell was Drax, the reason I woke up feeling rested.

Turning to my other side, I plucked my phone from my nightstand and saw it was eight. Far too early to be awake, a little early for getting the winery ready for guests... unless you had magic, and then it was far too early for that too. Beneath the time were six text messages, three in the Coven of Misfits chat about the Full Moon ritual tomorrow night when the moon was truly full, two from Lucy cancelling our plans and then re-instating them, and one from an unknown number.

Unknown Number: I'M ON MY WAY TO HELP WITH YOUR SENSORY CHALLENGES AND FARM EQUIPMENT, SHOULD BE THERE IN TWENTY.

143

I stared at the message and tried to remember who was coming and if I knew about it.

Me: THAT'S NICE. COULD YOU MAYBE... ELABORATE MORE?

My brain worked at digging up some memories of last night. Drax had held me while I fell asleep, after cooking me dinner and spending the whole day helping at the winery... which was a legal nightmare... Someone was going to come and help... because someone had suggested an enchantment to help with my sensory overload, but it had seemed more like a platitude than a genuine offer. Like a suggestion you make with no intention of following through. Like, we should get drinks or let's get together, I'll teach you how to use Excel.

Unknown Number: LOL. IT'S KACI. RACINA SAID YOU NEEDED HELP WITH NOISE-CANCELLING TECH MAGIC AND YOUR TRACTOR. I WAS GOING TO HAVE A LOOK AT YOUR CAR, BUT I HEAR SOMEONE ELSE IS ALREADY HANDLING THAT.

Once again, I was at a loss.

I went to the kitchen to pour water in my coffee maker, only to find it already ready to go. Another little gift from the dragon to jumpstart my morning... it was starting to weird me out, so I turned the coffeemaker on and declined to think about it any longer.

I chose a mug from my cabinet and then stared into my fridge, looking for inspiration. Many people who loved coffee loved it as it was, but I loved my coffee with enhancements. Like creamer, or flavor shots, or something that cut through the bitter acid of boiled bean water to provide me with the magical property that was... caffeine.

And in the winter: warmth.

Me: I... REMEMBER SOME OF THAT. WHAT'S WRONG WITH MY CAR?

My phone started having seizures on my counter, and I panicked.

Kaci was calling me.

I did not answer my phone for people I knew. If a doctor's appointment needed to be made, I held my breath while I dialed and worried about breathing into the phone like that 90s horror flick. So, I held my breath while speaking until I almost passed out, then gasped for breath into the air like I ran a marathon. Answering the phone for a stranger was unthinkable... Who was this monster?

Holding my breath, I stabbed the accept button and whispered, "Hello?"

"What do you mean by 'what's wrong with it'?"

Well, at least she skipped small talk.

"It was sitting outside just... yesterday?" I hadn't looked for it, but I couldn't imagine someone coming all the way out here to steal my secondhand early 2000s Subaru. "I'm pretty sure."

"No... Your heater is broken, it hasn't had an oil change in two years, your tires are bald, and your radiator cap is broken. Also, seven hundred other things Sue noticed when she went to get keys made. Artie took your car and some guys with the pack are trying to make it drivable again." She harrumphed in disgust at the state of my vehicle. "Honestly, it's a wonder you aren't dead."

"I didn't know Sue knew so much about cars. I thought she was a teacher... or maybe a grant writer..." I was still scared to breathe even though the phone was on speaker and now at least a foot away from me. I stared at my coffeemaker and willed it to brew faster, watching Corky strut in. His ginger fur glowed majestically, mocking the fact a stranger was pressing against my comfort levels before I was even awake.

"I think you're missing the point. Did you ever even maintain that car?" She was laughing at me, the sound of her vehicle traveling on a roadway in the background.

"It wasn't really mine?" I asked, practically jumping up and down with excitement when my coffee maker beeped. My mug was filled with the true elixir of life before my next breath and after a long satisfying drink, I groaned in relief. "I mean, it is now. But... it wasn't."

"What?"

"I rode a Kawasaki Ninja... But it snows here and there's mud, so gran insisted I take the Subaru with the winery... Insisted is a bit strong, she said she didn't need it so I might as well drive it so I didn't die."

"I meant what are you doing and why are you making sounds like that? My wife will kill me if she thinks I'm listening to shit like that from a woman half my age."

"Sorry, you called me pre-coffee." I took another drink and tried to control the noises of satisfaction that threatened to escape. Corky leapt onto the counter and started threatening a mug full of pens with gravity. "I need to feed my cat before he destroys something. Anything you need me to have when you get here? Coffee? Water? Tools of some kind?"

"Oh, honey." Her turn signal clicked. "I'll see you in a bit."

Kaci ended the call, and I stared at my phone on the counter. Corky yelled loudly and I snapped to attention, filling his bowl with crunchy cat food and verifying the water in his dish was clean. Once I'd confirmed he was set, I refilled my coffee and carried it to my bedroom. Opening drawers, I tossed a bra on the bed, followed by a pair of jeans and a shirt screen-printed with the winery's logo.

Gripping the hem of my sleep shirt, I pulled it off and folded it up to rest on my pillow for tonight. Trudging into the bathroom, I did the morning routine and went back out to don the day's apparel. It wasn't gay, but it promised to keep me from getting arrested, and there was a tiny rainbow.

Once all my bits were covered, I searched out my thickest socks and the boots I rarely ever used, knowing I'd need them to trek out to the equipment shed. I finished my second cup of coffee and carried the empty cup out to the kitchen. Filling it one last time from the pot, I looked at the clean pan from dinner last night.

"Should I bring Drax coffee as a thank-you?" Corky was done with his breakfast, yowling as though he hadn't been fed at all.

"That will not work, kid." I drank my coffee, still wondering what the niceness protocol for people who help you sleep is.

Beside the front door was my flannel coat and a puffer jacket, and I debated which to wear out to meet Kaci. The equipment barn wasn't too far out there, but I wasn't sure how long we'd be there. Corky howled.

"No dice." I placed the now empty cup in the sink, grabbed the puffer jacket and pulled it on, relieved to find gloves in the pockets. Sliding my hands into those, I unlocked the apartment and looked back at the angry feline. "You staying or going?"

He flung himself dramatically on the ground.

"Suit yourself."

Loping down the stairs in my boots, I emerged into the small vestibule and went left toward the janitorial closet and away from the tasting room. On the other side was a fire door that spit me out into a gravel drive where I usually parked my car. Stepping out into the too-bright light, I let out a small scream and stuck my hand back inside the door before it slammed shut. Hanging on the wall was a ball cap I kept for just such occasions, and I pulled it on, threading my ponytail through the opening in the back.

"Where's your car, love?"

I screamed again, clutching my chest and spinning around to face Drax. "Stop sneaking up on me!"

"It's daylight." He moved closer and invaded my personal space. "How can I sneak up on you in daylight?"

"I was blinded by the excessive sunlight. Also, being sneaky is not light dependent. Weren't you leaving?"

He held a small container out to me, and I looked at the glass dish like it held poison.

"I was. Where's your car?" His hand remained extended, and the smell of fresh garlic and leeks tickled my nose with peppers and bacon.

"Artie's people have it. I guess Sue found a bunch of things wrong with it yesterday and now it's in the automotive repair land... Kaci will probably fill me in when she gets here. What's that?" I asked, unable to ignore the container in his hand anymore.

"Rashers and boxty. I made extras, thought you might want some. Figured we slept together, so I owed you breakfast. Who's Kaci?"

I stared at his hand, the container, and then his face.

"You... made extras? On purpose or on accident? Also, you didn't sleep. You left."

Rolling his eyes, Drax gripped my biceps and stroked down my arm until he had my hand palm up in his. "Just eat it, *mo doineann*. I promise to sleep the entire night with you another time if it helped you get rest."

I could smell the potatoes through the lid and my stomach grumbled audibly. Chuckling, he pulled the lid off and showed me there was a fork inside.

"It did." I ogled the food for a long moment. The smells were as tantalizing as the man who'd made the food, but I still hesitated. Drax snuck his hand in, gripped the fork and scooped up a bite of the potato cake and bacon. He lifted it to my lips, eyes meeting mine and daring me to refuse.

I opened my mouth and let the fork slide in, immediately sliding into bliss.

"Oh, goddess, that's good." I moaned, reaching for the fork. Drax had a death grip on the utensil, and his eyes completely shifted to his dragon's. "Drax?"

He gathered another bite, taking my hip with his other hand and drawing me against him. I gasped at the feeling of his fingers sinking into my soft flesh and he slid the food into my mouth. Chewing to the same rhythm of his fingers kneading my flesh, we kept unflinching eye contact—me and the dragon.

"Let me feed you, love."

In the gold of his eyes, I saw flashes of sweaty flesh, a heated gaze, and a flash of teeth. We sank deeper into each other, every forkful traveling less and less until I was practically eating directly from his mouth.

"Tempe." He breathed, and I leaned in for another bite. Gold bled to green, Drax fighting to come back, but he didn't pull away as my lips moved toward him. My brain screamed BAD IDEA, but my memories flashed to last night, to his words, to waking up to find he'd made coffee, and I wanted a taste of more than just his food.

Don't say no. Please don't say no.

"Yes?" I swallowed my last bite to the sound of the fork clattering against the empty glass container. I glanced down, staring at his hand and the empty container in mine. There was a wine barrel by the door, and I pushed the container onto it. There was nothing between us anymore, my body flushed against his as I waited for him to say something. His body reacted to me the same way I reacted to him and I appreciated the feel of him against me, but I needed more.

"I... we..." Our eyes searched each other for hesitation, answers to questions we hadn't asked while sharing heat and air. This time, his pure green gaze stayed unperturbed by the golden dragon he kept inside. Drax was the one in charge in this moment and, unlike his dragon, I couldn't predict what he wanted.

The man wrapped his other hand around my waist and slid it under my jacket to press into my back. I tilted closer, the skin of my cheek barely scraping the stubble on his chin.

"I have to tell you something." Uncertainty marked his face, and I wondered if it was about me, the winery, or something else. I watched his full pink lips move and begged the universe to bring them closer.

"OK." I felt the warmth of his skin under me. We'd gotten even closer. "Is it that you want to kiss me? Because..."

"It's about the day you were—"

Gravel crunched behind us, breaking the trance of my hormones. My face fell, and I tried to step back, but Drax tightened his grip, chin dipping to meet me beneath the ball cap. He ran his lips from the curve of my neck, awakening every nerve ending in my body until he reached the soft spot behind my ear and took a small nip with his teeth.

"I'll be back in a few days," he whispered. "When I get back, I want to take you on a date."

"Why?" I panted, trying to get my breathing under control. "We already live together."

"Courtship, love." His lips brushed softly against mine and then a gust of air pushed me backward and he was gone.

Lips tingling, cheeks flushed, I looked up to see a stunned woman in her 60s standing at the corner of the building.

"Well, damn."

Took the words right out of my mouth.

CHAPTER
SIXTEEN

Kaci was a short witch with pink hair and more rings in her ears than orbit Saturn. She wasn't the same age as my gran, but she had definitely seen a few dozen birthdays. She was built for manual labor, short and stocky, and dressed for the same in coveralls, plaid and denim.

I had absolutely no memory of ever meeting her, but I doubted I'd be able to forget her twice.

"Hi, I'm Tempe." I offered, extending my hand once life returned to my limbs and I could operate my feet and make words. Despite my complete mental shutdown, the flesh movers carried me around the corner to greet the woman standing in my parking lot beside an older model... green thing. Kaci accepted the handshake, shaking once without looking away from where Draigus had disappeared.

"Was that a fucking dragon shifter?"

I snorted a laugh and nodded. Without any additional info, I decided I liked her.

"That's Draigus, or Drax. Pain in the ass and co-owner of this place." I let out a sigh that was a bit too dreamy, for the subject matter. I was far too easily swayed by something as basic as being fed delicious food, having him build shelves, and a chaste kiss.

Though he'd also made me coffee, kept me warm until I fell asleep, got me into my bank account, and cooked me dinner, so maybe I wasn't being *that* easily swayed.

Also, I'd done some shady shit for food that only tasted half as good, and that man hadn't even made it himself.

Compartmentalizing those thoughts, I turned to Kaci and then to the tasting room, and finally out toward the farm as a whole. She had come over to help with sensory overload and the farm equipment, but faced with the prospect of providing direction and asking for help, I didn't know where to start.

"Do you know how rare dragon shifters are?"

I glanced back at her, head tilted in confusion.

"No?"

"Very rare. I don't have stats, but the numbers are not very high."

"They aren't? He and his godfather are both dragons, though by the time I met his godfather, he no longer shifted. Or perhaps he never did... My mom never talked about him and gran barely talks at all except to make demands. He and my gran were fated, but he came along when my mom was a teen, which ended up in her leaving and then pregnant. Or pregnant and then leaving? Either way, my interactions with him have been limited. Whenever I was around, he wasn't."

Kaci frowned.

"Have you seen his fully transformed dragon?" She continued, and I decided that if this line of questioning was going full steam ahead, I was going to need additional coffee. Moving toward the tasting room door, I silently willed her to follow me.

Not with magic, just mental projection and hope.

No way was I capable of magic post Drax induced lust haze and pre-coffee round two.

Kaci trundled along behind me, her short legs needing to take two steps to my one. I used magic to unlock the door and propped it open for her to follow behind me. On autopilot, I ducked behind the counter and started a new pot of coffee.

"I've seen his wings, and I've seen him fly, but never the full dragon. Fairly sure I saw him silhouetted across the moon once —" Right after I was a statue... The thought crashed into me, and I froze in place, wondering if that was why he'd been evasive last night... wondering if that's what he wanted to tell me.

"Was he huge?" She asked, and I blinked at her.

"I've only seen him with pants on, but I think it's above average from what I've felt?" I was still thinking about the full moon, the dragon, Arran's reaction, and Lucy's assertion that he'd been angry, and just kept talking. "It felt impressive against me this morning, and the other night, assuming it wasn't something in his pocket and he was turned on like I was... what?"

Mouth hung open, Kaci was now the color of the tomatoes in my greenhouse and getting redder. A key social cue had passed me by and I was flummoxed. How could she ask a question and not want the answer? My face must have captioned my confusion, because she shook her head with a small laugh.

"I meant his dragon, Tempe! But boy, do you not mince words!" She fanned herself. Nodding my understanding, I studied the coffee pot and watched it slowly fill with bean water. "I'm mostly into the ladies, but now I'm worried about making eye contact with a man I've yet to meet officially."

"Oh... Do you want to meet him?" My head tilted to the side as I assessed whether or not I thought he'd be kind. Just because we were making progress doesn't mean I was ready to go around subjecting strangers to him. Neither of us excelled at human interaction, and I couldn't imagine worrying about what both our faces were doing.

Though *courtship* meant public outings, the more terrifying prospect was subjecting me to people. Perhaps I could sell him on the idea of Netflix and chill... I need to buy a TV.

"Maybe someday, I'll let you know. Now, the dragon?"

I blinked at her, trying to clear the idea of a paperback and chill date. Probably that was just parallel play and not something adults did... maybe if it was the same book? Or was that a book club? I was already sweating through my T-shirt and he hadn't even asked me out yet.

Kaci cleared her throat, and I remembered she asked me a question... about something.

"What was the question?"

"Your partner's dragon!" She threw her hands up in exasperation and I tried not to melt from embarrassment. "Is it massive, like normal dragons in books you can ride? Is it like an enormous lizard? Are you going to live out Anne McCafferty dreams and use him like a fighter plane in the fight against evil?"

There was a new thought... "Right, sorry. I might have seen his dragon... maybe. Honestly, I can't be sure it was him... or even a dragon. But yeah, the shadow was big if the memory is real... although it was a full moon, so maybe it can't have been."

"What else could it have been?" Shocked, she could follow my stream of words; I considered the possibilities. There really weren't any, but the full moon shining when I woke up really made it being him less and less likely in the light of day.

Kaci slid onto one of the bar stools, her legs kicking beneath her while spinning a menu beneath her index finger. Knowing her son shared my sensory aversion, I started cataloguing her behaviors. Fidgeting, easily distracted, but hyper focused on a topic once introduced to it...

"Not sure. But I don't trust all of my memories from that day. So Racina mentioned your son had sensory issues?" I prompted, diagnosing her with ADHD despite a complete lack of clinical qualifications and background information. One of my roommates in college had behaved similarly without an official diagnosis and we found it was easiest to communicate when I redirected us to the prudent subject. "That you'd worked some tech magic to help with sound?"

I poured myself a mug of coffee and offered her one.

"Oh! Right! Sorry, got distracted. So..." Wrapping her hands around her coffee mug, Kaci took a long drink. She looked around the tasting room, her eyes pausing in the corners and along the higher eves and exposed beams. "Whew, you have quite a drafty echo chamber in here. Do you find it difficult to heat?"

I pointed to the space heater that died.

"We get by. That died two days ago, but mostly, the space heaters get the job done. Maybe if there's time later, you can take a look and see if my toes can be spared. What are you thinking about the noise? We have a sound system if you have like... a white noise program we can play underneath the music. Or..." I stared into my empty coffee cup and tried to think of something else that might make me sound smart but came up blank.

"Oh, no. It's easier to regulate the energy of the space than to balance unknown noise levels. For example, my son has a necklace that he wears in public spaces that essentially brings down the volume and the energy of the surrounding people. Like lavender essential oils, but effective. Around our house, though, and spaces he's in all the time, we have... like a plug-in air freshener, but instead of detecting smells, it detects triggers and sends out a counter wave. Like blocking an alpha wave with a beta wave... or was it the other way? Meh, either way, the trigger is still there, but it's dampened. Does that make sense?" She jingled as she moved, her piercings tinkling against each other as her body twisted side to side in the chair.

"No. But it sounds like you know what you're doing. Could you help me make a similar necklace? We might have a problem with the room." I looked away from her and drank my coffee, worried about saying too much and needing a break from watching her. Kaci was in perpetual motion, and it triggered my anxiety. Either I wasn't doing enough, or I was moving too slowly, but watching Kaci was not an option.

"What's wrong with the room?" She spun on the stool, absorbing the peeling plaster, the new shelving, and the empty spaces that no longer held wine. A teal wave slid out, cresting into the room and disappearing like a tide. "That's unusual."

"It's... probably cursed. Or haunted. Maybe an enchantment to steal magic, but why gran would need it... Either way, even if we could work magic in this room that didn't get sucked in, I get a lot of bridal parties. They don't like being dampened, shushed or quieted in any way." I pointed to some confetti cocks that somehow remained, wedged between the planks of the floor.

"Oh, no, it does nothing to the people being noisy or energetic. Just the triggered person. So, if anyone else in the room also has sensory issues, they'd feel relief. But people who naturally accept all manners of socially extreme behavior would be completely unaffected."

I was fairly certain she used the phrase 'social extremism' incorrectly, but not certain enough to comment. Kaci's solution sounded like a gift from the Goddess, but if it was so simple... "Why haven't I heard of anyone doing anything like this before?"

She scoffed, and I forced myself to look at her. "Because the magical community doesn't treat neurodivergence any better than the normies do. Just look at Maple" –I gave her a questioning look — "Your gran?"

Crap, how often did I talk to anyone who actually knew gran and called her by name? It was as foreign as hearing Arran call me Liv's kid. A reminder that in this sphere, I was the planet out of orbit with the rest of the system.

"My gran?" I asked, drinking my coffee and trying to piece that info in with my own memories. We hadn't been close, but I had never really been close to anyone. Some women declared themselves a girl's girl and would have a woman's back no matter what. Others were all about getting that D, and it didn't matter who or what they stepped on in the process.

I was a cat person. Not a person who necessarily loved cats, but the human version of a cat. If I chose to associate with humans, it was at my whim and with the constant caveat that I could wander away at any moment. When pushed to remain longer, I was not above using teeth and claws to escape. It wasn't a failure to understand human behavior; I understood it too well. All the nuances of language were lost on me, but the blatant lies and half-truths etched in their brows and lips were impossible to conceal. Observing people had taught me you couldn't trust their words and asking the hard questions got you uninvited from social gatherings.

Simply put, I made people uncomfortable, and they exhausted my patience.

And that was *before* my mom died.

"Honestly, I get that her mate thought I was the absolute worst, and he warned Drax before he got here. I noticed my resident dragon cataloguing my behaviors and mouthing their names. It was irritating at first, but he did it without judgement, so I decided he was an info-seeker. But I didn't really get that extreme distaste from her... I didn't get much of anything. Most days, I thought she was out on another planet. Did she have a problem with you, too? I can't imagine ADHD is any better than AuDHD in her world if what you say is true."

Kaci paused, studying me.

"I mean... um... so you know about farm equipment?"

Her face broke into a smile, and she nodded.

"I do, yes. But let's take care of this first. And yes, Maple found me taxing once Damien came into the picture, which is why I rarely came by after you left. But while you lived here those few summers and your mother was in recovery, we had a good time looking up facts about plants and playing hide and seek. I recognized a kindred spirit in you while you were living here, but I couldn't stand Maple's constant old world, *you can fix your brain if you just try harder* mindset. It was the most closed-minded bit of bullshit I'd heard in a long time, and coming from her after all those years of her standing by my mom and offering wisdom, the things she said about Liv, your mom, when she never had before."

Her smile brightened, her hands taking mine with palms facing upward. There was so much to piece together from her words that I found myself more skittish with unfamiliar touches than I'd been recently. After all the unsolicited touches from Drax, I hadn't thought this issue was still an issue, but apparently, he was special.

"I never lived here before, aside from spending a few summers here in high school to learn the trade since 'only peons needed viticulture certificates', but I got the impression I wasn't all that welcome. And I don't remember you being here..." I tried to steady my breath after being unwittingly touched.

"Sorry, I forgot to ask. But you were here when you were... three to five, I think. Your mom was on her first stint in rehab, and your gran was the only family she had to send you to. I think Damien, her fated, didn't like you around, so you weren't here per se as much as you could have been." Kaci traced a rune on each of my palms and then closed her eyes. I joined her, because it felt rude not to and tried to follow the subtle murmuring. All the word vomit washed over me, but I couldn't make sense of it. I had no memories of being here as a child. No memories of this woman, or my mom in rehab. She'd needed rehab but never gone... or had she? No one ever talked about her, and my memories were taking on the edges of TV show caricatures, blanks filled with after school specials... magic pinched me. Ordering me to pay attention.

Ordering me to focus.

Heat filled my palms, warmth arcing between the left and filling the right. As the heat intensified, Kaci's words became louder and clearer. In a language I could not identify, I let my magic feel the intention and provide a translation.

Restore balance, protect from unwanted stress.
Counter the shadow. Bring forth a light from within.
Comfort, peace, home.
A safe place to just be.
"So Mote it Be."

The heat boiled over and then cooled into something solid and weighty. I opened my eyes to stare at a silver metal linked chain with a disc pendant laying across my palms. A design was etched into the pendant, but it disappeared in the valley between my hands.

"Place it around your neck and tuck it in your shirt, dear."

Kaci spoke with her eyes closed. "It's effective if people see it, but it's personal. Looking at it will probably reveal things to you that even you may not know about yourself. My son did not look at his until he was nearly eighteen, wanting the chance to develop as a witch without that insight, shielding the necklace from his sight."

"Eighteen? How old is he now?"

"Twenty-five."

I followed her guidance, slipping the leather strap over my head and tucking it away. The idea of not looking at it made my skin crawl with anticipation, an itch to fill an unknown knowledge void that I couldn't seem to tamp down.

"It's gone. Racina made it sound like he was six."

Kaci opened her eyes and studied me.

"Compared to her, we probably seem that way." She leaned back, and I heard her back crack. "The room will be much easier, but you'll have to do the heavy lifting on this one. If we can't trust the walls, we'll need to find objects to place around the room. Can we trust them on the shelves?" She nodded to the fresh wooden structures Drax and Artie had built.

"We can try... We'll probably need to work the enchantment outside and carry everything in to be safe. Speaking of things my magic isn't working on... where did we land on the dishwasher, washer, dryer, and space heater?"

KACI WORKED on catching her breath while I gazed at the tractor and prayed no one would ask me to do any more magic today. In an emergency, it was possible, but it was bound to be ugly.

It was about a half mile from the tasting room to the barn. Though normally a pleasant walk, six inches of snow had made it a trek with heavy resistance to our boots. The small inclines had turned into slippery slopes, and we'd struggled to maintain purchase even with the Yaktrax I'd pulled from the garage. My face was flush, cheeks tingling with cold and exertion as I tried not to offer the shorter woman help a fourth time and see if she'd meant it about stuffing snow down my pants.

Having spent the morning working magic and climbing ladders with her, I had no doubt she was both capable and willing to exact her revenge. When her badass tech witchery didn't fix my appliances, she got down on her hands and knees and did manual repairs. Which gave me an absurd amount of confidence she could dismember me and use my corpse to fertilize the vines.

"This is what I've got," I puffed out, watching my words float away on a cloud of steamed breath. The walk hadn't been as hard on me, but I still wasn't in *trek a half mile through the snow and breathe normally* shape either. "I think that's for tilling... maybe. And that's for... pulling. That does... something."

I stopped talking to suck in air. Before us was a tractor, I was certain how to work at least that much, and then it got a little dicey. Beside it was a contraption that reminded me of the thing that killed Shredder in the Ninja Turtle movies, a bunch of discs sliding against each other on a flat top attached to a tow hitch. Beside it was another tow hitch with two long cross beams and a hook that might have gone in the ground, and beyond that was a forklift, a contraption that might make barrels somehow, and a conveyer belt for... corking, maybe?

Though I thought all the bottling equipment was in my basement—pun intended.

Corky appeared beside us, looking disgruntled and not the least bit out of breath.

"No one told you to follow us, dude." I chastised him as he leapt out of the snow that had coated his legs and belly. Despite being damp, he landed on the cold metal wheel well of a large... thing. Farm thing... it wasn't the tractor, but it had an engine and wheels. I ambled over and looked at the levers, the metal seat and the buttons. A levered arm that hinged had a weird little claw that faced the driver, and a scooped bucket seemed to be the only tool operated by the trio of levers. "Do you think this is what inspired Wolverine's claws?"

"Wow..." Kaci breathed the word with equal parts amazement, insult, and condescension. I glanced at her, noting she was mostly upright, and her breathing had evened. "You have never worked on a farm a day in your life. That's a backhoe."

"That's a little insulting. Back or front, you shouldn't call people hoes."

"No... the thing you're leaning on is a backhoe." She laughed, and I raised an eyebrow at her.

"It was named by an ass man, wasn't it?"

"Who the hell knows? Wanna tell me what happened to the equipment?" Kaci propped a hand on her hip and I sensed judgement.

"What do you mean? It's old!"

"No... I mean, it's been a couple of years since I've been out here. I did the occasional tune-up on this stuff, but the way it looks right now..." She shook her head.

"I didn't have anyone to work the farm last season, and I don't know how to do this stuff. So it sat. I didn't mean for it to get—"

"Tempe!" She put her hand on my arm, and I looked at her grease-stained nails. "You wouldn't have needed anyone to help you with harvesting. The equipment is magic. But there's no magic left in there and either she poured rust and degradation on it, or someone sped up the decay. Because these weren't this old looking before."

We both surveyed the backhoe and contemplated how the equipment looked when I was here before.

"Do you think the magic got absorbed from them like the winery?" I looked at the nearest piece of equipment and scraped off a piece of rust. "And would it damage the machine underneath once the magic was gone?"

"I couldn't tell you. If it did, then maybe everything breaking inside isn't a sabotage spell, maybe it's the weight of the enchantment destroying the structure. Let's see what's under the hoods and then order some dishwasher parts. Sucks that magic doesn't work, but I know how to do things the old way."

Nodding, I tried not to dwell and fall down another rabbit hole. If the enchantment was ripping the winery apart, how much longer did I have before it was gone?

CHAPTER

SEVENTEEN

DRAX

THE JAGGED ROCKS CUT INTO THE GREY SKY AS I descended from the clouds in the perpetual mists of Ireland. From above, the land was an endless mass of green, with no sign of the endless farms, wandering sheep or mystical beasts who called the land home. It was as much a mirage as the human shell surrounding my dragon—an illusion of something far more persistent and mundane than the teaming life underneath.

Far off the Northern Isle, a small mass of earth waited for me. Surrounded by water and the boat wrecking crags of igneous lava and scoria that built around it, the place was accessible only by air and there was not much to see to tempt a human to land.

A few hearty trees had persisted amid the scorched and flat-tened rocks. They grew sideways with brittle needles, providing less of a canopy than the shadowed warning of inhospitality beneath. Alongside large stones and sand there were elongated bluffs, but nothing as stark as the desolation the space offered.

I'd spent seventy years without leaving this island, until my godfather summoned me to America, but it was not a home-coming to return. Though my mother was still alive and well along the emerald shores, I had not returned to her house since being split in two. She'd warned me not to go with Damien and I

163

did not wish to disappoint her with confirmation of my ignorance.

When all of this was over, curse or nay, maybe I could go home. Maybe Tempe could meet my mother and together they could discuss what a loveable eejit I am.

Maybe I could earn the right to be lovable.

My boots touched down on the desolate surface and I stared into the storm clouds, allowing my wings to pull back into the flesh of my back. No matter the season, the clouds lingered over my prison. The only safe place for my curse to transform from the words of a dying witch to an inescapable truth of my design. His spell echoed off every rock on the island, a broken record of the consequences of fighting someone else's war and buying their lies.

"Until you learn to love,
Live in the humanity you deny,
For every life you willingly snuff out,
Every full moon you will decry-
I'm only a monster, there is no doubt."

His bloody corpse haunted every rock face and scrag tree.

I waited, sensing the moon's ascent in the sky with growing weight in my gut. There was about an hour until the spell took effect, and I sat on the smooth flat stone beside the shelter and tried not to remember the bloodied man who'd chanted the words. But it was as futile as trying to stop the tides that batter the rocks.

The entire war in Ireland had been futile, and none of it had been mine to fight. The promise I was protecting my kin, my people, had all been a lie. But I was in too deep, looking down at the witch cursing me before I allowed my claws to come forward, plunge into the witch's chest and pull out his heart, the last few beats a discharge of electrical pulses occurring in my palm. I'd felt power and vindication, taking a single life to save thousands.

I'd stormed into the house behind him for the weapons and soldiers I'd been assured to lie on the other side. It was to be a coup, one that would save countless innocent people and I would rest easy knowing that I was on the side of right after months of questioning. But there had been only a woman and five children, one of which not yet old enough to hold his own head.

I left everything behind and tried a thousand ways to die, only to discover it wasn't possible. Nothing could kill a dragon but the death of his mate and, as it would happen, mine hadn't been born yet. And now that she was here, I would fall on a thousand swords if it meant sparing her so much as a paper cut. After all her pain, I could allow her to endure no more.

Face in my hands, I scrubbed them over my eyes. For a century, the images of bloody corpses and the lives I'd stolen consumed me. Every trip to this island was a nightmare on repeat, with faces blending into a mask of human agony that I was certain would haunt me until I grew moss and became absorbed into the cliff side.

This time, however, I saw her face. My love. *Mo doineann.*

Anam cara, Tempe.

Her smile and voice telling me facts about her, her family, grapes... Cooking her breakfast, rebuilding her shelves, helping her learn her business—it all seemed poor repayment for this small ray of sunlight in the grey cold emptiness of my life. I wanted to tell her, to confess to the bond and let her decide, but if she didn't want me, I couldn't leave. Not until I knew why the winery was stealing and storing magic and if there was a larger threat looming over her.

Nothing escaped Tempe's notice. She cared for everyone, but how do you care for someone who lost their humanity every twenty-eight days? How do you love someone when the reason their life fell apart is the same reason yours did—the same man is sucking the life out of all of you? She deserved to know who was behind the problems with the winery, but what if she thought I was the one causing them?

I needed to know who had installed the enchantment before I came to her with it.

"I should let her go," I said to the gathered clouds. The

warmth of her lips still lingered on mine, the feel of her body, soft and pliant against mine, a memory I'd carry on my skin with the permanence of a tattoo.

Thunder rumbled across the sky with a streak of lightning that fired into the sea. A war waged in the clouds that matched the war waging in my head and my heart. It was ultimately up to her, but how do I just dump the truth on her head like a bucket of ice water when she's already frozen?

"Will never let her go," my dragon snarled, and I felt the first slips of my control.

"What about what's best for her?"

Lightning crackled once again, and he fought back, at odds with the truths of life. *"We are what's best for her!"*

A searing pain cut through my chest, a liquid chill that split me in two, and I felt myself pulled free from the body I inhabited. This time, though, it was different. Instead of being pulled into the void, I felt myself being pulled toward something new, somewhere new. My mind was leaving the vessel, but I was being called and directed away from the darkness. For a moment, the dragon and I melted into one, as we were at birth, and a single clear thought broke through the haze.

"Something is calling me home."

Awareness departed and everything grew smaller, my true shape emerging to fill the island. Steam hissed from the fire blowing through my mouth as cool air filled the space beneath my wings and I rose higher to see the dragon's shadow cast on the ocean's surface.

"Salty sea."

"Hunt."

"Soar."

"Mate."

"We will have our mate."

EIGHTEEN

TEMPE

"I'M SORRY, WE'RE CLOSED." I TURNED AROUND FROM the bar at the sound of the opening door, ready to be met with some pushback only to come up short. Sue stood in the doorway, her tiny frame dwarfed by the large bank of shelves Drax and Arran had built beside it. "Oh! Sorry, come in. Lock the door, please?"

The leader of the Coven of Misfits obliged me, clicking the lock into place. The soft, steady, tap of her winter boots tracked the room while I counted the till and took tasters out of inventory, closing everything out for the day. "The shelves look wonderful."

"They did a really good job." I confirmed, stacking the last of the used glasses into a dish tray for the 39th time, not that I was counting, and carted it into the kitchen to place in the big dishwasher and swap it out with the clean ones. When I exited, Sue was seated at the bar holding a rag, her hand empty palm up, waiting for a glass to dry. "You don't have to..."

"I know I don't. Which is why I didn't ask if I could, I told you I was. Now, a glass, Tempranillo. I will not ask again." She issued the command in my full name and lugged the dish rack over to her wearing my shoulders as earrings. Once I placed it beside her, I moved my stool across from hers and grabbed my own cloth to polish the ones she dried.

We worked in concentrated silence for a while, the squeak of water pulled across glass and the clink of it set against the stone countertop the soundtrack to our activity. Halfway through the rack, I caved.

"Where's Max?"

"My offspring is sitting with him. He's not a fan of car rides after dark and the road up here is a bit harrowing." Her nails clicked against the glass. "Also, he feels your cat is a bit of a dick."

We both looked at the oversized orange feline reclined by the register. The tip of his tail swished and twitched, and I wondered if he was pleased or irritated with the revelation. Three more cups passed between silence and I tried again.

"What's on your mind, Sue?" I moved the glass I'd just polished to the counter behind me with its friends for tomorrow's guests.

"Not much. You?" Her eyes met mine, a single eyebrow lifted in challenge.

"A lot, but I'm not the one who drove up a mountain to dry glasses." I lifted my chin to the cup in her hand, lips pressed together.

"You could tell me what's on your mind, Tempe." Her rag squeaked over another glass.

"You could tell me why you drove up here." I set it down, polished and sparkling, on the soft lining with its friends. She kept her face drawn and arms crossed, not continuing until I caved. "Chance called today. They confirmed the winery is in my grandfather's name, but the records after his death still need to be chased down and the statement sounded literal. Like the deed was in the hands of a jackalope they were trying to catch up with, or maybe a cheetah? At the very least, the place and the money belong to my family since there's no record of sale. But without the deed, I don't know what percentage I'm entitled to and how much I can change. Drax left this morning, which I assume you know, and we learned yesterday the place is sucking magic out of me and everyone who uses it within the building so everything has to be done the normie way. The buildup of magic in the walls is probably what's breaking everything, and I can't take any of it back out. You're up."

Sue exhaled heavily, the chuckle at the end shaking her chest a little. "I thought you might be lonely with Drax gone and I came up to keep you company." Clink, she set down another glass and I picked it up. "Also, as I'm the reason your car was carted off, so to speak, I thought you may need a ride somewhere. Kaci told me about the magic and the walls, as well as the farm equipment."

The polished glass joined its friends. "Where would I need to go? My lawyer owns a phone and my accountant doesn't have a corporeal shape, so I'm as connected now as I was before you took the car. Added bonus, Drax bribed people to bring me over sixteen bags of coffee, for both upstairs and downstairs, so I'm set for like... a week."

Last glass dried, she set down her rag and studied me. In the interest of equality, I studied her back. Her eyes were still sharp, cutting into the soul of those who sought her out. The shoulder length greying hair on her head was in a loose bun at her neck, and she still hadn't removed her large warm coat.

"Where indeed... you don't often leave this place. Does that seem normal to you? Never meeting people?" Her blunt nail clicked on the counter, tapping emphasis on each word in her question.

"I met the people in the coven?" I crossed my arms over my stomach, cold washing over me with a parade of ants pinching my skin from the inside. "And I meet customers."

"You hate customers." She tilted her chin down, arms crossed. "And aside from Penny and Lucy—who have to force you out—you don't spend time with the coven."

"Not all of the customers... I like the ones who drink their wine, speak very little, buy some and leave." I backed farther away from her as I talked, trying to increase the distance between me and her growing disapproval. "And I love everyone who doesn't leave glitter dicks on my floor." I avoided her claims about coven members because I had no counterpoint. Socializing was not my forte. I preferred to be at home, with my books and my cat enjoying the company of quiet. I wasn't against someone doing these things with me, but people in general, wanted to go outside.

Where there were *more* people.

Her lips twitched, but she didn't smile. I'd been hiding on this hill, exhausted and depressed, for over six months. It was the first time I realized people noticed, cared, and intended to put an end to it. Unfortunately, I didn't want anyone to put an end to it. Why was everyone trying to fix me?

Rising to her just over five-foot height, Sue strode to the walls and pressed against them. "You're correct in your assessment that Kaci came by and told me about the enchantment. That it had sucked the magic out of your farm equipment, and you were worried it would cause structural failure, though you failed to voice it aloud to her, the concern was on your face. It seems you conducted a test and confirmed your own suspicions." Teal whisps left her hand, small embers of magic that were immediately absorbed. Devoured into the building itself to feed an invisible beast. "She also told me that Drax left this morning and she witnessed a kiss. You did not mention the kiss, Tempe."

I fisted my hand on my hip, heat rising up my neck. "It just happened, and I was working. I still don't know if it's the building, the space around the building, or rats in the walls. We figured out that spells that touch the winery proper are used as feeder magic and drain the caster over time, which is why my shields are down, Mr. Spock." My chest heaved and I found myself struggling to catch my breath. "I didn't mention the kiss because it's personal. Yes, I conducted some tests, trying to isolate the source and reverse the charge, but obviously that failed."

"I was always more of a Bones than a Spock, but I appreciate the reference." Her hand appeared on my shoulder, and I looked up at her from the floor. My arms wrapped around my knees, and

I rocked slightly, trying to keep the anxiety inside. I wasn't ready to fall apart, but I also wasn't going to give up. "It looks like the enchantment is confined to the building, but any active magic done inside is absorbed. The reason your spells to stop the decay aren't working is because inert matter is not meant to hold more than one magic at a time, and it is filled to the brim with the absorption enchantment."

"Can you remove it?" I tried to see the walls from my space on the floor. "My attempts did nothing but make me tired."

"I'm not sure. In general, only the caster can remove an enchantment this complex. Either by choice, by force, or by death." Her face swam and the edges of my vision went a little fuzzy. "For now, I recommend any magic you need to do be done outside."

"What about Samuel? He can't work without his glamour." My eyes closed to stop the earth and the room from spinning opposite directions. "I can't do this without him and we can't close on Saturday and Sunday."

"Hmmmm..." Air brushed past my cheeks, and I felt her on the far side of me. "Maybe there is something else we can do for him. I'll have a think about it."

I nodded.

"Did I ever tell you about my husband?"

My eyes opened and I rolled my head toward her. She offered me a hand up and I carefully accepted, letting her guide me to a bar chair. We took seats beside each other and she passed me a tissue from a pack in her pocket.

"He was a normie. As are all my kids. We had fifty years together before he passed and through it all, he never shared a single feeling. I know he loved me, and the kids, but he was more or less closed off from expressing anything. I'd had the mistaken impression that it was because he didn't feel anything, but it turns out he felt too much, and he kept it all inside. I found a journal after he died, filled with all the thoughts and emotions he couldn't speak aloud."

She wiped some moisture from under eyes and I passed the tissues back.

"I'm sorry, that sucks." I shifted in my seat, scratching at a spot on my lower back that started to itch. "At least he journaled, though? Heard that's healthy..." I got up and grabbed a freshly cleaned cup and some water, placing it in front of her. Pouring another for me, I drank it quickly and took another.

"Yes. And you remind me of him." She took a reasonable sip of hers, running a finger along the rim to make a low whistle. "I wanted to tell you not to keep the feelings, the thoughts, the things you need, on the inside for fifty years, Tempe. Let people know how you feel *now*, including your dragon."

"I... I don't know that I have..." I downed my water and wished it was tequila as I backed away from Sue. "Feelings."

Her lips twitched slightly as my phone buzzed on the countertop. "I believe that is the calvary, come to force you out of your shell. I'm merely the advanced guard to prevent you from tricking them into staying here instead by escorting you to the bar."

"The bar? What bar? Why would I go to a bar?" I ran out of room to back away and was now just trying to make myself smaller. My shoulders hunched to protect my neck while I furtively checked the exits and calculated the distance to escape and whether or not she'd catch me first. "They're loud, sticky, and full of people. Why is it always up to me to change and leave my comfort zones and not everyone else to just let me be myself?"

I physically shuddered from my head to my toes.

"Because you're miserable. Tempe, why are you constantly distancing yourself from other people? You are not an island, no one expects you to live alone up here. And yes"—she held up her hand when I opened my mouth— "I know Drax is here, but you hold him at arm's length as well."

My tongue stuck to the roof of my mouth and the room was too warm. Under her intense scrutiny, I'd have preferred to be left in the Sahara with only a plastic bottle of water. "You don't need to worry about me, I'm fine."

Her penetrating observation suggested doubt. "Except I do worry about you and now that I know the bags under your eyes are from this winery sucking the life out of you, I will not sit idly by and let you stay here. If you're fine, then you will change into something suitably festive and join your friends at the bar. I believe it is thirty degrees outside, so I recommend pants, but wear what makes you happy."

"Pajamas make me happy! Please, no!"

"I'm not sending you to die, Tempe. It's a bar with your friends, to not be in this place that is literally killing you. And it's a bar, I doubt you'd be the first to wear your pajamas to it."

I opened my mouth, but no sound came out. I cleared my throat and tried again. "What if they realize I'm different and stop talking to me? Brevity tends to be my friend when it comes to human interaction…"

"You really do believe that," she said after a moment. "Everyone in this town is 'different', Tempe, and while your brain may not be operating on the same software, there is absolutely nothing wrong with it, or you. If you truly cannot handle the bar, they will change activities, but if you never put yourself out there, no one will see how wonderful you are."

"Easy for you to say." I headed toward my apartment, muttering to myself not incur additional anger. "Everyone in your family didn't abandon you."

DRESSED in a tight black V-neck sweater and jeans with my hair curled and my make-up attempted, I returned to the tasting room for departure. Sue studied the walls, making notes in a book, before picking off a piece of the cracked plaster and tucking it between the pages. She turned, stumbling back a half step and then collecting herself into her normal stern demeanor.

"What was that?" I gestured to the book and the small patch

of missing plaster on the wall. She relocated a display bottle in front of the patch and gestured me forward.

"Just a paint sample. You look lovely." She tucked the notebook into her coat pocket and approached the door. "Are you ready to go?"

I patted my pockets, finding my wallet and house keys. "Phone?"

"By the register." Sue gestured to the device I'd forgotten when I'd gone upstairs. I crossed the room to collect it and saw four messages in a group chat with Penny, Lucy, and Naomi. The wood nymph and her water sprite wife weren't able to get a sitter, but the other two witches were ready to let loose.

Phone tucked away, I looked around the room one last time. "I guess I'm ready."

Sue led the way to her car, and I followed. Using a key to lock the tasting room felt a lot like having sex for the first time, weirdly intimate and kind of gross. I assumed I would get used to it, the door lock—not sex. I'd figured that one out, but the winery would be better if I could break the enchantment.

Snow crunched under my boots, and I carefully navigated the frozen slush and ice to avoid falling on my ass when the dumpster rattled on the far end of the lot, echoing off the building and surrounding woods. A dark shadow stretched from behind and I felt my magic start to build in my fingertips. I moved closer and the shadow grew, with pointed ears and an extended neck. I let my magic dissipate into me and spoke softly. "Come here puppy."

A head popped out. Red and scraggly, the animal had floppy ears and a damp coat. I took another step closer and he took off, running around the building toward the cave side entrance. I followed at a slower walking pace, taking care on the downhill slope that rounded the carport, until I was on vineyard level. Drax's cave entrance was slightly illuminated from the interior winery lights, casting a small amount of light along with the full moon above onto the ground.

Two of the small bowls I kept in the barrel room sat on the

ground, and I walked over. They were both empty. I frowned at the dishes, the cave entrance, and the vast landscape of snow and vines. "Why would he let you stay out here?"

I picked up both dishes and carried them in through the cave, filling one with water and the other with meat and veggies from the fridge. I carried both back toward the cave mouth and set them just inside, checking that the barrier would allow the dog in. Taking one of the folded blankets out of a basket beside Drax's bed, I set it up near the dishes with the space heater. Drax had never bothered to plug it in, so I found an outlet and set it up a safe distance from the bed and anything flammable with a quick protective spell against being knocked over.

"Tempe!" Sue's voice echoed around the vineyard, and I poked my head out.

"One second!" I gave the set-up a final look and then hiked back up the incline, sweaty and winded from the effort.

"What was that about?" She led me to the car and climbed in, the heater already going full blast.

"I think Drax was adopted by a stray, and he forgot to tell me." I leaned on the door, hoping to catch a glimpse of the dog before we left.

"That tracks. The two of you seem like the type of people that get collected." She huffed out a breath, pointing the car down the hill. Before I could question her statement, a large shadow crossed the moon, temporarily blocking the light with a winged impression and a long tail.

CHAPTER
NINETEEN
TEMPE

Whoever dreamed up the concept of a bar should be murdered. Not regular execution style, single shot to the back of the head, but strung up by their ankles in heavy chains and subjected to ten thousand tiny cuts—salted and not permitted to cauterize. As I predicted, the place was loud, sticky, and filled with too warm bodies in too small a space. Lucy and Penny were posted at the door and forcibly dragged me inside to sit at a high-top table to the left of the dance floor.

Full Moon Saloon looked like the love child of Sir Elton John and *Twilight*, the books, not the movies. Every moon phase was painted on the wall, the current phase illuminated with a touch of magic. Caricatures of wolves, dragons, sirens, mermaids, and all other supernatural creatures were painted on the wall beside the door, pockmarked with dart-holes from the unsatisfactorily depicted. Stars and moons were inlaid into the tables with resin, and the stools glowed in the dark with glitter in the black seats.

A long wooden bar ran halfway up the right side of the bar. Beyond it was a sea of bodies that were either seated or oddly hinged. Left of the entrance was a small dance floor and even more tables, where fewer people felt the need to congregate. It was a kindness that we took one of the seats, but I was concerned as the night wore on, the desire not to stand was going to outweigh the need to be farther inside.

"What are you drinking?" Penny was wearing a loose top and tight jeans, looking like a bohemian cowgirl. Lucy had swapped her witches hat for a flat ironed look that went with the fire-engine red halter and black jeans she had on. Neither looked uncomfortable, and neither looked willing to let me get up unescorted for fear I'd bolt out the front door and never be seen again. "You look like a tequila sunrise girl. And you look like a candy apple martini."

Lucy nodded at the martini. I tried not to throw up on people's shoes as my stomach lurched and the lights stabbed at my retinas.

"Where's your necklace?" Lucy asked and I leaned into her without opening my eyes.

"My what?"

"Your necklace! That Kaci helped you make. Where is it?" She spoke a little louder, her voice carrying over the music and the banal chatter of the masses. It was not as banal as a normie bar from my college days, no one had a robot hand stuck on their penis story, but turning back into a man in the middle of town square and showing the senior's yoga class your ding dong, wasn't significantly more supernatural.

"I forgot it at home." I dropped my forehead to the tabletop, the sticky lacquer surface unpleasant to the touch.

"Did you forget your magic at home?" Penny arrived with drinks and her signature attitude. "Because I'm pretty sure you can summon it to you. This is a supernatural bar."

In front of me, the drink had two distinct layers, red and orange, and smelled potent. Though it had been a long time since I'd had anything besides wine, my fear of my family's addiction issues sat much higher in priority than my desire to party.

"Tempe?" Penny's hand covered mine and I followed her arm up to her face. "You don't have to drink it and we don't have to stay here."

The lights dimmed and a drag queen took to the stage. "Ladies, Theys, and Every Which Ways! Welcome to tonight's performance of Howling at Your Full Moon! We have ten performances tonight, and at the end, you better put your palms, paws and claws together to help me pick a winner to take home the coveted Full Peach Trophy!"

Howls, claps, whistles, and cheers filled the bar, the mass of bodies toward the back surged closer to the stage I'd missed. "I'm your host, The Fabulous Fangerella, and I'll be keeping you company between the acts."

An enthusiastic dance chant began, and the host worked her hips seductively, dropping down low in six-inch heels. Impressed, I took a sip of the drink in front of me and pulled back. Tongue hanging out, I wiped it against the top of my mouth to get the burn off. Penny leaned in, speaking directly into my ear. "Do you need to go?"

"No." I pushed the drink toward her. "But that's disgusting."

On stage, Fangerella was crawling on all fours to a person with their neck exposed. Her fangs were on full display, and I watched in amazement as she wrapped a hand around the "victim's" neck and sunk her teeth in. The whole bar got a contact high off the lust wafting off the bar snack, and when she retreated, the victim looked rode hard and put away wet.

"Fuck." I fanned myself with a cocktail napkin and Penny laughed. "Unrelated, I'm going to see if the bartender serves something that doesn't double as acid reflux in a cup."

"Get your necklace. This is gonna get loud." She held the stool so I could hop off and then I wove my way to the bar, trying to avoid physical contact with strangers and not miss a second of the incredible dance skills on display.

I bounced off a solid wall of humanity and felt myself falling. A hand snaked around my waist and hauled me up, pressing me against a muscular frame of raspberry and cedar. "You OK?"

"Yeah." I stepped back and looked up at the bearded man in front of me. He had on a flannel shirt, jeans, and was holding a glass of beer that didn't appear to have lost a drop. "Thanks, and sorry."

We both stepped left, and then right, laughing when we were still in the other's way. "How about I just stand here until you leave?"

"Ladies first, as the saying goes. I promise not to move." He made a show of holding his arms close to him while I passed, holding his breath with puffed cheeks and robot posture. Once I stood at the bar, I put my back to the wall and used the solid plank as a ground. Visualizing the pendant where it sat in my nightstand, I remembered the weight of it on my neck, the cool feeling of the metal against my skin, and...

"Sorry, I... Wow, that's cool." The mountain man was in front of me again, reaching for the necklace. Beer wafted toward me on his breath and his heat caged my body in, making the small space even tighter. "Can I see—"

"No!" I made to step back but collided with the wall. His hand approached with a mission, and I didn't have anywhere to go. Sweat slid down my spine, heat curling through my belly with a bucket of worms while I worked harder and harder to angle away from the impending doom of the stranger.

He froze and I breathed a sigh of relief.

"I'm not ready for people to..."

He was no longer moving at all. Beside me, the bartender had two hands wrapped around one shaker and another two pulling beers from the tap, but he'd also become a statue while the beer kept pouring out into the cups, overflowing into the tray with a dull slap of liquid on metal. Everyone facing him was completely immobile and I walked through the crowd with every muscle tensed, sweat beading along my hairline as "I Need a Hero" continued to play but the performer was frozen in a dramatic lean.

Gripping the necklace, I sent a seeking ring out into the room. Every person was alive, but instead of living at a normal pace, they'd slowed down to almost not moving forward at all, something unheard of... except... in dragons?

Was there a dragon nearby? Could they slow down everyone else?

I ran outside, checking the street with shaking hands and a tremor working its way through every muscle of my spine. Cars and passersby moved normally, completely unaffected by the spell attached to the people inside the bar. Even in the parking lot, patrons preparing to enter weren't impacted, but would they be?

Desperate, I sent out another spell and found something larger. So large it took over an entire rooftop, but shadows kept it completely out of sight. Golden orbs glittered in the full moonlight, and I pushed my magic at the void. The maroon smoke shimmered, and a pleasurable vibration slid over me, turning into a crimson wave that washed over my skin and stole the last of my anxiety.

Behind me, the music stopped inside the bar. "Looks like the music skipped! Let's try that again folks!"

The song restarted, and the pulse of life vibrated outward. It hummed and slapped at my nerves, the necklace doing little to counteract the rush of blood burning through my veins and making my brain fuzzy. A gust of wind skittered across my face, tangling my hair and sending the snow dancing across the lot.

Crunched crystals of ice pulled my eyes away and I turned to see Lucy and Penny crossing the lot. "Are you OK?"

My eyes went back to the rooftop, searching with sight and magic, but the dragon was gone.

"Yeah... I'm... I think I need to give that tequila sunrise another try."

CHAPTER

TWENTY

TEMPE

"How does it feel?" I looked Samuel over, his satyr half on full display, and frowned. "And how do we test this?"

He shrugged his shoulders, continuing his opening prep for the day. "I trust Sue and Andrea, I'm sure it will be fine. You need to relax."

I wrung my hands, the anxious mother on her kid's first day of school. "Don't tell me to calm down, Poofy Pants. Do you know what's at stake? Don't walk away from me, young man!"

Samuel laughed and decided to just ignore me. In his defense, it was the fourth time I'd made the declaration. In my defense, I did not want to stand in the parking lot to memory charm normies if they saw a horned half-goat pouring wine. While I trusted Sue and Andrea, I did not trust magic done in and around this building.

Their plan was fairly simple and built on the framework of the spell Kaci and I built. Using the same method, we'd created a necklace for Samuel that passively changed his appearance for non-magical beings. It was a somewhat complicated, wearable, mirror that only reflected back to you what you are in the version of someone else. Because it was passive and functioned as a mental shield to the viewer, it wasn't recognized by the enchantment that

181

haunted my business. As an added precaution, we'd modified the same items counter-balancing the stimulus triggers to do the same.

The only limitation was I didn't have a normie handy to test the magic and the anxiety of what-if was giving me a damn ulcer. Moving to the customer side of the bar, I paced back and forth, tapping the tops of each stool as I passed. My legs twitched to run or collapse, but instead my shoes tapped against the floor, counting the seven steps each way, waiting for a normie to walk into the winery and either have a tasting or have a "holy fuck magic is real" meltdown.

Outside, the weather reflected my mood. Slushy snow fell, turning the ground into greyish-brown puddles that froze into filthy slush. Wind whipped the naked trees, tapping the branches against each other in a loud counter-rhythm to my stool tapping.

Samuel stopped behind the bar, sharing a visual exchange with Corky that suggested one or both of them was *this* close to having me committed. The cat faced me, paws crossed, tail upright and twitching, while Samuel took the position beside him to observe my descent into madness.

"I saw you at Full Moon last night." Samuel leaned against the counter, and I jumped, eyeing the exits. "Hell of a disappearing act."

"What? Who? Me? I didn't disappear." My voice squeaked at the end and I cleared my throat to try again. My fingers tapped the stool nearest me, pinkie to index and back again. "I went outside for some fresh air, but I came back in. I saw all of the performers. Sabrina was my favorite, doing *Every Little Thing She Does Is Magic* with puppet Salem. No idea the drag scene here was this happening."

"Not then. When Lenny cornered you by the bar and I thought you were going to try to dig your way out through the floor. I was on my way over to help you and next thing I knew, you were gone. Care to explain?" He crossed his arms, tucking one hoof over the other to offer me his undivided attention.

Penny and Lucy had done something similar, but the bar was incredibly loud when they asked, and by the end, everyone was too drunk to remember. I shrugged my shoulders to pop them and cracked my neck, preparing to... share.

Just the thought forced another shiver to roll through me.

"What do you know about dragons?" I picked up a rag and wiped down the pristine counter to keep my hands occupied. "Dragon shifters, I should say... are there non-shifter dragons?"

Samuel's head cocked to the side, and I shut my mouth. "I don't know about non-shifter dragons, but the only shifter dragon I know is Drax and he shares about as much as you do. My Nan said back in Ireland, there were a fair amount more of them. Not terribly social, they were also not very violent with a few exceptions. One or two clans were known for their fiery colors and tempers, but most were content to fly and help where they could. Rumor was they helped build some of the old castles to have something to do. They'd reach mating age and stop aging, like rocks, never bleeding or getting injured, or experiencing pain. So they'd get bored and enter the normie populations, doing feats of wonder as either presumed gods or 'strong men' until even that lost its novelty. Then one would either meet or take a mate, and they'd rejoin the timeline to get older—aging at whatever rate their mate did."

My rag stilled, and I pictured the bright red dragon magic Drax shared with me. His brilliant crimson wings and easily triggered temper... some things added up that hadn't before. Still others could only be answered by the man himself. "What happens if they meet their mate after they took one?"

Samuel shrugged. "No idea, maybe they just never get one. What's all this about?"

"Time stopped last night, for everyone in the bar, but me. Every living creature slowed to not only no longer age, but no longer move. Like the magic that holds them at mating age but applied to everything in the building. Outside, nothing was affected... It was like when I got anxious and Drax appeared, I panicked and..."

"The dragon appeared? You saw him?" Samuel's chest leaned toward me, the spirals on his horns coming into sharp relief.

Twisting my lips to the side, I shook my head in the negative. "I saw something, a large shadow on a rooftop, but... I think felt him. Is it weird to feel him?"

Samuel opened his mouth and closed it again. Once, twice, on the third time I rolled my hand in the universal "out with it" gesture.

"Don't kill me, but the two of you are bonded." He held up his hands when I leaned in to argue. "Hear me out. You are bound to this building by the 'inheritance', you feel the other one, share magic, ideas, and somehow, he easily connects with you where everyone else struggles. Whatever the reason, you're linked together. It makes sense that if you were scared, he'd find you and try to help."

A ring from the newly installed front door bell announced our first customers and I stiffened, praying to the goddesses no one screamed when Samuel walked out from behind the counter.

"Good Morning, Ladies! Are you in for a tasting? Celebrating something special?" His upbeat smile penetrated his voice and I peeked over my shoulder. A group of normies, female... one wearing a veil shoved her way forward.

"I'm getting married!" Two of her compatriots shot off poppers and glitter dicks rained down on my floor.

"Mother fuckers." I grumbled quietly, reaching for the broom while Samuel led them cheerfully to a large table in the corner. In the dimmed sound provided by the spells, I let my mind wander to everything he said, and everything he didn't.

Either by proximity or necessity, Drax and I were joined together. But was it forever?

THE TICK, tick of the clock on my nightstand stole the minutes until I needed to be at Sue's house for the full moon coven meeting. As a digital clock, it shouldn't tick, as the symbolism for my impending doom, it was unfortunate that it hadn't exploded yet.

Beneath the clock, my drawer glowed with a warm summons. I tugged the drawer gently open to see the necklace Kaci and I made, lying face down in the drawer. After I'd gotten home last night, I'd just tossed it in on my way to the shower and I still hadn't looked at the message. If it revealed something internal and fundamental about me was flawed, it would be old news. Except... It's one thing to think the universe cursed you, or that you were a curse to it, and another to see it inscribed in metal as a message of unwavering confirmation. On the other hand, if it said something obvious, like death before decaf, I would be horrified at how big a deal I'd let it become.

"Merrow." Corky cooed, and I glanced at him on the small chair beside the large windows that look out on the winery. His eyes fixated on the sky, the full moon shining brilliantly onto the land with enough illumination to cut through the night like a second daytime. The day's storm clouds had disappeared and in their place were a million stars and the glowing orb of the moon at the end of its cycle.

I approached him, the persistent tug in my chest insisting I go back, making me aware the necklace would not be ignored but my healed scratches were equally insisting that the cat would also force the issue of my attention. Of the two, I considered blood loss more life threatening than a minor discomfort in my ribs. Together, we leaned against the window to peer out, my face beside the cat's, only for my breath to immediately fog up the glass.

Sighing, I unlatched the metal clamp and pushed up on the frame. None of my windows had screens, a fact that troubled me in the insect infested summer but was fine in the winter. I stuck my head through the opening and looked out into the chilly night, enjoying the cool air against my warm, damp skin. The wet braid on my neck instantly felt less sticky, and I took a deep inhale of the cool air.

Beside me, the cat put two paws on the sill and poked his pink nose through the opening, whiskers twitching. Something in the distance had captivated his attention, but my remedial human vision couldn't see a thing. I studied the ground, searching for shadows like the one I saw last night but there was only the brilliant reflection of moonlight on snow.

There were no paw print tracks tonight, the food I'd left for the stray eaten and the blankets mussed. I'd refilled it before coming up to get ready and I crossed my fingers that the dog had stayed warm and dry through today's slush storm.

"What are we looking at, dude?" I asked him, but he continued to stare out into the night as the lion king—surveying his kingdom of everything the light touches. "Alright, well... I'm going to keep getting ready."

I walked back to the nightstand and pulled on the necklace. Tucked into the black long sleeve top, I considered removing it to look when my phone alerted a message from Lucy that she had arrived to take me to the full moon celebration.

Ducking into the bathroom, I checked my appearance one last time. Hair braided, black shirt over dark wash jeans, comfortable walking shoes, minimal makeup and tiger's eye jewelry, everything was as good as it was gonna get. Walking back out, I grabbed the velvet sack of stones I need to recharge, an empty wine bottle filled with water, my phone, wallet and keys, stuffing the last three in my pocket. Scooting Corky back inside, I shut the window over his howled objections.

"Sorry, kid. I can't afford the heating bill to leave the window open, even if I might be a millionaire. You coming with?" He gave me a long, slow blink and lifted a single paw for cleaning. "Sure. That makes sense."

Passing through the doorway, I paused in the kitchen to grab a tote with a couple of bottles of wine and my cup of water. Struggling to keep it all balanced, I made it to the door before the cat reappeared and sniffed at me in distaste.

"My apologies, your highness. Please, allow me to hold the door for you. I'm not carrying a bunch of crap or anything." I juggled everything to make sure his tail cleared and then pulled the door closed to lock with the key on my ring.

At the tasting room door, I repeated the process with the bags and a key before Lucy appeared to take some of the items out to the car.

"Thanks! This whole key thing sucks. I can't wait to magic the shit out of this place again..." I turned my back on the winery and stepped off the porch, following Lucy to the rear door of her car. When I was level with her, I realized she wasn't moving. On the car seat, Corky was frozen mid-lick, paw raised to his mouth.

I reached out into the night, pulling at the threads connected to my friends until I found the ancient power that held them in stasis. An invisible mass sitting on top of the winery held everything still again but not so I could escape. He wanted to... enjoy a moment?

My brain stuttered. It wasn't my thought, but I was certain of it anyway.

Tugging each thread, I used my magic to add more weight to each one. Making it heavier and harder to hold on to until, one by one, they snapped. Under the crumbling spell, I peered at the rooftop, waiting to see him.

A large, merlot colored dragon with emerald lined wings lay coiled on top of the winery. Piercing gold eyes connected with my own in an unblinking fascination. The look coursed through me with heat, desire... possession. Flames licked through the night between us, hanging in the air and heating every inch of my being.

"*I'll be back tomorrow,*" I promised him as Lucy finished loading the car.

"Hurry up and get in! I'm freezing my nips off!" Lucy shivered and slid behind the wheel.

"Yeah, of course." I rounded her car and opened the door, taking one last look at the rooftop before I climbed in.

CHAPTER

TWENTY-ONE

DRAX

A SHARP STABBING BEHIND MY LEFT EYE ACCOMPANIED my normal return to consciousness. A rough grit of damp sandstone rubbed against my cheek, the air warm and... foul. Wet fur and digested fish with a persistent scraping of teeth... My eyelid slid open to meet nose to nose with a hairy beast licking my face, a vague memory surfacing with each fishy lap of his tongue.

"How the fek did ya get to my island, dog?" I tried to get enough strength in my arms to shove it away from my face, but all I managed to do was get my fingers stuck in the hair. The reddish fur was wet and matted, sticking to my palms while beneath it, the beast's bones were prominent enough to count.

"Ye need a meal." I struggled harder, this time to exit my shelter and attempt to hunt food for both of us. It was surprisingly warm and well-lit for my island in January, a fact that led me to open a second eye and put even more energy into rising. "Didja swim here?"

Sitting upright, my elbow collided with something wooden. When I turned, my hand knocked over a small stack of books. Inside, my dragon refused to rouse and help me with seeing in the dark. Without his vision, I was no more magic than the sack of potatoes leaning against...

189

"Potatoes?"

Turning to my left, I inhaled and gathered Tempe's scent along with that of fresh laundry and the faint musk of a cave.

"We're home?"

Staggering upright, leaning a hand on the wall for support, I ambled toward the mouth of my cave and looked out at the grapes. The setting sun was giving way to a large amber moon that hung low in the sky, it's rising as unstoppable as the tides it pulled from the still water below.

It was still full.

We had returned a day early, my dragon content and resting... but how?

I kicked a dish and stumbled slightly. Two bowls sat out beside a folded blanket and the space heater I kept in the corner. Small remnants of food still littered the bottom of one, and the other held fresh water. Tempe's scent clung to the area and I glanced at the dog.

"Yeh trying to con another meal out of me?" I reached down to ruffle its ears, noting the dog food and treats stacked on the dresser. "I don't need a dog. You should know that I'm absolutely rubbish at caring for myself, much less people and other livin' things."

The beast flopped over and rolled on his back, showin' me his bits. His tail thumped against the side of my dresser while I noted the completely concave belly and lack of meat on his ribs. "*Rogaire gadhar*, yeh look a mess. What's the plan here? I leave every twenty-eight days."

A scream cut through the cave with a crack and a skittering of sound. I raced out and into the barrel room, shifting my hands into claws as I went. Immediately inside the cavernous storage room, Tempe stood beside a barrel, glass shattered on the floor around her with a deep red liquid pooling in all directions.

"What happened?" I flew over and grabbed her, patting down every inch of her searching for where all the blood had come from while trying to figure out if I should fly her out through the cave or through the winery. Where did witches get medical care? "Where are you injured? Speak to me, love."

"Mmm...rrmmm..." Her voice came from far away.

"Is it your tongue?"

She smacked my arm, prying my hand away from her face. "No, it's your hand over my mouth, Fireball! Put me down! Geez, don't come back early if you're going to go nuts."

I placed her on the ground, hesitating to let her go. There were no injuries, healed or otherwise, adorning any inch of her perfect flesh. At the smell of her, my dragon sat up, growling softly with need.

"Seriously, let me go. I need to clean up the glass." Tempe shoved off my hands and started toward the back wall only to come up short.

"What's happened? Are you OK?" I gripped her waist again, trying to check her over again, but she slapped my hands away from her.

"Come here, baby." She crouched low, extending her hand out in front of her with her back to me.

"What... did yeh hit your head... oh, the *rogaire gadhar*." I let out my breath, feeling my heart race as I continued to picture scenarios where the dragon had ripped her apart. Or the winery had fallen down and impaled her.

"You really adopted a dog." She glanced up at me, her brown eyes through her lashes a sight made in the fires of my darkest fantasies.

"Yeh've been feeding him." I crossed my arms, wondering at the protocol of shifting myself in front of her. Her unwavering gaze on me from this angle was not something I'd forget.

Rogaire gadhar bumped his head against her hand and she gave him her complete attention. Running a hand down his back, her brows creased. "I've been feeding something, but I hadn't seen him. He'll need a bath... and maybe more food? I'll have to find out what's normal for..."

The dog was back on his back, showing off his bits with his

tongue hanging out. Corky strutted over, looking down on the beast disdainfully before swatting him on the nose and then cleaning his paw in disdain at the water and filth encountered. *Rogaire gadhar* rolled back over and cowered.

"That was rude, Corky. Be nice to Rogue."

The dog licked her cheek, and she pressed a kiss to his head. With easy grace, she stood and walked to the dryer, grabbing a towel from beside the appliances and dropping it on the dog's head. He stumbled away from her, drunkenly moving around until he collided with my leg.

The black nose worked its way out of the towel, sniffing at me until he was close enough to lick my hand. I quickly worked the towel over his fur, rubbing away the worst of the water and filth. In the end, his fur stood on end, like that seagull after styling his hair with a fork in that children's movie about mermaids and octopus witches. His neck was unadorned, a sure sign that if he had a person, they didn't care enough to safeguard his return. I looked up at Tempe to see her sweeping up the broken glass, eyes steady on her task.

"Has something happened with mate?" The dragon voiced the question but I didn't know how to speak his words to her.

Silence stretched between us, and I dried the dog to occupy my hands. I was scared to ask her if something was wrong and find out my returning early ruined her plans. If she had plans... *What if she had plans with another man?*

"Then I will rip him apart!"

Tempe dumped the broken glass in the trash can and then turned to me, hands clenching and unclenching at her sides and tapping against her thighs. "So... listen..."

Rogue escaped the towel and lay on my foot. His light brown eyes looked at me with joy, an expression not mirrored in the woman across the room.

"I'm listening, love. What's wrong?" I carded my fingers through the dog's fur to keep from pulling out my own.

"If you have a... person. Out in the world. And that's where you're going. You can bring them here." The taps on her thigh picked up pace. "No hard feelings about that whole kiss, date thing. You don't…"

The building anxiety in my chest notched higher, and I felt like a bleedin' lightweight on a bender. I didn't know why my dragon was gone or if he'd return. If his return would be safe for her, or this dog, or the winery that was already crumbling from magical overwhelm and now, if my reckless kiss before leaving… *fuck, I kissed her.* I told her I wanted to court her and now I was acting like an idiot who'd never asked a woman to date.

"Are yeh sayin' you don't like me, love?" Rogue leaned in a little closer and I took his comfort. "That you don't want to date me?"

"No. Just… I saw something interesting last night and I did some asking around. Dragon's are frozen in time until they meet their mates, which I knew. But they also don't bleed." She couldn't keep still any longer and started moving around. She grabbed the mop bucket and filled it with water, starting to clean what my nose recognized as wine. "You bled."

My breath caught and I tried to think on my feet, but I couldn't form words around the pinch in my throat.

"You bled in my office the other day. Which means you've met your mate, but you were surprised. Do you not know who it is? Or are you hiding from them? Is it because of me? Or were you hoping to have both? Because seriously—"

"Would yeh like me to answer or are yeh just going to continue tying yerself in knots, love?" I stood up and crossed to her, taking the dirty mop and water back to the utility sink beside the fridge. "What makes yeh think it isn't you?"

"What?" Panic filled her eyes, they bounced around the room and her fingers dug into the luscious curve of her thigh. "No… how? We haven't… have we?"

"Why would yeh immediately think that I had a secret family and not that you, the women I've been spendin' all meh time with, is my mate?" I moved toward her, seeking her heat and warmth while Rogue and Corky retreated. "Yeh've immediately taken to this dog, named him, the same way yeh've named me, but only one of us seems to have convinced yeh they're worth the energy."

Her eyes flashed something dark, a warning to tread carefully.

"Strays wander in and out, love. Getting attached will only hurt you in the end. Filling his space with comforts will not make the appeal of freedom lessen, but yeh've already done it and here he sits, ready to pledge allegiance to you and that arse of a cat." The look on her face continued to darken the longer I spoke and by the time I finished, she was more fire than my dragon. "Why do you doubt the same of me?"

"So you want to leave?"

"I never said..."

"I filled your space with comforts, but you need your freedom. Flying off once a month won't be enough and eventually you'll want to leave forever?" Panic rose in my chest, my own words thrown back in my face. It was easy to see how she'd make that leap, but I didn't intend to leave her. I'd bloody said I wouldn't leave her. "It's not a hard extrapolation to make, Draigus! I'm pretty smart for someone dumb enough to get excited about the prospect of a date. I doubt you because if you can put words to the advantages of being a stray so eloquently, you clearly still consider them advantages."

"Nay, lass, I was talking about the dog! And I said he didn't want to leave! Said I didn't want to leave."

"Were you?" Anger rolled off her in fiery waves, singing the air with sulfur, and the dog flattened its ears, seeking protection behind me. Now she advanced on me, her anger pushing us backwards into my cave. "Because everything you said could easily apply to both of you!"

"No, *mo doineann*." My magic rose to lick against hers, pulling me toward her. "I meant what I said about working together, about courting yeh. I was making—"

My feet carried me into her space until we stood toe to toe.

"You were making an assertion that I should trust you and not 'just a dog'! But he's not just a dog! He's a living creature that needs our help. If you don't want him to live with you, he can come live with me! There's plenty of space in the apartment you didn't want, and mine! But if you don't see the parallels between the attributes you applied to him and the ones that still apply to you, let me draw them for you!" Her hands sparked her deep red magic, letting the smoke fill the air in crisp lines. "You own three outfits and before I came along, you kept them in a duffel."

A red duffel appeared in the air.

"You slept on a cot until I put this bed out here. And I put that cot out here before that bed, so you'd stop sleeping on the damn floor!"

A cot appeared. Then the full moon, the winery, a map of Ireland.

"You don't call anywhere home, you fly off every full moon, you've made no appearances in the winery unless everything is going wrong, which I'm thinking is part of your plan to seem like the great savior now that it's falling over. And you're telling me that wanderers never settle as we're standing in your literal outdoor residence because you can't handle the heat of indoors even though it can be literally any temperature because of AC!"

"It's too fekkin hot for me to live indoors, *mo doineann*." I grabbed her hand and pressed it to my face, slid it down over my chest where my heart was pounding, and back up again. The magical figures dissipated, a red magical haze coating us in a shimmering splendor. "I'm not avoiding yeh, preparing to run away or plotting an escape, it's just too hot. Even with AC, the lack of air movement and darkness makes it too warm. If my godfather still actually shifted, his arse would have slept out here too! I show up when everything's gone wrong because yeh summon me with your distress, because you might be my mate. But you're so bloody scared, I don't know how to tell yeh! I don't know how to tell yeh that the only reason you're standing here is because I brought you back."

"Brought me back from where, Drax? I never left! I never leave! I'm always the one left standing, alone, when it all crumbles around me. It hurts too much to keep caring and hoping, do you understand?"

Swallowing hard, she turned away. Fear and longing coated my tongue, a feeling I knew too well.

"I brought you back from near death, Tempe. I kissed you under the light of the full moon, opening our bond, to save your fekkin life after staring at your lifeless form for thirty six hours. I'd never do anything to hurt yeh, but if you want me to make you feel something... If you want to know what it's like to be swallowed whole by desire... and fear of losing something yeh've just begun to have..."

She wriggled against my grip, but I kept hold of her wrist, inhaling the scent of her skin. Beneath the soft flesh, blood pounded harder and faster, making the smell stronger. My sight shifted, from normal to the intense planes of my dragon, and I felt his heat moving closer to her as I fixated on the juncture of her neck that would carry our mark.

She pressed against my chest with her other hand, and I captured that one as well. I held them both while she raged against me with the worst Irish accent I'd ever heard. "You could have told me 'Tempe, I have to live outside because I'm a daft dragon. I appreciate all the work you did to make indoors livable, but if it's all the same ta yeh, I'm going to live like the dwarves in snow white'. You could have opened your mouth and said something before two days ago! Instead of playing the strong silent Drax the Dragon. You could have told me you're the reason I'm not a statue any more."

"And you could have come to me for help with literally anything instead of forcing me to invade yer bubble until you had no choice but ta let me do something. And you act like bein' a statue was the best day of yer life, why would I admit to takin' it away, even when your life is worth living? It's bad enough I let yeh call me Drax, but yeh won't even have the decency to let me help ya? To claim me as essential to your world? "

"It... You don't like it? Why didn't you say anything?" Her ears turned pink.

"That's what yeh focus on? The bloody name? I showed up and yeh decided what meh jobs would be, and then yeh decided I wasn't fit for any of it, and then all I ask is for a chance to prove I'm worth your time and yeh focus on the fact I didn't like the bloody name?" I backed her against the wall, both of her arms at my mercy. I pushed them against her chest, shamelessly rubbing her erect nipples with my fingers. "Yeh just started doing and doing until yeh burned yourself out. And then what were yeh gonna do?"

"I don't know!" Her breathing was ragged, her scent swirling in the air. "I never know what I'm doing! Does that make you feel better? If I admit that I care about you but I'm scared that you only want me because proximity and necessity forced us together and when it's all sorted you'll regret everything, will you feel better? Will that make you happy?"

"No, lass." My control snapped like a twig in the barren wood. My dragon punched forward, his heat flicking against her flesh. I took both her wrists in one hand, shifting my fingers to claws, with a violent thrust, I anchored them into the stone above her head. Tempe pressed her thighs together, shifting side to side. "No, love. The admission does not make me happy. But it does make me see that I have even more jobs to do than I thought."

"What jobs?" She pressed against me, fighting lust and feeding it all at once.

My eyes dropped to her lips, back to her eyes, her thighs, and her hands manacled to the wall beneath my clawed hand. I licked my lips, wishing I'd ripped her clothes off first, but terrified she'd run if given half a chance.

Despite her obvious desire, my beloved was still a flight risk and if I relaxed my grip, she'd run. Embarrassment and fear clung to her, the stench of a pickled herring on a salad of blubber.

"Do you want to make me happy, lass?" I stared at her mouth, her chest rising and falling, nipples scraping against me. Waves of lust and want rolled off her and I could taste her desire. She wanted so much, but only from me.

Only I could give her this.

Mine.

"Y-yes?"

"Promise to stop acting like everything is up to you to fix. Yeh have to interact with the fekkin world more than just when it annoys yeh."

"Who else is there?" Her whisper made me think we weren't just talking about the winery.

Pressing my nose along the length of her neck, I inhaled deeply. Memorizing every little breath, every whimper she made when I switched from smelling to tasting. Her legs squirmed, and I knew I was wise to pin her to the wall.

You can't run forever, love.

"Have a little faith in me for some jobs, and that blasted satyr you hired for others. Plenty of people want to help and support yeh, but you're too scared to let them. I see yeh've started, it's time yeh let them do it all the way. No push back. Since we're here, it looks like there's a job for me right here..."

Beneath my lips, her soft flesh was warm and trembling. The faint twinge of salt, wine, and lemon cleanser clung to her skin, her pulse scattering between each dip of my head and the flick of my tongue. Her breasts were rising and falling rapidly, peaked nipples brushing against the thin fabric of my shirt.

"This job is all mine." I growled against her skin while my hand found the button of her jeans. The fabric was thick and form fitting, testing my resolve to not destroy her property as I fought to lower the garment without having to lift my head away from her collarbone. "Are you going to stop me?"

"But..." Her eyes rolled back, irrational rationalizations fleeing with each flick of my tongue.

"Tempe? Are ye going to tell me I'm not qualified for this job?"

Her head shook side to side, and I jerked her pants harder. I pulled them up against her pussy, enjoying the gasp she made when I made contact, giving her friction and just a little burn.

"I need the words, love."

"N-no. You are qualified for this job."

"Do yeh want me to do it?" I rubbed her pants against her again.

"Yes." A breathy moan slipped past her lips.

"Good girl."

Pulling harder down, the fabric slid beneath her hips, taking the neon rainbow underwear with it. Pausing my assault, I leaned back to take in my prize. The soft swell of her belly, the smattering of dark hair on the mound of flesh I would taste another time.

"Alainn," I whispered. "So beautiful."

"D-" I leaned in and pressed my mouth to hers, feeling her confusion meld under desire as her lips went from stiff to yielding. Then demanding, as she took control, and her tongue plundered my mouth. With my free hand, I took hold of her flesh, massaging the folds at her hips and up her ribs until the soft fabric of her undergarment blocked my path.

My dragon snarled and shoved up, delighted when it slid up easily and the heavy weight of her breasts spilled over into my hand. Flicking a nipple, I shoved a thigh between her legs, letting the wet heat permeate my trousers and keep my place warm while I explored her upper half. After a quick pinch, I switched sides and Tempe began moving back and forth along my thigh, seeking release. I dropped my hand and slammed her hip into the wall.

"What did I say about letting other people do their jobs, Tempe?"

"I needed more." She let out a desperate gasp and I lowered my lips to her ear.

"Then you should ask."

Digging my fingers into the wall more firmly, I spun her around. The curve of her ass pressed against my cock, the soft flesh cool to the touch and dimpled from the rock wall. From this angle, I had complete control and a feast for my eyes. Everything was on display and available for me to touch and sample as I pleased.

It was fucking addicting.

My hand wrapped around the front and dove into her heat. The arousal immediately coated my fingers and sent my dragon into a tailspin. We needed our scent on her and I rubbed my still covered cock on her ass while I found her clit and pinched it.

She let out a small scream.

"Do you like that, *mo doineann*?"

"Uhhn." I sped up, pressing into her ridge and rubbing her liquid arousal over her again and again until her legs started trembling. Using my knee, I spread her wider and propped her right leg up. The glistening pink of her entrance shined in the light and my fingers spread her lips to dive inside. I slid two fingers into her channel, her body clenching around me.

"Drax, more." She begged me and it was everything I wanted.

I slid another finger inside while scraping my teeth over her neck, fighting the mating urge to mark her skin.

"I want... to touch. Pants." Her ass pushed back, seeking my erection, brushing against me. It felt too good, my eyes rolling back into my head, my dragon fighting to devour her whole. I pulled my fingers out, smacking her ass cheek and leaving her own need sparkling on the reddened surface.

"Whose job is this, lass?"

Keeping her pinned in place, one leg raised with mine, I reached around and slapped the other side. She cried out in pleasure at having her pussy slapped. My hand went back to her ass, slapping it again just to feel her spasm against me. The skin was so warm, so ready, and in her silence, I spanked her a third time and jerked my knee up, spreading her wider.

Making it hurt.

Showing me what was mine.

"Who is in charge?"

"But-"

I smacked her twice, smoothing the sting and digging my fingers in as more of her arousal dripped down her leg. I couldn't resist taking a finger up her thigh and scooping some up, letting the salty taste coat my tongue while she watched over her shoulder. I popped my fingers out of my mouth and shoved them past her lips, letting her taste how much my mouth watered at the promise of having her inside me.

"No, but lass, aside from yours, which I have already smacked red for disobedience. Who is in charge?" I pumped my fingers past her lips twice before taking them out, forcing her to answer.

"You are." She breathed the words, and I put my fingers back in her mouth. When they were good and wet, I slid them out and down to her slick core.

"And who will fekkin decide how much ye get?" I rubbed around her clit until she was shaking with the effort of holding still and waiting for me to touch her where she needed me most. My storm was trying so hard not to rage against me, and it was working us both over, bringing the need higher. *"I fucking love this with her."*

"You."

"Good girl," I whispered, and slid two fingers back inside, twisting my palm to rub her sensitive ridge with my thumb, and she immediately screamed in relief. Her core clenched around my fingers, and I wanted her tight channel around my cock. I wanted to feel her on every inch of my skin until I couldn't remember what it felt like to not be touching her. "Don't forget again."

I kissed her harshly, tugging her bottom lip with my teeth before letting it go and dropping my face to her neck, suckling at the juncture.

Tempe dropped her head, letting me make her feel. Her hands stopped tugging against my restraint, her breathing evened out at a needy rasp, and she gave herself over to us. The electrical shock slipped through us again, but with it, my dragon slid across the bridge, flames kissing the edges of her skin, dancing in the moonlight over and around us both while her magic twinned around him.

It was fucking beautiful.

My hand sped up, and I added a third finger. With my thumb on her clit, my leg holding her wide, I had a beautiful view of her entrance and her ass.

Before long, I'd come in both, and she would be mine for eternity.

"I'm gonna..." She gasped and I pinched her clit, leaning into the place where my shirt rode up and our flesh pressed together as if my cock were buried in her instead. "Draigus!"

Her orgasm ripped through both of us, my dragon roaring forward as my release coated my leg and hers dripped down my fingers. I stroked her through it as more of my other hand shifted to the red-scaled beast. Her arousal dripped down her leg, my hand, and my teeth elongated, threatening to puncture my lip.

Tempe's ass brushed my cock, and I shimmered around the clothing.

"Fuck," I jerked away, Tempe tumbling to her knees.

"What?" Her wide eyes stared up at me from the floor, hazy lust warring with confusion and loss. Then her teeth flashed, and I saw my dragon fangs, ready for her to mark my flesh in return as the dragon fire danced around her and scales shimmered up my leg.

"Go," I told her, backing away. As the moonlight touched more of me, the dragon grew stronger and fought me to return to her.

To mark her. To fuck her. To claim her.

"But I want-"

"No! Don't fekkin question me, Tempe. I said go!" I roared, stumbling backward until I felt the mouth of the cave and stumbled out of it. Falling until I shifted fully and took off into the night.

CHAPTER

TWENTY-TWO

TEMPE

Suffocation weighed down my chest, stealing my air and making it impossible to get out of bed. It was not a task I normally wanted to accomplish, but today I was incapable in more than just spirit.

The weight pressed against my ribs, pushing all the air out of my lungs until it felt like I was drowning. Cruel sunshine stabbed through my eyelids, beckoning life and activity to spring forward, but the weight was too much.

Nothing had ever felt this painful, this heavy. In flying away from me, leaving me half naked on the floor, he'd stolen my air. The feeling hadn't just been his body leaving mine. Something had been physically ripped from me when he flew away, leaving sharp stabs of agony in my mouth, my hands, everywhere he'd touched ached with both loss and stinging torture.

But the weight seemed to grow with each passing moment. Getting sharper, warm, damp and... panting?

Warm, wet sandpaper scratched up my cheek, and I swiped at my chest, colliding with something large and hairy.

"Ugh, I thought I was heartbroken after one orgasm." I told the *rogaire gadhar*, as Drax had so uncreatively called him. Since he was quite the scoundrel, I decided Rogue suited him and I

203

would leave the name in place. "Now I know I just need a bigger bed if I'm going to keep taking in strays."

Nudging the dog, I pushed him left while I went right until a yowl cut through the morning with the same fierce point as the sunlight. With a glance, I confirmed that I'd only almost placed my head on Corky's rear left paw and not actually committed the treason for which I'd been accused. "Excuse you."

The cat declined to move off his pillow. I inched slightly closer and took a clawed paw to the ear, his version of a warning shot. I wiped at it with the back of my hand and there was no blood, his version of mercy as well. "I still need to get up."

He showed me his fangs.

"Ugh, I give up!" I stared at the side of my room where a fabric chair sat covered in not quite dirty clothes. They'd been worn once for a few hours and were too dirty to put amongst the clean clothes, but too clean to send through the laundry and hadn't yet reached the correct occasion to wear again. I wasn't supposed to use magic in the winery, and so far my energy had surged as a result, but I was between a rock and a claw-place. Closing my eyes, I pictured myself standing beside the chair. "One, two..."

The air shifted, a chill tickled my bare feet, and I opened my eyes.

"Kind of worked." My dresser loomed above me, the laundry chair an inch from my hand and precariously loaded from this angle. Even my magic wasn't ready to stand up, an omen to stay in bed I studiously ignored because I was going to finish testing at least four varietals, so help me Hecate. I felt the heavy pinch of extra magic leaching out of me, and tried to remember magic was to be used sparingly. I hauled myself up from the floor, wondering if there was another method of inert magic that could shield spells in this apartment from being absorbed. The dog and cat immediately rose, stretched in the animal cat / cow poses and leapt gracefully off the bed to stand beside me. "Seriously? You couldn't have done that ten seconds ago?"

Neither answered me, so I led us out to the kitchen. The ache between my legs reminded me I had crossed a line with Drax, and he... ran away. My kitchen wasn't as bright as my bedroom, the lack of sun letting in more shadowed thoughts... large, winged shadows that didn't belong to the man whose face held the expression.

The giant dragon on the rooftops hadn't held his expression either, but the feeling of the dragon moving through me last night was the same as the magic holding Lucy and Corky in place. It was *like* Drax, but not him. Like he had an alter ego... or a brother?

A loud yowl from below and a soft whimper alerted me to the audience that wanted things–namely food. "Right. Feed animals, make coffee, *then* worry about the mysterious dragon secrets that my housemate is keeping from me."

Since coffee needed prep time, I started by adding water and grounds to the machine. Once the switch was flipped on, I grabbed the spare dog dishes and food from my table and prepped Rogue a water dish, a food dish, and Corky's breakfast.

As the reigning asshole of the house, he leapt up and began dining immediately while the large reddish dog sat patiently with drool hanging from his lips. I placed the dish in front of him with a head pat and he immediately started scarfing the food as though any meal could be his very last.

My phone had a seizure on the counter, and I startled. A photo of Grim took over the phone with Penny's name and I wondered if she knew I was just thinking about her. The woman had not only given me a supply of pet food and dishes for downstairs, she'd also insisted I take extra dishes and food. Because the dog would find its way into my apartment, I couldn't summon food from elsewhere in the winery, and her canine was too spoiled to eat regular food anymore.

Despite the earthworms in my gut, I answered her call. "You know this behavior goes against the millennial code, right? If one more person calls me unbidden in the morning, I'm gonna start hexing them." My rant continued, because I still didn't have coffee in my mouth to make it stop. "Nothing life threatening, but that rubber ass spell you did on Yasmin's husband sounds pretty damn good."

"Where the hell were you last night?" Her anger flowed through the line and my anxiety spiked in my chest.

"Here, why? What's wrong?" Sharp claws scraped up my lungs and I fought for air while willing the coffee pot to brew faster so I could have some before danger hit.

"Where is here, Tempe? You didn't call us after you teleported home, claiming to have enough magic, and when we drove by to make sure you were OK, there were no lights on in your apartment." The muffled stomps of her stockinged feet over the line were interspersed with the sound of coffee getting sipped into her mouth.

"What time did you drive by? I was in the barrel room, bottling... well, sampling. And then I was with Drax. Then I was in my apartment, which is where here is." I ruffled the dog's ears, his big brown eyes looking up at me with adoration and manipulation. "How much breakfast do you give a really skinny stray?"

"Depends on the breed. What do you mean 'with Drax'? He's not supposed to be back." Silence filled her end, and I could picture her stopped, waiting for answers with the practiced patience of a predator luring prey. "Unless something big and important happened and you forgot to fill in your bestest of friends even though you promised to work on that."

I swallowed back the guilt.

"He... we didn't get to discuss the whole reason why he was back early. Just his having a dog and why I named the dog and trusted it not to leave but I always expected him to abandon me." I opened the cabinet to grab a coffee mug, accidentally opening the one over the stove. Inside was a blue bottle, roughly the size of a port bottle, beside the box of rice. I took it down to put with the other glass and then opened the door next to it to grab a coffee mug.

When I set the mug down, the bottle was back on the shelf by the rice.

"He actually asked you that? What did you say?" Penny paused on the other end just as the coffee maker beeped. I forgot the bottle and closed the cabinet. "Have you not had any coffee yet?"

"Working on it now. I told him he had a number of marks in the 'going to leave' column and also he was a people and people are untrustworthy. Then we got into an argument, one where he pointed out I never let him do any of the jobs I gave him and fought him on the ones he gave himself. Then he told me it was his job to make me feel, pinned me to the wall, gave me an orgasm, turned into a dragon and flew away." My coffee was ready to drink by the time I was done and I took an extra-long pull, killing the contents in a few swallows and immediately going back for seconds. Girl talk wasn't my forte. Reading filthy books, cool. Watching porn, also fine. But using my words to say the things out loud? Somehow impossible. So, I just poured out the words like sewer water and hoped whoever was listening owned a filtration system.

Silence filled the line and I pulled the phone away from my ear to see the call was still active.

"Sorry... that's... That's a lot to process."

I drank my second cup of coffee and let her process, walking over to the armchairs and sitting down. Corky jumped onto my lap and Rogue looked at the neighboring chair, his paw lifted in uncertainty. "Go ahead, you can sit there."

The dog jumped up and curled into a tiny ginger ball. I stroked the fur on his head.

"He needs a collar... probably a leash. The bed we put in the wine cave is working out... might need one up here." I made lists out loud, the switched to petting the cat in my lap before he cut me. "How's the processing going"

"Like I wish it wasn't super early on a Monday when I have to go into work, and I could Irish up this coffee." I heard her moving around on the other end.

"Do you have actual patients now?" Excitement bubbled up

in me for my friend. She'd been struggling to find a place in the Hollow when she moved back and while they accepted her, they didn't really accept the whole "mental health matters" mindset.

Surprise, surprise.

"Some, yeah. But we'll get back to that. I should tell you that my dad talked to Drax the same day he talked to you, but he wouldn't tell me what they discussed or why when he came over to return Artie's car, his kilt was covered in dust." I heard the jingle of a collar on her end and pictured Grim's large flat head in her lap. "Did he mention anything to you?"

"The day we did the drunken séance? No. But the next morning, he was standing over my sleeping form all 'let's fix the winery', so maybe your dad inspired him... There's something I should tell you about the other night at the bar." With a single finger, I stroked Corky's fur, one way and then the other to see the shifts in orange. "Time stopped for everyone but me when I was cornered by a guy near the bar. When I went outside, I thought I saw a dragon on the roof, and I think I saw it again the night of the full moon. I wondered if it was... another dragon, but I realized last night that it was Drax. Samuel said we're bound together, and Drax implied I'm his mate, but what if he doesn't want this bond? What if he chose it because he had no other choice? Or because he's tired of being alone? Or worse, what if someone else chose it for him and that's why he's here?"

"Would you rather he not have any choice at all? That the universe chooses him for you?"

I picked at a random black hair on Corky's back, trying to pluck it between my nails. "Do you like that the universe chose Artie for you?"

A heavy gust battered against my window, and I snuggled into the arm of the chair. I wanted more coffee, but it was in the kitchen, and one cannot displace a cat that has sat upon you. Similarly, I also wanted a fuzzy blanket, but there were no cozy throws in this apartment or winery.

"Tempe, the universe fated us to each other, but I chose him.

And honestly, he chose me. When he sat down next to me in junior high, the one kid willing to sit next to death, he made a choice. Maybe it led to the mate bond, maybe it was an early recognition of it, but at the end of the day, it still feels like a choice. Which means you have to choose, too, Tempe. Do you want Drax?"

"I..." The room was warm and blurred at the edges, the ground moving farther away like Alice through the looking glass. I was falling and there was nothing to catch me.

"If you could choose anyone, would you choose him?"

"It's not that simple..." I stuttered.

"It is, Tempe. I promise you it is. You just have to listen to your heart."

The windows rattled again, and I looked up. A large figure loomed on the other side of my French patio doors, and I screamed. The phone fell from my hand, the handles rattled and then the doors pushed open to reveal Drax, standing in front of me with dark circles under his eyes in last night's clothes.

"I'm so sorry, love. Please tell me you're OK?"

CHAPTER

TWENTY-THREE

TEMPE

"TEMPE?" PENNY ASKED FROM FAR AWAY, BREAKING THE trance.

I relocated my cat and found the device, holding it to my ear. "Drax just flew in. I'm going to get more coffee. I'll call you later?"

"Yup. Follow your heart."

I snorted at her and the call beeped twice before going dead. Since the cat had been relocated, I got up and went to the coffee maker, gesturing with my cup toward the man beside my open French doors. "Want some?"

He pulled back, nodding slightly. "Are yeh gonna poison it?"

"Too much effort. Also, the poison is on backorder." I refilled my cup and grabbed a second one from the cabinet. Filling it with coffee, I added creamer to both without giving him the option of drinking it plain. Partly as an act of petty defiance of his right to choose what went in his coffee and partly because no one was permitted to drink black coffee in my house. "It's also a waste of coffee if you don't drink it all before you die."

When I was done, I handed him the cup and took up the armchair I'd vacated. This left him the choice of either forcing Rogue to move, sitting on the floor, or continuing to stand awkwardly like a half-dead statue. "Thanks, love."

210

I saluted him with my mug and took a long drink.

"I feel I owe yeh an explanation."

I snorted at him, offering an eye roll and trying to decide if I wanted to throw in a 'No shit, Sherlock' for funsies.

"Fair point." He reached behind his head, scratching the back of his neck while looking up at my ceiling. "Yeh remember that I used ta murder people and yeh joked the island was my prison?"

I nodded, drinking my coffee and pretending not to check out the smooth expanse of skin presented to me at eye level. The man had abs and an adonis belt, both kryptonite to the female gaze. With all my effort, I looked away, fighting the pull.

"They were targeted people. At the time, I was told they were hiding weapons, that the other side was planning on imprisoning the magical creatures and using us as enslaved weapons. As one of the most dangerous species, it was my duty to the country and the weakest among us to join the IRA and fight." He dropped his hand and stared into the mug. Taking a drink, he grimaced but didn't comment. "For years, I believed in every mission I was sent on. I didn't fact check, didn't do an audit, just flew off and murdered whoever they said. Then I started to notice gaps in information, people who looked like those I promised to protect being the ones I was sent after. I asked questions, Damien got mad, said he couldn't explain everything to me. One day, that person turned out ta be a witch protectin' his wife an' kids. With his dying breath he cursed me, fancy words that meant nothing until the next full moon."

Drax carried the mug to the kitchen and set it down. Hands shaking too much to keep holding onto it, he switched to pulling food out of my fridge. "The first time it was like going on the lash and waking up in a field in yer knickers with a black eye and some woman's number on yer hand. I had no idea what happened, but an entire house burned to the ground and nay one person could tell me if I'd done it. I exiled myself to that island where there was no one I could hurt, and I go back there every full moon since being called here by Damien because I'm still not safe."

Several eggs were cracked into a bowl. He then chopped vegetables on a cutting board, and slid those in, scrambling everything with a dash of salt and a splash of milk. A pan warmed on the stove and with a few droplets of water, he confirmed the temp, added oil and started cooking the eggs. About halfway through, he flipped the omelet and sprinkled shredded cheddar inside. Once the second side was cooked, he folded over the egg, and cut in half to divide between two plates.

"I was called before the war tribunal, a witness to the war crimes committed by the supernatural IRA partners. There were several of us recruited to the cause by Damien, tricked into fighting for both sides. Unlike me, however, the others hadn't been duped into making yet another bad deal." His jaw worked as he stared at the food, offering me a plate and a fork while lost in another space and time. "Damien hunted me down, tracking me to where I was hiding on the island to keep people from getting hurt–but it also meant I did not know what was going on with the magical community. The man said I owed him for the riches I'd amassed in the fight, though I had nothing, and for the dragon stolen from him for losing the war. I hadn't known at the time it was a punishment for his crimes... I swore a blood oath to grant him one act of service."

The bite I'd just taken turned to sawdust in my mouth. "This was his repayment? Asking you to come here?"

Drax nodded, taking the seat Rogue had vacated. "I'd thought it was to protect his investment in the winery, or that the mate bond had softened him and he was looking out for her, but after spending time here, I don't know that either of those things are possible. He's nay one to soften and based on what I've seen, yer the only one invested."

"What do you think his reason is, then?" I forced down the bite in my mouth, using coffee to make myself swallow. "Was he hoping I'd go insane and murder you? Or did he ask you to do something else?"

Drax shot me a look, and I stuck my tongue out at him to infuse some levity into the heavy conversation.

"Don't threaten me with a good time, love. Damien is a leech. One of his talents on the battlefield is taking energy and strength from his opponents, so that the harder they fight, the stronger he gets. The tribunal bound that power." He took a few bites of his omelet without really seeing it. "But I'm worried that somehow the enchantment here is linked to him. If not his power, a family member or an acquaintance he recruited. Your gran's magic is on the signature, but he's the only one I've known to want and crave power enough to request such a thing from her."

"What about you?" I looked into his eyes. "What did he ask you to do?"

"Nay a thing love."

"So you're saying you and your dragon are basically two completely different people every full moon and Damien forced you to be here so he could steal your power while also stealing the power from everyone who visits?" It sounded crazy, enough magic came through here that Drax's contribution would be inconsequential. I couldn't voice my real question, the truth I was scared of, that he'd asked him to be my mate and keep me distracted. "Why would he need you for that? Is he trying to make you weak or is dragon magic different?"

"It's the same magic, love... as far as weakening me... that remains to be seen. My dragon and I are not just two people every full moon, love." The warm magic slid inside me, dancing in a slow sensual samba with my maroon smoke. "We're two people all the time. No one has been separated from their dragon, not in the known history, but I've essentially become two whole entities sharing a body. Constantly wrestling for control, and every full moon, for all three days, I lose it. When I'm especially weak, he has a bit more freedom while I lack the strength to fight him, but there's nay much benefit to exhausting me unless yeh want the dragon in control."

"Can't anyone help you... pull yourself together?" I smooshed melted cheese together to make my point.

"They won't while I'm indebted to Damien. He's considered a war criminal, and they cannot trust someone in his debt." Drax pushed around the last few bites of egg on his plate. "I spent the better part of the last seventy-five years on a tiny island off the coast of Northern Ireland, hiding where I can rampage without harming a soul. Now I'm turning up here early, a power similar to Damien's presenting under Maple's magic, and I was myself for the full moon for the second time in a decade... because of you."

"Did he ask you to mate me?" The question finally slipped out.

Drax slid out of his chair, setting his plate on the coffee table to kneel in front of me and between my legs. "Nay lass. Everything between us is because you are who and what I dreamed of. You have to know that I didn't want to leave yeh last night. That I'd never leave yeh unless I thought you were in danger. I do not trust the dragon half of me with you." His hands slid up my thighs to wrap around my waist. "You are the most important person, and I cannot lose you."

"Does he have a name?" I threaded my fingers through Drax's hair. "Your dragon, does he have a name?"

"Why would he have a name, love?" The man looked up at me from between my legs and I tried not to let my lust-y hindbrain take over. "He's me."

"If you aren't the same person anymore, then you should call him something else." The dragon danced in my veins. "I'm voting Draigus, because it mean's dragon and that name never suited you... not to me. And when I came on your hand last night, he's who I felt."

Golden eyes flashed back at me.

"And I was thinking..." I started, staring at the coffee in my mug. I wasn't sure if I believed him about the mate bond, wasn't sure I believed he hadn't been asked to make this connection, but I did believe his dragon was not as easily manipulated.

"Never a good thing for me." He joked, and I stuck my tongue out at him. "Are you saying that you need to compare Drax and Draigus?"

"I'm saying I want to meet him." I leaned in and kissed Drax on the nose. "Today."

"Tempe, I'm not sure..." His fingers massaged my outer thighs, and I barely resisted giving in to his earlier invitation of seeing if I liked the man or the dragon better. I was willing to bet this winery it would come up a tie. But if the dragon was as invested as he was, maybe I could believe him.

"I am. You say you don't know what he'll do, but I do. Because what he did when you came back on Friday—"

"Friday? I came back the same night I left?" Fear tightened his grip on my legs, the whites of his eyes two bright around the green irises.

"Yeah... you didn't know?" I pressed myself in closer to him, sliding his fingers loose to lace through mine. Icy stone danced on my tongue, his fear potent enough to freeze me through. "I went to a bar with the girls and a drunk guy cornered me. He stopped time so I could escape. Then on the fullest moon, he stopped time just to spend time with me. I think Draigus has a crush."

Anger, confusion, and relief flickered across his face. "Aye lass, he does. And it's not just him."

"But, he was on the rooftops. I want to see him up close and personal. If you're going to date the Incredible Hulk, you need to meet Bruce Banner." I tapped my index finger to his nose. "Boop."

He stole my hand out of the air, kissing my finger, then my palm, working his way up to my wrist, elbow and ending at my neck when he nipped gently and sucked, leaving a hickey and a wave of liquid desire pooling in my belly. "Which one am I, love? The scientist or the beast?"

Our lips hovered near each other, waiting for an answer to connect. I leaned in, taking the soft pink invitation and falling into the temporary bliss of his kisses. With our mouths locked together, I let my hands explore the muscles of his arms, the breadth of his back and the soft pillows of his ass. I pulled away slightly, feeling him harden against my thigh. "Do I get to meet your dragon?"

Drax slid his lips along my jaw, biting the soft spot just under my ear so I arched into him and the ridge of his cock rubbed me through his pants. "Do I have a choice?"

I dropped my mouth to his neck and delivered a hickey of my own, kissing my way back up to whisper in his ear. "Not if you want to find out exactly how wet you're making me."

"Fekkin she-devil. Fine, after dark, you may meet the crimson scourge." He gave in and rocked his hips against me. "What should we do until then?"

"Taste test wine and plot some bottling. First, I need to find a new wine thief, otherwise I'm screwed. And since it's your fault I lost mine, you get to help me hunt one down." I flopped back on the couch. "Life was so much easier when I could fix shit with magic."

Drax drew his brows together. "Why the hell would yeh need to steal wine, love? We have a hundred barrels downstairs."

Sincerity radiated from his eyes and I couldn't help it, I laughed. Leaning in, I pressed my lips to his, softly at first, before leaning into it. The soft way he moaned and the subtle parting, inviting me in deeper. I fell into the moment, wishing it could last forever.

Maybe Penny was right, it didn't have to be that complicated. If his dragon proved to be as attached as he claimed, then maybe I didn't need to be so scared.

CHAPTER
TWENTY-FOUR

DRAX

Two hours later, Tempe and I stood in the barrel room. Her replacement wine thief, a glass contraption with a pour spout on one end and an opening on the other with finger grips in between, sitting on a table beside the barrel she was tasting yesterday.

"I think that one operates... this thing?" Tempe said, pulling on a joystick. Nothing happened, and the forklift remained motionless. She tried pushing it instead with the same result before going to the other side of the console. "Maybe this one?"

She jabbed a button and once again, nothing happened.

"None of that does anything and you have to stop touching the equipment." Kaci walked into the room wearing coveralls soaked in water, her hair pasted to her face and a bead of water clinging to the tip of her nose. "I brought you a wine thief. You are supposed to be drinking. Why isn't she drinking?"

The older witch narrowed her eyes at me, somehow reminding me of my mum despite being younger than me. I lifted my hands in surrender, showing her the keys I'd nicked.

"I'm doing my best over here, ma'am."

"Erhem!" Tempe fisted her hands on her hips. "If you two will stop discussing me like I'm not in the room. I need the forklift to move barrels. I tasted that one and it's ready to bottle. So I need to move it off the cradle, and then I need to find all its friends and put them in a section with it. Then I need to—"

"Shhh…" Kaci held up her hand. "I don't care what you need the forklift for. You can't use it. But you have him, and he can lift heavy things and fly. Go nuts." She snatched the keys from my hand and stuffed them in the front of her shirt.

"She makes an excellent point, love. I'm here to help and I don't know the first thing about how wine should taste, but I'm excellent at manual labor." My chest expanded and I flexed my arms, peacocking like a dumbass to impress her. "Use me, Tempe."

Kaci pointed a finger in my direction. "Good man. I need to shut off the water. Your dishwasher's a fucking asshat. If you need to tinkle, do it now."

"Ah…" My head lowered and I felt my ear burn slightly. "What's 'tinkle'?"

Both women paused mid movement, arms at unnatural angles to look my way. "You've…"

"But it's…"

"Do you need to take a piss?" Kaci tossed her hands in the air, the bark of laughter Tempe let out in response echoing around the concrete chamber. "Or a shit, but tinkle specifically refers to the first."

The fire burning on my cheeks could have cooked a dozen eggs and my legs felt made of jelly. It was not often women discussed bowels, but something about being confused in front of Tempe made this all the worse. I wanted her to think of me as competent. Instead, the lasses were doubled over, clutching at their bellies with laughter while I fought the urge to squirm.

"Right… I'm uh… good thanks." I reached my hand behind my head, rubbing the back of my neck while the dog and cat returned to join in the spectator sport of my humiliation. "I'll just… be over there, then."

Tempe reached for my arm. "Please don't be embarrassed.

Kaci has a kid, so she was using kid language on you assuming you're the same age as I am. It's hard to remember that despite how you look, you're older than all of us and not used to modern terminology... though having to explain why we need cute words for bodily functions makes me question the practice. It shouldn't be funny, but... well... tinkle? Tinkle, tinkle, little toilet, how I wonder what's in your pot?"

I felt my chest jerk with laughter.

"What are we laughing at down here?" Chris poked her head over the balcony, short black hair and ear piercings making for an almost masculine female. "And why is no one working?"

"Tinkle!" Kaci called out to her wife.

"If you get it on the floor, I'm not mopping it up. I just cleared the water off the floor and I'm tired of mopping."

Kaci beamed up at her, the shimmer of affection in her eyes carrying her away from us before her feet did the same. "Thanks babe. I'll be up as soon as I turn off the water. You two" —she pointed a finger between myself and Tempe— "get to work."

"Yes ma'am!" Tempe joked, saluting her with two fingers to the eyebrow. Kaci responded with a single finger and the women walked in separate directions.

I joined Tempe beside the barrels, noting three stood alone in curved wooden racks while the rest were stacked in pillars approaching the ceiling. Each bore a small piece of paper on the end emblazoned with the winery logo, the year, and the name of a grape. The writing was neat and perfectly penned, but not one I recognized.

"I already tasted those." She gestured to a dozen barrels at ground level. "Well, one of each type, to see if it's ready... and they aren't. The best way to do this would be a re-org / taste-test where we get the matching varietals back into the same stack and then separate ready from not ready."

I read the barrel in front of me and pushed it in line with its friends. The next one had the same name and year, allowing me to just put it on top of the other without much effort. Number three was the same but the stack was now over my head and I shifted my wings free to fly it to the top of my new column.

"Muscled dragon show off."

"Not showing off yet, love. But I can take off this shirt if you need..." I reached for the hem, pulling it up over my abs.

She slapped at my hand, laughing, and rolled her eyes, giving me a playful shove. Before she could pull her hand back, I took it, kissing the place where her wrist and her palm met. The contented sigh went straight to my dick, and I had to drop her hand before I got carried away.

Again.

When we were together, I wanted more. Denying myself for months, both before I opened the connection and after, had been a fresh kind of hell, but this limbo was worse. She knew we were potentially mated, but not that I hadn't chosen her, and not that it was done to save her life. Fate had decided not only who but when, and I wasn't ready to lose these moments getting to know her.

I wanted the whole thing, beginning, middle, and the end. Not to skip straight to, 'this is my future, and you have to get on board, or I die alone... exactly when you do'. I wanted her to choose me, to love me, not to question if it was real or the mate bond. If it was real or pity at my lack of a future without her.

Wondering if she'd have made this same choice if the universe hadn't willed it.

It was like the gods had spent the past hundred years crafting my perfect partner, the antithesis of everything I had been, and gifted her to me when I was ready to give up on all life. It had not been a coincidence that her company battered against me, challenging my fortitude, but she was the storm I would bottle and brave daily. Knowledge I'd felt in my bones even before that moonlight kiss that brought her back from the land of statues and opened our bond. But I'd spent over a hundred years learning exactly what I wanted and needed, and she was right fucking here.

If I wasn't what she wanted, could I spend another hundred changing into him?

I flew to the top of a stack, hovering beside the wine to read its name. "2021 Syrah?"

From up here, I could see her looking at something on the table. Her fingers traced a line of text and then her chin tilted my direction. "Bring it down!"

Hefting the massive container, I deposited it onto the wooden rack in front of her. Climbing onto a step stool, she removed a small plug and inserted the glass contraption. Once she placed a finger over the end and withdrew the tube, it was filled with wine. Tempe released it into her glass and studied the colors.

Swishing, swirling, then she scribbled in her notebook, took a sip, scribbled some more, and took another. "This one is ready to go... maybe we should start a 'to be bottled section' over there?"

She pointed to the area beside a complex setup of stainless-steel equipment I suspected was meant for bottling, though I hadn't the foggiest how to turn it on. Obeying her wish, I grabbed a wooden rack in one arm, the barrel under the other, and deposited them across the room where requested. "Perfect! Now when you see any other 2021 Syrahs, you can place them over there."

I looked at the label, nodded, and made a mental note.

"Bring me something new, dragon shlepper!" She teased me, and I gave her a dark look. "This is so much faster than a forklift. What would I do without you?"

"Aye, aye, captain." I rolled my eyes but smiled at the easy admission. Maybe she only needed me to move the wine, but she still needed me. If I could get her addicted to the feeling of coming on my fingers, tongue, and cock, that would be two things she needed me for.

"You've been quiet," she said, and I glanced at the woman who took up all the space in my head and heart.

"Sorry, just thinking about this winery. Its name, your gran and Damien, building it after she'd had her chosen. What did she do before my godfather arrived?"

Tempe blinked and looked away, standing over the new barrel with her glass tool. My witch dipped the wine thief into the barrel, covered the top and when she removed it, there was wine filling the cylinder. The sample was transferred to a glass and allowed to aerate for a few moments "Gran didn't build this place with Damien. It was her and my grandfather's winery first. I learned my mom grew up here from Penny's dad but my mom never talked about her dad, and he was obviously gone before I was born. Since my mom left with her fling and her bun, I never got to spend much time with the people up here to learn about her. As far as I can tell, though, she was different before. Happy, maybe? Sometimes when people talk about her, it's like they are talking about 2 different people, but I've only met one of them." Tempe shrugged and a muscle in my jaw twitched. I picked up the barrel she'd just tested and, with a quick shift, flew it back to the top of the stack. "Why do you ask? Thinking about mates?"

She looked at me out of the corner of her eye and I scrunched my nose, remembering her question from this morning. She believed I chose her as my mate because that was Damien's price. That it was a product of proximity and desperation, not genuine love, fate, or the magic of her existence.

I'd have to change her mind before sealing our bond. "Thinking about the name Love Potion on the Vine, and where it came from... wondering if we should change it like the lawyer suggested. Wondering if we're cursed. If Damien has a brother trying to steal magic on his behalf."

She nodded, testing the new wine I'd brought to her. "I think the name is a play on the words of an old song, though I don't know the significance to them. I've been thinking more and more about changing the name... It just feels like the last nail in the coffin that ties me to my family. Like I'd finally be giving up on them. Or maybe just finally letting go of the imaginary *what if* I held onto of who they could have been."

"You've got a new one though." I gestured upstairs, the implication being Kaci and the others who had visited. "And you'll always have me, even if yeh decide not to date me, I'll stalk yer shadows and haunt your dreams. Whether you stay with this winery or abandon it, I'm with you, love."

She jerked back, arms flailing on the stepstool. "Leave? Why would I leave? We can't leave! Where would we go?"

I steadied her on the stool, my hands staying on her waist until I was certain she had her legs beneath her. "Anywhere we want, love. Yeh are not bound by the choices of the past. If the enchantment is crushing you, walk away from it. Let it fade and crumble, there's no reason to kill yerself when the place is trying to do it fer yeh."

Mouth pulled to one side, she considered my words. "I'd rather you not stalk me. If the dating doesn't work out, I'd like to think we can be friends."

My heart contracted in my chest, but I nodded anyway. There was nothing I wouldn't agree to to keep her.

Silence stretched between us, thoughts whipping through the lines on her face as she contemplated my words. Stuck for something to do with her hands, she picked up the wine thief and dipped it into the barrel in front of her. Her throat bobbed, and I watched her drink another sample, eyes half closed, considering the contents and making notes in a notebook.

"What are yeh looking for?"

"Characteristics of the grape and the vintage. Different varietals are expected to taste a certain way, and different years have different hallmarks based on the weather." She swished and sipped and made notes before nodding that I should stack the barrel with the four others that were ready to be bottled.

"Did you learn about that in yer school?" I asked, flying her another. Sweat was startling to drip between my wings and I made a mental note to work out more if I was going to continue to be a substitute forklift.

"No. Gran said viticulture was for amateurs and I didn't need school. I learned this from a sommelier book where he basically admitted everything is made up and relative." She shrugged and pulled another sample.

"Then what's the fekkin point?"

"To make sure it tastes good. Are all your manly dragon muscles tired? Do you need a break?" She taunted me, and I slapped my hand hard across her ass cheeks twice.

"Bad girls don't get to come, Tempe. Might want to consider that before you keep pokin' the beast."

"Yes, master." She bowed with faux sweetness and a batting of lashes that sent me from semi-hard to rock solid in seconds. My dragon surged forward, and I saw her breath catch at his gaze, heart pounding in unfiltered desire. Her fingers twitched, a sign she could feel him and wanted more.

A stampede of scales and fangs raged inside at the notion, but I pushed it down.

Blood pounded in my ears as I listened to both our hearts beat in tandem. Longing for release and the need to see the task at hand through splintered my concentration and I fought to keep myself still while the dragon paced through my blood, demanding we take her.

"I need another taste."

Tempe and I had stopped moving and were simply staring at each other's lips. Hers were slightly parted, air moving in and out slowly. Warmth radiated off of her, sparkling between us, her tongue darting out to add a layer of moisture to her mouth.

Giving in, I pressed my lips to hers. It started innocently, another light kiss like before, but the taste of grapes and her sweet skin was an aphrodisiac. Tempe was my own personal drug and after a single hit, I needed more. We dove in together, tongues twisting together while I slowly walked her backward. Each step brought us under the balcony, where an upright barrel sat at the perfect height to plunder her lips and rub my cock against her core.

Absolutely perfect.

Exploration with her mouth turned to exploration with her hands as she roamed my chest, my stomach, sliding under my shirt to brush along my scarred flesh. Each ridge a battle wound that hadn't bled, each touch a healing caress against the humanity I'd lost. Her touch was an invitation to do the same, letting my hands wander up her shirt, squeezing her flesh and sliding my palms along to the back where I could invade her soft leggings and grip her ass.

Mouths still fused together, I drew her closer until the ridge of my cock was pressed along her opening. Despite layers of clothing, I rocked into her. Fucking her mouth with my tongue the same way I wanted to use it on every inch of her flesh, every sensitive nerve ending and opening she'd grant me.

I would pillage every entrance until she only knew the sensation of being filled by me.

Hands going up, I went for her nipples. Seeking to tweak them until she came against me. Just as I reached the underside of her breasts, I was thwarted by a constricting bit of fabric pressed tight to her skin.

"I hate modern clothing," I growled, tempted to tear it. Tempe laughed against my lips, removing her hands from my shirt to wrap them around my neck and pull me into a hug. Not satisfied, but content in her arms, I held her back and breathed into her ear. "Later, when you sit on my face, yeh will be naked and I will take whatever I want."

She shivered against me.

"Why does it have to be later?" She whispered back, pressing her pussy against me and grinding hard enough to leave zipper indents in my cock.

"Fuck, lass, all those jokes about trying to kill me might have not been jokes after all."

"Er hem," Kaci said, and Tempe jumped while I held her against me and looked lazily to the side. The older witch was wearing a mischievous grin beside us, and I had a feeling she would have let us carry on if there weren't things to discuss. "If you two are done dry humping each other, we have to head out. The washer works for now, but I'm leery about its ability to hold up under intense use and there are a few other things to go over before we leave."

Tempe's face disappeared against my shoulder, her flaming cheeks warming my chest. Embarrassment wrapped around her like a veil, and I dug my fingers into her sides until she started giggling.

"I dun know about dry, but yeh. We can come upstairs if you are going to be a nosey cock block, acting the maggot and embarrassing my queen." I nuzzled into Tempe's neck one last time, inhaling plum and sandalwood.

"Queen, huh?" Kaci asked, and I looked at Tempe to see her response.

"Only a queen has a dragon in her castle, and I've never had a *gra* for princesses."

She blushed again, but didn't tell me to stuff it. I kissed the tip of her nose, grateful that we didn't need to fight to be together, at least not at this moment.

"Aww... that's so cute!" Kaci exclaimed, made heart hands and bounded away. When she was halfway up the stairs and we hadn't moved, she paused to shout down at us. "You have five minutes, so do not think you can carry on."

"Your friends lack boundaries, lass."

"We're your friends too!" Kaci called as she disappeared back up the staircase. My heartbeat kicked up at that. Friends? We were friends?

"Don't question it too hard." Tempe pressed lightly against my chest. I took a step back and helped her down, her eyes fixed on the bulging front of my trousers. "Shame to waste that."

"Aye, but where you are, there's more, lass. So people just... make yeh their friends here?"

"I guess? I'm not sure of the rules, but Sue said we seem like the sort of people who get collected and the longer I'm here the more I think she's right. Even my cat collected me from the side of a dumpster."

I followed the sight of her ass up the stairs, colliding into her back when she stopped suddenly.

"Hey Drax, about what you said before..." She chewed on the inside of her cheek, hesitating slightly. "I want to stay."

I leaned in and pressed a kiss to her lips. "Then we'll stay, love."

CHAPTER
TWENTY-FIVE
TEMPE

After Kaci had walked us through her repairs, we said goodnight to both her and Chris while the sun began its final descent.

"Holy smokes, it's dragon time!" I did a happy dance and Drax laughed.

"Aye, love. Go take a shower and change into something warm."

"What, why? Are you trying to get out of this?" I stabbed him in the chest with my finger. "Because if you are—"

"No, lass. I'm just covered in wine and sweat and thought yeh might be as well."

I poked my head down my shirt and gave a sniff. "Fine. I'll be back in ten minutes."

I darted toward the staircase without a backward glance, tearing off clothes as I went. Once in the apartment, I made a beeline for the shower and did the fastest scrub down without the aid of magic in the history of this bathroom. Patted dry with the towel, I pulled out jeans, a long sleeve, and a hoodie, thick socks and fuzzy boots and returned to the barrel room just as Drax exited his shower and I came to a screeching halt.

The white towel slung low across his hips gave a glorious view of the abs and adonis belt I'd been ogling, but what caught my eye was the scars. They crisscrossed his flesh from the end of his shoulder to disappear into the top of his towel. "What the hell?"

Drax's Adam's apple bobbed, and he looked away. "War, love. Leaves its mark whether or not you bleed."

He walked into his cave and I went after him, moving a little slower to give him a chance to get dressed. Our barrels were spread out, a tricky dance to navigate, and by the time I got to the cave, he was pulling on his shirt. "Drax."

Guarded, he met my gaze with his shoulders hunched.

I walked over, slid my hands under his shirt and pushed it up. I kissed each scar I saw, infusing love into the violence that tore him apart. "I'm sorry you went through that."

"I deserved it, love." He stroked my cheek.

I released his shirt, keeping my palm pressed against him while I cupped his face with my other hand, bringing him down two inches to my level. "No, you didn't. And when I see Damien, I'm going to kick his fucking ass."

His chest rumbled under me and he leaned in to steal a kiss. "I would pay to see that."

"Tickets go on sale after I see your dragon, Fireball. If he's not as magnificent as this version of you, the cost goes up significant-ly." I bit his neck softly and he rumbled, a smile ghosting his mouth as he pulled away.

"Then I guess I'dbetter be impressive." He offered me his hand, and I took it. Hand in hand, we walked through his cave, Drax pausing to grab a backpack and slung it over one shoulder. A "stay " gesture was issued to the pets, they took up posts on his bed before he led us out into the sunset.

A light breeze blew over the vines, rattling the bare branches beneath the setting sun. Pink, purple, and orange streaked across the sky, columns of light breaking through the clouds at the right angle to look like a tear between the universes. West of us, the still near full moon hung in translucent purgatory, waiting for the sun to finish its show for the day.

Taking a long inhale, I let the scent of earth and snow fill my lungs. Wrapped around it was the smoky stone of Drax and Draigus underneath, and the weight of potential magic just waiting for the tipping point.

"Yeh good, love?" He wrapped his arms around me from behind and rested his chin on my shoulder. Warmth permeated my hoodie, making everything cozy and relaxing.

"Yeah. Just... It's beautiful out here. Sometimes it's easy to forget with the business crap and the shitty people, but... the vines, the mountains, snow, moon, air... they're beautiful." I let out a sigh, snuggling closer to him for another moment to just breathe it in.

"Aye." He pressed his lips against my cheek in a quick kiss. "I forget sometimes that life is the point of living this long. It's too easy to let it just pass you by."

Nodding, I took one last deep breath before stepping away and gesturing him forward.

"Now take it off, Fireball. I need to see all the beauty and you've never stripped for me. I'll even sing you a song. I've got a lovely bunch of coconuts dededelee..."

My crude demand stole a laugh from his chest. The heavy look of concern that had settled between his eyebrows wiped away on the next breeze. "Did you just ask me to strip, love? And sing?"

Nodding, I crossed my arms and let out a whistle.

"Take it off, daddy!"

His eyes darkened, a new level of need dripping off him.

"If you want to make it through this evening with those pants, lass, you will not test the bounds of my self-control." He warned, setting the backpack down beside me to stretch and let his shirt ride up.

"Now who's being a tease?" I swallowed my drool, and he smirked. I flipped him off, gesturing to the backpack. "What's this?"

"Picnic. Thought we could go out to this spot I found fer supper, if yev no objections. Hate to ask, but can yeh carry it?" He raised an eyebrow, and I hefted it onto my shoulders. Despite being a fairly weighty bag, I was too excited at the prospect of a picnic to care that I needed to carry it. "You'll want to step back for this part."

Taking a few steps back, I saw him scan the ground and the grapes for clearance.

"Do you want me to hold your clothes until you change back?" I wasn't actually planning to give them back when he shifted but didn't want them to get wet in the snow. If he started to shiver, I might let him have his undies back... or warm his cock up another way. Depended on my mood.

"Cute, love, but these clothes shift with me. It's why they're all I wear. Did yeh not notice they're magic?" I shook my head, and he smirked again. "Too busy fondling my knickers to notice the enchantment? I guess I can forgive yeh, considering how badly you've wanted me all these months."

Before the retort could leave my lips, Drax's body was disappearing.

He began with his spine, neck growing in length, as well as his back, until his head was forty feet from the end of his tail... he has a tail! Arms and legs had become clawed feet on the end of reverse joint limbs. Nose elongating into a snout with wide nostrils beneath glimmering green scales, it was his eyes that pulled me in.

The golden dragon eyes of Draigus I'd come to know so well these past few days.

Another step back allowed me to take in the whole picture. His skin and scales were a deep red that was almost a match to the color of my magic. In the fading light, it shifted between a rich burgundy to a deep crimson that nearly disappeared with the growing darkness. Besides the green scales above his eyes, the underside of his wings was a sparkling emerald with intricate Celtic knots that looped through and around each other in a never-ending pattern. I would need an eternity to study them—

even if they weren't absolutely massive. Drax's wings extended three rows of grapes each, each articulation point hinged with serrated claw.

Deadly, beautiful, he was the same man I knew on a grander scale.

Head swinging around, the smooth red scale brushed against my neck. Ridges and heated breath stroked my face as he nuzzled against me, my arms wrapping around to hold his head closer. With my nails, I scratched the spot between the emerald eye ridges, the dragon rumbled beneath me in an unmistakable purr that brought me equal parts joy and contentment.

"Hi." I pressed my forehead to his, feeling the full magnitude of the beast who'd been moving through me for months.

He snorted and I laughed, my hair tickling my neck in his warm breath.

"It's nice to see you up close." My fingers ran along each surface, memorizing the textures and colors. "You're living art, Draigus."

His teeth nipped at my neck and arousal flooded my core instead of fear.

"Frisky. I guess you should trade with Drax so we can go on our picnic." I kissed his snout. Instead of a transition beneath my lips, I felt a ridge of scales between my legs.

Draigus had his tail pressed against me, rubbing the knobby bones against my jeans that transferred every sensation straight to my clit. Three strokes in and I was panting against his face, the golden eyes shifting back to green. Both of them were here and, based on the increased pace, it was a shared idea to torture me into bliss.

"Draigus." I hissed as an orgasm swept through me the same moment my feet left the ground. Tail giving one last stroke between my legs, I was deposited in front of his wings with my soaked core pressed against the base of his neck. The change in altitude didn't lessen my sensitivity and the new position was just as effective. "Shit!"

A rumble went through me, the bastard laughed and pushed me closer to another release.

"Oh goddess." He shoved me forward into his neck and I wrapped myself around him. I pressed my face into the scales and tried to focus on something besides the growing pleasure inside me. With a downward thrust, I fell forward again, only this time the air blew past me with force, and I peeled my eyes open to see the winery disappearing below us.

"Flying... we're flying!" I clutched him tighter and tried not to panic about the lack of seatbelts. "I'm going to die... I'm going to..."

Draigus swooped down, sending me sliding forward along his back ridges. The pleasure was instantaneous, and I moaned.

"Not fair."

He did it again and my eyes slid closed to lock in on the sensations that weren't my impending death. The air took on more pine and fewer agriculture scents; I heard running water, smelled a slight sulfur tang, and with another swoop, we were back on land.

My eyes slid open. We'd gone up a mountain to where the air was significantly cooler. Just as a chill sent a shiver through me, I spotted billows of steam coming from a ring of rocks that circled a small underground hot spring pool. Full night had fallen, but the moon's light cast an endless glow around the partial clearing, and I could see clearly that most of the area had escaped snow fall under protecting tall old growth pines.

Solid ground was under feet, and I glanced back to see the dragon only to be met with the smoldering gaze of my Irishman.

"Did you enjoy your ride, love?" He joked, sliding the back-pack from my shoulders and setting it down. Unzipping the top, he pulled out a thick outdoor blanket and placed it down beside the hot spring.

"It was decent. But too short. You should work on your endurance." I smirked and saw his dragon flash. He was on me in an instant, hands pulling down my jeans while pressing me into the blanket. Mouths collided in a demanding kiss that promised to bruise while his fingers plunged into me.

I was over the edge after three pumps, and he laughed against my mouth.

"So should you love. You should also work on that smart mouth of yours if you don't want to end up with a red arse." He leaned back, pulling my pants back up and giving me one last kiss before sucking my taste from his fingers.

"Have you considered the possibility that I like annoying you?" I breathed, not ready or able to sit up yet. "Your punishments are my idea of a good time."

"In that case..." He pulled more items from the backpack, stew and warm fresh bread, joining the bliss of smells around me. "I should feed yeh so we can get on with my revenge."

Pulling me upright, I was propped against his side with my back along his ribs. Beside us, he had set up a small camp stove heating a tureen of Irish stew, crusted soda bread, and a bottle of white wine. Two bowls were already dished, bread inside the rim, and stemless glasses beside them.

"When did you make this?" I asked, accepting the bowl and glass. After a small sip, I set the cup down to scoop up some soup with the bread and take a huge bite. "Fuck, where did you learn to cook like this?"

He shook under me, laughing again, and I sat up to allow him use of his arms. Instead of picking up his food, he reseated me between his legs, so I was still resting against him while he ate one handed off to the side.

"My ma taught me. I can't make much beyond traditional Irish with simple ingredients. Irish stew with lamb is easy, soda bread, rashers, and anything with potatoes. It's simple enough to set in the pot to cook while yeh go about your day, though modern technology would make it easier, I still stick with the stove. I'm not sure slow cookers and instant pots will ever be my thing."

I lamented the empty food bowl in front of me. Sad that I hadn't spent more time savoring every bite.

"Don't look at an empty bowl like it kicked your puppy, love. There's more as I suspected yeh forgot to eat today after I forced breakfast on you." He leaned forward and spooned more in the bowl, adding another chunk of bread to it. "I'm guessing your mom didn't teach you how to cook?"

I swallowed the bite in my mouth and waggled my hand in a kind of gesture.

"She taught me some. When she wasn't..." I swallowed the lump that formed with a sip of wine that turned into a gulp. "Drunk. Sober, she was a great cook, and a decent mom. But when she gave into the demons... it was like a switch was flipped. Intentionally helpless and incompetent, we switched roles and I spent all my time trying to clean her messes. Mostly the internet taught me recipes, and I fiddled with them until I liked the food. Swapping out flavors and textures until they didn't make me gag."

I ate some more stew, considering the carrots and potatoes.

"I used to want to open a restaurant. Grow the food and create dishes with it that people would travel for miles to eat." I laughed dryly at my dream. "Nothing I made ever tasted half this good. Glad that dream died early."

Drax didn't offer any platitudes, he just rubbed my arms and shoulders while my memories surfaced and floated away. "I think if you still want it, it's not too late to go after it. I've had over a hundred years to cook, love. But I don't think jobs that place you at the mercy of the public are really what you want, do you?"

I sighed again, finishing my meal and wine.

"Did you really cook the last seventy years though?" I teased, scooping soup and bread into my mouth. "It's not like there's stoves to heat food on an island."

He pressed his mouth together and looked at me sideways. Turning his head, he let a small stream of fire out of his lips into the night sky.

"Sure. Sure... fair point. But what would you cook?"

"Fish mostly. Do yeh like fish?" He scooped up some soup of his own and I shook my head.

"Nope. I think it's disgusting. The smell, the texture, the taste. But something like 20% of the world's primary protein source is fish, so more for them. What did you want to be when you were little?" I asked him, knowing that my lack of knowledge about early 1900s Ireland was probably going to limit my understanding of anything he had to say. Bowls set on the blanket beside us, he leaned back and took me with him. Rolling over, I pressed my ear to his chest, listening to his even heartbeat while his arms held me tight. It was warm and comforting here, filled with food and the knowledge he was here for me.

"Dragons live so long, never knowing at what point we'll rejoin the timeline, that we rarely give regular thought to what occupation we'd do. When Damien asked me to join the IRA, I was certain that it would make me more noble, more worthy, but I was far too young to understand what was asked of me and my ma hadn't the courage to stand up to him when I refused to heed her warnings. Perhaps she saw the steps into the future, that it was part of my path and journey. More likely, she was ready to be rid of me. I haven't been home since I was cursed and I'm not sure she knows I owe him a debt... I pray she never learns that I'd been so naïve."

"Tell me about your family. You mentioned your mom, what about your dad?" I drew little shapes on his chest, absently linking the scars. "Are all of you dragons?"

"I din know, never met him. When I was a lad, it was jus' me and me mum. She's an emerald dragon, very sensible. Kept me in line, made sure I finished meh studies, and always had an ear to lend for me and those with troubles around town." His fingers threaded through my hair, twitching the edges to brush against my ear. "Never met her fated as far as I know... though I haven't spoken to her, I'd fly past her house on occasion. She's still in the same village, though it's modernized some, the same house, I've nay seen her with another."

"Why not? She's your mom. I'm sure she still loves you." I squeezed his torso. "Did she tell you anything about your dad? Was he a red dragon? Did he die? Samuel said red dragons are known for being rage-y. Is that true?" I fired off questions and then stretched my jaw yawning. Too much wine and activity wearing me down.

A rough scratch drifted from above me, his body rocking in time to the sound of stubble on his palm. "Nay, she never mentioned him, or what kind of dragon he is. When I'd ask she'd say that he's not worth knowin' and I'm better off. Only red dragon I've ever known is Damien, and he's a fair bit rage-y, came along when I turned eighteen and when I left with him, she said it was a bad idea. I didn't listen to her."

I swallowed, a tear sliding down my cheek for a mother who lost her son. "Does Damien's dragon look like yours? Or is it a different shade of red?"

Crickets chirped around us, the warm spring burbling in the rocks behind us. Tilting my chin up, I checked Drax's face. All his muscles were scrunched, deep in thought.

"I dun think I ever saw it. When I asked, or suggested he come with meh on a raid or a mission, he'd have a meltdown."

"But he wasn't bound until after he forced you to fight for the IRA, right?" Drax's hand paused in my hair, his other arm propped his head up to study me.

"I'm honestly not sure. Yeh think he was bound all along? I didn't cost him a bloody thing?"

I shrugged. "It's a possibility if you never saw his dragon... He seems like the show-off type, doesn't he?"

Drax paused, anger coloring his cheeks the same red as his dragon.

"Fucking wanker." He dropped back to the blanket, pulling me in tighter.

I laughed at the exclamation. It felt inadequate for the betrayal committed, but I got the feeling Drax had come to terms with the man's lies and fuckery long ago.

"So why didn't you call the whole thing off after the council told you he was a criminal? Cancel the godfather-ship?" I asked, assuming it wasn't like the mafia. If it was the mafia, he was screwed. Everything else seemed optional. "Tell him you were wrong, you owe him nothing and he can 'sod off' or whatever?"

Drax laughed at my sleepy crap Irish.

"Love, I'm magically bound to him. Until my blood debt is repaid, I cannot go against him unless it will cause irrevocable harm to another. He cannot ask me to harm life, but he can stop me from helping, use my power and my magic to damage that which others hold dear until they beg for death. Most of our lives are just waiting for someone to give us a purpose, and it never occurred to me to just wait that out in quiet solace. This is my punishment, but I think it worked out." He pressed a kiss to my forehead as I drifted off, mentally planning a research party to cancel his debt. "My repayment was to come here and work the winery in his place. Because of him, I have you. And I could not have asked for anyone more perfect than you, Tempe."

"Me either. Maybe your mom did know it would work out. You should call her." I hummed, drifting off to sleep.

WE SLEPT for three hours before Drax forced me awake.

"No... five more minutes." I tried to burrow in deeper.

"We need to get back to the pets, love." Drax lifted me off the blanket, placing me on his back like a monkey so he could fold it and return it to the pack. "It's going to drop below freezing, if we don't go now, you'll turn into a block of ice."

I rubbed my cheek against his neck while he added the dishes and scraped my teeth on his jaw when he zipped it shut. "Now what?"

Drax slipped the backpack on my arms and set me aside. "Stand back."

His shift was nearly invisible under the cover of the trees.

Before I could lay down again, his tail lifted me onto his back, pressing me into his neck until I hung on tightly, contemplating the possibility of choking him in this form.

Before I could lean too heavily into sleep or murder, we were back amongst the vines. My head was too heavy to move, and I clung to the dragon neck hoping he'd let me use him as a bed. Instead, I was lifted by the arms of the pack and when the pressure released, I was cradled in Drax's arms being carried back into the winery through Drax's cave.

Corky gave a plaintive "meerrroooww" and Rogue's puppy eyes were all the more pathetic with his droopy ears. I reached my hand out, trying to pet him, only to already be on my way into the barrel room.

"Yes, we will get you fed. One step at a time, we must all get upstairs." Drax's voice rumbled beneath me and I heard the sound of dog claws ticking their way up the stairs behind us. In the tasting room, he checked all the locks one more time, and then ascended the last staircase to my apartment.

Drax set me on the bed, pulling off my boots, jeans, and sweater. Cupping my cheeks, he leaned our foreheads together. "Are yeh gonna be able to shower and take yer medicines, love?"

I nodded sleepily, standing up to peel off my underwear while he watched and took a new pair into the bathroom, tossing the dirty ones at his face. "Go feed the floofs."

When I exited the bathroom five minutes later, the pets were in bed and Drax was standing in the doorway, waiting for me. His fingertip traced a droplet of water from my temple down my jaw, along my neck, and into the divot of my collar bone.

"Are yeh ready for bed, love?"

"Mmhmm. You gonna stay with me?" He toed off his boots and reached for the hem of his shirt.

"I was hoping you'd ask." When his boxer briefs were all he had on, he crawled into bed and I followed him. Using the water he left on the bedside table, I took my medicines and turned into his chest, studying the Claddagh ink on his left pec.

"That's beautiful. When did you get that?"

"You're beautiful, love. Rest now. I'll tell you about it in the morning." His arms wrapped tightly around me, the windows open to let in the cool air, I felt myself drifting into sleep with a smile on my face. Even without being able to use magic, Drax had made the day magical.

CHAPTER
TWENTY-SIX
DRAX

WATCHING MY MATE SLEEP, I MARVELED AT HOW strong and fragile she looked. Lying there in the moonlight, stroking her hair, I felt the fool. My mum was in Ireland, alive and well, and shame kept me from her. Meanwhile, this woman couldn't get her mother back and I could see in her eyes how much it hurt to know I took the privilege for granted.

Out of pride.

"I'll call her tomorrow." I promised quietly, not wanting to wake Tempe. I let my gaze stare out at the moon until my eyes drifted closed and a fitful sleep welcomed me.

THE MORNING DAWNED BRIGHT, sunshine blinding me from the open windows of Tempe's apartment.

"Fekkin hell, no wonder you wake up pissed." I shielded my eyes with a forearm, wondering if I could hurl a pillow hard and far enough to hit the sun. Beside me, Tempe had a pillow covering her head to block the wet nose of Rogue, who was trying to force her out of bed for his canine needs. Her squeals were muffled, but his nose burrowed deeper for every retreat she made.

"Ugh... we never should have had all these kids so close together. Ruins the morning after date nights." She screamed again as his nose found its target.

I laughed, kissing her cheek and sliding out of bed. I pulled on my trousers and boots but didn't bother with the shirt. Despite sleeping indoors, the open windows and freezing weather had kept it comfortable and I started to think we could split our time, sleeping up here in the winter and in the cave during the summer. It would be the perfect balance of our needs... assuming she wanted our life together.

I closed the windows and led the dog through her apartment, pausing to power on the coffee maker I'd set up last night. We walked out while it burbled on the counter, down the stairs, and through the tasting room to escort Rogue to the tree for relief. I stood beside him, watching the window. Tempe rose from the bed, her standing frame in full view through the open curtains stretching in the smallest tank top and underwear imaginable. I could see where my fingers had held her open, the small nibble my dragon had taken, and the exact spot I'd mark her as mine forever.

As soon as Rogue did his business, we went back inside, and I walked into the apartment as Tempe emerged with sleep shorts over her underwear, but nothing more added to my second favorite outfit.

"Morning..." She yawned, grabbing coffee cups from the cabinet and setting them on the counter. Then pet dishes which were filled with food and distributed while the coffee maker finished. I poured the caffeine into our cups and settled her onto a barstool facing the counter.

"I was thinking..."

"Never a good thing for me." She tossed my words from the other day back at me.

"Brat." She smiled around her coffee mug, and I shook my head. "I think we should re-do this place for yeh. Get rid of some of yer grandmother's shite."

She spun on the barstool, turning to face me. I stepped

between her legs and looked down at her, marveling at the gentle curve of her neck and the round tops of her breasts. I traced a black leather cord into her tank top and pulled out a metal disc from between them.

"Where did yeh get this, love?" I asked, tracing the runes etched on the surface while my heart beat faster, pounding in my chest.

She joined me in looking at the necklace, brows pulled together. "I made it with Kaci. It's meant to help me with over-whelm... I never looked at the pattern before. She said it would give insight into my being or something. Doesn't look like anything, though, does it?"

"Yeh don't see anything?" I turned the necklace in her hand. "What about here?"

My finger traced the points for her.

"Does that say dragon?" She pulled it from my hand, rotating it more. "And Doherty?" She looked up at me, lip trembling slightly. "You're... you're the safety I need to feel at peace?"

I dragged my knuckles along her cheek, skin trembling beneath my hand. A vein in her neck jumped, her throat working on the words she'd just said aloud, marrying them with what I'd told her.

Mate.

"Do you need to talk about it?" I let my thumb trace her lips, leaning in until my forehead rested against hers. "Do yeh need me to go away and give you a minute?"

Her arms snaked around my waist, pulling me in closer. Lips pressed against mine, first gently and then picking up steam until her tongue was sliding in and out of my mouth. She moved her hips in time to the thrusts of her tongue, pressing my thick ridge against her core where the heat warmed more than just my flesh.

I held her close, letting herself find her rhythm, her words. Fingers tangled into her hair as I held her mouth against mine, loving her taste. She angled her head back to come up for air.

"No. I want you. With me." Leaning back in her lips found

my neck, and then her teeth. Her fingers had slipped lower into my knickers, hands sliding around the front. One unbuttoned my trousers while the other dipped lower and brushed against my cock.

I gripped her thick brown hair pulling her face back up to mine. My lips sought hers out, pressing soft kisses first to one corner and then the other. Slipping my hands into her shorts to caress the skin of her arse, I pulled her forward until she was flush against me. "I'm yours, love. To do with as you wish."

Her fingers wrapped around my shaft and pumped twice, my pants falling to the floor while I left soft kisses along her jaw, leading to her ear, and taking a nip at the soft spot beneath to hear her moan. We joined again, my mouth swallowing her moans as I pressed my fingers lower, toying with her dripping entrance. When I started to move away she gripped my cock hard and broke the kiss.

"More."

"As you wish." I toed off my boots and stepped out of them while I returned her kiss, never once losing the rhythm of her mouth against mine, licking and sucking the taste of coffee from her lips. Pressed against me, her nipples pushed against her shirt, rubbing my chest. I pulled it off with one hand and dropped my mouth to the dusty rose peak, sucking one into my mouth while my other hand tweaked its twin. With her head thrown back, the column of her neck was on full display and my dragon slid forward.

Not yet.

Her grip on me tightened, dragging my hips closer to hers so she could grind against me in time to her strokes. "Drax."

Her breathy request came with an extra strong squeeze and I dropped to my knees. Her shorts and knickers came down with me and I was eye level with the most perfect pussy I'd ever laid eyes on.

"Mmm... breakfast." I growled, lifting her leg onto my shoulder while sliding her to the edge of the stool, and inhaling her scent. Salty, sweet, and just a little tart, I stroked my tongue from her ass to her clit. Wrapping my lips around the sensitive ridge, I tongued her into my mouth and sucked. Her hands slid into my hair and I gripped her other thigh, lifting it on to the opposite shoulder so her ankles could lock behind my head.

"Oh fuck." Her exclamation spurned me on and I sucked in the sensitive bundle, using my tongue to flick her in time to the thrusts of her hips. Then I slid into her channel, fucking her with the tip of my tongue while the flat kept pressure on her clit and she rode my mouth.

Tempe's core clenched around my tongue and I knew she was close. My fingers replaced my tongue in her channel, fucking her hard while my tongue flicked her clit with the same urgency fingers thrust into her, before sucking hard and humming her name against the most sensitive part of her while curling my fingers upward to reach just the right spot.

"Drax!" Her scream shook the coffee cup on the counter and she came apart around me, shaking, the spasms choking my fingers and coating them in her wet release. I stroked her through it, and when the last tremor subsided, I slid them out and licked my fingers clean, gently lowering her legs.

"Good girl, coming on my tongue." I swiped my mouth with the back of my hand.

Tempe was splayed out on the counter, a feast for my eyes and I found myself leaning in to taste her nipples. Sucking the one I'd missed earlier. Her fingers carded through my hair and she pulled my face toward her.

"I want your cock inside me, Drax." She spoke into my lips, kissing me hard while her hands sought the thing she requested. "Please?"

I looked at her lips, swollen from our kisses and wet from her own release. "Are you sure?"

"Yes. Please?"

There was no hesitation in her eyes. Sliding my hands under

her back, I pulled her against me pressing her torso to mine. "Hang on then, love."

I carried her to her bedroom, her lips kissing my jaw, teeth scraping my neck, while her hands pulled my hair. By the time we made it the eighteen steps, I was about to combust and I dropped onto the bed with her on top, letting her have control.

She shimmied down me, pulling down the knickers that had somehow survived the journey and throwing them across the room. Her tongue took one slow lick from my balls to my head and I grabbed her by her hair, pulling her face to mine.

"The first time I come in you, Tempe, it will not be in your mouth."

She smirked, running her hand up my chest to cup my chin, leaning in close. "Then you better fuck me, Draigus."

Called up from below, the dragon surged forward and took hold of her hips dragging her up until her wet core was dripping over my cock, the underside rubbing her ridges.

"Have yeh got protection?" I gasped, wrestling for a moment of control, while the dragon insisted that after 70 years of celibacy we had nothing to contaminate her with.

"Witch. So... magic birth control and I haven't had sex in a few years so.... You?" She slid along me, distraction stilting her words while her hands played with her nipples and I slid her off my cock to impale it deep inside of her. "Oh goddess, you're huge."

"It's been seventy years, love, so yeh might have to show me what you want."

She rocked her hips, rolling her wet, hot channel over my shaft, every movement a new version of heaven. My hands slid up her belly to her ribs, taking her tits from her hands and sitting up to suck on them while she gripped my shoulders. The new angle hit deeper and I could feel the sudden shift in her posture.

"Mmm... Fuck me..." Tempe thrust harder, rolling her hips faster.

I took hold of her thick thighs, lifting her slightly off of me to drive into her. I slammed into her over and over again, feeling my building pleasure in the base of my spine while nonsensical sounds slipped past her lips and I switched nipples. Her hands on my shoulders slipped down, her mouth dropping to my neck and I felt her teeth scrape against me.

"She wants to mark us."

With a final thrust she clenched around me, spasming and jerking wildly while I exploded into her, filling her with my cum. We rode through the waves, until spent, she collapsed on top of me, still rubbing her clit against my pelvis.

"Fuck that was good." She licked a line up my neck and I chuckled.

"Better than good, it was fekking perfect." I kissed the top of her head, holding her close to me.

"Should we spend the day here, getting you caught up for the past seventy years?" My cock twitched, still inside her.

Shaking with laughter, I shook my head. "Nay lass. We have to open the winery today and yeh were gonna see about hirin' out a bottlin' service."

"Boo..." She pouted into my chest and I tickled her sides until she was writhing against me, panting and aroused. "You suck."

"Yeh have first hand experience of all the places I suck. Hop in the shower and I'll get breakfast ready." Rising, I pulled on my undergarments and tugged Tempe up, smacking her ass toward the shower. "Off with yeh."

"Aren't you going to shower?"

"I'll wash you off of me when I get to have yeh again." I pulled my trousers on over the underwear.

She flipped me the middle finger and disappeared behind the door. I went into the kitchen and pulled down the pancake mix, reading the instructions before mixing the powder and water in a bowl. They didn't seem that hard, but I was on pancake number four, and so far I'd given all of them to the dog.

"Why the fek is this so hard?" I snarled at the pan, flames threatening to melt the plastic handle of her cookware.

"Woah, Fireball." Tempe stepped in and turned down the heat on the burner, adding oil to the pan and starting the hum of the little fan over the stove. "We've got enough problems with this place without you trying to burn it down."

"There's two ingredients in these bloody things, how the fek have they gone arseways?" I felt off balance and on edge. A simple burned breakfast impacting more than it should.

"What's wrong, Drax?" Tempe's hand cupped my cheek, running her fingers down the side of my face, and I kissed her palm, inhaling the smells of plum and sandalwood that flowed through her. With that simple act, she settled the fire in my chest and balance was restored.

"I... love..." Her breath held in her throat, and in the silence, sound carried from just outside. The stairs creaked outside her apartment, and I faltered. Stepping away from her, I shifted one hand into a claw and placed myself between her and the front door as another stair groaned on the way up.

"What's happening?"

"Someone's coming up the stairs..." She moved me over and stood beside me, her magic at the ready around her, despite the steady drip of the walls sucking it away. "Stand behind me."

"Fuck that. Stand beside me." She snapped, and I couldn't help it. I drew her into me and kissed her hard.

"I love you, Tempe."

She froze like a deer in headlights; the door handle jiggling just before it shoved open, and her magic slammed into the wall beside it.

CHAPTER

TWENTY-SEVEN

TEMPE

GRAN MAPLE STOOD IN THE DOORWAY LOOKING LIKE A caricature of a witch from the 1960s. From the half-moon spectacles perched on her sharply pointed nose to the severe bun knotted at the crown of her head, I would have been less surprised to see her in wizard robes than the hippie skirt and peasant blouse she wore instead.

"Maple." Drax lowered his chin in her direction, but the rest of his body held tension like a depressed spring under load, one that threatened to spill out into violence if you let go.

My hands shook, fearful over the potential violence warring with the shock of his confession. He loves... me? I pushed the thought toward my "for later" box, but it fought back. Screaming to be heard, to be commented on.

"Retirement has had... *little* impact on you." The sarcastic undertones wove through Drax's voice and I waited for understanding to sink in. Gran had been gone when Drax got here. Everyone had been gone, besides me. How much could he possibly know about her from before she left to live closer to the equator?

The woman's face remained the same, an overly large smile that didn't touch the dead eyes resting above them. I'd seen more

249

animated puppets made of wood, but this one still had a chest that rose and fell with the steady rhythm of the living. Several seconds stretched on, the three of us trapped in a stand-off without rules.

"Are you going to stand there or come over here and say hello?" Gran held her arms open, an invitation for a hug that looked performative. Hesitation stunted my feet, making their journey slow and spastic, the irregular slap of flesh on vinyl flooring loud in the otherwise dead room. We weren't really a hugging family, but I was a pathological people pleaser and that kept me moving forward when every cell in my body told me to run away.

Cautiously, I gave her a quick one-armed hug, stumbling backwards, my bare feet catching on the entry rug and twisting in transit. Left leg crossed over right, I spun around and nearly collided head first with the floor, saved only by hand on the counter. From my lower perspective, I was on level with Maple's weekend bag beside her, but magic meant that it could be filled for a week or a month.

Drax loves me, my brain shouted. I got myself back upright and retreated into the kitchen and the safety of coffee.

"Hey..." I looked down at my bare feet and then at the calendar on the wall. Tomorrow was the anniversary of mom's death. The day before her birthday, I relaxed slightly. The timing of this visit, though inconvenient, at least made sense. "Are you here for the anniversary? I didn't have anything planned besides visiting her stone and saying some words. But we could go out to the gravestone together and then, I don't know, share a meal?"

A sharp look of confusion impaled me, cutting deeper than any silence from the past few months.

"What anniversary?" The confirmation stole my air, her placid smile still firmly pinned to the robotic features. "Did you get married?"

Either she forgot her only daughter's birthdate, its nearness to her death date, or she simply didn't care. Mom had always gone on drunken ramblings of her mother throwing her away when she remained without magic after her father had passed. There was a lot of resentment towards her fated, but... she forgot? Who the fuck forgets when their only kid died?

"Mom?" I tried to get my voice to sound firm, but it was brittle and broken. My hand was gripping the counter, fighting the urge to break off a piece and throw it at her.

"Your mom never got married. She had you and she died." Gran walked toward the kitchen table, draping her purse on the chair to stare blankly at her own wall art. "But I don't know why we'd celebrate that."

An acidic burn crept up my throat, matching the heat that burned its way from my toes up to my palms. "Her death anniversary. It's tomorrow, Maple!"

"Tempe, that's not until February!" She waved dismissively, and the lump in my throat blocked my airway. Lightheaded, I oscillated between wanting to pass out and wanting to scream. Every nerve ending in my body dulled, cauterized with the heat of her indifference. Instead of losing sleep, haunted by memories, the woman had carried on as if the life she'd birthed meant... nothing.

"It is February," I whispered.

"What? Speak up, Tempe. No one can hear you if you mumble." She planted her hands on her hips and looked down her nose at me.

"I said it is February! Can you hear me now, or should I get a skywriter to caption it with subtitles?" My bones rattled, clacking together with sharp jarring pains to my jaw. Memories and betrayal were looping around my neck, trying to strangle the life out of me.

Gran had forgotten.

Drax placed a hand on my shoulder, the room slowing in its rapid rotation. He'd set aside his own rage, slowly reeling me into him until I was no longer forced to bear the weight of my own spine. He depressed his thumb into my shoulder, trying to release the growing tension in my muscles before they strangled me. We simply stood there and watched as she observed her own home for the first time, despite everything being the same as she left it.

Maple strutted over to her floral armchair, giving it a disapproving sniff and eyeing Corky on the neighboring chair with reproach. "Cats should not be on furniture."

"And parents should know when their kids were born. And more importantly when they died!" Drax snapped, wrapping an arm around me and pointing to the calendar. "Yeh can' have lost all the calendars bein' *delira and excira* on the lash, can yeh?"

Waves of heat flooded off of him and into my frozen frame. Every breath came with a suppressed scream and the burn of unshed tears, his heat forcing me to breathe when I was ready to lie down and quit. My heart was jump started, his pulsating dragon fire shocking me once, twice...

"I beg your pardon, son, but that is entirely inappropriate. Tempe, are you going to let him talk to me like that?" She shooed Corky, who gave her a long, slow blink before lifting his leg and going to town on his man parts. "Your cat is being disrespectful, as well. Are there any decent men in this household? How can you possibly allow this?"

"It's bein' a cat. They aren' known for listenin'. What are you doing here, Maple?" Drax held me up in his arms. My legs had given up supporting me, but my heart was still working, still beating.

I just wasn't sure it was beating for me anymore. Affection for Drax rushed through me with every steady thump. An unprecedented need for his company, affection, and, in this moment, support, as my world fell apart, leaving fissures along my insides that slowly dripped liquid ice.

My gran was here, in time for the anniversary of my mother's death, and she didn't fucking remember. Instead, she'd strolled in and started criticizing everything and everyone. Not hearing from her for months could have been passed off as so many things, but sitting before me, I was confronted with a hideous truth.

People were right to hate her, to say that she was a callous and dismissive woman who treated people miserably. No one who'd met her liked her and it was for a reason.

The woman was awful...

"Where's Damien?" Drax asked. Guilt and fear whisked across her face. If I hadn't been staring at her, I'd have missed it, but seeing her express an emotion wasn't the sudden shock I wanted it to be. Wasn't the urge I needed to jumpstart my will to survive.

"He went to the wine cave to seek you out first." The words were undercut with the burn of lies and distrust. "I'm sure you'll catch up with him soon enough. We can all just stay here and have a nice chat until then."

"Drax..." I didn't want him to walk out the door and leave me here, but if she wanted us all confined, there had to be a reason.

"I'll go meet him then." Drax hugged me tightly, squeezing my hand, he leaned in to whisper in my ear. "I'm never far from you, love, and I can be where you are in a moment. We're in this together, mo doineann."

His warm lips brushed my temple, the heat of his breath tickling my hair. When he pulled away, a large chunk of something heavy inside me went with him. Being without him, even for a moment, was like having my flesh ripped away and I gasped.

His dragon's eyes flashed, the pain mirrored in their depth. "I'll return."

The door clicked shut behind him, gran softly swallowing but forcing her heart rate steady. They were up to something, but I wasn't certain what there was for them to be up to. The winery and the wine were all as they had been, falling apart but surviving. Just like the people who worked here. Unless he met whoever had placed the enchantments on the walls, there wasn't much left he could ruin.

"That wasn't necessary. He's just having a look around before finding us up here." She shifted in her seat but remained steadfast, pretending to have no cares while Drax hunted down her mate. I wasn't sure if mate non-verbal communication was a thing, if she warned Damien that Drax was looking for him, or if that was just a shifter romance novel thing. "Surprised to see you two doing so well together."

"Hmm... why is that?" I asked, not really listening. My ears were trying to pick up sounds of a disturbance or signs that Draigus might need my help. If another dragon was in the winery, would he be stronger than mine?

"Well, I just didn't think the business would do that well and Damien said Draigus..." My eyes snapped to her. The business had done well under her for years, so why wouldn't it do well under us? Unless... "Can I get some coffee, Tempe? You know it's rude not to offer your guest a beverage. I raised you better than that."

I took a long, slow blink and glanced at my empty cup, thoughts colliding into each other like a molecular bombardment experiment. It seemed rude to deny her, but it was also the perfect amount of petty to say no just because.

"I didn't raise you to ignore people, either!" Her outburst pulled free one of my own.

"You didn't raise me. Honestly, no one did. But mom, Liv, she did what she could." My grip on the mug tightened and Rogue slunk into the room, sitting beside me with his head on my leg. Fingers twisting through his amber ale fur, my mind wandered to a night my mom had come home drunk.

She'd been sober for two months. It was the most days I'd seen her smile in years... I must have been ten. Before she'd left for work, the house phone rang. We almost never answer it, but that time she did. Almost like she'd been forced.

At the end of the call, she was off. Upset, confused. Her boss called a few hours later, she hadn't come in to work. Hours later we were on the floor of the bathroom, her eyes watering, body weak, she was crying. *Why can't they just leave me alone? No matter how far I go, it's never far enough.*

At the time, I thought she meant alcohol, but staring at my gran... *what if?* The old refrain echoed around my brain with the hollow chords of a well-worn record. Still... *what if?*

"Tempe?" Maple intruded into my memories, and I raised an

eyebrow at her. Letting Rogue go, I walked over to the coffeemaker and refilled my cup. "Are you going to bring me some coffee?"

Shaking my head, I headed back toward the bedroom and gestured for the animals to follow me. It had been a long path to acceptance, but I was done pretending we were family.

Drax, Rogue and Corky were more family than she had ever been. At least I knew loving him wouldn't crush me... shit. I loved him.

I loved him and I didn't say it. But there was still time.

"It's your home, not mine. Help yourself," I called behind me. "I have to get dressed."

CHAPTER

TWENTY-EIGHT

TEMPE

Maple sat across from me at the small coffee table in the apartment, her face blank except for a placid smile that would creep out The Joker. From one moment to the next, her eyes lost focus, regained it, gave a look of panic, and then appeared serene and beatific.

If I'd had a mouth swab drug test, I'd have stuck it in her cheek just to see if she was on something.

When I'd come out of the bedroom after getting dressed, she'd still been sitting in the arm chair. I'd had a moment to calm down, a moment to collect my thoughts and decided that if she wasn't my family then I didn't care if she got hurt. I needed answers and this might be the only way to get them. I needed to know why she was powering the magical vacuum and who she was working for.

"So, if you're not here for mom, what are you here for?" I took a drink from my coffee, annoyed that I'd given in and made her a cup. Instead of drinking the coffee, she held it like a prop, waiting for the director to instruct her what to do with it next.

"I used to live here. There was much less fur." Her brows drew together in a scowl. Corky shifted on my lap, daring her to say another word about him. "My daughter always wanted a pet."

"Mom wanted a pet?" It was the first time I'd heard this. My entire childhood, I'd begged for a furry friend, but my mom always appeared terrified and appalled. I thought she hated animals and only ended up with Corky when he adopted me outside my apartment in college during a storm. "She never got one."

"Of course she didn't. He would have killed it." Gran's sharp tone pulled me back, her narrowed expression flashed blue ice shards, cutting through the trance and clearing her mind. "She wouldn't have taken on anything that could be used as a threat or a weapon. It was what made having you so hard."

I pulled back against my chair. "Having me was hard?"

"Of course it was. Love was a weapon..." Her eyes glazed over and the smile returned, smoothing all her features and taking ten years off the woman in front of me. "Oh my, talk of weapons. Could I have some more coffee?"

I blinked at her, long and slow, pinching my thigh to check if I'd fallen asleep. "You... still have a full cup. You haven't drunk it."

She looked down at the mug in her hand and back at me. "I suppose I haven't. But it's cold now. Could you dump it out and get me a fresh one?"

Corky looked in my eyes and let out a soft "mrrrrow?" And I shrugged at him in return. Usually, the woman was quiet and stern, but something was off. I took her cup and started toward the kitchen, lifting it to my lips to drink instead of dumping it out because, come on—coffee.

"No!" She jumped to her feet, hands raised, a jet of plum magic zapping the cup.

I startled, bumping into the counter and dropped the cup. It crashed to the ground, spilling its contents with the sound of breaking glass. Coffee splashed against the cabinets and across the floor, dripping and pooling with a fragrant and sticky mess that didn't align with the hazelnut I brewed. "What did you put in here?"

"Hmm?" She was seated again, hands folded in her lap.

My hands shook slightly, eyes staying on the woman as I grabbed the wet pads for my mop and started swiping at the mess. As the coffee disappeared, the class pieces formed a neat pile, and I scooped them into the dustpan to dump in the trash before wiping the cleaner off the floor with a wet washcloth.

Gran didn't move through the whole process. She sat statue-still, hands un-moving, a robot powered-off and waiting for someone to reboot her. The brown leather handbag hanging on her chair had the flap open, a small blue bottle peeking out that looked familiar, but I couldn't place it.

"Are you OK?" I narrowly resisted the urge to wave my hand in front of her face.

"Yes, dear." She didn't look at me. "Just waiting for coffee."

"Sure." I stared at her for another minute, but she didn't move. The coffee pot was empty, and I went into the cabinet to get replacement grounds. A blue bottle was blocking a bag of coffee, and I moved it to the shelf below, grabbing a bag of coffee at random and closing the cabinet. When I turned around, her purse was closed, and I couldn't remember what I'd seen inside.

"Gran... why did you enchant the winery to steal magic? Who's getting the magic?" I poured water into the coffee maker without breaking eye contact. Or eye to ear contact, since she still wasn't facing me, but a muscle beneath her eye jumped and her cheek bunched. The hands in her lap clenched around each other, fingers white and strangling one another while her mouth worked without sound. "Gran?"

"Women don't need to do magic with men around." Her voice sounded sincere, but I suspected if she could choke herself, she might have. Instead, her hands shook to the magnitude of a 7.2 earthquake. "My purpose is to be of service. It was requested of me to create and build the spell that haunts these walls, and I alone can harvest it, to the dismay of my benefactor."

I stared for so long in silence, the coffee maker beeped its completion. Her statements didn't align with what I'd read in the grimoire, a woman who loved magic and experimentation. She

believed in the power of science and magic and now she was...
this?

Instead of throwing up, I chose a new cup from the cabinet and placed it on the counter. After I added coffee, I put in a small dollop of cream and a cube of sugar. I carried it back to her and this time, when I set it down, she picked it up and easily took a drink.

"Who's the benefactor? Who asked you to do this?"

"You look so much like her." Her eyes softened, clearing only to glisten with tears. "I miss her so much and it's my fault. All of this."

"All of what? Miss who?" I searched the room for something to explain the sudden shifts.

"Your mother, Tempe. He wouldn't just let her go once he learned of the stipulations, but you were too powerful to take." Her hand reached out, cupping my cheek and stroking a damp spot under my eye. Just as quickly, she jerked back and pulled away when my phone trilled on the counter. "Oh, look at the time!"

I checked the phone display and saw Chance's name. Picking up the phone, I swiped the call active. "Hang on. Gran, where are you..."

"Back to Damien. I should see where he is. Goodbye!" She left the room without another word, leaving her purse hanging on the chair.

"What was that?" Chance sounded as confused as I felt.

"Maple... maybe. Or the pod person, on drugs version. What do you need?" I scrubbed my hand down my face, trying to make sense of what the hell had happened with that first mug of coffee.

" Can you meet... right now?" Chance didn't sound any more excited than they had a moment ago. "This isn't really a phone conversation..."

But what if?

"Yeah. Do you have a place in mind?"

The apartment door creaked open. Before my fight or flight

could kick in, I sensed the man on the other side. His person became an extension of mine, be it the forced proximity, physical intimacy, or just our magic recognizing the other, my nerves settled, and I could think.

"Meet me on Sue's porch in five?"

"Yeah." They clicked off the call and I dropped the phone back onto the counter. Drax was wearing his usual cargos and T-shirt, hair a little shaggier, beard freshly shaven, and eyes holding secrets of a thousand miles.

"Damien was down by the barrels. Searchin' the walls for some'in. Are you leavin'?" His face was blank, a practiced indifference, but the gold of his dragon peeking out said it was not a calm inquisition.

"Yeah. To meet with Chance. They didn't say what it was about, but didn't sound positive about it. Did you see or sense a second dragon? Someone they might be working with? She said someone made her do the spell, that it was her job to be of service, but she couldn't tell me whose service."

Drax shook his head and I deflated onto the counter, waiting for the energy and willpower to deal with this. "She—Maple—said, talked, about my mom. Briefly, but..."

"But..." His nose worked, pausing over the trash bin. "Were you in the garden?"

"No, it's February. The garden is frozen, why?"

Drax lifted the lid and sniffed more, picking up a piece of the broken coffee mug. "What happened to this?"

I shook my head, the coffee mug already forgotten. "Gran had a cup of coffee I made for her, but she wasn't drinking. Then she asked me to pour it out because it was cold. I was just going to drink it but she scared me and I dropped it, breaking it and spilling it. What's wrong?"

"It's laced with belladonna, Tempe." He looked between me and the broken cup. "Did she add anything to her cup?"

"I... I didn't add it." I shook off some brain fog and my phone chimed. "I need to go."

Drax crossed the room, wrapping his arms around me, and pressed a kiss to my lips.

"Sorry, love. We'll talk when you return. I'll see you at opening. Remember, if yer late, I might have to talk to customers, and you'll never see them again."

"The horrors. Thank you." I sighed, sticking my phone in my pocket and grabbing my wallet. "Do you think gran was trying to poison..." I let the thought trail off. There would only be two options and neither of them looked good.

He squeezed my hand, and I swallowed the lump in my throat. "No matter what, I'll be here when you get back. I'll always be here for you, love."

"Thanks... and Drax?" He glanced at me. Holding my magic like a chicken, ready to disappear the moment the words were out, I made sure to look him in the eyes. So he'd know I meant them despite my anxiety. "I love you too."

And I let go of the thread to disappear.

CHAPTER

TWENTY-NINE

TEMPE

MAX MET ME ON SUE'S FRONT PORCH.

"Hey babes." I scrunched his ears, nails raking against the thin coat of his neck above his emerald, green sweater. The dog's company soothed my shaking hand on the heels of my confession. My brain was in denial that I said it, but my heart... It finally felt like something had gone right. "This is nice. Rob an Irish sheep?"

Chance opened the door and summoned me inside before the Doberman could respond, but I suspected the dog hadn't needed to rob anyone. With his delicate nature, squishy face, and adorably over-sized paws, even a sheep would give its wool for his sweaters.

"Do you just... go around talking to animals?" Chance asked, their suit a pinstripe blue today. "Like, are you still hoping to be the Disney princess and not the witch? Because that ship has sailed, Tempe."

"Wow. That's a hurtful stereotype." I delivered in my most cutting voice. "You know, they were all witches. The real villain was the writers who pitted women against each other over a man."

"Someone's been reading feminist blogs." They stepped aside, and I walked into Sue's house. It was different in the daylight. Incense still hung in the air, but the natural light brought color and an ethereal glow to the space that was absent in the evening

262

hours. Sun catchers sent rainbows scattering across walls, carpets, and Max, who was now lying on the hard surface hallway. "Mom said we can use the office, just in here."

They led me to a room that opened just before the staircase. I'd always believed it would be a closet, and the hooks in the hall were for the convenience of the coven, but...

"Did you say mom?" I asked, stumbling on the short step down from the hallway into the sunken den. "Like... figuratively?"

"No." They laughed, flopping onto the couch and stretching out. "I burned all the pictures of me growing up and technically I work outside the hollow with the rest of the non-magic folk, skipping the holidays for solo time. But this house is outside the hollow, so I can visit as I please. Thought she told you I was dog-sitting?"

"Non-magic?" Corky strutted over to an armchair and perched on the center cushion. With all seats occupied, I dropped to the floor and sat criss cross applesauce like a child. "She said offspring but I never pictured you..."

Chance visibly winced when my hip popped. "Yeah... you thought I was a witch?"

I shrugged and offered a nod. "I thought I detected magic coming off of you. Honestly, though, I've been off my game. Too much magic getting sucked out of me." I scrubbed my face as the front door opened and Sue came in. "Hey."

"Hey, mom." They offered her a two-finger scout salute that was moderately sarcastic.

"Such sass, Chance. I'd ask where the hell you got it from, but I look in the mirror every morning." She entered the room and gave them a quick kiss on the top of their head, doing the same to me as she passed. Unwinding her scarf, she hung it on a coat rack with her personal coat before materializing a kettle, cat strainers, and loose-leaf tea to fill the strainers from somewhere behind her desk.

"Witchcraft!" Chance hollered, laughing at their own joke.

Sue flicked a bit of magic across the room that appeared to flick one of the lawyer's ears.

"So much sass." She put water in the electric kettle and turned it on. Adding bags to each cup while a knot in my chest tightened at the playful interaction. "Now, Tempe..."

I blinked her direction, fighting the feelings of loss and jealousy at the easy affection that had never been my life.

"Oh, sweetie." She started over, but I held up a hand.

"It's fine. I'm fine... just..." I sucked in air and blew it back out. "Bad brain day."

"It's still morning," Chance whispered, and their mom magically performed another ear flick that had me chuckling. "What, it is!"

"Gran and Damien came back this morning. She'd forgotten mom's birthday and when I almost drank poison, she started talking about how someone would have killed a pet and used it against her but I was too powerful to go against and I don't know what's real and what's... I don't know because she's like Dr. Jekyll and Mrs. Freaking Stepford Wife."

Silence stretched through the room, and I glanced up to check they hadn't both turned and run back out on me. Chance's eyes were a bit too wide, and Sue was chewing her cheek, neither on their own a bad sign, but both telling me I came to the right place for answers as the kettle whistled.

"What did you do?" I asked, and they both spoke at once.

"I cut off her access to the business account aside from what I assumed was her monthly stipend being transferred to an external account in her name."

"I scried to see if I could force the true source of the winery's enchantment to reveal itself. That's why I took a sample of the wall."

Both answers overlapped and blended, neither a complete explanation, but both were enough to explain part of the problem. Chance had taken access to the large amounts of cash away and Sue had forced them to return through the magic cast.

Rising, I shut off the piercing shriek of the kettle and poured the steaming water into all three mugs. Based on the smell, Sue had chosen English Breakfast, which was not coffee but at least had caffeine. Swirling the cat tea strainer, I placed lids on the other two cups to steep while I played with mine. The clear liquid steamed while swirls of tea colored the water, and the sun broke it apart in a multitude of colors. It was all layered together, but the outcome was something dark and not really what I wanted.

A metaphor if ever there was one.

"Tempe... I..."

"Why did you invite me into your coven?" I asked, not looking up from the tea. "I thought gran had forced you but..."

"No. Quite the opposite, actually. We approached you after she left, concerned that you were left alone on that hill without connections or introductions. Knowing her had been our entry point, but... your gran hasn't been part of our community since Jake died. His death hit her hard and then it felt like the next day, Damien was there. Her true fated mate." Sue picked up her tea and the one for Chance, squeezing my forearm as she passed. "We honestly hardly ever saw her after he came around."

"Do you know for sure it was fated and not chosen? That he didn't just... take her when she was too weak to fight him?" I kept my eyes on the tea.

Sue sucked in a breath, Chance making sounds of interested detachment. "That would be a deplorable thing to do. But no, there was no proof it was fated. We all assumed based on how quickly it happened..."

"Arran said it was a winery before, and my mom liked to work with her dad up there. Do you know about that?" I glanced up and quickly back down, certain I would cry if I looked at them for too long.

Sue took a sip of her tea collecting herself from the initial horror. I followed suit, making a face when it was not coffee and tasted like bitter nothing. Chance stood and grabbed a honey bear, squeezing a generous helping in both our cups before stirring with his steeper. "I've been waiting for you to ask... I was starting to think you'd never be ready to know about them.

"Jake and your mom used to spend hours in the grapes, planting, and learning all about them. Your gran wasn't really one to get her hands dirty, but she knew the science of blends and branding. They named it after the song they danced to at their wedding, *Love Potion Number 9*. It was a long running joke between them. She claimed he stole her heart, and he said with her magical potions, he didn't have a chancce."

I felt myself smiling, wondering what life would have been like if he'd lived. Wondering if one day Drax and I would have cheesy stories about wedding songs and dragons. Goosebumps peppered my arm, reminding me that despite being new, everything with him felt... right. A knot formed in my stomach at the thought of him up there with Damien, alone.

"Your gran was a chemist, one of the smartest women around, while your grandad was a farmer. Jake's connection with the land is probably why you are such an extraordinary garden witch. He was a human, but their love hadn't been contingent on power or skill. The winery was their dream, a balance of their love and skills, your mom the prodigy of them both with no magic."

"She said gran hated her when her magic never arrived. She was running to escape their disapproval..." The memory from this morning multiplied in my head back through time, other moves. Other drunken nights and alarmed calls that turned into downward spirals. "I thought my mom resented my magic."

"That doesn't sound like the woman I knew before, though she had a couple decades on me and Liv a few decades behind. That winery was thriving before he passed, and she was more than capable of running it after him. Any changes that came to her personality, came after his death."

"Is it not now?" I looked at Chance, who shook their head.

"It is now, but I can't go back far enough to see what the financials did before. You might have to ask the accounting dorcha for that one. But I did some legal digging, especially when

I wanted to find out the land ownership rights. Legally, so long as a surviving member of the family wants to run it as a winery, the property can't be anything else."

Returning to my seat on the floor, I crossed my legs and took another drink of the leaf water. Honey had helped, but it still sucked when compared to other beverages I could be having right now. Coffee, wine, Draigus... OK, the last one wasn't a beverage, but I could possibly have him right now.

"If she could run it without him, why is Damien involved at all? Why wasn't he just a couch potato who let her do the work? It doesn't sound like he had a choice if the property had to be a winery."

"I think he might have, but I wasn't speaking of him." Sue said, and I jerked my neck painfully to look at her. Sharp stinging tingles ran up and down the thick muscle and I gripped it with my hand.

"What? Who then?"

"Your mom owned half the winery. Despite everything, women couldn't be joint owners of a business when that winery was opened, and your gran was never listed on the deed to the property. Neither imagined life without the other, so it never made sense when laws changed to do anything about that. It was legally considered separate property. When he died without a will, Idaho inheritance law made it so she only inherited half, the rest belonged to your mother... and now you."

"How the hell do you know so much about this?"

Sue shrugged, sipping her tea and looking out the window.

"I was there... perhaps not as there as I should have been, but I was very young and listening at the door when it all went down. The look of anger on Damien's face, your mother's fear..." She shuddered softly. "I was worried harm would come to you when you visited as a child, but Kaci said your magic protected you. That you'd survive to-"

Her previous statement sunk in while I processed the new ones.

"Wait, what? I wasn't willed the winery, it's mine? Outright? And Damien has no power to force Draigus to be there? Blood oath be damned?" A fly would enter my mouth, but I couldn't seem to close it. "Why didn't anyone tell me?"

"I think you may be hyper-fixating on the wrong..." Sue started, but Chance cut her off.

"If I may?" Chance tapped their mother. Pointing to a picture on their phone. With an eye roll, she magicked it into the room beside us.

"Couldn't you have brought that over in, like... a briefcase or a satchel?" I asked, looking at the half-dozen file folders and judging Chance hard to avoid thinking about all the truth bombs just dropped on my head.

"Nope. Ruins the line of my suit." They gestured along the side of their body. "I had to go back to the paper archives to find this. It was never digitized, but the business was owned and registered before, that's how Idaho tax law came into play to grant your mother that ownership share. Then after she ran away, that's when the whole thing went into fraud land."

Without a concrete thread to hold on to, I just sat on the floor. Considering everything they'd said, I couldn't be sure my mom was the monster I'd made her out to be. Maybe distancing herself was protecting me... What if gran...

"Here we go." They pulled out a document that looked older than both of us combined. "The original business was opened with the stipulation that the land could only be transferred if no descendants, by birth or adoption, wished to continue running it as a winery and wanted to repurpose or re-sale the land, basically what I said before. Any new owner needed to conduct business as such for a year minimum before waiving ownership, unless the business failed or would cause irreparable physical, emotional, or financial harm to the owner or their descendants."

I took the page and skimmed the arcane language that was denser than Tolkien. It included the word "whereas" more times than I'd seen printed since that summer I worked as a file clerk for Paso Robles City Council reading ordinances.

"This has my mom's signature on it..." I commented, reading a sub clause that was added in newer ink and dated a year before I was born. "It says she does not now, nor ever, intend to waive her ownership. Her intention was to stay and work the land..."

Swallowing, I let it all wash over me. Trying not to look at any one piece for too long.

"And this... Is this an attempt to have my mom placed under Damien and Maple's Guardianship? Granting... Damien the Power of Attorney?" I asked, Chance nodded, and I chewed on my lip. "Why the hell was he trying to Britney Spears' her? There's no file for custody of me... they just wanted to make financial decisions for her... citing substance abuse and risky behavior..."

Dropping the papers, I scrubbed my hands over my face. If you don't care about someone, you just want control of their interests, what could he be after? Power? Money? Add to it the magic being sucked into the walls, and power wouldn't make sense anymore. So long as we kept casting in the building, he'd have power. And there was a million dollars in the business account, why not take it and run? Was there more money to be had? But if the winery went under, he'd lose the magic... unless he only needed the magic for one thing... something big...

"How valuable is our land?" I asked Chance, and they shrugged.

"I can text Numbers. It's the only way we communicate. Why? Are you going to sell it after everything?" They looked a little disappointed, and I shook my head.

"No, but if it's enough money... if my magic protects me, but mom didn't have any... Maybe dying was her way of protecting the land, making sure I inherited part of it. If everything was fine until my grandfather passed... How did Jake die?"

Sue pulled her lips between her teeth, wiggling her nose in concentration.

"It was... unexpected. Medical, I believe, but not something that made sense. I'd need to ask around. Why?"

"What if..." I swallowed the urge to silence myself. Just this once, it didn't seem impossible. "What if he didn't die? What if his death was arranged? Then Damien makes Maple his mate when she's too depressed to fight him and he takes hold of her magic. Somehow, he links up with another leech dragon, and they start stealing magic from everyone who comes in, storing it in the walls. But it drains them too, while they live there, so they pull me in instead. I make money, but it's not as much as he can get by selling the land and the business needs to go under and I'm not failing. So he brings in Drax... why? To make me fail? And there was no other dragon with them. And what do they need all that power for?"

My heart stammered, Draigus's face floating in my mind's eye. His name is on my necklace, his lips on my skin. He said he loved me... and I meant it when I said it back.

"There's something else I need to tell you about leech magic." Sue's hesitation filled the air with thick anticipation. "I was doing research in the old library. Leech magic is a special talent that belongs to one particular clan of dragons, the red dragons from Northern Ireland."

"So whoever is helping them has to be related to Damien? But no other dragons were there. What about the other red dragons?" I scratched between my shoulder blades, itchy and restless.

"Gone. There were only two clans, and Damien's family destroyed the other. All red dragons are part of his clan."

I pictured Draigus, his arms around me as he told me that being here was his repayment for the blood oath. That Damien ruined his life and was a monster.

"Are you saying Drax is... Damien's family? Couldn't he have been part of the other clan before Damien killed them?" The thought made my guts churn but I liked that prospect better than the first.

"Not unless he's six hundred years older than he says he is. I'm sorry Tempe, but Damien is a lot closer to your Drax than he should be."

CHAPTER

THIRTY

DRAX

Opening came with no word from Tempe, but far too many words from Damien.

"What are you really doing here, Damien?" I leaned against the wine barrel, staring at the man who had scripted me into service. My godfather was an old Irishman from before the times of synthetic fibers. His wool pants were brown and red plaid, the button down a brilliant white, his suspenders and shoes a matching dark brown leather. The jaunty page boy cap on his head hid the thinning hairline, but it was still more red than white where it peeked out below the rim.

If I wasn't mistaken, images of him were in history and soci-ology books, wearing this exact outfit.

The clothes made him look like someone's pop-pop and not what he was, the perfect disguise for a deadly, manipulative bastard several centuries old. Battles, both written and unwritten, held traces of his claw marks-painted red with blood he spilt. Men and women turned over their souls to his charisma, only to find themselves dead or despised at the end of an unjust war.

"I live here, boy-o. Or did ya forget this winery is mine? You're staying here at my invitation." Damien's smile displayed a set of sharp dragon teeth. A feature he shouldn't have—as was the

272

magic drifting off of him in subtle waves that beat in tune with the subtle circles Maple weaved standing beside him. He'd touched every inch of the wood in this room, growing stronger while more of the wood splintered beneath his touch. "It wasn't a real inheritance, I'm not dead. Yeh owe me."

Arms crossed, I huffed out a breath and looked away. It was the same line he'd given every time he showed up on the island, inviting me to join yet another fight, but there was nothing worth fighting for. Not until Tempe. "It's not yers, yeh don't own it. Tempe's family owns it. Yer jus' squattin here like a layabout. And what more do I owe yeh? I'm here, aren't I?"

"Watch yourself, sonny. The magic in the walls, the money in the till, I could live off this for years, and you're hardly necessary." His fangs flashed my way, souring my stomach. "But it's not enough. I have bigger fish to fry."

Maple drooped forward, her plastic smile melting into a marionette without a puppeteer. Heat flashed through me and my dragon came forward, ready to defend us—only to be tugged at and plucked by the man before me. I pulled the dragon back, churning in my gut made worse by the overhead lights bursting in and out of focus.

"What are you doing?" I staggered back, leaning onto a barrel with my hand pressed against my chest.

"Testing. Looks like it's not time yet." Damien shook his head. "Your witch pulling her magic has set me back. No matter, it's only a matter of time."

"How are you doing this? They bound you!" My heart hammered, the dragon inside trembling and cold. He was not one to be tricked or manipulated. "Who are you working with?"

Damien let out a low, cruel chuckle. "There's power not even they control, if you find someone strong enough to energize it. I only had to take a mate with power and land who was too heartbroken to stop me. And wasn't it just lucky a witch cursed you to get me exactly what I need—a free dragon already sharing my bloodline."

Maple jerked up, laughing with Damien and smiling with pain in her eyes. A moment of clarity showed through and I reached for her only for the window to snap shut. Everything in her closed off and she went back to being Damien's shadow while we climbed the stairs to the open winery. He moved, she moved, he laughed, she laughed. The brilliant scientist, the witch who'd married a normie and raised a child who loved to garden, was gone. All the fight had left her—after all these years, she couldn't fight anymore.

Damien had taken the beautiful mate bond and twisted it as he did everything.

The old man took the stairs back to the tasting room, leading Maple while I trod slowly behind them. Just before I entered the kitchen, a small burst of dragon fire delivered a note to the ground before me. Startled, I immediately checked for witnesses, but the normies were out of sight. Collecting the paper, I entered the tasting room.

"Maple!" Cathy Jo called out, her cat sweater rapidly approaching us as I scanned the room for any sign Tempe had returned.

Samuel worked the Tuesday crowd with effortless charm, a decidedly light load all things considered. The satyr had become something of a friend to me, and it was a relief to have him while I waited and an added source of dread when the older dragon eyed him like a meal to be chewed up and spat out. A clawing sense of dread worked its way up my chest with every moment Tempe was gone, tightening sharply the longer she stayed away.

"Cathy Jo?" Maple asked. Our group shifted and the older woman joined our small group. She was about seventy, maybe eighty, and had a small bit of magic, but not that of a witch. The two hugged, Damien giving his mate just enough of herself back to converse. "How's your stained-glass business?"

"It's amazing! You should come see it!" She tugged on her hand, but Maple turned back to Damien, seeking permission.

"Yeh should both go." I gestured toward the front door. "See the town, grab a cup. The winery will be here."

Damien's eyes alighted on the note in my hand and I quickly stuck it in my pocket.

It wasn't the best idea to set them out in the world, but it was a worse idea to have Damien here. Every second I shared with him, I could feel myself getting weaker, the winery losing magic, and a growing sense of rage for what her grandmother endured. Hopefully Tempe wasn't in town, wasn't where he could get to her. Tempe was my only concern. The town could fend for itself.

Rogue stood beside me, lending me his calm to not shift completely and attack the man. Maple, Tempe's only family, would feel any pain I gifted the arsehole who ruined our lives. Hunting him would not solve our problems, it would only hurt Tempe in the end.

As their figures retreated, I opened the note clutched in my fist:

We have verified your suspicions, but it is not a new player. You must end his life this time, now that he's mated there can be no more warnings.
Send proof when it's done.

THE AIR LEFT my lungs and I sat heavily on a stool.

The only way to kill him was to kill Maple. He was already killing her soul. He'd reduced her to a magical battery, and somehow used her to take back a power bound by the tribunal. He shouldn't be able to leech, but he was doing it and using her magic to expand, to turn objects into sponges that only he could wring.

"Feck... how?" I scrubbed my hands over my face.

The questions raced around my mind while Samuel danced between the tables and the clock counted the seconds Tempe was gone, ticking away on the wall. It had been too long, too long since I'd seen her. "Samuel, I'm going to go find—"

The door blew open, slamming against the wall behind it.

Tempe burst into the room, the wind raging around her despite the still trees outside. Samuel's eyes flashed alarm, then settled on me with an apologetic look. Carefully setting down the tasting bottle, he let out a long, loud whistle, stomping his hooves. A shelf of glasses rattled, quaking in place before crashing to the ground. The ground beneath us quivered and patrons stood in alarm.

"Sorry everyone, I think we'll need to close and investigate the pipes. Please enjoy the tastings you've had and visit again soon." Samuel's voice carried around the room, infusing charm and lust to urge them further, while wide eyes and an elevated pulse betrayed his panic.

"Mate scares him?"

People gathered their things, moving past *mo doineann* without seeing her.

Tempe stalked toward me, predatory and seductive, a huntress come for her kill. Once she was within range, her hand gripped my throat, closing in around my airway and pressing in against it. Magic pounded against the bar, rocking the glass bottles in a symphony of sound, but it caressed my skin as gently as when she stroked my most intimate parts.

"Am I to understand you're angry, love?"

Instead of battering me, shoving me around as she intended, the magic tickled my flesh. Her maroon sparkle danced with my burgundy dragon, their path taking them around the room in a beautiful symphony of colors. Our twinning flames finally together as they should be, her confession earlier was the second to last barrier to our joining.

The sight gave me an erection that was now pressing into her abdomen. While the magic was sucked into the walls, feeding Damien's plot.

"Why aren't you bleeding? You should be in agony!" Her rage took on a needy edge, the shift imperceptible to anyone who didn't know her. "You deserve to suffer for lying!"

"I do. But if you're attempting to strangle love, you're going to need to press harder." I leaned into her palm, taking my own oxygen against her hand. The rasp had nothing to do with the pressure on my throat. If she kept choking me with her curves pressed against my dick, I was going to come in my pants, rip hers off and then come again all over her ass after destroying her pussy.

I could smell her red, violent anger, but her eyes watered and the tremble in her hands disagreed. My love was hurting, but she seemed inclined to only accept violence.

"You betrayed me! You're helping him, you're his family, and then pretended you loved me so I wouldn't find out that only red dragons of his lineage are left! That only red dragons are leeches! You fucking monster!" Her violence simmered, lust pushing against it. Violence and sex too similar for her to fight the bond with my dragon already partly inside of her.

"I'm not a leech! I'm no kin to him! Are you going to make me pay for crimes long past?" I leaned into her hand, feeling the rush of losing air. My thigh went between her legs, and she ground against me, unaware. My Tempe could not admit that she needed my connection, but her body knew. Knew that she craved me to steal whatever pain had been revealed to her. "But before you slay the abomination, let's make one fucking thing clear, I've never betrayed you and I've never lied to you. I love you. All of you, so whatever you've learned that upsets you, if yeh can't use your words, yeh'll have to accept mine."

"Liar! You... You helped him. You said this was his price! Why else would you be here, if not to distract me, to soak up all the magic in the building so he could harvest it? You could harvest it for him with your red dragon leech magic? You say you don't have it, but how else can you explain the spell? My gran is split into pieces and yet her magic is fueling this enchantment. If not with your help, how is he doing it?" Tears sprang to her eyes and something in my chest cracked. "You can only exist if you're part of his clan."

"I've helped no one but you, *mo doineann*." I took hold of her wrist and pulled it tighter against me, my other hand snaking around her waist to pull her tighter. "You are the only one I answer to. The only one I love. All I want is you. He's using her magic to power his talent, one I thought he lost."

"Tell me why he's here! If you're not doing his bidding, why haven't you left?"

"Because I love you, Tempe. I told yeh I loved yeh and I wasn't lying. The universe chose you as the mate for my dragon and I chose you as the woman I love. The fucker is here for the money and the power." I felt him pull at my dragon in my memory, felt him pulling energy from Maple until she collapsed. "He needs magic, but the war tribunal took his. He's using me to keep access here, and I think... I think he wants my dragon but after we stopped feeding the magic into the building, he needs to take it."

"What?" She pulled back, but I wouldn't let her go. Pressed against me, she was where she was meant to be, and I couldn't allow her to leave. Couldn't risk her getting hurt and leaving me. "Why does he want your dragon? It's part of you, he can't take it!"

"He may be able to... when I was separated, I think it became possible. At least before I opened the mate bond. But my dragon belongs to you, Tempe. He will only answer to you. Do you choose us back?"

Her anger ratcheted back up, heat and fury on my behalf. My woman was prepared to fight, but Damien wasn't here. "Where is he? I'll kick his ass."

"I sent him an' yer Gran into town with one of her friends." Heat flicked out at me, and I wanted to grasp it, pull more out of her until we could consume the passion that raged within. "Do you choose us back?"

"You sent them out there? What if they hurt someone? He's draining the life out of this place!"

"Aye, and that's why I sent him away. So he couldn't hurt yeh. So he couldn't drain the life out of you, love. Now answer me, do you choose us back?"

"What about everyone else?" She shoved at me, but I wouldn't let her go.

"I don't care about everyone else. I care about you." I bit the shell of her ear. "Only you, Tempe. You are my concern, my priority, my mate. I knew you'd be back here, the beasts are here, fuck everyone else. Do you choose us?"

Her breaths grew ragged, her control cracking under waves of desire. "But..."

"But what?" I stroked my hand up her ribs, down the side of her thigh. My dragon paced in my head, his teeth overtaking mine as I fought for control. Fought her for permission to love her. "Are yeh saying you'd sacrifice us for everyone else? You don't choose us?"

"No but..." She trembled... scared for us, for the town. Terrified of a past come back to haunt her.

"But nothing, Tempe. You are mine to love and protect and I will not lose you!" My hand locked around the back of her neck keeping her face close to mine.

"I don't belong to anyone." She panted into my ear, and I smirked.

"No?" Flames licked the edges of my vision, and I stopped fighting my dragon. For once, I was letting him have control instead of fighting. It was time she understood how much I've held back for her comfort. My hand around her waist drifted lower to cup her heat from behind, working her back up. "Secure it."

"What?" She squirmed and pressed against me, my fingers stroking her through her leggings.

"Lock down all the entrances." I took my hand back and stepped away, unwrapping her arm from my neck until I leaned against the opposing side of the bar. I felt her magic lock down the building as she watched me, her chest rising and falling. "Clean up the glass. For the beasts."

I heard it rattle into the trash can. Her hands clenched and unclenched at her sides, fighting the urge to touch me, to give in and admit she was ours.

"Good girl."

Tempe whimpered, and I wrapped my hand around her throat. I dragged her forward, lips pressing against hers in a bruising kiss. Rough, violent, she bit me and tried to shove me away, but my palm stretched from her throat to the back of her neck and held her lips to mine.

"So you don't belong to me?" I growled against her mouth, scraping my teeth on her lip without mercy. Spinning her around, I bent her over the bar, shoving her ass in the air. "You aren't wet and craving my cock again? You don't choose to be with us over all else?"

"It's just lust." Her voice cracked, and I smirked at her face pressed into the bar.

"Are you certain?" My hands were in her leggings, pulling them down to her ankles and bringing my mouth to her dripping core. The beautiful pink ridges were coated in need, and I buried my nose against her before taking a long swipe with my tongue from her clit to her ass.

Then again. She quivered beneath me, shaking with anticipation.

"No." I pulled back and slapped her ass. The flesh rippled and turned bright red. "No, you don't get to come until I hear you say it, *mo doineann*. Until you understand how fucking difficult it has been with you here every day, trying not to take away your choices as everyone else has. How hard I've fought to support you and not force fate while you fought your desire. Fought against love at every turn."

I slid one finger in and stroked her, feeling her clench around me. Wanting more, but she wouldn't get it.

"I'm here because I was promised answers to my curse for fulfillment of a blood oath. But I stopped caring once I brought you back to life, because *you* are my life. I love that my dragon goes to you. I love that he can support you when I cannot and I don't want to take that back."

Dropping back down, I crouched between her legs and twisted to lick her clit without breaking the rhythm of my single finger. Sucking the sensitive bud into my mouth, her taste flooded my mouth, and I popped off while dragging my teeth against her.

"No coming!" I snapped, taking it out on her other ass cheek. "You were fucking everything I dreamed up for seventy-five fucking years alone on an island. This pussy, this ass, your kindness, the way you light up sharing weird facts and the hope you once had, even when the light had gone clean out of you. But still, I held back. Let you take the lead. I cannot hold back anymore."

My slick finger slid easily out of her, and I flipped her over, tearing the center of her leggings to stand between her legs. Brown eyes wild, hair going in all directions, she looked out of control and desperate, a mirror of my own inner turmoil while I pretended to be in control.

"Putting that light back in your life has been my sole purpose for months, even as I failed miserably to make a dent in the shadows. Because you refused to stop holding back from me."

Her hand reached for my trousers, and I slapped it.

"Yeh said you loved me, then you come in here and attack me. Is that love to you?" I stroked two fingers into her slick heat and then slid them into her mouth, forcing her to taste. Forcing her to understand that this was what we did to each other. "Is it love to get upset and start yelling without talking?"

A beautiful insanity.

"Do you taste how bad yeh want me, Tempe? Do you understand what control I've exercised?"

Her eyes slid half closed, tongue and lips working over my fingers with dedication. The sensation belonged somewhere much lower, and I pulled my fingers out of her mouth to slam back into her pussy. Desperate for more space, I opened the snap of my cargos and watched her greedy eyes stare with anticipation.

"Yeh know yeh want this cock, again, love." I shoved my pants and boxer briefs down, letting my cock spring free and hang heavily between us. A mewling sound escaped her mouth, practically begging for a taste

"Please?" she begged, and I could not deny her. I could not deny her anything.

Angling around the counter, I let her mouth wrap around my head and suckle once before I pulled away. Walls clenching, I could tell she was close, and I pulled out of her again. Licking my fingers clean this time, I saw in her eyes how badly she wanted this. How badly she needed this angry, rough encounter to let out her hurt.

She needed to feel everything at once and the look in her eyes said I was her safe place. An irritated scream came out of her lips.

"How do you feel, love? Desperate? Helpless? Empty?"

Nodding, she licked her lips.

"That is how you've made me feel since I saw you, frozen as a rose quartz statue amid the vines. If you need to feel pain, anger, pleasure, heat, you ask me. Do yeh understand? I will be this space for you, but you cannot beat it out of me."

She nodded again and her eyes shined with tears. "Please?"

It wasn't just a plea for relief, it was a desperate desire for love. To not get left behind again. She wanted to belong somewhere.

"Your magic knows you're home, love. Look at it. Look at dancing with my dragon. It's always known we'd be here for you." I grabbed her chin and turned it to our magic, her eyes widening as they moved together.

Her magic tugged me closer, her lips sliding around my cock again. I let her get the whole shaft past her lips, bottoming out to the feeling of her throat clenching around the base. My fingers, still slick with her arousal, slid lower, and I pushed against her anal ring, pressing a finger past it while she moaned around me. I pumped into her mouth, adding another finger to her ass.

She needed to feel out of control and I needed to feel all of her around me at once. We needed to claim every intimate part of her. She was my everything, my lifeline. I pulled out of her mouth and stilled my hand, listening to her pant, fighting her magic that tried to bring me back to her.

"Say it."

"Mine." She panted.

"Say it." I slid myself past her lips again and pulled out.

"Yours. I'm yours."

I rammed myself past her lips, my fingers fucking her ass while she gasped at the fullness. I pulled out again.

"Last chance, mate. Do you choose us?" Tears threatened to spill out of my eyes, looking down on my perfect wild mate. I couldn't live without her, but I couldn't force a life on her she did not choose.

"Yes." She gasped. Magic swirled around us, pulling us together tighter. "I choose you."

I slid back inside her, relief flooding my chest at last.

"Do you like that? Are you a good girl who likes to be fucked in the ass while sucking cock?" Her eyes rolled back, and I knew I wouldn't last. A tingle built in the base of my spine, my balls tightened, and just as I felt her coming, I pressed my thumb against her clit and rubbed until she crashed around me. Her orgasm crested as my cum shot down her throat in endless rivulets.

"That's right, mate. Drink my cum, every fucking drop, is yours. Forever. I promise."

CHAPTER

THIRTY-ONE

TEMPE

Drax tried to step away, but I fisted his shirt and dragged him down to me.

"We are not done."

His taste still coating my tongue, I devoured his mouth. Forcing him to taste himself back while I craved more. Instead of shying away, being repulsed by the same action in reverse, he embraced it. There was no halfway, no double standard. What one of us did, we both did, and there would be nothing we hadn't done by the end of the night.

Drawing away, I looked him in the eyes, seeing hesitation and concern.

"I was a good girl. And I believe good girls get cock. Give me my cock. If this ass and pussy are yours, then that cock is mine and I demand you give it to me."

My demand sparked him back to life, lips attacking mine without mercy while my body left the bar, legs wrapped around his waist as we descended into his cave. Relishing the feeling of the zipper of his pants digging into my legs, his quickly hardening cock rubbing against my ass, and I needed all of it.

I needed the punishing pleasure. Needed to feel the pain and the love, to process the grief and the loss in intimacy without

284

words. Wherever the danger lurked, this moment was ours and I was holding it with both hands.

I deserved love, deserved this, and he was fucking mine.

My back slammed into the cave wall, and his mouth left mine. Gold and green eyes flickered back at me, both halves of his whole fighting to claim me. Heavy with lust, I ground my core against him while he held me against the wall.

"You think you're a good girl who gets cock?"

"Yes. Now. I need you, now." I slid up and down against him, my hand fisting in the back of his shirt to pull it off over his head. When his arms got in the way I used the same enchantment that let it shift with him to pull it off around him.

"So demanding. If I refuse?"

"Then I'll tie you to the bed and impale myself on your dick until I come all over it and leave you lying there, wanting. Don't fuck with me, Fireball." I spat the words at him. If he'd flinched, been alarmed, I'd have taken it back, but his hips thrust against me. His cock sliding against my clit. "This dick is mine, remember?"

He rubbed himself against me.

"Tempe, if I start... there may be no stopping." He tore my shirt down the center. Lifting a nipple to his lips, he sucked it between his teeth and tugged until I cried out. "I may mark you."

Despite his objections, his body refused to challenge my words. It knew what I wanted even as he tried to remain in control. I needed him to lose control of himself... and take control of me.

"Then do it," I pleaded, letting my hands thread through his hair. "Give me the rest of you. Because you have all of me. Take control. Do your job."

His Adam's apple bobbed as he swallowed hard.

I kissed him hard and dragged his lip away with my teeth. Before I could finish, he had me on my hands and knees on his bed. Removing the scraps of my shirt, he carefully removed my shoes to toss the scraps of my leggings and underwear. His boots and pants disappeared in the next moment, laid bare for me to enjoy before I was pressed back into the bed.

"I'm going to destroy your wardrobe, shiorghra." Taking hold of my ponytail, he wrapped it around his palm and pulled my neck backward, his other hand pressed between my shoulder blade to keep me bent before him. "And I'm going to fekkin wreck you, so that no one before me will ever exist in your mind as there will be no one after. I will fuck every thought out of your head except how many orgasms I can give you."

In one smooth motion, his thick cock slammed into me from behind. Despite having it in my mouth and the work he'd done with his fingers, it was almost too much. Pulling all the way back out, he slammed into me again, forcing me to cry out as he held on to my hair.

"You like that?" He asked, doing it again. When I could only moan, he brought his hand down hard across my ass. "Use your words, Tempe."

"Yes."

He brought his hand down on the other side, jerking my head back to give him access to my clit on the front while his lips traced my ear. Tugging the shell, his breath tickled my flesh and sent chills running down my skin, adding to the pleasure.

"Yes, what?"

Drawing out until only the tip remained, his body collided into mine. The rough slam sent a jolt of pleasure up my spine, through my core and shuddered into my nipples. I wanted him in both of my holes, filling me, invading all of me until I couldn't breathe without feeling him inside me.

Couldn't exist without feeling his love.

"Yes, I love your cock slamming into me."

Drax did it again, pinching my clit and forcing a shudder from my lips. He stilled his cock inside of me, refusing to move even as I throbbed around him, needing more. He slid out, flipping me over to look him in the eye while he teased my opening.

"Please, Draigus. I need you inside me."

He slid into me again, tugging us chest to chest as I bounced on his cock, and he thrust into me.

"I want to hear you scream to the world while you ride my cock. Tell them who makes you feel this good, tell them what you want buried inside of you, *mo doineann*. Whose job is it to wring every drop of cum and control from this body?"

"Only yours, Draigus... Drax. Only you, forever."

"Good girl." Drax captured my mouth in a burning kiss that set fire to my lips, radiating outward until my body was an inferno. A gathering need built in me; I wanted him everywhere. Inside me, around me. Part of me.

I released his lips, feeling him trail kisses down my neck.

"Mark me. Tell everyone who I love." I clenched around his cock, chasing the building orgasm. His mouth lowered to the juncture of my neck, hand sliding between us to give me just a little more stimulation. With a tilt the opposite way, I gave him permission to sink his teeth into me, release crashing into me with the binding of us together. Another built immediately on its heels, his mouth sealing the wound, and I exploded again.

Dragon dancing around inside of my veins, I felt a new pleasure clambering higher. The dragon was investigating every inch of my heart and mind, caressing me from the inside out until a third orgasm hit, and I gushed all over the sheets, his thighs, and the cock I would ride until I died.

Blood rushed to my head, my mind blacking out and little bursts of light exploding on the edge of my vision as I felt his release shoot into me. Breathing heavily, we collapsed backward onto the bed, tangled together, exhausted, but our bodies breathing together as one.

"Drax?" I asked, my voice hoarse and raw.

"Aye, my love?"

"Was I supposed to bite you back?" Laughing, he squeezed me even tighter as he withdrew from my opening. Immediately, I felt his loss and reached to put him back, but he took my hand and kissed the inside of my palm. Draping me across his chest, he pulled a soft fleece blanket over both of us, and I felt two dips in the mattress as our furry army joined us. Stroking my hair down my back, he pressed a kiss to my temple and another to the new mark he'd left on my skin.

"Next time, *anam cara*."

He stroked my hair, bringing me back down. Sunlight streaming in, the first bright point in the day.

I looked at Drax, his face contorted, body too stiff for what we'd just done. "What's wrong?"

Head shaking, he tried to pull back, but I gripped his jaw, pulling him to me. The muscles beneath his skin trembled and the bed grew cold. His raging heat was replaced with a bone deep chill and the sun outside went out. The magic that pulsed through the walls above us slithered away and absolute silence descended. "Drax?"

His face cracked a fraction, and a sharp pain burned through me. The dragon cowered in the corner, my magic a shield, protecting him from the broken glass shredding us from the inside out. I let out a scream.

"Come out here, boy-o!" Damien's voice bounced around the cave, my scream dying under his deep baritone. "If yeh don't, you'll both suffer. You know what I want and thanks to that little show your girly put on, I have the power to take it."

"Don't go." I gripped his arm, but he was already standing. Pulling on pants, a shirt, and boots. "Why the hell are you getting dressed? He'll kill you!" Another wave of agony crashed against both of us, and I bit back a sob while he breathed through the pain.

"He can only kill me if he kills you. As long as you're safe, I'll endure." With immense effort, he slid the wall into place, shielding me from the pain. "I have to go or he'll keep hurting you."

"He'll keep hurting us both either way! You can't! You can't go out there and fight him. I can't lose you." I gripped his shirt, pleading. "We could run and hide… and start a new life. I'll leave all of this and protect you."

Drax pressed a kiss to my lips. "There's nowhere I can hide from him, love. I'm bound by blood until this is fulfilled. You won't lose me. I simply have to survive longer than he does."

"What if you don't?" He set me aside and I shouted. "What if you don't?"

He swallowed and shook his head. "I will, *anam cara*. The question is if you'll still love me after what must be done."

"What must be done, Drax?"

Petting Rogue and Corky, he stiffened his spine and strode out into the premature darkness. "Drax! You noble fucking bastard!"

I shoved myself up, wiping tears off my face. I would not sit idly by while someone else fought for our future. Sub arctic concrete bit my feet, reminding me I was naked and partially frozen in the most outdoor location one could be without being outside.

"Crap!" The sharp sting of cold burned through my skin. I jumped back on the bed, thinking the warmest clothes, socks, and boots I owned onto my body from upstairs. Instead of the usual pinch of energy, it felt like a melon baller had scooped half of my power out for a single request. I sagged against the bed, feeling the weight of my emotions, of the sex, of being marked, and behind it all, a large power source just outside. It was growing stronger, sucking the life out of everything it touched, and my own magic wilted further against the assault. The flavor was familiar, familial, and inside my head, Drax's dragon still partially hid but echoes of agony traveled down the line.

My mate was being tortured. "Fucker."

Corky and Rogue started to stand, but I waved them back down, hand shaking to the same beat as my racing heart. The cave dropped another five degrees, and both animals started to shake for a different reason.

"Shit!" My teeth chattered and I wrapped them in every

blanket on the bed and every one from under the bed while my feet wanted to run to Drax; wanted to run upstairs and hide. I placed a kiss on both their heads and turned on the heater full blast beside them. My heart wanted to run to him, my mind wanted to stay with these kids. I paced for a second needing something to do while I figured out what to do, and I felt the shield spell tremor. I paused, staring at the cave opening, while my magic was slowly sucked out of the barrier. The only protection I had to offer the two animals in my care was gone.

Without it, there was nothing left to do but fight.

"That fucker! I'll be back." Bundled up, I stepped out of the cave and encountered a burst of wind that stole my breath. No definition of *cold* I'd experienced could compare, the snow on the ground had turned into solid sheets of ice beneath my feet as I was pulled closer and closer to the source of the power vacuum.

Life had ceased around me. While I could normally feel the trees, the forest, the animals moving around on the rim, even the vines had gone quiet. Everything was holed up in survival mode.

How cold is it? Cold enough to kill the plants?

I stared at the grapes. How long could they survive like this? Valleys didn't get this cold... Anything below 15 Fahrenheit would destroy the plants... permanently.

My feet stopped, a glowing orb above the grapes dragging in the night and cooling the air. It stole the heat, the life, and...

"Drax?" I whispered, running to the slumped figure at its base. My feet slipped on the ice, sending me skidding and careening, but I kept going as fast as I could. The closer I got, the better my view. One figure became two. Two figures became two kneeling and one standing between them, his entire focus on the glowing ball above him, was Damien.

Snow crunching beneath my boots roused Drax first, his eyes wide as he mouthed at me to run, but no sound came out. Beside him, my gran's catatonic form was lifeless, but I could still sense her heartbeat.

Get out of here, Drax spoke in my mind, and I felt his dragon moving through me. Alarmed, I lost my footing. A patch of ice hit perfectly beneath my heel, and I went down. Sliding on my back like a member of the luge, I glided forward to rest at Damien's feet.

His inhuman eyes glinting in the moonlight, he smirked with fanged teeth.

"Just in time. You brought me my dragon. Perhaps yeh'll serve as a replacement battery as well, the older generation is losing its luster."

CHAPTER

THIRTY-TWO

TEMPE

ICK CRAWLED UP AND DOWN MY SPINE. THE DRAGON IN my mind slammed against the walls to be let out, to fight for my safety and Drax, but he was trapped. My form didn't shift and Drax... I looked at my mate, forced to kneel beside the man with his shoulders squared, hands bound behind his back. Pain flashed across his face, the screams he kept to himself, written in the lines of his body.

The picture of grace under fire as blood seeped from a slice along his shirt.

Gran was on her side, no longer able to keep herself upright. A pale red flowed out of her and into Damien as he stood beneath the golden ball. Glimmers of the woman from earlier flashed in her eyes, back and forth, the woman and the puppet warring to send a message.

"Nothing to say, young one? Perhaps you approve of the idea?" A slimy smile slithered across his face, flames dancing on the edge of my vision. Drax's dragon warmed me from the inside out, lending me his strength and his fury, but I held it back, kept it in. "Or perhaps you think this fool will save you?"

A leather clad shoe connected with Drax, his abdomen taking the hit in a solid blow that rattled my bones but did little to the static figure. My dragon simply continued to kneel, his head hung to stare at the ground.

Why doesn't he fight? I asked the dragon, uncertain if it could hear me.

Because we cannot love, this is part of our debt. Blood and honor bound to obey until the terms of the oath are fulfilled.

Defeat wafted off of him, both from his dragon within me and the man trapped on the ground beside a monster. One who'd tricked him out of his youth and saw to it he spent a hundred years afraid of himself. Anger turned to rage, and liquid fire dripped from my fingers. Wrapping all the magic around me in a tight coil, it built and built until, with a final crescendo, I let it burst from my hands.

Deep burgundy flames shot out, obscuring Damien. His agonizing scream was joined by my grandmother's, and I pulled back, the old woman writhing on the ground with tears in her eyes. Her skin reflected in the moonlight, second-degree burns marring her skin and weeping openly.

"That's right, girly." Contempt twisted his face, victory lighting his eyes. I ran toward my gran, only to collide with a solid mass of energy. Feet slipping on the ice, I skidded backward, landing on my ass several feet away. "I own her! Yeh cannot touch her, cannot save her, and cannot kill me without taking her with."

Drax lashed out from where he was held down, and I watched the force that bound him. There was a note of basil and ethylene glycol coating the back of my tongue, a memory from when I was little and learning to master the craft with gran in rare moments she tolerated me.

Is he holding you with her magic? Drax nodded against the binding, hearing the question I asked his dragon within me. On the ground, gran's eyes fluttered open, the night growing colder while she continued to lie burned and desperate on the ice. Life was draining out of the vines, out of the woods. Unchecked, his frost could destroy the entire hollow and every mortal in the region.

"What do you want?" I rasped, rising from the ground. Gran was family, my family, and I had read her grimoire from cover to cover. A small footnote mentioned familial magic. Gran had been trying to find a way to share hers with my mom, to give her a spark so that she could go to school in the hollow where she thought it would be safer.

"This land, lass. Are you daft? It's worth millions to developers. With that kind of money, I could buy an army. Start another uprising, buy an idiot bureaucrat and pass orders to expand my power until I own this country. Money can buy yeh everything in America. Everything but morality and intelligence, which the majority haven't, anyway. Every fortune I've earned has been captured. Your mother was almost incapacitated, her share almost ours to sell, until she took her life to pass it on to you."

My gut lurched while my mind fought to stay afloat, I needed to remember what the book said. I had already figured out he wanted money. This wasn't new information. I knew my mother's addiction was not her fault alone, and suspected her death wasn't an accident...

"Bitch laced her booze with poison, screaming how I'd never have her father's land. She didn't know I had ways of manipulating an unlovable, fat witch with a brain disease. That I had a century old dragon in my pocket who was just as lonely, just as desperate. And now he's mated with you." Damien twisted his clawed fist, and I felt a sharp, piercing spear sluice through me. "Tell me, lass, did you feel that? You will feel every bit of pain I inflict on him until one of you gives in and gives me my dragon! I didn't sire this useless sack of flesh not to benefit from him! Getting that witch to split them was child's play, but weakening him to take the dragon has been decades of effort."

Thoughts froze in my brain.

"Sire? Sired him?" I shouted while Drax looked on helplessly from the ground. There was no resemblance between his kind moss eyes and strong honest heart and the man threatening to rip him apart. "You created a son to scrap him for parts?"

"Aye, lass. It was nay hard to take his mother to bed, but she wouldn't give him over." The orb glowed brighter and my chest trembled with silent convulsions. I needed to focus, to save Drax, but... would I... would we... have to kill his father?

My fingers tapped against my leg, fighting not to hear him, not to feel the pain, to just survive the next ten seconds. Then the ten after. Another wave of bone crushing agony whipped through me and I felt the dragon begin to rage, sliding back toward Drax.

"Don't do it." I warned him as I fought to hold both him and my magic inside.

Gran's findings had been that familial magic could not be transferred if there wasn't already a supernatural well to receive. Her study had been conducted with another witching family, one whose daughter had power, but not as much as she should. They'd gotten her into the school... My mom had no magic to speak of, and remained on the outside. A fact that was used to bully her when Damien came along.

Damien, who'd learned first-hand from the Reich what our current regime was attempting to replicate. All men like him were the same—arrogant narcissists who believed that they deserved more and better than everyone. Including a son to steal the essence of to strengthen himself.

While he orated his genius—shit talking to me–trying to turn me against Drax, I zeroed in on the metallic coil wrapped around his ball, grasping at the thread. A tenuous twine that wound around Drax, looping through Damien, and sapping the life out of Maple. Slowly, I unraveled it, absorbing the power. Taking what belonged to my family and returning it to us, generations of knowledge and wisdom filling my chest. But more than knowledge, with her magic came memories. Stories and flashes from a life I never got to see.

Gran watched my mom and grandfather in the field, planting and playing with worms. Sat at the kitchen table, gran teaching Liv to balance an equation in sixth grade science. Stolen moments of love and light between my grandmother, my mother, and my grandfather. Beauty and affection that transcended everything else, until Grandpa Jake died.

Everything swathed in black. Tears and midnight ice cream. A stranger with sharp eyes and then watching her family from the outside. Gran had loved my mom with her whole heart, and tears burned my eyes. The knowledge of a woman gone before I met her was almost as painful as the loss of the one I'd had.

Her whole life with Damien, everything he did, she'd been trapped behind an invisible wall. Watching and unable to help. Maple had watched him bully her daughter into running, the rock musician who was my father, a victim of her misused magic that my mom had not wanted. It wasn't love, or lust, it was assault. But she loved me anyway, though she couldn't let Damien find out. The fear in my mom's eyes when she looked at me, while Maple tried so hard to protect her with hands tied behind her back. There was safety in indifference, and when that failed, she took her life.

My mom died for me... and now I'd have to kill for her.

This man had ripped apart families for centuries... but ours would be the last one. I could only hope that Drax would forgive me for killing his father.

Just before the spool of magic emptied, resistance jostled the line. A small jolt that shut up the diatribe emanating from the man before me and cut off the stream of memories. Tears frozen on my cheeks, I searched for the line.

"What are yeh doing?" Damien pulled back, his own murky shadow swallowing the navy shimmer. As it got eaten up like Pacman dots, Drax slipped through the barrier. It was enough to free him, but I was losing my grip on the line.

"Yeh think you can take power from me?" The navy line turned maroon, and my energy dwindled. Inch by inch, he was sucking the magic from me, from gran, and I threw up a wall to keep him from taking Drax's magic. From absorbing his dragon and becoming whole. Beside him, gran's form fell free of her cage, as I took up the job of feeding his crimes. "I'm a leech, lass. Even as a dragon, I could absorb magic, absorb power. You cannot fight me. I will win! And once the dragon I bred to replace my own is mine, I will be unstoppable."

With one last look toward my dragon, I saw him rise beside the older man. Steady on his feet, fingers elongated into claws, he took two menacing steps forward and I sent fire down the line.

"Fuck!" the old man screamed, his hands singed in scalding blisters, while my gran shuddered in pain but made no sound. Very little life emanated from her and I tried to figure out how to unbind them. "Yeh bitch, I will..."

Drax leapt forward and, with a flash of his claws, tore a chunk of flesh out of the man's face. Above us, the golden ice orb continued to drain life from everything it touched, my own magic getting pulled from my chest even as Damien pulled from his end.

"Tempe", gran's voice in my mind was weak. It floated on blue clouds of carbide that dissipated quickly. *"Tempe, help me stop him."*

I looked over at gran, the real Maple looking back at me. Love, regret, and pain carved into the lines of her face, a masterpiece no artist could recreate. Her body wasn't moving, only her eyes held life, and it was fading. Already, her legs were showing signs of frostbite and her hands no longer moved.

"He can keep me alive as a battery forever. Please, we must end this."

Drax released his wings, dragging Damien into the sky while he attacked both the magic and the man. With every blow he landed, Maple's body shuddered, but she no longer tried to fight the pain. A steely acceptance filled her grey eyes, she embraced the pain as her punishment for all she could not control.

"How do I stop the spell? How do I unbind you?" I stood up and pulled my magic to me, gripping at the threads of energy that withered away. Even as I gathered power, it quickly was sucked away into the golden orb above us. The spell had evolved, pulling in both life and magic. Whatever needed to be done, had to be done without supernatural power.

"You can't, but I can." She showed me an image, a glass bottle that was similar in size to a port. It was short and blue, a copper stopper in the end. *"I need this bottle. It is in the cabinet above the stove. You've probably tried to move it, but it will still be in the cabinet above the stove."*

I'd seen the bottle. So many times, I'd been tempted to toss it, or had moved it only to find I'd put it right back where it was. Started to investigate the contents but always got distracted. Always found something more important or interesting to focus on... which now appeared to have been on purpose.

Damien fell to the ground two feet away from me, his body creating a loud thud that reverberated across the ice. Pulling the bottle forward in my mind, I channeled my magic... and felt it get sucked away into the ball above us. It had been a longshot, but my hopes for ending this quickly disappeared on a freezing wind that carried frost across the ice.

"Fuck." I turned back to the winery, eyes watering in the wind and cold. Even in ideal weather, it was far. With a promise to Drax and Maple that I would be back, I said a prayer to the goddess and started running.

CHAPTER

THIRTY-THREE

TEMPE

T HE CAVE ENTRANCE WASN'T PROTECTED BY MAGIC. MY barrier was sucked away and swallowed by the orb, and I made a plea to the goddess that nothing dangerous had found its way inside. Breathing heavily, I walked through as fast as I could, waiting for the cat and dog to join me. Even with Drax's bed, I stumbled, eyes caught on the lump with four furry ears.

Corky and Rogue were still, their energy levels even lower than when I left, despite the blanket and space heater to keep them warm. I stroked a furry head with no response, the soft heartbeat barely thrumming beneath the surface, losing enthusiasm with each beat.

"Fuck, no!" I whispered, running again. In the barrel room, I stumbled up the steep wooden steps, stopping for a kitchen knife as I burst into the tasting room and made a hard right to the staircase at the rear.

"He's stealing the life of our animals." I cried, not sure who I wanted to hear me. I stumbled up yet another staircase, the knife in my hands scraping against the wall. When I reached the landing, I stared at the new lock that opened without magic. "Where's the key?"

I ran back downstairs, a sharp pain cracking through my ribs, and a large body slammed to the ground outside. *"Drax?"*

"Just a scratch."

He was full of shit, but I didn't have the energy to fight him. I shoved the tip jar off of the counter, pennies and nickels hitting the ground—no key. I pulled open the register drawer, checking under receipts and the till bag.

"Where the hell is the key to my apartment?"

"Floor." His grunt came with a sharp pain in my shin, and I cried out. I dropped to my hands and knees, crawling along the counter until I found it with a few leftover scraps of clothing. Clutched between two fingers, I carried the key up the staircase. After two tries, I finally got it into the deadbolt, turning the lock. With another breath, I felt for Rogue and Corky.

Not good. They were running out of time. I swiped the tears from my face, running into the kitchen, I climbed up onto the counter to reach the topmost shelf. I threw bags of pasta and packets of seasoning on the floor, searching until I found the blue bottle behind the box of white rice next to the coffee.

As soon as my hand grasped it, a gnawing sense of wrong clawed through my gut.

"Maple needs you." I whispered to the bottle, carefully tucking it into the inside pocket of my jacket. Whatever was inside needed to make it there, across a quarter mile of ice, with me falling and shattering the container. My energy lagged, the over-whelming feeling of dread and loss pummeling me. "Goddess, grant me strength."

On a deep breath, I walked down the stairs, scared to run and more scared of falling. Exiting through the front door, I ran to the carport and pulled out the keys to my motorcycle. Firing up the engine, I climbed on and skidded down the drive, revving the engine loudly to cut through the growing silence of death surrounding the winery.

Ice tried to mis-align my tire, but I kept the bike under me as the ground shifted from pavement to dirt. Every brain cell I possessed was reassigned to keeping my fast twitch muscles operating the bike, anticipating and observing dangers and reacting. So long as I stayed in the moment, one step ahead of breaking every bone in my body, I couldn't think about anything else.

If I couldn't hear the thoughts, no one was going to die.

I raced up the vines, using the floating ball of magic as my guide. What was originally beach-ball sized now appeared as big as a hot-air balloon, growing brighter by the heartbeat. My energy was being pulled into it, along with everything else, and I twisted the throttle.

Faster, harder, no holding back for tomorrow. If I failed, there would be no tomorrow... for anyone.

My eyes turned to the fight. Damien had stolen part of Drax's dragon form. He was down to one wing and claws. Though he could remain aloft, he lost the agility needed to fight. Instead, he was focused on the ball, every attempt to find a weakness met with a clawed revenge from the older man.

Distracted, I missed the telltale shadow, a rut the same size as a wine barrel, and my front tire pitched into it. Flying through the air, I turned around, hugging the bottle to me and tucking my chin to protect my neck.

A sickening crack echoed through the night as my rounded spine landed on a patch of ice ten yards from where Maple lay.

"Tempe!" Drax screamed, his voice loud in my head and all around me. Air strangled in and out of my chest, but I could still breathe. I put up a wall around my pain, keeping it from him and from myself.

"I'm OK." I groaned and tried to sit up. But my core stopped working and the pain in my torso resisted. I shielded the sensation. *"Fuck."*

One long track of ice stood between me and my gran: the least friction surface imaginable. Spinning like a top, I pointed my head toward her, braced with my heels and shoved.

Every rib in my torso screamed at me that this was a shit idea, but my broken body served as a sled down a row of grapes. Under the ice were rocks, bumps, and ruts, each jostling what was six broken ribs, at least. Air came in constricted huffs, and I suspected a punctured lung. It hurt, but none of it hurt as much as knowing that if I failed, everyone from Corky and Rogue to the residents of the Hollow who had become like family would die.

Too many lives for something as inconsequential as pain. Pain is just suffering... or weakness... My thoughts jumbled, teeth chattering in the cold, and I knew I would lose consciousness soon.

Moments before colliding with Maple, I dug in my heel and whipped to the side. Her head was inches from mine, eyes closed, chest barely moving.

"Gran?" I breathed, sliding my hand out to her. Frozen fingers met, and she flinched. Blue eyes wild, she looked around in panic before settling on me.

"Tempe." She reached for my cheek and I slid toward her on the ice until I felt the gentle caress. "I'm so sorry. I was too weak to fight him at the time, marked with loss he took me as his mate but I was not his."

I swallowed the lump in my throat. Despite the cold, my heart was pounding in my chest, and it was too warm. I wanted to rip off my clothes, my skin, the fiery crawling sensation of ants running over my body.

"I know gran. I think he killed grandpa." The whisper was carried away across the ice. "I should have seen it sooner. I should have done something to break the bond between you. Maybe, once you're free, we can start again?" A tear froze on my cheek, and I pulled out the blue bottle.

"I think he did too, but once he was gone, there was nothing I could do to bring him back. I will always be proud of you, Tempe. I could not speak to you myself, but I watched you, and I was proud. You have done nothing but make this family proud." My throat closed, the sound trapped with emotions I couldn't name but had always wanted to feel. I passed her the blue bottle, only for her to shake her head.

"Open it and pour it down my throat."

I jerked away, crying out in pain at the sudden movement. "Why?"

"My hands." She held up two trembling palms. Above us, the fight continued while I tried to remove the stopper. Damien had taken another piece of Drax, his tail now attached to the other man, and I knew we were running out of time. If Damien got the full dragon, I wasn't sure we could stop him with the contents of a bottle. Twisting, tugging, the cork refused to come loose, my own hands too frozen to manage. "Take the ice, break the top."

Looking around, I found a frozen rock. Gripped in my palm, it burned my skin, and I gave it a hard whack against the neck. Blue glass scattered on the snow, and I stared at the milky white potion. The rainbow swirls in the surface reminded me of dish soap and chemical cleanser.

"What does it do?"

"In my throat, quickly." Her command echoed around in my head. The switch jarred me into action, but she leaned back, eyes closed, mouth open. Angling carefully, I put one edge to her lips and let it dribble in. Slowly at first, and then faster until there was nothing left. *"That's my girl. This will happen quickly, I'm so sorry."*

"Now what do we do?" I fought to sit up, but she placed her hand on my chest, holding me in place. Gran graced me with one last look, apology and peace in one. Eyes wide, a single tear streamed down her face and the bottom fell out.

"Now, my sweet Tempe, I die."

CHAPTER

THIRTY-FOUR

DRAX

MIDAIR WITH MY CLAWS AROUND DAMIEN'S NECK, I heard Tempe scream. Her body was hardly moving, but I felt her despair as thick as my own through our bond. Dropping the man, I watched him fall to the ground, his bones crushing under the weight of his fall. Flying to my mate, I went to lift her, but she just shook her head.

Crying, she reached for Maple, begging her to change her mind. My dragon came back to me in pieces, my wings and tail, and realization slammed into my chest.

Maple had sacrificed her life to end Damiens.

"No, please! You can't!" Tempe's tears froze in place on her face, but the air was warming. Above us, the spell was growing dim. "I just got you back."

"It's the only way, my love. I'm sorry we didn't get more time. So proud of you. Always proud of my girls." The older woman held her cheek. They lay side by side in the snow, but while Tempe grew stronger, the light in Maple was fading with the spell above her. "You are everything Liv wanted. She loved you so much. What he did... had us do... was far worse than this death will be. I hope you will forgive her, and me, for leaving you. We never wanted to leave you."

304

"You don't have to die." Tempe choked on her own agony, and I had no idea how to help. I couldn't hold her, couldn't save her gran. I was powerless to do more than stand here and watch her say goodbye to yet another family member.

"I do. He isn't my mate, Jake was the only one who ever could be..." She sucked in a breath, fighting to finish these last words. A blue bottle glimmered in the dying light; my dragon's nose worked to identify the poison... flashing to all the times we'd seen and moved it in Tempe's kitchen. This was her plan, her way to end this when the time came, but someone else had to give her the poison. "He bound us together, forced me to comply, to stay alive. To keep you girls alive, it was all I could do. I could not end my life, he made sure of that, and he could not die so long as I lived. Take care of her, Drax."

I nodded, my own tears stinging the corners of my eyes. "Always."

"I'll make an antidote... I'll... there's another way. Please?"

I stroked Tempe's hair, her voice breaking. I could feel her body was injured, my dragon refusing to let me move her. We would need doctors... eventually. My letter from the war tribunal sat folded in my pocket.

"Some men can only be stopped by death. They do not respect law, they do not respect life, only power. And death is the only thing that can stop them from seizing it. I only wanted to survive for you to have love..." She struggled to get out the words, but I felt the weight of her gaze. The responsibility being passed to me to care for the woman between us in place of an entire family stolen away by my own.

Ice crunched behind me, and I whipped around. Damien was limping toward us, vicious and snarling. A shard of glass in his hand, eyes on Tempe, to destroy her for stealing his self-proclaimed destiny. My mate held her grandmother, counting her heartbeats until the end.

"Damien." I rose and held up the letter. The dragon's fire ink glittering in the light, his first inklings of fear. "For your crimes against this family, this community, and violating the terms of your punishment, you have been sentenced to death." A flick of my wrist, and my dragon's claw was deep in his chest, ripping out the rotted heart he didn't deserve. Shock marked his face, and below us, Maple took her last breath.

I placed two drops of blood on the letter, mine and his, watching the thick parchment burst into flames that were carried off into the sky. Above, the golden spell exploded into the brilliant light of the early evening, while my mate lay shattered on the frozen ground, clutching Maples's hand, scared to let go and accept the truth.

She'd lost the last living member of her family, and she'd never truly gotten to know any of them. I'd taken my own father's life, and felt relief.

"ARE you certain you're ready for this, anam cara?" I asked for the thousandth time. Tempe had been allowed out of the hospital two days after Maple's passing. She had eight broken ribs, a punctured lung, and a standing appointment with Penny to work on her grieving issues. Arm held against her, inhaler in her pocket, and a pissed off expression on her face, my mate gave me a death glare.

"Ask me again and I will break *your* ribs, Fireball."

I leaned down to press a kiss to her temple, my hands subtly checking her stitches. Immediately she softened, the cat on her lap and the dog beside her doing wonders to keep me alive.

"I missed the anniversary, but I still need to see her. To see both of them... I..." Swallowing, she struggled to find more words, giving up with a shrug. "They died... for me. Us. Everyone... I... need this?"

Tears burned my eyes and I nodded. Lifting Corky up so she could stand, I placed him on her uninjured shoulder. Rogue stood as well, preparing himself for what was going to be a longer than necessary walk. I'd offered to drive her, as had everyone else, but she insisted she needed to walk. To travel the path to see them as part of the journey of remembrance.

My job was just to hold her hand. To carry her if necessary, but to make sure tribute was paid.

Limping through the vineyard, we said goodbye to the old plants. It had been too much for them, and they hadn't survived. We'd start over in the spring as soon as the last frost passed. Neighboring wineries run by normies had thought it was a centralized polar freeze and offered to dig out some saplings for her in the spring. The magical folks nearby were already planning something a little bigger, but I'd made sure to accept both offers on her behalf.

We said goodbye to the forest. Damien had killed several acres within the tree line, most of the animals had long since left for the winter, there were only trees to suffer the price. Those too would be replanted in the spring, with Tempe planning a clearing and rebirth ceremony for the fallen. Another task the neighboring witches from the hollow had been more than happy to help with.

Finally, we started up the hill. A family cemetery lay at the top, one that held a memorial for her mom, her grandfather, and the generations before them, with a new name added to the stone. I'd cremated the remains, saving them for the spring when the ashes could be spread through the vineyard to help the plants grow.

Tempe had offered up a spot for Damien. He'd cost her everything she loved, but learning he was my father meant he was family. I'd readily declined and deposited his burned remains in a volcano where he'd never be part of anything again. When she was better, I'd tell her about the tribunal, about the relief I felt when he died with my hand around his heart, but it wasn't for today.

The four of us sat on the bench, staring at the stones. Rogue whimpered softly until Tempe stroked his ears while the cat looked at him disapprovingly from his place on her shoulder. The names were carved in different scripts, Maple's in my own with the aid of dragon's fire, but they were all together now.

Neither of us spoke.

"I've never been good with loss..." Tempe breathed. "Never really understood death or goodbyes or cemeteries. But I'm glad they're all together. The four of us will never meet in this life... maybe in the next?"

I wrapped my arm around her, pulling her against my side.

"Do you think the tribunal will overturn your curse now that you don't owe a debt to Damien?"

Swallowing, I looked at her. Despite asking a question, her brown eyes remained fixed on the tombstone, a memory of all the family members he'd stolen from her. The man had left his mark on both of us, but hers would always watch from a hill above the house.

A reminder of what was lost.

"I don't want them to. It's not a curse to share my dragon with you." She looked over at me, and I pressed a kiss to her mark. Draigus slid across and warmed her cheeks, letting me feel her sorrow. "I can't think of myself as cursed as long as you're here."

She leaned in and kissed me, her tongue plundering my mouth. Needing the connection after loss. My hands slid over her body, the cat jumping down indignantly when she climbed into my lap. Taking special care to keep her ribs steady, I let her rock gently against me while I kissed all my love into her.

Before I could rip through another set of her garments, the phone in my pocket buzzed.

"Blasted device," I cursed, pulling it out and attempting to poke at the screen. Words appeared in a box and I scowled at it.

208-700-0000: EVERYTHING IS READY.

"Rain check, love. There's something I need to show you."

"Is it in your pants?" she asked, rocking against me.

"Sadly, no. Hang on to that thought, though. Hold on to the

cat." I placed Corky in her arms and looked at the Irish setter. "Yer gonna have to show me how fast yeh can run."

Releasing my wings, I grabbed onto my woman and held her against me, flying us slowly over the field while the dog pounded the dirt happily below us. Landing softly in the parking lot, I set Tempe down and rubbed Rogue behind the ears. A half-dozen cars filled the lot, and I gave her a small smile.

"We have a surprise for you."

"Who's we?" She eyed me suspiciously and tried to peek in through the window.

"Open the door and see for yourself."

THIRTY-FIVE

TEMPE

Pain and irritation took turns at the front of my mind as I turned the handle. I wasn't really up for visitors, but I knew the cars in the lot. Fighting myself, I pulled open the door and plastered a fake smile on my face. Everyone meant well and I could stand to talk to a few of them.

All thoughts disappeared when I walked into the new tasting room. Cool sage walls replaced the faux plaster, the floating shelves were re-hung in an artful diamond pattern with live succulents instead of fake flowers, and surrounded a portrait of Corky and Rogue made of sliced corks. The bar was still positioned in the center, but the countertops were redone in greens and blacks. The barrel tables were repainted with scenes of dragons and sorceresses in castles on green mountains. Once crowded wine racks were redistributed, the new ones Drax and Arran built attached to the enchantment free walls that were no longer cracked and threatening to collapse. The barrels I'd marked for bottling had been bottled, corked and were sitting at the ready, on the shelves and behind the bar, with a band new menu printed out.

All relabeled with a new name, brand, and logo–drawn to perfection by Leila.

A smiling portrait of my grandparents with my mother as a child looked approvingly out from the wall, the haunted guardians of this chaos. A black light flicked on and a skeletal ghost underlay drowned out their portrait, a morbid and creepy effect that somehow made the painting more bearable.

"How?" I asked, tracing the label on a bottle of merlot. It was a deep gold with flecks of emerald making the same castle scene with a sorceress on a parapet beneath a flying dragon, our logo now two bottles crossed at the tip, corks unrealistically exploding from the top like crossed firing pistols, beneath a jagged font: Two Corks in a Curse, all in a deep glossy black. "How did you create all this?"

I looked from face to smiling face, overwhelmed and emotional. Tears stung my eyes, and I wanted to cry, and hide, hug them, and drink until I was numb. Drax moved in beside me, wrapping an arm around my shoulders and pulling my back to his chest in a one-armed hug taking care with my ribs.

"Breathe, anam cara. Breathe," he whispered, and I choked some air into my starved lungs, wincing as it pushed against my ribs. Chin on my head, he laced the fingers of his other hand through mine, and we took it in, together.

I nodded my agreement, clutching his forearm across my chest.

"It looks like something out of a storybook. Do you think people will like it?"

"Yes," Samuel declared, and I nearly jumped out of my skin as the Satyr appeared in his natural form. All the same enchantments were in place, to help with overwhelm and protect the magical from view, I could sense their low level hum working in the background. "We have done a soft launch announcement on socials and used a few tricks to redo the billboards. Interest and engagement are up to 300%. Most people saying that it looks more like the boss bitch they've seen working here."

"We didn't have socials... so 300% of nothing isn't exactly a feat..." I muttered, and Penny flicked my ear with a bit of magic. "Ow!"

"You had socials. Samuel made them when he started here. Do you even use the internet?" I swallowed at her scorn and withdrew into Drax like he was my personal cave of safety.

"Not for human interaction... mostly I read fanfic... and buy stuff." Naomi, Kaci, Lucy and Chris all nodded in understanding while everyone else looked baffled at my self-control. "I don't have a lot of friends from before I came here to stay in contact with and I'm not big on sharing, so..."

"Well, good thing you have me!" Samuel danced around like he should play a pan flute and it made me nervous for him. Lucy's cheeks tinged pink, and I wondered if I should hook them up or if they might already be hooked up... *Future problems.* "I think we can expect a full house tomorrow."

A woman with brown hair and a pale complexion moved through the group and Drax stiffened behind me, his grip on my shoulder tightening.

"Ma... I... This is Tempe." He didn't move toward her, nor did he release the stranglehold he had on my collarbone. She nodded, weary as she glanced around the room.

I extended my hand, pulling Drax forward with me to the pounding of his heart against my back. "Hi. I'm sorry, I don't know your name."

"Fiona." She accepted my hand and the touch was familiar. Draigus slipped through me to greet her and I felt the emerald green flash of her other half. Head cocked to the side, she looked between me and her son. "I suspect it's been an interesting seventy years."

"It's been an interesting seven days... I think the seventy in between were a little... fishy." I joked and then immediately regretted it. No one knew about his island or the fish, and now I just looked like a weirdo...

Fiona chuckled softly. "Yes... My son ate far too many fish on that island. If I hadn't planted the vegetables in the neighboring wood, he'd have likely gotten scurvy."

"Planted?" Drax breathed, still rigid as stone behind me. "They... I didn't... I thought I foraged them."

His mother stepped closer and touched his cheek, the stone behind me melting back into a man under her touch. "Nay, love. You were not the only one keeping tabs and doing small deeds for the other. I was just far less obvious. I was worried when you came here it would be harder to keep the woods stocked, but then Tempe just... picked up where I left off. Even before she knew you were her mate. You'd better not cock this up, son."

Everyone in the room laughed and Samual appeared beside us. "Speaking of... don't smile!"

He snapped a picture of me and Drax, nodding his approval.

"Brooding cursed lovers. You two will be the perfect image for this winery." He started swiping and tapping while I looked down at my sweaty and snow-covered clothes. They'd given me a sling to protect my ribs, but I lost it at some point the same day I got home.

"I'm not wearing a bra."

"You can't post her picture with..." Drax was cut off when Samuel turned the phone. The image cut off at his arm, my fingers wrapped around it while we were looking at each other with love, longing, and the sadness that comes when you experience the loss of an ideal that never was.

And the relief when the worst has finally happened and you survived.

With love.

He'd applied a filter that darkened everything, made it moody, and imprinted the logo in the bottom corner. "Bloody hell, that's..."

I didn't know what it was either, but I liked it.

"That's us. Dark, cursed, a little broken... but surviving and in love. With the family we made."

"If you think it's too soon..." Lucy started, hesitating as she checked with Penny.

"No... I..." I looked at Draigus, hoping he'd fill in the words I couldn't find. "I think it's time to let go of the past. It's not helped us once to avoid it or try to make it right."

"Agreed. I love you, as you are. I think it's time we left other people's dreams and expectations behind, love. Let's embrace what we are: cursed and stuck together." His eyes bored into mine, heavy with meaning. "Forever."

"Forever," I confirmed, capturing his lips in a kiss.

ABOUT THE AUTHOR

Noelle Rider is a fiction author writing romance with plus-sized female leads and their furry friends. She is one of two authors under the Perry Dog Publishing Imprint, a one woman, two dog operation in Idaho... for now. My dogs are Perry and Padfoot, the furry beasts shown above. They are well-loved character inspiration in all things written and business.

If you are interested in joining my newsletter, please subscribe on my website, PerryDogPublishing.com

You will receive A Bite in Afghanistan, the prequel to the Sharp Investigations Series, as a thank-you for joining. I only have one newsletter for mental health reasons, so both romance and mystery are on there! If you only want one in your inbox, follow Perry Dog Publishing on all socials to stay on top of the latest news... and pet pics.

ALSO BY NOELLE RIDER

Witching and Scheming : A Huckleberry Hollow Romance

Pumpkin Spice :A Pumpkin Valley Novella

COMING SOON...

Blood Widow: A Reverse Harem Revenge Thriller w/ E. N. Crane

FOR MORE CAFFEINE ADDICTED HEROINES WITH DOGS, CHECK OUT HER OTHER PEN NAME: E. N. CRANE

www.ingramcontent.com/pod-product-compliance
Lightning Source LLC
Chambersburg PA
CBHW060900210726
48293CB00006B/1888